I0730355

PROPHECY OF STORMS

CURSED BLOODLINE PROPHECY
BOOK ONE

CINNA - STONE

CONTENTS

Cover Designer: Etheric Designs

Editor: R. A. Wright Editing

Formatter: R. A. Wright Editing

ISBN eBook: 9781764316200

ISBN paperback: 9781764316217

PREFACE

This book contains content that may be distressing for some readers, including but not limited to:

- Harm befalling an animal/pet (shown)
- Attempted rape of an adult woman (shown)
- Physical abuse by a father-figure (mentioned)
- Torture of children in a cult-like community (mentioned)
- Past child abuse (mentioned)
- Oxycodone (incidental mention)
- Grievous harm to a child (implied)

This book also contains LGBTQIA+ representation. If you're likely to be offended by non-binary characters or pronouns, a male angel falling from heaven and entering a female vessel, or sex scenes that don't contain the endgame love interest, this might not be the place for you.

Xx Cinna

ONE

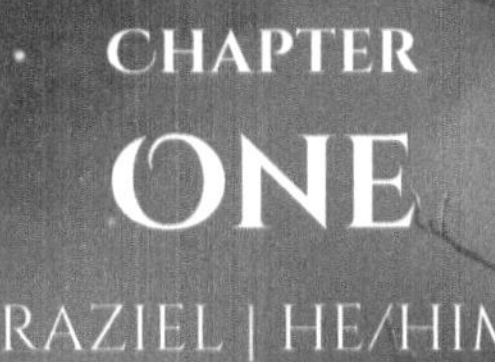

Two angels, a priest, and a rabbi walk into a bar. I know there's a joke in there somewhere, but as they walk toward me with barely suppressed rage glinting in their eyes, I'll be damned if I know what it is.

"They can't still be mad?" I wonder aloud, then down the last of my bourbon, embracing the harsh sting.

"The rabbi caught you deflowering his daughter behind a dumpster," Cherry, Purgatory's finest bartender, reminds me with a salacious smile. "Not that I blame her."

"You know, sweetheart, when you look at me like that, it makes me feel cheap." I slide my glass toward her. "Another refill?"

I turn from the bar and open my mouth to greet the rabbi when a fist hits me square in the face. My ears ring, and I find myself lying on the dirty bar floor, peanut shells digging into my cheek. Talk about a punchline. I rub my jaw to soothe the ache while trying to ignore my wounded pride.

"A smart man might have thought twice about showing his face around here." The priest squats beside me, making the sign of the cross. No one has ever accused me of being a smart man. "I'll pray for you to find your way, my son."

"I wouldn't waste your prayers," a familiar voice says. Footsteps sound on the hardwood floor, and a pair of golden-armored boots appear in front of me. I move to a kneeling position and dust myself off.

"My lord," Reign says in greeting, and I find myself meeting the eyes of the second commander of God's army. "You've seen better days."

Haven't we all?

"What are you doing here, Reign?"

"We're looking for Sahari." The corner of her mouth lifts into a bemused smirk. "You've got nuts on your face."

Sighing, I wipe the shells from my cheek. "Why the hell would I know where Sahari is? Aren't you supposed to be her lapdog?" My remark earns me a kick to the back, and I again have the pleasure of peanut shells cutting into my skin. "Let me guess. You brought the little one."

I hiss as Nina grabs a fistful of my hair, pulling me to my knees. "Give me a reason to end your pathetic existence, I beg you."

"Let him stand, Nina." Reign waits until I'm on my feet to continue. "Do you have any idea what's going on back home?"

I dust myself off again and fall back onto my barstool. "I don't know if you noticed, but I'm not exactly a regular in the family group chat."

Ignoring my sarcasm, Reign continues. "We're on the brink of war, Raziel."

"It must be Tuesday." I gesture to the bar. "Take off your cloak. Sit down, let me buy you a drink." Smirking, I glance at Nina. "Not you. I don't like you." Ignoring her aggressive hand gesture, I turn my attention to the bartender. "Your finest bottom-shelf for my friend."

"Did you hear a word Reign said?" Nina exclaims, her palm hitting the bar top with a bang.

I stare at the scarred hand, feeling my irritation grow with every waning second. "Sahari. Blah blah blah. Brink of war. Does that sum it up?" It's unwise of me to provoke the vengeful angel, yet too sweet a temptation.

"Would you two please cut it out," Reign begs, her tone unusually exasperated. "Raziel, when was the last time you left this place?"

"It's been a while," I admit, taking in the familiar surroundings. "It suits me, wouldn't you agree?"

I resist the urge to smile as I take in their appearances. The golden cloak and armor of Reign's uniform hide the white markings upon her flesh, while Nina's are on full display. They tell the story of their creation. Bonds forged, wars won and lost; the battles that made them legends, and honoring those who perished. If the runes were written in script, they would read, "Serve thy Lord God, the Almighty Father, and deliver justice upon his enemies." I know their story well, having marked their flesh myself. The now blackened runes on my own wrist are a permanent reminder for all to see. I blink rapidly, refocusing on the matter at hand.

"Why would Sahari come see me? We haven't spoken since the hearing."

Reign scans the bar, her gaze lingering on the priest as he not-so-subtly tries to eavesdrop on our conversation. "It's not safe to talk here."

"That's too bad." I pick up my bourbon, only to have it set back on the bar. Nina points to the door as if I were a disobedient dog. Her expression promises bloodshed should I refuse. "You forget your place, little one."

Even sitting, I tower over her, but I'm not foolish enough to think she's intimidated. The last time we fought, we destroyed what remained of an abandoned village, and it took an army to separate us.

"Call me little one again," Nina seethes, gripping the handle of her short sword, "and you'll find yourself crawling into the next life."

A dark chuckle escapes me as I meet the warrior's gaze. "I let you have the first shot; I won't be so forgiving with the second."

"Give me one reason—"

"Enough." Reign's tone is pure command as she looks first to Nina, a silent discussion passing between them, then to me. "I only need a moment of your time. If you still wish us to leave, you have my word, nobody will bother you again."

I pick up my drink, empty its contents in one gulp, and slide it back across the bar, the now empty glass symbolic of my existence. "You've got ten minutes."

"Thank you, my lord." Reign bows deeply, then straightens. "If you'll follow me."

Reluctantly, I follow the warriors outside.

"If you plan to kill me, you've chosen a prime location," I say, half joking, but as we trek farther into the wooded area, the red eyes in the darkness seem to glow brighter.

"Purgatory has made you paranoid, Raziel," Reign says. "Your life is not in danger."

"Someone might disagree with you." I wink at Nina as I lean against a tree. Nina flashes her teeth in agreement. "What brings you to my humble abode?"

Reign gestures to the space around us. "Are you able to ward the area? What I'm about to share with you cannot leave this forest. Even the beasts have ears."

Curiosity piqued, I call upon my God-given gifts, the power humming to life after lying dormant for so long. The familiarity of it causes the ache in my chest to lessen. I'm relieved to find it still there after all this time.

"It's done," I whisper, breathing easier for the first time in centuries. While it should have been a welcome release, it only serves to remind me of what I've lost.

Reign releases a breath and straightens as she meets my gaze. "We haven't heard from Sahari in seven days. Someone is killing angels. We've found the partial remains of three, but over the last few weeks, dozens have gone missing."

I'm not sure what I expected her to say, but nothing prepared me for this. "Where's Father?"

"Father abandoned us centuries ago," Nina says, her eyes tracking my every movement. "No one has heard from him since your hearing."

Looking between the two angels, I find myself lost for words. "I don't understand."

"None of us do," Reign offers. "When did you last speak to our father?"

I remain silent.

"Exactly," Nina says. "Father is gone. It's up to us to keep things going."

I send out a prayer for guidance, for answers, for a sign my mistakes will not destroy more lives. In return, I receive silence.

"Days after Sahari disappeared, Nina found an intruder in her office. When confronted, he attacked her."

"What happened to him?"

"He ran into the pointy end of Rainmaker," Nina says, two fingers tapping the ruby embedded in the handle of the legendary sword. The gem shines brighter at the touch of its master.

"You didn't think to question him first?"

Nina shrugs. "I gave him options. He chose death."

"What's done is done," Reign interjects, bringing my focus back to her. "Don't you want to know what he was looking for?" She reaches into her cloak and pulls out my journal. "Apparently, whatever this contains was worth his life."

"Have you read it?" I take the journal and flip open to the first pages, my fingers caressing the angelic runes of prophecy.

"It's not any language I recognize," Reign says. "We assume the intruder—and whoever sent him—knew what he was looking for."

"The journal disappeared before the hearing," I tell them, reading the familiar words. "*As it began, so must it end.*"

"The bloodline prophecy." Nina's eyes widen. "This is your journal? *That's* why Sahari was coming to see you."

"Could Sahari have read it?" Reign asks.

"Enough to figure out the context," I admit, spying Sahari's handwriting written down the sides of a few pages. It was a poor translation of my own language, but I understood. "She'd have known it was one of mine."

Sahari and I had spent centuries together as friends, and later, lovers. There wasn't a journal in my library she wouldn't have recognized upon sight. I reread Sahari's message again and again.

Something is hunting us.

If you're reading this, it's already too late.

It had been too long since I took flight, and yet, as I look to the sisters in front of me, exchanging hopeful glances of what this meant, I knew it was time to return. I unfurled my wings, and the leaves on the ground rustled at the shift. The beasts in the shadows retreated, as though they had forgotten who stood amongst them.

Having to leave Purgatory after five centuries felt as if acid had been poured over my flesh, leaving the skin blistered and seeping. The urge to return and drown out the pain was all-consuming. The vision of my failures and the memory of blood coating my hands played in the back of my mind, a stark reminder I'm an outcast from my people. I force myself to think of Sahari and those that had gone missing in the absence of our father. With that thought, we took flight.

Before long, we were within sight of the city, and the parliament —seven seats for seven holy beings—which was now encased in a pristine glass dome. We land alongside a path surrounded by red poppies. I kneel to get a closer look and run my thumb across the petals. "These are new."

Reign's voice is soft as she comes up behind me. "Every time an angel disappears, more bloom."

I gesture to the glass structure. "Why does the House of Parliament now resemble an upturned fishbowl?"

"That's what you want to discuss?" Nina seethes. "You have the attention span of a human."

Reign sighs. "Give it a rest, Nina."

Nina sneers at me once Reign has passed us. "You're still a useless fool."

"And you're still an annoying little brat."

"Enough," Reign snaps. "Nina, return to the camps and spread word of Raziel's return."

Nina stares at Reign in disbelief. "I'm not leaving you alone with him."

"Raziel is no threat to me," Reign assures her, squeezing her hand kindly. "I know you're scared, Nina—we all are—but if Sahari is alive, we must work together to be reunited."

"And if she isn't?" Nina whispers. "What hope do any of us have if Sahari has met true death?"

Reign's face remains kind, and she reluctantly drops Nina's hand. "Raziel and I will meet with the others. When you've collected yourself, return to the sisters and tell them of Raziel's return, then report back to me."

I watch the warrior continue back down the path. Her wings expand as she takes flight, and I'm struck at the beauty. In the glow of the sun, her marbled white feathers show strokes of black and gray, as if caressed by an artist's brush.

"She's usually so delightful," I remark sarcastically, only partially teasing, though I regret it as soon as Reign turns to me. Her eyes are cold, and her expression ruthless. "Sorry."

"The bloodline is a touchy subject among the sisters," Reign reminds me, grief filling her own eyes. "Walk with me, Raziel."

Silence falls between us as we approach the parliament house.

Finally, Reign breaks the silence, saying, "If Sahari truly did fall, it wasn't something she saw coming."

"There's no sign of her?" I ask hesitantly.

"None," Reign admits. "Do you think it's possible she's gone?"

"None of us are truly immortal." I look around at the field of red poppies with their many meanings, from times of war to eternal sleep. "*As the flowers bloom, so shall they die.* If our father wanted us to be invincible, we'd have been created so. We bleed as the human's bleed, and if it bleeds, it can be killed. It keeps us humble."

"You're not making me feel better."

"I'm not trying to make you feel better, love. I'm being honest with you. No one is truly invincible, including Sahari. Having said that, Sahari is the greatest of God's warriors. I've fought at her side, as well as yours, from the beginning, and I've watched angels fall in battle a million times. I always thought if the day came when either Sahari or I fell, we'd be there to see each other go."

Reign is quiet for a long time. "She loved you."

"I know."

The guilt of my crimes weighs heavier on my chest with every breath taken outside of Purgatory. Reign stops, and I turn to her, seeing the question in her gaze. "Ask."

"Why did you do it, Raziel?" Even after all these years, I still don't have an answer to satisfy her curiosity or soothe her grief. "Why did you betray us?"

"She was my friend."

"Friends don't betray friends." Silver tears fill the corner of Reign's gaze.

"It's complicated." As love often is. What else is there to say? Even after all this time, I still don't know how to tell them the truth. I still don't fully understand what happened myself.

"Try telling that to Isaiah and Gwen." I stiffen at the mention of their names. "Gwen is dead because of the actions of your friend."

"You don't think I know that? None of us knew the fate of that day, and if we did, we wouldn't have gone. I wouldn't have put their lives in danger."

"After all this time, you're still blinded by your affection for the witch." There's pity in the warrior's gaze as she looks at me. "She never cared for you, Raziel. I doubt she's ever cared for anybody but herself."

That wasn't true, though, because there was one person Claire McCoy cared for more than anybody else—her twin, Silas.

Reign sighs. "I don't know why we're still discussing this. None of it matters now."

If the past has taught me anything, it's that it is never truly forgotten. Memories linger until the quiet hours of the morning... or until you reach the bottom of your ninth bottle of top-shelf whiskey. Then, given the opportunity, they slap you in the face.

Reign rounds the corner, and we're met by Michael. He's leaning against the side of the building, sharpening his sword as we approach. He lifts his mischievous gray eyes to mine.

"It's good to see you again, brother," he says, rising to embrace me. "I had bet Reign wouldn't be able to drag you away from Purgatory, or that sweet little bartender. Not all of parliament will be pleased by your return, but my men and I will follow your leadership."

Reign moves to stand at Michael's side. "The Iron Sisters and I also stand with you. The parliament needs a leader."

"I'm not here to lead," I say, looking between the two of them. How long had it been since the three of us shared space?

"Raziel—"

"Nobody should be following me after... everything," I say, cutting off the objections. "The two of you have managed thus far. I'm here to figure out what happened to Sahari and the others."

Michael's expression hardens as he takes a step toward me, the action intended to intimidate. I feel my lips twitch as I resist the urge to smile.

"Intimidation doesn't work on me, brother."

"If you aren't here to lead, will you follow?" Reign asks, placing a hand on Michael's shoulder.

I laugh. "I didn't say that."

"Translation—you're going to be a major pain in my ass," Reign counters. Before I can reply, a scout rushes toward us. "What is it, Eli?"

"They've found another body."

TWO

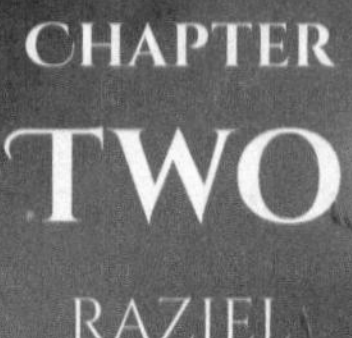

I lift the cloth to reveal the bloody remains beneath, then lean closer, assessing the damage. His throat has been torn out. The clotting around the wound suggests it happened after he died.

"Teeth marks," I say to the young scout peering cautiously over my shoulder.

"Is that smell coming from him?" Eli asks.

"He's been baking in the sun for hours," Uriel offers. "The other half of his intestines are over there."

"It's not that," I say, ignoring the commentary. I press my fingers to the wound, then bring them to my nose. The putrid scent of sulfur burns the back of my throat as a faint memory from my time between realms flashes through my mind.

"Do you know what it is?" Eli asks, covering his mouth as he stands to move away.

"I can tell you it wasn't an angel"

"Shifter, maybe?" Uriel suggests. "Could one of the spirits escape the crypt and go mad?"

"Can't hurt to ask."

"What else could it be?" Uriel's brows pinch together in concentration. "No animals in these woods are capable of this level of violence."

The torn limbs, gashed stomach, and what remains of the intestines and forearms looks to have been shredded by claws. Other wounds aren't jagged, but clean. Too clean, as if they'd been made by a surgical blade. And to top it all off, his heart is missing. I rise. "I don't think it was a shifter."

"Has this sort of thing happened before?" Eli asks, his gaze jumping between the two of us.

"Never."

There's a first time for everything.

"I have a friend who works day shifts at the crypt. I'll make a call." Eli goes to leave, but I gesture for him to wait as I address the gathered patrols.

"Until the threat is identified, no one is to travel alone. Check in on your friends and spread word of the new curfew. No one is to be out after dark unless directed otherwise."

I dismiss the patrols and decide to put some distance between myself and the remains. Uriel follows me into the woods, heading toward a cliff overlooking an expanse of lush green. "Not to contradict you, brother, but Michael wanted this kept quiet. Won't a curfew incite panic?"

"Not that I need to remind you, brother, but I don't take orders from Michael," I say, unable to keep the bite from my tone. "If those more vulnerable are aware of the threat, they'll stay vigilant of their surroundings."

"Is it true Sahari suspected a connection between the prophecy and current events? What are your thoughts on everything you've seen so far?"

My only thought right now, dear Uriel, is that I'd kill for a whiskey. Of course, I don't say that aloud.

"It's too soon to tell. The timing for the prophecy is imminent, there's no denying that, though I struggle to see how this all connects."

"What do you think killed my messenger back there?" Uriel asks, a knowing look on his face. "I saw your reaction, Raziel. You have your own theory."

"It was a hellhound." I watch for his reaction. "I didn't say it in front of the others because I didn't want to panic them."

"You did the right thing." Uriel gestures back toward the corpse. "The implications of what that means . . ."

"It does not make sense, yet I know it to be true."

"There's only one way something like that gets through the gates."

"I know," I say, confirming Uriel's thoughts. "We don't say anything until we've gathered more evidence."

"I'll have the body taken to my lab and examine it myself." Uriel steps closer. "What if Sahari came to a similar conclusion?"

"If she did, that would narrow down the suspects."

"Meaning?"

"Aside from God himself, there are only three archangels with enough power to open the gates and fight Sahari, and I'm one of them." Uriel's reaction has him taking a step back. "Sahari said war was coming. I can only think of one archangel who'd benefit from such a thing."

I walk over to the cliff and look out over the ravine. The breeze picks up, and I close my eyes as the fresh smell of pine trees and river water washes away the putrid scent of decay and old blood. Footsteps sound through the undergrowth. I turn my head at Michael and Eli's approach and nod in greeting.

"Brothers. Eli, tell them what you told me," Michael says.

"I checked in with my friend who works at the crypt," Eli explains in a rush. "There was an attack just after shift change this morning. The afternoon shift arrived and found the front door open and the guards dead. It appears only two levels were breached. They're still investigating, and most of the spirits have been accounted for, however, there are eyewitnesses who say some of the spirits were taken."

Uriel's head shoots up. "They've taken spirits?"

"Yes, sir. Who would do that?" Eli asks.

"More importantly, why?" Michael asks. "What do they want with them?"

"There's more," Eli pipes up as Uriel's wings unfurl to take flight. There's always more. Eli shifts uneasily. "A recent change to the database organized the floors by bloodlines. It was thought it would bring peace to the spirits knowing they're with kin. The two floors breached in the attack are from the McCoy bloodlines. It houses the witch's family, including those royal Fae who immigrated to Earth a few centuries ago. And the twins . . . they're gone."

Missing and murdered angels, the twins' disappearance, and now spirits . . . I don't like where this is going, but I know by the look in Uriel's eyes we are on the same page. "It's got to be the souls."

Uriel nods in agreement. "I'd wager they're collecting ingredients for a spell."

I gesture back in the direction of the corpse. "His heart and liver are missing. What kind of spell requires human souls and the heart and liver of an angel?"

Uriel shakes his head. "I need to consult my books."

"I need you to visit the crypt," Michael says. Too far gone in my own thoughts of the past, it takes me a moment to realize he's speaking to me. "Speak to the survivors, review the footage, and bring me something I can use to track these bastards down."

"Raziel?" Uriel's voice is cautious as he places a hand on my shoulder. "Do you want me to come with you?"

"No," I manage to say, swallowing the bile in my throat. "You need to examine the body. I'm fine."

I step back off the cliff and let gravity drag me down, not bothering with goodbyes. The ground races toward me, but I unfurl my wings at the last possible second, catching the wind and soaring higher as I fly to the crypt to piece together all the information I've discovered.

Hellhounds in heaven, a possible rebellion uprising with a leader strong enough to open the holy gates, and a prophesied apocalypse. Heaven's most beloved vengeful angel is missing, along with a dozen others, including the most powerful witch in history and her equally powerful shifter mage of a twin brother. And whoever controls the hellhounds is also collecting ingredients for a spell using the souls of the most powerful bloodline in a millennium.

What the hell is going on, and where the hell is Claire McCoy now?

THREE

The last time I visited the crypt, it was a simple cabin in the woods. Now, it resembles a luxury hotel. The guard at the door bows his head as I approach. "Welcome back, my lord."

It takes me a moment to place the angel. "Joshua?" He smiles wider at the recognition. "It's been a long time."

"Indeed. Things must be pretty bad if they sent you."

"Raphael had a hair appointment," I say, taking the gloves he offers. I'd hate to get more blood on my hands.

The interior of the crypt is cold, and the scent of sulfur lingers in the air. I examine the bodies of the deceased in the hall as I make my way into the heart of the crypt, where the inhabitants should be at peace in their cells.

Each spirit is assigned their own room big enough for their cell—a holographic casket with ancient runes carved into the surface that usually houses the slumbering spirit—and a few pieces of furniture from their time on Earth. It creates a sense of home so they can rest peacefully. Instead, spirits wander from cell to cell, muttering nonsense. Every other corner contains a spirit cowering in the shadows, clutching at their skulls, tears streaming down their pale faces as they whimper for someone to protect them.

An old lady wanders past but stops and tilts her head to look at me. "Darkness is coming, mister. He will bring the storm and destroy us all."

"What's your name, ma'am?"

"Ms. Maeve McCoy."

"It's nice to meet you, Ms. Maeve," I say quietly, offering her my hand. "Would you like some help getting back to your room?"

She looks back down the hall. "I miss the sun."

"As do I," I admit. "It's not quite the same, is it?"

"No." She takes my arm. "She warned us they'd come."

"Who warned you?" The woman lifts her gray eyes to mine, tears filling them. "Maeve?"

"My grandmother," she admits, leading me to a room. "She visits us sometimes."

Claire. That shouldn't be possible.

"When Claire visits you, is she here physically?" I guide Maeve into her room. "Or does she visit you while you're in the cells?"

The old woman's eyes droop as she struggles to stand. I lift her into my arms, and she snuggles in closer and yawns. "I'm so tired, mister. So tired."

"It's okay," I whisper, as I carry her the rest of the way and lower her into the cell, then brush the hair back from her forehead. "Be at peace now, Ms. Maeve."

"Psst." I look to the doorway, where a child waves for me to follow. In a flash, he's gone, and I run from the room and skid into the hall. I turn my head left, then right, finally spotting him at the other end. He giggles as he runs away from me. "Come on, Raziel! Chase me!"

His laughter contrasts eerily with the blood and death around every corner. I find myself getting lost in the maze. Spirits walk by me, muttering and cursing the noise. I spin in a circle as a tiny hand tugs at my furled wings. His hand flies to his mouth as he giggles, then disappears again.

"You're so slow!" the boy taunts. "I thought archangels were supposed to be fast!"

I turn down an empty hall and throw my hands in the air when his giggles fade. "Come on, kid. I don't have time for games."

I'm about to turn when the door at the end of the hall opens and sunlight fills the room. The smell of the ocean and the crash of waves assaults my senses. I'm drawn to it. As I get closer, I'm reminded of a simpler time, far away from here.

"It's a glamour," a figure explains from the shadows, raising a hand as if to brush it away. One moment, there was a floor-to-ceiling window overlooking cliffs above the ocean, and the next, a gray cement wall. The scent and sounds disappeared with the illusion. I turn to face the emerging figure and still upon the sight of the ancient witch. "Do you know who I am?" she asks.

"High priestess of your coven, you sacrificed your life to bring your granddaughter back from the dead after her brother fell on the battlefield during the Great Fae War." Those events had taken place five hundred years ago, though it felt as if it were only yesterday. "It's an honor to meet you, Elsbeth."

The old woman stands before me with sadness in her eyes. "I'm glad you finally came. I have waited a long time to meet you, Story-teller. I was told to give this to you." She reaches her hand through the brick wall and retrieves a letter with my unbroken seal. "Do you recognize this?"

I swallow the lump in my throat and straighten. "No, I don't," I say, reading Reign's name on the front, in my own handwriting. It was quilled with my feather, inked in my blood, and yet I hold no memory of it. I feel a sense of urgency, like time is running out. I search my memories, call to the forgotten secrets locked within my mind, but only a whisper floats back to me. Yet another mystery to solve. It's time to go.

CHAPTER

FOUR

RAZIEL

I've already taken my seat when the rest of parliament file into the grand hall. Upon seeing me, whispers of curiosity and outrange echo off the marble walls.

"Why is he here?" Raphael asks, pointing a finger in my direction. "For all we know, he's in cahoots with the enemy!"

I touch my heart and smile, knowing it'll irk him. "I've missed you too, brother."

The glare he levels at me would turn most angels to stone. Unfortunately for the two of us, I thrive on conflict and get a sick kind of satisfaction out of pissing him off.

"Crawl back into the pit from whence you came," Raphael retorts. "You're a disgrace to your own kind."

"Find new material, brother." I shoot him a wink, then turn my attention back to the archangel at the head of the table. The room is filled with politicians, warriors, and the leaders of God's armies. It's been almost five hundred years since I've seen some of their faces. My heart sinks as I see how far we've fallen.

Raphael, never one to be ignored, slams his hand down on the marble tabletop. "I demand the traitor be removed."

"If my presence intimidates you that much, you're welcome to leave." I sneer as he moves toward me. "We both know you can't match me, brother. Don't humiliate yourself."

As I rise to meet his challenge, Uriel catches my arm and squeezes.

"Sit." Michael's voice, low and threatening, carries through the room. "I'll only say this once. Reign and I have requested Raziel's presence. If he gives an order, you follow it. If you have an issue with it or him, you're welcome to take it up with him, but don't come crying to us when he puts you on your ass."

Stone-faced, Raphael takes his seat, and I purse my lips, fighting the urge to smile at him. I settle into my seat and look to the front. Reign clears her throat, and the meeting is called to order.

"News would have reached your camps by now that Sahari is among the missing," Reign declares, meeting the eyes of every warrior in the room. "The night our commander disappeared, she'd been to visit the cells where Silas and Claire McCoy were imprisoned. She reported their disappearance to me, then went to Purgatory to retrieve Raziel. She never made it there, nor home. Raziel is here to help."

The crowd begins to stir, and I listen to their accusations. *Why would she seek help from a traitor? Did Sahari believe he was responsible for the crimes? How do we know he didn't kill Sahari and dispose of her body in Purgatory?*

"Despite his past mistakes," Michael says, "Raziel is still the Lord Keeper of Secrets, Prophet, Protector of the Word, and the Bringer of Hope. He is the right hand of God, and the most powerful archangel amongst us. With the bloodline prophecy in play, we need him."

Reign cuts in and surveys the restless room. "I have my sisters searching for Claire and Silas McCoy. We've yet to locate either."

"Have you been to their cell?" Uriel asks me.

I shake my head. "No. I was forbidden from ever setting foot on the island. Reign informs me there were no sign of a struggle, but while I was at the crypt, one of the spirits said she'd been warned about the attack, and the information was repeated by several others."

"The witch's lapdog likely helped them escape." Raphael spits in my direction. "Why don't you ask the traitor where he's hiding his lover?"

"If you spit at me again, brother, I will rip out your tongue," I say in a bored tone, tilting my head back. I lock eyes with the arrogant bastard. "How you've gone this long with it still intact is beyond me."

"Raziel," Michael interjects. "What did you find at the crypt?"

"Hundreds of the guards are dead. It's still unknown how many souls are missing, but I can confirm those taken from the crypt are from the McCoy bloodline. The witnesses I spoke to swear there was someone inside their head before and during the attack, sifting through memories, looking for something."

"How was the witch able to travel between her cell and the crypt so freely?" yells an angel from the gallery. "Wasn't she confined? Or do we let all our prisoners roam?"

"The runes on her cell could only do so much. Claire McCoy is the most powerful witch to exist in three millennia. Make no mistake, brothers, Claire chose to be compliant all these years. The moment it wasn't convenient for her to do so, she acted, and once news of the slaughter at the crypt reaches her, she will seek vengeance for her kin."

An angel hisses from the crowd. "How many more of us have to die while you protect her, traitor?"

Rage boils within me as I seek the angel who'd spoken. He cowers beneath my gaze, and I release a fraction of my power in his direction. "Perhaps you'd like to stand up and say such things to my face. If not, I suggest you keep your mouth shut in my presence, or risk losing more than your tongue."

"Raziel." Reign brings my focus back to her. "How was the crypt infiltrated?"

I debate whether to tell them, but there's enough evidence that it's no longer a theory, but a fact with dire implications.

"Hellhounds." The room falls silent, then erupts into chaos. "The stench of the beasts lingers in the air," I say, keeping my tone level. "Hellhounds can't just stroll in on their own. They were let inside and unleashed upon the crypt."

From beside me, Uriel says, "I finished the examination on my messenger—"

"We have more pressing matters at hand, Uriel," Raphael urges. "I'd like to discuss the possibility of war."

Uriel glares at Raphael. "How can we prepare for war when we don't know who our enemies are? I've examined the body. The heart and liver were removed while he was still alive, and there were also traces of sulfur on his remains."

Reign's gaze shifts between me and Uriel, looking unsettled. "You're telling us there really are hellhounds in heaven?"

"I have a theory." I cringe, already regretting opening my mouth. "The timing of the attacks is strategic. The veil is thinnest during this time as we approach the prophesied apocalypse. This one particularly, because it's a part of the McCoy bloodline. Whoever controls the hellhounds is using it to their advantage, but I believe it serves to be a distraction. We're under attack, and the perpetrator is one of our own."

The mere suggestion causes outright chaos. Angels jump from their seats. Fear, panic, and outrage at the accusation spreads through the hall like a pox amongst humans. That's my cue to leave.

I stand up, and Uriel rises, a questioning brow raised. I reach into my jacket and withdraw the letter for Reign, then lean in to speak to him. "Wait until she's alone to give it to her," I say, then sneak out the side door and into the garden.

Nina sidles up beside me. "It's nice to see you making friends," she says.

"Don't you have someone else you can annoy?"

"Reign kicked me out." Nina shrugs. "I hate those meetings, and besides, I heard some big-shot archangel is enforcing a rule that none of us are allowed to wander on our own. It looked to me like you were about to wander, so . . ."

"I don't think they'd mind if I went missing."

"Don't get needy on me, Raziel." Nina punches my arm as her wings lift her into the air.

Nina still wears her armor, but with a halter belt that carries her throwing blades. The buckles travel along both her thighs to where her two short swords sit. Twin star rubies glisten in the handles of her short swords, matching the large star ruby in the hilt of the sword across her back—Rainmaker.

Nina is small, but in battles past, Rainmaker has sliced through warriors like a hot knife through butter, and from the sky the blood of her enemies rained over the battlefield to soak those still fighting upon it.

Now, she looks back at me with a mischievous grin on her face. "I'll race you."

"Is this your way of apologizing?" I ask, spreading my wings and following her into the clear sky.

"If kicking your ass in a race to the lake is what you consider an apology, then sure."

"Last to the lake pays my tab at Purgatory?"

"Deal."

I ignore the annoying angel and give myself over to instinct. My heart races, and adrenaline courses through me. I'm still laughing as I hear Nina's cry of frustration from behind me.

"Cheater!"

I spot the lake in the distance and dive, not slowing as I hit the water and glide along the bottom, then break the surface and span my wings as far as they'll go.

I can feel the wind between each feather, the chill of the lake water, and smell the bushes surrounding me. I'd missed this feeling —this sense of belonging, even amongst all the animosity. The tips of my wings break the surface of the lake, and the water ripples out from their touch.

Nina's laughter brings my attention back to her, and I watch as her wings fold back and she pierces the surface of the water. She cuts through it like a spear through air, spinning and twisting as she travels beneath me, then winking as she comes up and takes a swipe at me with her wing.

Rolling out of her reach, I spin and catch the wind, letting it carry me higher. Smiling to myself, I spread my wings and fly. I cannot remember the last time I felt this weightless.

Being in Purgatory makes you forget the good in your existence. It sucks away all you once cherished and dulls your senses until you simply exist, wallowing in misery. I hadn't realized how much it had affected me until this moment.

Hello, Raziel.

Startled at the mental intrusion, my wings catch the breeze, bringing me to an abrupt halt.

By the lake.

I spot the redheaded witch and her brother. *How did you escape?*

Was it supposed to be hard?

The pull toward her is undeniable. I look ahead and see Nina soaring high in the sky, totally unaware of the fugitives lurking below. I aim for the trees and land lightly before Silas and Claire McCoy.

She's as beautiful as the first time I met her. Her petite, slender body is hidden beneath her royal-blue coat, and her red curls hang loose around her, but it's the darkness in her eyes that almost brings me to my knees. "Claire."

"It's time to go, Raziel," she says.

"I don't think your pet is happy with you, sister." Silas flashes a toothy grin, as if the thought pleases him. "What's wrong, Raziel? Did you think she'd come alone?"

I bite back a snarl, ignoring the arrogant bastard. "You wiped my memories."

I remind myself I once loved this woman. That she was not my enemy, nor to blame for my choices. I can't let myself think about the sacrifices I made for her. I put my trust in her, risked the people whose lives I cherished above my own. I betrayed my family to help reunite her with hers. Because of that, I spent centuries in Purgatory, denying myself freedom and connection.

I strayed from my destiny to walk alongside her, and it brought ruin to my people.

I should've been stronger.

Raziel?

I stiffen and turn to her in rage. "Stay out of my head!"

"We don't have a lot of time," she pleads. "You have the journal. Please, give it to me."

"It's gone," I tell her, watching as fury simmers in her green eyes. "Perhaps you'd like to explain why I don't recall writing those prophecies?"

"Your little friend has found us," Silas warns, turning his face to the sky.

"Don't look at her," I snarl, ignoring Nina's arrival as I step closer to the seer. "Explain it to me, Claire. Explain why you wiped my memories!" *Why did you betray me?*

She seems genuinely shocked at hearing my voice inside her head. "How did you do that?"

"You opened the door." I smile cruelly at her. "You're powerful, Claire, more powerful than anyone will ever truly understand, but you're not the only one with the ability to walk through minds."

"I will hurt you," Nina snarls at Silas.

"You're welcome to try," Silas counters lazily. "I'll swat you like a fly, little angel."

I turn my head to find Silas blocking Nina's path to Claire and me. Nina's face is red, and she's got her short sword at Silas's throat.

"Put down the sword, Nina."

Her eyes snap to mine. Rage, betrayal, disbelief, and hate fill her brown eyes. "I should've killed you."

Silas muses thoughtfully. "You'd kill the only male standing between you and extinction?"

"What are you talking about?" Nina and I ask in unison, sharing a glance.

"The prophecy you dreamt of was brought about by the fall of parliament," Claire answers. "The kingdom will call, eternity falls, feathers to ash. Those same words from the original prophecy warned Silas about our fates. You came to me asking for my help to prevent the prophecy, and for centuries I have done what I could, but once Sahari fell through the veil, there was nothing more to be done."

Nina gasps at the mention of Sahari.

"It may bring you some comfort to know she's alive and on earth," Claire says.

"Why wouldn't I try to prevent the prophecy myself?" I ask her.

"You couldn't," Silas answers. "Not without tipping off the leader you were onto him. You came to us and asked us to wipe your memories until it was time. Now they can be returned."

"You expect me to believe you wiped my memories *because I asked*?"

Silas shrugs. "Believe what you want, Raziel. It doesn't change the truth."

"Wait," Nina whispers, tilting her head. "Do you hear that?"

Silas turns, drawing his own sword. "Claire?"

"It's too late. They've found us."

Claire, Silas, Nina, and I form a circle in the center of the clearing as the ground beneath us begins to shift. The air grows thicker, more putrid. "Rogues."

Nina's head snaps in my direction, but whatever she's about to say gets caught in her throat. The look on my face makes her still and turn back to scan the clearing, squinting into the distance. "Raziel."

"If things go south, you fly." I spin my sword through the air as the bush ripples with energy. "That's an order."

"It's too late for that." Silas raises his sword, and a storm thunders in the distance as lightning sparks over his weapon and down his arms.

"I'm not afraid of a fight," Nina snaps. "What is that stench?"

Déjà vu hits me as adrenaline for the battle ahead fills my veins.

"Hellhounds," Silas says with a chuckle. "Just when I was starting to get bored."

There's a smile in Claire's voice as she adds, "You always wanted a puppy."

"Ha. Arriving in three . . ." Silas sounds almost gleeful as he begins to count down. "Two . . ." Beside me, Nina unfurls her wings from her back and takes to the air. I smile, sinking into the battle lust and preparing to unleash myself upon the rogues. "One."

FIVE

RAZIEL

A battle cry sounds from behind me, and the wind shifts as I turn and catch the full force of the blade coming down on my sword. The rogue's teeth are stained red, his eyes black and consumed by rage unlike anything I've ever seen.

I hold him back with one hand, and with the other grab the dagger from my belt and thrust it through his jugular, then toss him to the ground.

I don't get time to dwell. I'm surrounded. Smiling at the rogues, I note their eyes this time. Not all of them show the blackness, but for those who don't, their eyes hold a lifelessness that concerns me.

I revel in the way my sword cuts through flesh, silencing their cries. One rogue angel appears out of nowhere, and I'm forced back by his sword as it pierces my shoulder. He pulls it out with a flourish. A feral smile lights his face as he says, "I've waited a long time to meet you, my lord."

The rogue, tall with inky black hair and blue eyes, inches closer to me. I ignore the searing pain radiating from my shoulder.

"You're the first angel to draw my blood in over a century," I remark through gritted teeth. "Though you couldn't have wanted to meet me too badly—I've been in Purgatory for a few hundred years now, and this is the first time we've met." I raise my sword as he closes in on me.

The wound to my shoulder throbs, and I struggle to keep my sword arm steady. His eyes narrow on the injury, catching the slight tremble of my sword. I need to end this fight quickly.

The rogue eyes me with arrogance. "I had no interest in dallying with a drunken fool. Now this is the Archangel Raziel I've been waiting for. Lord Keeper, Master—"

"You talk too much." I take the offensive and force him back, his sword meeting and blocking every advance. He was a skilled warrior once, but his arrogance has made him overly confident. I spot the opening I need, but as I move to strike, he rolls out of the way and comes up behind me, his sword cutting through the flesh of my back.

I cry out and stumble forward as I drop my sword. Time slows as my knees hit the earth.

Rogues scream, and blood rains from the skies as Nina cuts through one after another. It's a glorious sight, watching her in battle, her movements like lightning. She never stops long enough to be a target. Every swing of her sword is made with the intent to kill.

It's a sight I'll never forget.

Thunder rolls in, and lighting strikes the earth. Fire circles the clearing, forcing the hounds to retreat. Silas's sword pierces the heart of a rogue, withdraws, and swings through the air again to behead another. His eyes scan the clearing for his sister before he darts away.

I follow his gaze and allow myself these final moments to really look at her.

Claire doesn't need a sword to cut through rogues. She breaks their skulls open and turns them on each other without breaking a sweat, and yet she moves like a dancer, cutting through each one and bringing them to their knees. She delivers death with a smile.

If I'm about to die, her face is the last I want to see.

Claire goes still, and her eyes lock with mine. She screams, hand outstretched. Tears spill down her cheeks. A sword pierces my body, and I arch into the impact. Fire and heat engulf me, and her screams echo mine as the world around us goes up in flames.

The last thing I can recall was a world on fire, but when my vision clears, it is Silas's face I see. He kneels in front of me, his hands gripping my shoulders, and I can feel Claire's hands on my back. I taste blood as it fills my mouth, and I recognize the presence of death. Staring into Silas's eyes, the knowledge sinks in, and I cannot contain my amusement.

"What's so funny?" he asks, a reluctant smile on his lips. "Do I have something in my teeth?"

"Your face is the last one I'm going to see." I choke and hiss at the heat of Claire's hands on my back, then cry out in agony as the sword is ripped from my torso. "Make her stop, Silas. The battle isn't over, and she needs her strength."

"Don't listen to him," Nina tells Claire as she kneels beside me. "Heal him, do whatever you have to do." She sheaths her sword, the star ruby glistening in the surrounding firelight. I meet her gaze, and she bows her head. For the first time since I returned, there's no mockery in her tone. "I owe you an apology, my lord. It is an honor to fight alongside you again."

"You're only saying that because you know I'm dying." I scream at the pressure applied to the wound on my shoulder.

"Oops." Silas's grip eases. "Did that hurt?"

You're not dying, Raziel. Not today. Talk like that again and you'll wish you were.

Nina jumps to her feet and draws her short swords. "I can feel them out there, watching."

"They're waiting," Silas corrects, as howls ring out around clearing, the ring of fire the only thing keeping them back.

"Hellhounds," Nina whispers. "I've only ever heard stories."

"They're a lot worse than their legends." I climb to my feet despite Claire's protests. "And they're a lot faster than you."

"If you're trying to scare me . . ."

"I'm not," I admit, relieved at the distinct lack of pain. "We should flee while we still can."

"I've missed your pep talks," Claire murmurs as she moves to stand beside Silas. "I forgot how encouraging you are."

Scanning the woods, I see at least sixty rogues and three hounds. "What are they waiting for?"

"I don't know." Nina pauses as the ground beneath our feet shifts and cracks, splitting as tree roots snap free. Trees sway back and forth in the violent winds and the tremors running through the earth. "Silas?"

"That's not me." Silas takes Claire's hand. "We need to leave, now."

"We'll never make it," I argue, and turn to meet Nina's eyes. "I'll hold them back so the three of you can escape. I'll cloak you and buy you as much time as I can."

"That's not an option," Claire protests, as the fire circling the clearing is doused by rainfall. "Either we leave or we fight, but we do it together."

Silas, Nina, and I nod our agreement. Claire takes Silas's hand, and they're gone. My feet barely leave the ground before a scream penetrates the air. I pivot to see hellhounds tearing apart Nina's wings.

"Nina!"

I pick up Nina's fallen sword and behead the first hellhound. A chill runs down my spine at the sickening sound of bone crunching between the hound's jaws right before fire engulfs its body.

The second hellhound is pushed back by fire, and I kneel beside Nina. She's on all fours, her mouth parted in a scream as her tears salt the earth. I pull her into my arms and hold her, her blood staining my clothes as her nails dig into my arms.

"I'm sorry. I'm sorry," I murmur against her hair, tears spilling from my eyes. "I'll get you out of here, Gwen, I swear it."

I squeeze my eyes closed and push back the memories. This is Nina, not Gwen.

"Raziel," she cries. "I can't fly! I'll slow you down. You need to go and warn the others before it's too late. They need to know what's up here."

"It's too late for that, little one." I brush her hair back soothingly as I hold her. "I've got you."

Her body trembles as she lifts her head to argue, but her face pales as the clearing fills with rogues and hellhounds. The rogues stand shoulder to shoulder, their swords pointed at our heads. We're surrounded.

"Too late," Nina whispers quietly, and she squeezes my arm to stand. I hold her and attempt to shield her from harm, though at this rate, it's a pointless attempt. Her wings have already been torn to shreds. Her back presses to mine, and I feel what remains of her blood-soaked wings pressing against my own.

She trembles, yet she raises her sword to fight.

Nina is one of the greatest warriors I've ever fought with. Fearless, and at times reckless, but she's faced off against greater odds. She's not afraid of this battle. Had her wings not been injured, she might have reveled in facing off with the beasts. It would have been another story to mark upon her flesh, another tale for her legend.

In this moment, I don't like our chances of surviving to share that tale.

A shadow falls over us.

"Lower the sword, Nina." I cast my eyes up at the familiar voice of my brother. "I don't want to have to kill you."

"Raphael?" Nina stares in disbelief. "I should've killed him when I had the chance."

Wasting no time, Raphael turns his gaze to mine. His arrogance disgusts me. "You should've stayed in Purgatory."

"I've never enjoyed killing before," I confess through gritted teeth, "but I'll make an exception for you, traitor."

Raphael's smile widens. "You will die here today, Master of Secrets, and by the time I am done building my empire, you won't even be a blip on my radar."

Nina rolls her eyes and groans. "He's going to bore us again with one of his speeches."

I suppress a grin. "I have the same recurring nightmare."

"Enough!" Raphael sneers. "Where is the journal?"

Christ! I knew that damn book would be a pain in the ass.

"I have many journals," I muse. "You'll have to be more specific."

"More specific, huh?" Raphael narrows his eyes, and his jaw ticks in impatience. "Where is the journal Sahari stole from your library?"

"Oh, *that* journal." I whistle, looking to Nina as she mirrors my own expression. "He's looking for *that* journal."

Nina chuckles uncomfortably but plays along. "Why didn't he say so sooner?"

"I don't like repeating myself."

"Are you sure?" Nina mocks. "You seem to love the sound of your own voice."

"You will show respect to our master!" roars a rogue behind me, and I watch in slow motion as he flies forward, his sword raised. Nina drops. As the sword swings by her head, she shoots up and grabs his arm, snapping it with a sickening pop, then her hand drops to the short sword strapped to her thigh and she thrusts it through his neck.

"Enough talking. I've grown bored." Nina tosses the corpse to the ground at Raphael's feet while spinning her sword in her hand as she circles and eyes the remaining rogues. "Let's dance."

I smile at Raphael, raising my sword as he withdraws his own. "You heard the lady."

Lightning strikes a nearby tree, sending embers into the sky as it goes up in flames. The fire casts flickering light over us, while the storm rages and blocks out the sun.

Raphael runs forward, his sword raised, a battle cry on his lips as his men and hounds swarm us. Wind pelts against the warriors, and fire circles the clearing once more, forcing the hounds back.

I swing my sword to block Raphael's attack, and his weapon falls into the mud. I raise mine for the kill strike, but a solid wall of muscle hits me, sending us rolling across the clearing and into the fire.

I roar in agony as flames lick at my flesh and the jaws of one of the hounds clenches down on my collarbone, dragging me back to its master. I can hear Nina's screams, and Claire's, telling me to get up, to fight, but the pain is too much.

"Get him on his knees," Raphael orders, grabbing Nina's sword from the mud. "Bring her to me."

I'm forced to my knees before Nina, and Raphael circles her. She's kneeling in the mud, a bloody handprint around her throat. "You're truly magnificent, Nina. A waste of a soldier. I give you one final chance to change your allegiance."

Nina's eyes close, but when she opens them, she's reciting the story of her birth.

"Serve thy Lord God, Almighty Father, and deliver justice upon His enemies."

Nina smiles at me, winks, and makes her last stand. She throws her head back, hitting the rogue restraining her, then frees her arms and rolls through the mud, grabs the discarded sword, and beheads one rogue before burying the sword through the eyes of another.

I'm pinned and forced to watch as Raphael appears behind Nina, takes Rainmaker, and runs the blade through her heart.

"I will bring about a new world," Raphael whispers into Nina's ear. "Those who do not bow will share your fate."

Nina's eyes widen, and her lips part in a silent scream.

"Nina!" Her name is ripped from my throat, and the ground beneath me trembles with a power I have not felt in a long time. Raphael holds my gaze as a tear in the veil opens. Nina's eyes meet mine one last time as the light within them fades, then he throws her through like she's no more than garbage.

A rage unlike anything I've ever felt erupts within me. I feel only hatred for the angel in front of me; I don't even feel the moment the rogues break my wings.

Raziel! Listen to me!

The wind and rain sting like a thousand cuts, forcing rogues and beasts back. Bones break beneath my hands, blood coats my tongue, and limbs are torn from flesh. My wings drag along the ground as I stalk my prey, catching the rogues and beasts in my path. I feel nothing as their swords and teeth tear at my skin.

Beyond the bloodlust, I see Claire and Silas standing by the tear in the veil. Silas's arm is firm around Claire's waist, dragging her forward, but her head is turned back. She stares at me with tears in her green eyes.

The storm Silas conjured tears through the clearing, the winds making it nearly impossible to see any farther than an arm's length in front of me, but I run toward the veil.

Raphael roars the order: "Kill him!"

I find myself falling, the last thing I'm aware of a hellhound tearing its way through my flesh.

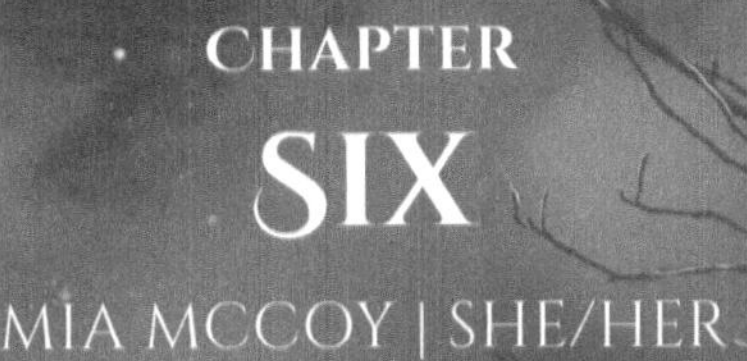

CHAPTER
SIX

MIA MCCOY | SHE/HER

My skin is gray and sickly in the mirror, almost transparent, with blue and black veins running beneath the surface. My red hair is dull and lifeless as it sticks to the sweat on my forehead and neck.

My green eyes are entirely black, made worse by the bags and veins visible beneath the skin. "What the heck is happening to me?"

I look like death, but all of that is secondary to the black blood gushing from my nostrils.

I choke as I turn on the taps, cup my hands beneath the running water, and lower my face to scrub at the blood, sobbing as manic laughter pounds and echoes in my head.

Soon. Soon. Soon.

"STOP!" I scream, clutching my head as the pounding gets impossibly louder. My fist connects with the mirror, and it shatters as the room spins, and everything goes quiet. I stare at my reflection in the shattered mirror. The blood is gone, and my skin is pale, with a sheen of sweat but otherwise healthy.

Am I going crazy?

Squeezing my eyes closed, I count down from ten and step away from the sink, my bloody fist clenching and unclenching as the familiar thrum stitches the skin of my palm back together.

Everything is fine. It was just a dream.

After I set the timer on the coffee machine, I slip into my runners and head out the door. I start every morning with a run. It allows me to shake off the nightmares from the night before and feel the sun on my skin.

The neighborhood is beautiful, especially after it rains. Twenty minutes in, the sun fades, and there's a shift in the air. The hairs on my arms and the back of my neck rise. I look up at the sky. Sure enough, dark gray clouds are rolling in from the north.

As if struck, all the air is sucked from my lungs and my heart is racing. If I didn't know better, I'd swear I was having a heart attack. My stomach churns as the memory of a dream forces itself to the forefront of my mind.

The white-haired girl is there, her appearance unnerving—as it always is—but she's been appearing in these dreams for so long that her presence has become a comfort.

The little girl is pale, with white, straw-like hair and big green eyes like those of a prowling cat. Her lips are colorless and thin, her expression set in a constant scowl that doesn't belong to someone so young.

We stand in a barren field, watching the storm as it rages and tears apart the world below, snuffing out the light of the poor souls not quick enough to escape its path. So many souls lost to the darkness.

The storm pulses as if it has a life of its own, and I can't resist the urge to touch it. Its magic is like a beating drum inside my head, pulling me into a false sense of peace. I raise my hand, and that's when I feel the storm reach back.

The wind comes for me, wrapping its talons around my throat and ripping the air from my lungs. Its magic is unlike anything I have ever felt within these dreams—pure and tainted all at once, seducing and terrifying. Unnatural.

I feel true evil corrupting all that makes me who I am, and in its place leaving every bad memory, intention, and regretful decision. It thrives on the guilt and horrors of my past, and for every life taken, the darkness seems to grow stronger.

All too slowly, I sink back into consciousness and feel the trickle of sweat sliding down my rigid spine. I focus on that sensation as I shift back into myself. My chest is heavy, and my heart races while at the same time feeling all too slow.

The darkness is coming.

I bring my knees up to my chest as I count down from ten.

"It's just a dream, it doesn't mean anything."

The lie is as old as time, as familiar as the white-haired girl in my dreams. I look to the gray skies and those angry clouds and feel the elements shifting with the approach of the storm. The ground beneath me shakes. The wind seems to rush around me, and the trees surrounding my path whisper warnings with their rustling leaves.

It's coming.

Run.

I spend the entire run home convincing myself that it was just a dream . . . that I can outrun the reality of what's coming. As I walk through the door of my home, the smoke alarm goes off, and the stench of burning plastic and burnt coffee assaults my senses.

I run into the kitchen and curse at the sight of the coffee machine shooting out sparks and smoke. As I reach the power outlet to flick the switch and pull out the plug, the damn alarm on the machine goes off.

I know it's irrational to feel betrayed, and yet, I stand there, glaring at the offending machine and wondering what else could go wrong today. I carry the machine out to the bin before I finish getting ready for work. Thanks to my breakdown earlier, I'll be late. And now I need to stop for coffee on the way too.

After a quick shower, I dress and buckle my belt, adjust the straps for my holster, and check the safety switch on the gun before I strap it in. I have to stop myself from taking the third gun and tucking it into the back of my pants.

"It was just a dream," I remind myself.

I grab my badge and close the safe, then head back to the kitchen to grab my keys and purse before heading out the door.

Of course, it couldn't be that easy. The garage won't open, so I have to climb into the bed of the truck and open the garage door manually, locking it into place with a screwdriver.

"Please start," I beg, turning the key in the ignition. Grateful when it rumbles to life. I'm not even surprised when I get to my front gate and find the electronic opener is fried.

Later that afternoon, I sit in my office, glaring at Garry, the IT guy, as he attempts to restore order to my computer. Garry has been at it for two hours, and I don't know who is more annoyed—me or him.

"That look isn't going to get this fixed any quicker, McCoy," Garry snaps, scratching the back of his neck. "Go get a coffee."

"That's what you said an hour ago," I mutter, scrubbing at my face before I look at the clock on the back wall, which also stopped working before I came into the office. "What the heck is going on with technology today?"

"It's the storm—"

"What are you talking about?"

Garry didn't look up as he explained. "My wife says there's a storm coming. She's been yapping about it for months, ever since that meteor shower— going on about what we need to do to prepare, and how we need more bottled water. I swear if I hear the words 'clean water' one more time, you might be arresting me next. The woman's nuts, but she's more accurate than the weatherman most days."

"What else does your wife say?"

"Just that," he answers, his head still buried beneath my desk. "She's been hoarding supplies for the last six months. You'd swear it was the end of days the way she talks. Though, she woke me up this morning because of a nightmare about some storm."

Thunder strikes the earth, splitting the ground in two. Fire ignites and people scream as monsters slither from the darkness and corrupt the souls of the living.

"Did she mention anything about a white-haired girl?" I ask, despite my better judgment and knowing the answer.

Garry stills beneath the desk and looks back at me in surprise. "How'd you know about that?"

"You should listen to your wife, Garry."

The man stares at me, and somehow, I can see the realization in his gaze. "You're one of them, aren't you?"

"You should go home."

"The storm . . . is it real?"

"Go home, Garry."

I don't even bother to pack up my desk; I grab my bag and head to the elevator. If the world doesn't end, I'll deal with the mess tomorrow. The doors to the elevator open, but I hesitate and take the stairs.

After climbing into the truck, I toss my bag across the seat and rest my head back against the headrest. It really has been a disaster of a day, and I've more than earned that bottle of wine I've been saving for the weekend.

I start up the truck and leave the garage without issue. It's raining, and I can't help but think about Garry's wife.

A storm is coming.

I pull up to a flickering stop light and watch as mayhem erupts in the streets. Cars are either speeding or driving too slowly, and people run across the street and in opposite directions with newspapers or briefcases above their heads. Kids huddle together under the bus stops trying to avoid the rain, while others jump in puddles and shout at the sky with carefree expressions.

My back goes rigid, and a shiver that has nothing to do with the cold runs down my spine. I want to warn them, to shout at them to run for cover, but I can't.

Stopping at a red light, I bring up my sister's contact details and call her. *You've reached Abbie Redwood. Leave me a message, and I'll text you.*

"Hey Abz, it's Miz. I'm just driving home in the storm. Be careful and call me when you get this. I love you."

I turn around the corner and feel my heart crack open as the homeless line up outside of a shelter. They'll reach capacity soon, and the doors will close.

It's dark by the time I pull into my driveway. The gate to my property sits exactly how I left it. I contemplate getting out to close it, but as my hand closes around the door handle, I hesitate and watch as the raindrops slide down the window.

Something tells me it would be a very bad idea to go out into the rain.

I continue down the driveway and pull into my garage to repeat the process from this morning, closing the garage door manually before heading inside. The stench of the coffee machine's betrayal is still pungent in the air. At that moment, there's only one thing to do —pour a glass of wine.

I'm halfway through my first glass of wine and cooking spaghetti when the entire house shakes as lightning strikes the earth outside. I stumble, dropping my glass as my hands go to my ears to suppress the ringing.

Lowering my hands, I realise a car alarm beeps in the distance. I turn off the stove and do my best to clean up the wine and broken glass, then remove the bottle of wine from the fridge and wander to the window to look out over the driveway.

I pull back the blinds and stare out at the storm. The rain pelts the window with an audible tap, tap, tap against the glass. I press my hand against it. Tiny vibrations shoot up my arm and leave behind a tingling sensation.

I can just make out the end of my driveway and the lights of the house across the street.

My attention is drawn to the streetlight on the edge of my property. A figure stands beneath it. Lighting strikes again, and for a moment, everything around me goes still. The lights above flicker and then go out.

The darkness is suffocating, and my heart races. Lightning strikes again, lighting the entire house in blinding flashes of green, blue, and white. I pull my shaking hand back from the glass. The reality finally sinks in that this isn't a typical storm.

"This isn't real." I choke on the words as the storm rushes toward me, suffocating.

Maybe I'm dreaming. No, it can't be a dream, otherwise the girl would be here too. She's always in my storm dreams. The taste of iron returns, and I sway on my feet, stumbling forward. I catch myself on the window frame and look up in time to see a figure emerge from the storm.

The streetlight stops flickering, and my eyes focus on him. It's so dark outside I can barely make out his features, but he raises a hand, and with two fingers, waves at me.

In the blink of an eye, he's gone, along with any remaining light. I swallow my fear and turn from the window, ignoring the storm as it rages outside. Feeling my way through the darkness, I return to the kitchen where I left my phone on charge.

I scream as I kick my toe on the edge of the breakfast island. "Arrhh! Where the bloody hell did that come from?" I curse, slapping the marble benchtop as if it was somehow its fault for being where it has always been. I feel around the island for my phone and hold it up triumphantly. My hands still shake, but I manage to press the home button, and another crack of lightning hits the earth right outside my house.

After unlocking the phone again, I notice the time. It's only 5:15 p.m. That can't be right, surely. I look out the kitchen window, confirming what I already know to be true.

Please, God, let her be alright . . .

Before I can hit send, lightning strikes the house, and the phone explodes in my hand. The room is lit up just long enough for me to glimpse the damage done. It's a surreal moment before the pain hits. My hands are shaking, covered in blood, with shards of glass embedded in the torn flesh of my palms.

I'm unable to hold back the tears as it dawns on me that I'm stuck until morning. Even if I could drive with my hands like this, there's no way through this storm, and being caught out there isn't an option. Even if I could call for help, there's no way I'd risk someone else's life. It's too dangerous.

Making my way upstairs to the ensuite, I leave a trail of blood behind me. My bedroom door is ajar, and I kick it open and wander over to my bathroom. Trembling from the pain, I take a moment and force my fingers to grip the doorknob. From the cupboard under the sink, I grab candles, matches, the first aid kit, and the bottle of vodka I keep hidden in the back for when things get really bad.

I do my best to ignore the agony of my hands as I light the candles. Vodka first, first aid second. When it feels like the world is ending, it's important to know your priorities.

The candles provide enough light to assess the damage done. My left hand took the brunt of it, but my right was cut from the glass screen.

Two hours, a bottle of vodka, and a warm bath later, I snuggle beneath my blanket and listen to the raging storm tear apart the world outside.

Again, I try to convince myself that it's just a storm, nothing unusual, but as I drift off to sleep, the little girl from my dreams is standing at the foot of my bed.

SEVEN

MIA

I stand in the desert. At least, that's what it will become many years from now. There won't be anything left of the modern world. This will all be another lost city buried beneath sand. Occasionally, scavengers will find remnants of old buildings, scraps of paper, and metal, but they'll have no comprehension of what any of it is.

The wind picks up and gathers sand in its wake, swirling it higher and higher into the sky. I cover my face, looking for refuge, but there's nowhere to hide. The wind hits me, and I'm lifted—tossed and thrown around like a rag doll.

I try to scream but only inhale sand. My arms flail as I try desperately to grasp a hold of something, anything, but only air and sand slip through my fingertips.

My heart races, and my chest feels tight. I'm sitting upright in bed, but I can't seem to slow down my panic. It was just a dream. I drop my head to my hands, and it feels so heavy. My eyes are dry and rough, as if the sand from my dream manifested into reality.

I'd like to blame the vodka, but the dream was too fresh, too real, and it comes back to me in flashes. A cold chill travels down my spine. I want to scream in frustration. Angry tears fill my eyes as I lift my head and stare at the ceiling.

"Why are you doing this to me?" I scream, unable to help drowning in my own self-pity. I've been having these dreams my entire life. I remember most of them. Over time, certain dreams fade, and I know when that happens it's because their particular fates have changed.

I don't know how I know this. I just know.

The storm last night wasn't new. I'd lived through it a thousand times, but this felt different. I remember the man standing beneath the streetlight. I remember the lightning. I stiffen as I lift my hands, remembering the blood, the splintered glass, the cuts and burns and the throbbing as I cradled them to my chest and fell asleep.

I kick off my blanket and crawl out of bed, hesitating as the ground beneath my feet seems to shift, then make my way over to my bathroom. Closing the bathroom door behind me, I lean back against it for support. I toss the bandages into the bin and inspect my hands, running my fingers over my palms in disbelief. Those injuries couldn't have been imagined.

My eyes wander over to the little bin beside the toilet, and I practically throw myself onto the tiles to dump the contents on the floor. Bloody tissues, used alcohol wipes, and tiny shards of glass scatter out onto the tiles in front of me.

Counting backwards from ten, I resist the urge to throw up. Once I can stand without risk of falling, I move over to the shower and turn on the water, but I find myself wondering whether or not it's safe.

In every ominous dream I've had, rain has fallen from the sky and flowed through the earth, leaving death and corruption in its wake. Staring at the running water, I hold out my hand like I do in the dreams, and for the first time, I feel the otherness reach out from within.

The water is tainted with darkness.

Run!

The ringing intensifies as I stumble from the bathroom. I dress quickly and grab my guns, ammo, and badge, trying to ignore the pull from the other room. The ringing grows louder, making it impossible to focus or register the empty space that used to be my staircase. Suddenly, I fall from the second floor and into the ruins of what used to be my living room.

I groan as I roll onto my back and stare up at the gray sky. The pounding in my head finally stops, the ringing an echo as the sounds of my surroundings filter in. I pull myself to a sitting position and take in what's left of my home.

The storm had destroyed it trying to get to me.

The ruins of my life are scattered throughout my property and beyond. Where my neighbor's houses should've been, there's nothing but rubble. It's as if a tornado swept through the area and flattened everything in its path.

I look back at what little remains of my home. How did I sleep through the destruction? Correction—how did I survive it?

I pick my way through the wreckage, digging through what remains of my garage. Among the wreckage, I find my hunting pack. It's a habit to restock it after every camping trip, so there's still plenty of supplies, ammunition for the rifle, my spare handgun and ammo, and enough food and bottled water to last a few days.

Locating the weapons safe, I retrieve my rifle and backup gun and clean out the ammo supply. I shoulder the rifle and buckle the holsters. I make sure my flannel hides the gun from sight before I gather up my pack and secure it into place.

As I pick through the wreckage, I can't help but think of my adoptive father, Jonah. My biological family was murdered by religious zealots when I was eight years old. I escaped and lived on the streets for a month before I ended up in the foster system. That's where Jonah found me years later.

Jonah collects descendants from the McCoy bloodline. He called us his "special children" and raised us on the Redwood compound—

essentially a prison camp for kids like me and those gullible enough to follow his law.

I could almost hear his voice. *"The end is coming. Never forget what you've learned here, because you'll need to rely on the skills you've got to survive."*

Right now, he'd be gathering his followers, bragging about how the end of the world had finally come and God would judge all who doubted him. I chuckle and roll my eyes at the thought, though the irony is that he hadn't been wrong.

It's time to go. Keeping a low profile, I head into the bush. My first instinct is to check on my neighbors, see if anyone needs help, but the same voice that told me to run tells me to stay out of sight. The fences separating our properties are electric, and with the electricity down, that means the fences are too.

At least in theory.

I search the ground and pick up a three-foot-long stick, then take a few extra steps back, aim at the fence, and throw. Nothing happens. The stick bounces off the fence and lands on the ground. After I clear the fence, I continue into the neighbor's territory, scanning my surroundings for any signs of life. As if things aren't bad enough already, this area is known for wild pigs.

I'm halfway across the property when I hear shouting, followed by the sound of a barking dog, then a gunshot.

Don't do it, I argue with myself, even as I head in that direction.

My neighbor lies unconscious on the ground. His son stands over him, his shoulders shaking and his arms outstretched as he tries to catch the family dog. The dog moves out of the teenager's grasp, his growls and pained barks mixing with a long whine.

I've seen this same teenager ride to school every day, his little dog running alongside him to the corner and back home once he was out of sight. Afternoon would come, and this same dog would make his way back to the corner to wait for him.

The teenager was his best friend—his human—but now, it seems, the dog thought him an enemy.

Despite knowing the truth on a deeper level, I'm still in denial. "Thomas, are you okay?"

The teen's body goes rigid at the sound of my voice. He straightens and turns to me. If it wasn't for the unnatural color of his eyes, I wouldn't have thought anything was amiss. He's at total ease, his gait steady as he approaches.

"Thomas, stop." I bring the rifle up by instinct and aim for his head. "I don't want to hurt you."

He doesn't even blink as he takes another step. Behind him, the dog continues to growl but makes no attempt to get between us. Behind Thomas, his father groans and rolls onto his side, coughing and clutching at his chest.

My vision blurs, and the sound of drums echoes inside my head.

Blackest of hearts, the beast takes hold. The voice is neither young nor old, neither male nor female. It repeats the words again and again as the drums grow louder. *Blackest of hearts, the beast takes hold.*

"Are you okay, sir?" I call out.

"It burns," the old man manages to say, then he stiffens, locking his gaze onto the dog and kneeling as he reaches for the hysterical pup. I watch as the man lunges. It's a little too late when I realize I've made a mistake, because the next thing I know, Thomas is coming for me.

A grin splits Thomas's features, and I can see blood staining his teeth. Specks of green glimmer within his unnatural black eyes. I expected them to be void of emotion. Instead, it's as if I'm staring into the pits of hell as an all-consuming rage drags what remains of Thomas into its depths. "Thomas?"

I throw myself back to avoid his grasp, but I'm not quick enough, and the tips of his nails graze my cheek. I hit the ground and use the momentum to roll out of his reach. Just as I come back to my feet, the dog releases a high-pitched yelp, then falls silent.

I do my best to block out the sounds that follow. My stomach churns, and I reach for the gun tucked into my belt. This time I don't hesitate. I take aim and blow a hole through the sixteen-year-old's chest.

One moment, he was standing above me with black eyes, and the next, he was on his knees, his eyes a clear, brilliant blue. He opened his mouth to speak, but no words came. He fell face-first into the gravel.

I climb to my feet and move quickly to stand behind my neighbor, pull the trigger, and watch as his limp body falls over the dog's corpse.

I stand there for a moment and take in my surroundings. I've just shot a sixteen-year-old boy and his father, and the family pet was torn in half by its owner. Blood from all three stains the gravel. I look up at the sky and see no trace of the storm but feel a prickling at the back of my neck that tells me it's still out there, looking for me and those like me.

A bitter laugh rips its way from my throat as I turn my back on the dead. I've dreamt of countless storms, witnessed the new world build itself in accelerated motion—life, death, and rebirth—but how many times would this world allow itself to be remade before it too grew weary of the struggle and let itself be consumed by that which sought to destroy it?

I don't look back as I follow the gravel driveway back to the front gate. I need to find a way into the city.

Abigail and I might not share blood, but we are sisters in every way that counts. Jonah is Abigail's biological father, but his greed for power and land drove him mad. Still, she'd been subjected to the same training as the rest of us.

At the age of twelve, he'd brought Abigail and I into a room for an inspection. He made a deal with a man who'd just inherited a dairy farm from his father that upon Abigail's thirteenth birthday, they would wed in exchange for the rights to the land for Jonah's expansion.

The month before Abigail's thirteenth birthday, my social worker came for a visit, and I asked her for help. I told her everything. She wanted me to leave with her that day, but I refused to leave Abigail. She left me her mobile and promised to get us out of there, but there was no proof, and it was my word against the word of a respected member of the community.

A community Jonah had built around us.

The week before the child-bride wedding, the social worker drove to the estate, and Abigail and I snuck out of the compound. My social worker drove us to a bus station and handed me an envelope of cash and an address.

A week after we arrived at the safe house, we were told the social worker was murdered. I knew in my heart Jonah was responsible. He'd have been furious—not just because we'd run away, but also because we'd ruined his plans for expanding the compound.

I keep to the trees, hiding from sight as more of my neighbors wander into the streets with vacant expressions, black eyes, covered in blood, and carrying weapons. They seem to herd together. Occasionally, I see one wandering alone, but if there was a cluster nearby, they gravitated toward each other.

Even the animals were acting strangely, but it wasn't until I watched three rabid dogs hunt down a terrier that I realized the animals must be infected by the virus too.

I can't unsee the vicious attacks. The knowledge that animals were somehow infected made the situation even worse.

As I creep farther into the bush, I spot an abandoned pink bicycle with yellow hand-painted daisies on the basket. It'll have to do. Pausing only briefly at the sound of a stick breaking behind me, I pick up the bike and silently walk it past the smeared trail of blood into the trees.

My stomach churns as I look back down at the bike. Small, pink, the basket with hand-painted daisies and the patchwork teddy. I refuse to cry, to let those five little facts build a picture of some young girl falling off her bike and being dragged away.

Stop it.

Whatever monsters lurk beyond those trees don't matter. None of these people matter; not to me. I need to find my sister—it's Abi who matters—and together, we'll figure out what to do.

I don't want to admit it, but when I consider finding "somewhere safe," there's only one place I can be sure of. The one place we promised ourselves we'd never return to.

The compound was both our home and our prison. Just the thought of the place is enough to send me into a cold sweat. But I won't allow myself to think about it further, not now.

I walk the bike onto the road, making sure there's enough distance between me and the lurkers before I climb on. It's been a few years since I've ridden a bicycle. I barely get my balance before I hear the unmistakable sound of footsteps behind me.

I don't look back, peddling as fast as I can away from the infected, away from the memories and the home I'd made for myself and into a future full of uncertainty, a future of nightmares made real.

EIGHT

RAZIEL

Five centuries. That's how long it's been since I've inhabited a human body.

It's both strange and familiar, but all is eclipsed by the ringing in my ears as panic sets in. *I have fallen.*

The ground is hard, and gravel digs uncomfortably into the flesh of my back. What must be blood, warm and sticky, soaks into the clothing I wear.

While the vessel I'm inhabiting has been emptied of his soul, remnants of his life linger behind. Every new sight and smell triggers memories of the past. The scent of the alley calls to mind a similar place behind a childhood home—a place where he'd once played with his brothers—and the sight of blood was a reminder of the first dead body he'd ever seen. It would be the first of many.

All the faces and names come to me in a rush. Guilt, shame, and regret weigh heavy on the unbeating heart inside my chest. The faces of his children and a memory of the woman he loved most linger in slow motion at the forefront of my mind. At the moment of his death, he was angry, confused, sad, and scared, but he died knowing he'd tried to do the right thing.

With the memories still fresh in my mind, I sit up and wait for the ringing to subside as I try to gain my bearing on the new reality. I raise my bloodstained hands. Black ink covers old tattoos from wrist to elbow, with strange designs left unfinished.

The ringing in my ears subsides, and other sounds filter through. Sirens blare in the distance, and music plays from somewhere in the building above me. It's almost enough to overwhelm these new senses, but I try to block it out. I climb unsteadily to my feet, catching myself on the brick wall.

Placing a hand over the gunshot wound on my chest, I draw the bullet out and watch it fall with a click to the gravel at my feet. The torn and bloodied flesh knits itself back together until all that remains is a faded pink scar. I kneel by the bullet, blood soaking the gravel in the alley, and press my hands to the earth.

The first time I came to earth, my hands met rich soil, vibrating with Mother Nature's purity.

This time, the soil is buried beneath layers of rocks, cement, decay, and resentment. It speaks of global warming, pollution, political corruption, and greed. The state of my father's creation is at an all-time low.

Mother Nature recoils from my touch, and I'm forced to retreat, drowning in fury and resentment for this new world.

How did I get here?

The last thing I remember is Purgatory. Reign, Nina. Nina? What happened to Nina? I look to the sky. The sun is shining. There isn't a cloud in sight.

What happened up there? I can't stay here. I don't belong here! I won't stay. I need to go home. I need—

I unfurl my wings and immediately wish I hadn't.

Pain rips through my back, like flames tearing at my wings, shredding them with razor-sharp steel until there's only agony and fire. The force of it throws me forward. I catch myself against the gravel, gritting my teeth as I crush the rocks between my fingers into dust.

I lift my head, swallowing a scream for help as I realize nobody will come for me. I've never felt so abandoned in my entire existence. *This is what happens to traitors.* I open my eyes, forcing myself to examine the damage.

My wings are still there, but the damage is so severe I have to look away. Broken, torn, and shredded in places by God only knows what. The blood coating the gravel is now mixed with feathers and ash, still burning with the flames of the fall.

How did I survive?

Gritting my teeth, I fold away what remains of my wings and face the sky to speak to God.

Why am I here, Father? Why would you send me to this place?

I think back to our last conversation. It's been centuries since we spoke. My thoughts go to my brothers and sisters, recalling chaos as we gathered in the hall to discuss the missing angels. I can't make sense of what was happening. It's a haze, nothing staying in focus long enough for me to grasp.

The words *"As it began, so must it end"* echo in my ears. A trickle of fear creeps up my spine, and memories of a prophecy and a great war filter through the cracks in my mind. *What have I done?*

Three days after the fall, I stand across the street from an old brownstone. It looks the same, and yet everything is different. Today, there's a blue car with a cracked windshield and a pink ticket wedged beneath the windscreen wiper.

The garden looks as it did that day, only instead of Gwen kneeling in the dirt, tending to the garden, her husband is in her place. He's dressed in worn jeans, a white shirt, and a red flannel overshirt. He wipes away sweat with the back of his sleeve and calls to someone in the house.

A servant comes out carrying a pitcher and two glasses and sets them down on the table. With his back to me, Isaiah pours himself a drink, then fills the second glass. His voice sounds inside my head.

I was wondering when you'd show up.

May I join you? I ask, hesitating.

I suspect I have little choice, do I?

Nervously, I cross the street. My palms sweat, and I can't stop fidgeting with the lint inside my pockets. I unclasp the iron latch and push the gate open, trying not to fall to my knees and beg for his forgiveness as memories of the past come flooding to the surface.

The sound of Gwen's screams. Isaiah's promise to kill me. The betrayal that followed.

"You look like shit," Isaiah quips, his lips thin as he rubs his salt-and-pepper beard. His hazel eyes meet mine, cold and unwelcoming. "When did you fall?"

"Three days ago." I sit across from him and reach for the glass. "I wasn't sure you'd still be here."

"This place is all I have left of her." The words cut deep, and I can't meet his gaze. "Welcome back, Raziel. It would seem the consequences of your mistakes keep piling up."

"I didn't do this." His eyes meet mine again, and I don't shy away this time. "I need help, Isaiah. Something is wrong."

Chuckling, Isaiah brings his drink to his lips. "Oh, the irony."

"I *need* help." My voice catches in my throat at the memory of the last time I'd spoken those words in this garden. I knew there was the possibility he'd turn me away, but there's no one else I can appeal to. "Please."

His face is expressionless, but I see the rage behind his eyes, and his hands tremble as he balls them into fists. I can feel the power radiating from him. It prickles my skin and makes the hairs on the back of my neck stand on end.

I shouldn't have come here.

"So, the Keeper of Secrets comes to me for help," Isaiah spits through his teeth, followed by a dark, humorless laugh. "You're lucky I don't slit your throat and use your remains to fertilize the roses."

"Isaiah."

"I'm not finished," he growls, rising out of his seat. "You destroy everything you touch, Raziel. You were my friend once; my brother. There was a time I shared *everything* with you. Now, my biggest regret is that I didn't kill you the last time you came for aid."

I hang my head and feel the weight of my past.

"Not a day goes by where I don't wish the same. I'm sorry, Isaiah. I shouldn't have come."

"No, you shouldn't have," he spits angrily, then steps back. "Damnit."

"I'm leaving," I say, rising out of the chair.

He raises his hand to stop me. "I can't let you leave."

"Why?"

"She's waiting for you," Isaiah says reluctantly. "You aren't the only one that fell, Raziel. Sahari arrived six days before you, and she's not the only one."

"Sahari is here?" Somehow, the information doesn't feel new. "She's alive?"

"She's alive. You aren't the only one missing time, either. A lot of the fallen are reporting absent memories from their last day in heaven. What's the last thing you remember?"

"I remember Purgatory," I admit, searching through the haze. "I remember being with Nina and Reign."

Isaiah's eyes sharpen as he focuses his suspicious gaze on me. "Show me your wings."

"Show me yours," I snap defensively.

Isaiah rolls his eyes. "This isn't a time to be coy, Raziel. If you're truly one of the fallen, you'll have nothing to hide. You came here for my help; you believe you can trust me. I am asking you to give me a reason to trust you."

Unable to look at him, I unfurl my wings, or what remains of them. The barely healed wounds reopen, tearing and ripping, shredding through tendons and muscle, and the pain brings me to my knees. They hang like a dead weight on my back, drooping limply onto the grass beneath me.

The world tilts, and I feel myself falling, but before I hit the ground, Isaiah's arm reaches across my chest, catching hold of me. He presses a cold hand to a damaged wing as wind sweeps through, carrying ashes and singed feathers to the blooming rose bushes. Gone is the sweet scent that reminds me of home. Now all that remains is the stench of my failures.

"Don't be so stubborn," Isaiah quips as I attempt to straighten. "I've got you."

Genuine compassion laces his voice, and it feels like a knife to the heart. I don't deserve his kindness, not after what I took from him.

Ignoring his advice, I force myself to stand upright, though I'm still unable to fold away my damaged wings. "Does it not bring you joy to see me like this?"

"Like what?"

"Broken."

Isaiah speaks softly. "You were broken long before the fall, brother. Seeing you like this brings me no joy."

"Where is Sahari?"

"She is safe with the other survivors of the fall."

"Everything hurts," I admit, as a shiver ripples through my wings.

"Your wing is dislocated."

"I suspect it happened during the fall."

"Unlikely, considering the angle." Isaiah raises his hand to examine the wing. His healing powers send cold chills through the tendons, soothing the ache. "It looks to have happened during an attack. Your wings are completely shredded. Something with claws, maybe fangs, cut through flesh and bone."

Isaiah leans in and sniffs.

"What are you doing?" I demand.

"Do you smell that?"

"All I smell is burned flesh and burning feathers."

"It's sulfur." He sniffs my wing again. "That can't be right. Do you mind if I examine the wound? Something appears to be stopping it from healing."

I nod my consent and lock my knees to keep from falling.

"This will hurt," he says in apology, before digging the tips of his fingers into the open wound. His arm tightens to hold me upright as my body jolts forward at the rush of pain. "Whatever attacked you left behind a piece of itself."

"Is that what I think it is?" I ask through gritted teeth, unable to keep the trembling from my voice.

Isaiah helps me to the table, and I fold away my wings—what's left of them—before collapsing into the chair. White-hot pain shoots up my spine and settles between my shoulders. I watch as Isaiah grabs the pitcher of water and shoves his hand inside, rubbing whatever he retrieved clean of blood. He holds up a three-inch-long canine as thick as my own thumb.

Dread sinks in, stealing my words.

"A fang from a hellhound," Isaiah finishes, examining it closely. "This doesn't look good, brother."

"None of it looks good from where I'm sitting." I force myself to stand to examine the tooth. "I don't remember what happened."

"I believe you." He hands me the fang. "I don't think you were meant to survive the fall."

"I shouldn't have survived at all," I tell him, an unfamiliar sense of mortality sinking in.

"If you were any other angel, you wouldn't have," Isaiah says candidly. "I could use a beer. You?"

"A beer sounds great." I pocket the fang, then follow Isaiah into the old brownstone, unable to look too closely at the familiar wallpaper and the old frames hanging on the walls. "It hasn't changed."

Without looking back, Isaiah lifts his eyes to the chandelier in the foyer. "I modernized the chandelier. It's a pain in the ass to change the bulbs, but the cleanup is easier."

I can't help chuckling. "How very domestic you've become."

"Fuck you." Isaiah looks back over his shoulder with a grin, but it falls almost immediately, as if remembering why we are here.

The fireplace fills the room with a soft ambient light. A widescreen TV is mounted to the wall above it, and in the center of the room sits a tan leather sofa. A fully stocked bar runs along the back wall with two stools tucked in front of it.

My hands caressed the mahogany wood bar, tracing the worn markings as memories come flooding back.

Gwen sways to a melody only she can hear. She holds a glass of scotch, her nails painted a delicate pink that matches her dress. Her blonde curls escape the bun and frame her face as she dances. I watch from the doorway as her eyes open, her big brown irises meeting mine, and a grin stretches across her face. "Dance with me before we go, Raziel?"

"Raziel?" Isaiah snaps his fingers in front of my face as he holds out an opened bottle of beer. "Do you want a drink or not?"

I shake myself out of the painful memory, reach for the beer, and take a long swig. Everywhere I turn, I'm hit with memories of her—of them, and the life I robbed them of. I close my eyes and raise the bottle to my lips again. "Is Sahari here?"

"No." Isaiah pulls out the bar stool. "After you regained consciousness, what was the first thing you remembered?"

I take a seat beside him at the bar and think about it. "There was a moment after the shock subsided when I heard the words *'As it began, so must it end.'* It's a line from the bloodline prophecy."

"I know what it is." Isaiah's knuckles turn white around the neck of his bottle. "Why does everything always lead back to her?"

Ignoring his question, I focus on the possible consequences of the prophecy. "The prophecy changes depending on the players, but the one thing that remains consistent is the catastrophic events that will destroy and exterminate *all* life on earth."

"Are you saying we're as vulnerable as the humans?"

"Our brothers and sisters are falling from heaven, Isaiah. We're missing time, and you just pulled a hellhound fang from my wing. If we don't find our way home before the prophecy unfolds, we're as vulnerable to whatever chaos it brings as the humans are."

Isaiah clinks his bottle against mine. "To the end of the world, and the fools that damned us all."

"Maybe we can stop it," I say, as Isaiah drops his head to the bar and hits the bench with his hand.

"No, no, no!" He lifts his head and glares at me, the wrinkles around his eyes deepening. "No."

"But—"

"No!" he snaps. "I've seen this movie, played that role, and I'm not interested in the sequel. Hear my words, Raziel. I am not helping you clean up that woman's mess again!"

"We owe it—" Isaiah's fist meets my nose with a sickening crunch. I fall off the stool, clutching my nose as blood fills my mouth, and my ears ring as the room around me spins out of control. "Fuck!"

Isaiah stands above me, vibrating with rage. "I've given enough, Raziel. I don't owe it, or you, or this world, anything. It can burn for all I care."

"Isaiah," I plead, climbing to my feet and grabbing hold of his arm.

Isaiah's voice is low and menacing as he says, "I suggest you remove your hand, brother, or you might find yourself one limb short for the apocalypse."

Reluctantly, I let go of his arm. "Our people are in danger, and I fear the risk goes beyond that of an apocalypse."

"Maybe it's for the best." Isaiah throws his arms up. "I'm tired, Raziel. I just want it to be over."

"I don't believe that." I close the space between us. "If it were true, you wouldn't have kept this place going. You'd have killed me the moment I crossed the street."

"I didn't kill you because I'm under orders not to. Sahari is preparing for war as we speak. She's already in talks with the coven and the local packs about protection. You cannot stop the inevitable."

The news of Sahari's progress toward war does not surprise me in the least. She was created for war. *The* Avenging Angel, first of her kind, Goddess of Death and Commander of War. The only way she'd be able to function is to prepare.

"I still need to try."

"Of course you do," he says, defeated. "Your honor will get you killed someday."

"If I'm going to die, Isaiah, I'd rather die trying to help our people return home than see them destroyed in a war they cannot win against an enemy they cannot fight."

Isaiah shakes his head but sighs. "Let's get out of here."

"Where to?"

He holds up a set of keys. "I'm taking you to Sahari."

I follow Isaiah out to the garage, where he opens the door to a white car. I eye the metal contraption hesitantly. "You drive around in this?"

"Would you rather I carry you?" Isaiah smirks, his eyes going from the car back to me, and for a moment, it's just like the old days. "You aren't afraid, are you?"

"What? No. I just . . . assumed we'd fly."

"Flying would certainly be faster," he admits. "Not as much fun, though, and you aren't in a position to take flight right now, so I'd have to carry you. If that's what you want, sweetheart, all you need to do is ask."

"Get in the car," I growl.

TEN

RAZIEL

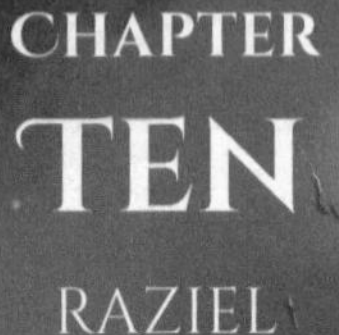

Angels began falling nearly two weeks ago. Since Sahari's arrival, their numbers have doubled each day. Those that survive make contact. The witches, who Isaiah informs me are our allies, have been tracking the fallen angels through the meteor showers since the first survivors appeared. He credits the coven for the survival of many of our kin, including Sahari.

I can't help but wonder who else is here. Sahari was powerful, left hand to God, and a member of parliament. She ruled in God's place, and in my place. Arguably, she had been the most powerful archangel in heaven. Aside from myself, which leads me to question, who rules in our absence?

"I know that look," Isaiah says, his knuckles white on the steering wheel as he glances at me. "What is it?"

"I was just wondering who's in charge." I look up to the starry night sky. "Has there been any sign of Reign, or Nina?"

"We found part of Nina's sword, but there's been no sign of the others."

"Rainmaker?"

A quick shake of his head. "It was one of her short swords. The steel was broken during the fall, so Sahari sharpened it down to a dagger. We're still searching, but the sword could be anywhere."

Flashes of a battle filter through the cracks of my memory. "I keep seeing a clearing. There's a fight, and I hear myself screaming her name." I fight back the emotions that catch in my throat. "I think I was with her when I fell."

"Do you remember anything else?"

"Not clearly."

"If Nina's injuries were anything like yours, she wouldn't have survived," Isaiah says, grief choking his voice. "You may want to approach Sahari with caution."

"Thanks for the warning," I say, blowing out a breath. "I was there the day our father created Sahari and the sisters. That kind of bond and loss would be like missing a fundamental piece of yourself."

Memories of Gwen hang between us. "If it were not for you bringing me back from the edge, I'd have torn apart the world and gladly let it consume what remained of me."

"Gwen wouldn't have wanted—"

"You don't get to speak her name. My wife is dead because of your arrogance. You gambled with our lives, with the life of a woman who loved you and would have done anything you asked, and you betrayed us like it was nothing."

"I will carry the guilt of her death for the rest of my life," I promise. "I don't know how many times you want to hear that I am sorry."

"Maybe I'll believe it when you stop making the same damn mistakes."

He pulls the car to a stop in front of a three-story cabin. The cabin sits in the middle of a clearing, with leaves covering the ground from the trees surrounding the property.

A young woman sits on the steps of the cabin, rising as Isaiah and I climb out of the car. Another figure emerges from the trees, petite and dressed in far too little for the weather, swinging a stick and swigging from a bottle of vodka.

"Ohhhh, look, it's the ass-kisser," the angel slurs. "I was wondering when you'd arrive to greet the Queen of the Fallen."

"Cut it out, Ester," the one from the steps says sharply. Then, to me, with a bow of the head. "Forgive him, my lord."

I keep my attention on Ester, noting the feminine vessel but the familiar presence beneath. "What happened to you, Brother?"

Ester stumbles forward, jabbing a chipped, black-polished fingernail into my chest, the stench of alcohol burning my eyes. I meet their cloudy, faraway gaze, the body a stranger's, the soul within anything but.

"That's the million-dollar question, isn't it?" He sneers through a mouth that isn't his, spitting a little with every word. "How are your wings, ass-kisser?"

"Crispy," I admit, ignoring the twinge in my back and Isaiah's abrupt snort as he chokes on his laugh. "Yours?"

Ester cackles bitterly. "She cut them off."

"What do you mean?" I ask, unable to properly process the information. "Cut them off?"

"When we found Ester, his wings were too damaged. Sahari made the decision to remove the wings to spare his life."

She *what*? Horrified, I look at Isaiah in disbelief. "It would have been more humane to cut his throat."

"Our numbers are depleted, Raziel. We need everybody for the coming war."

"Do they look ready for war to you?" I ask.

"Hey, assholes," Ester snaps, his voice slurred and razor-thin. "I've still got ears, you know!"

The angel from the steps gently lays a hand on his arm. "Sahari is waiting," she murmurs, nodding toward the cabin. "I'll take care of Ester."

"Thank you, Trinity," Isaiah says, already heading for the stairs.

"Don't keep our fearless queen waiting," Ester calls after us. "She might take more than your wings!"

Isaiah doesn't slow, but his voice is low enough for only me to hear. "We're not immune to the addictions of our vessels. Our wills are stronger than humans, but... we all have our own breaking point, too. Ester's drowning himself to forget what he's lost."

I glance back at him... too-thin frame, glassy eyes. "Is there nothing we can do?"

"Not until he wants help. And I've tried," His mouth tightens. "I have to warn you, Raziel. It's not a pretty sight inside."

"I didn't come this far to turn back. Stop being cryptic and show me."

Isaiah grips the handle. "Just remember, you asked for this." He pushes open the door and steps aside with a sweep of his hand. "Ladies first."

"Age before wisdom." I nod toward the darkened space beyond. "I'm surprised your vanity hasn't driven you to seek out a younger vessel."

Isaiah chuckles as he strolls past me instead. "Don't be jealous, Raziel. This silver fox hasn't failed me yet."

In the first room, witches tend to several survivors of the fall. I pause in the doorway, but Isaiah nudges me forward.

"It's best not to linger."

"What are they doing for them?"

"Whatever they can," Isaiah says, glancing inside. "The worst of them go straight to the priestess."

The second room smells of dust and exhaustion. Sleeping bags litter the floor, angels sprawled in various states of weariness. One lies on his back, staring at the ceiling. Another sits by the window with headphones on, absently flipping through a gossip magazine. A woman leans against the far wall, arm in a sling, scratches marring her otherwise flawless face.

In the corner, a boy sits on the sofa with a book in his lap. The vessel's voice sounds far too innocent and young, but the wisdom in his eyes leaves no doubt about the identity of this Archangel.

"Hello, Brother. I'm glad to see you survived the fall."

"Uriel." Relief rushes through me at the confirmation. "It's good to see you."

"Uriel fell the same day you did." Isaiah says. "His last clear memory was speaking to you in a field."

"I don't remember that." I admit. "Do you remember anything else?"

Uriel shakes his head. "Nothing else. I can sense the missing memories, flashes here and there. I just can't quite reach them."

"It's the same for me."

The angel on the sleeping bag speaks without looking over. "My last memory is searching for the missing." A dry laugh escapes him. "I found them."

"Every day, more angels arrive," Uriel adds. "Can you hear them?"

"I haven't heard anything since I fell."

Uriel studies with me concern. "What do you think happened upstairs?"

"I don't know," I squeeze his small shoulder.

"I've got people scouting for the fallen," Isaiah says. "We'll get to the bottom of this."

"When you say 'people', you mean witches?"

"And then some." He confirms with a grin.

"Our brother's choice of friends is questionable," Uriel says with a faint smile, "but we're grateful for allies in the war to come."

"We don't know what's happening, or who's behind it," I caution. "Let's not jump to conclusions."

"It's the bloodline prophecy." Isaiah rolls his eyes when I glare at him. "Don't look at me like that. You said it yourself."

"Bloodline prophecy?" Uriel asks. "It's happening now?"

Reluctantly, I tell them what I heard when I first fell, and what I believe it means.

"That doesn't bode well for us." The angel with the magazine says, tossing it aside. "If the twins are free, finding them will be impossible. Like finding a needle in a haystack."

"We'll find them," another voice cuts in from the doorway, a feral grin in place. "Which will make killing the little witch all the sweeter."

"What's your name?" I ask the newcomer.

"Clarence."

"Of course it is."

Isaiah snorts, covering it with a cough. "Sorry, tickle in my throat."

Ignoring Isaiah, I step in closer to Clarence. "I'll only say this once, so make sure to tell your friends. If you or anyone else goes after the McCoy bloodline, I will find you. And I will end you."

"You aren't the boss here—" His words choke off when my hand closes around his throat, lifting him clear off the floor.

"I am the Lord Keeper of Secrets, Prophet, Protector of the Word and the Bringer of Hope. I am the right hand of God, and you will obey me." I lean in, my voice dropping for his ears alone. "Otherwise, Clarence, I'll make you my bitch."

Isaiah's laughter follows as he slings an arm over my shoulder and steers me out of the room. "Damnit, Raziel, I try to hate you, and then you drop lines like that, and I'm reminded of why we were friends."

"The angels are out for blood, but they are not ready for battle, especially when we do not know who we are fighting."

"What would you have me do? They aren't like us, Raziel. They're scared, and angry. Most of them have never even seen battle. Power is the only thing keeping them in line and soon not even that will be enough. We're not in the capitol with an army at our backs anymore. This is earth." Isaiah holds out his arms. "This is all we have."

"I don't know what to do here," I admit, as we come to a stop in front of the door.

"Join the club." Isaiah slaps me on the back. "Get your free T-shirt on sign-up."

"If Michael is alive and on earth, we must find him." I cannot keep the desperation from my voice. "The angels fear him."

"There's been no sign of him yet."

"Speak to your people and tell them to be on the lookout. Get creative. If they can't find Michael, have Michael find us."

The door in front of us swings open. A blonde angel with gray-blue eyes stands there, rage simmering in her eyes as she greets me. "Hello, Raziel,"

"Sahari." A weight lifts from my chest at seeing her, but it's replaced with the guilt of the last century or more. "You have no idea how good it is to see you."

"It's good to see you too," she says, stepping aside. "We have a lot to catch up on."

~

Maps, books, and crystals litter the small room. Pillows lie scattered on the floor in the center, circling a bowl with ingredients for a spell. "When did you start dabbling in witchcraft?" I ask.

"Since I woke up in the vessel of a young witch." Sahari settles herself on the pillows in front of her crystals and book of spells. "Her name was Maya McCoy—a descendant from the bloodline. She sacrificed herself so that I could inhabit her body. The coven did not approve, but nothing can be done for it now."

"Good to see you making friends," I mutter, spotting a young witch glowering in the corner as she appraises me.

"You must be Raziel, the famous storyteller."

"That's Ava, my babysitter." Sahari scowls at the young witch. "This is the archangel—"

"I know who he is." The witch's scowl is unpleasant as she holds my gaze.

"Pleasure, I'm sure," I say, knowing there will be no pleasantries with the witch, then turn back to Sahari. "What's the last thing you remember?"

Sahari lifts her face, her eyes meeting mine. "My last coherent thought was of you. I needed to see you. I thought you could help."

"The last time anybody saw you, you were coming to see me," I admit, taking a seat on the pillows across from her. "At least, that's what I'm able to gather from my memories. It's all a little hazy after I left Purgatory with Nina and Reign."

"Nina." Sahari's voice cracks. "We found one of her swords."

"I heard."

"You don't remember anything else from before the fall?"

"Not enough to paint a clear picture." Hesitating, I clear my throat. "Before I fell, I vaguely recall being in a clearing with others. I think Nina was there."

"Was she alive?"

I search my memory, trying to piece it together, but I see nothing, know nothing, aside from the deep sense of dread and grief inside my chest. "I'm unsure."

Knowing fills Sahari's gaze as she sees the truth of it in my eyes. "But in your heart?"

"I don't believe she made it out of that clearing."

Silence falls over the room. Isaiah sits on the bed behind Sahari as I gesture to the room and all the maps. "What is all this?"

"I'm learning about this world." She follows my gaze. "Tracking the fallen isn't easy, especially once they leave here. Some of them have disappeared entirely."

"What do you mean?"

Isaiah chimes in from the bed. "I suspect someone is hunting the survivors of the fall."

"You've got to be kidding me," I growl, unable to help my frustration. "What the hell is happening?"

"We're at war." Sahari meets my gaze. "Whoever kicked us out of heaven wants to make sure we can't get back."

"After I regained consciousness, I heard the words '*As it began, so must it end*'. Do you recognize the phrase?"

"It's the bloodline prophecy." Sahari looks between Isaiah, Ava, and me. "Are you telling me this is because of the bloodline?"

"A few moments ago, I'd have said yes, but now I'm not entirely sure. The timing is convenient, and the signs are there. The storm is coming, and soon, but there might be a chance to prevent it."

"What a fool you are." Isaiah chuckles, though he is clearly unamused.

"It pains me to agree with Isaiah," Sahari adds, "but in this case, your idealism, while commendable, is imprudent."

Ignoring the others, Ava turns to me and asks, "What do you mean?"

"If the prophecy holds true, a great storm will tear through this world, leaving in its wake a trail of corruption and rot that eats through the very core of who we are. This plague won't just destroy humans, and it won't just destroy the earth—it'll destroy every living thing, and it won't stop there. You're right, we are at war, but it isn't a war we can fight if we're divided and fighting each other. It is a war that can only be won if we stand united."

Isaiah claps slowly. "How long have you been working on that speech, my lord?"

"Shut up, Isaiah," Sahari says. "War is what I do, Raziel. Revenge is my purpose. My sisters are dead, and the one responsible is out there killing those I swore to protect. What would you have me do?"

"I'm not asking you to stop hunting, Sahari. I'm simply asking you to consider the possibility of hope. If you help me stop this prophecy and prevent war on earth, I give you my word, I will ride at your side with an army to kill those responsible for the loss of our brothers and sisters."

"You believe we're fighting two wars?"

"I believe whoever threw us out of heaven wanted its most powerful leaders out of the way. They broke my wings and set a hellhound on me in the hopes I would not survive."

"A hellhound?" Ava questions, her disbelief clear in her voice. "Aren't they a myth?"

"Hellhounds are as real as witches and angels," I say, gesturing between the witch and me. "I wasn't meant to survive that fall."

"Hellhounds. You're sure?" Sahari asks.

I retrieve the fang from my pocket and hand it to her. "Isaiah pulled this from my wing."

Sahari examines the fang in disbelief. "Hellhounds in heaven? How is that possible?"

"I do not know," I admit.

"I've been thinking about it," Isaiah chimes in. "The only one ballsy enough to attempt it would be Lucifer, but he's still in the cage. Maybe his followers caught a second wind."

Sahari shakes her head. "It's not Lucifer."

"How can you be sure?" I ask, though I suspect she's correct. "It wouldn't be the first time Luci tried to take heaven."

"If it were Lucifer, we'd all be dead already." Sahari's eyes flash to mine as memories from long ago hang between us. "Thank the blessed heavens he's still caged."

Isaiah walks over to us, eyeing Sahari closely. "I'm sensing a *but . . .*"

Sahari takes a deep breath. "*But* someone has been breaking seals."

"That is just fucking perfect." I say humorlessly, and I rise to begin pacing. What purpose could anyone have to break the seals of hell? All too quick, the answer hits me like a ton of bricks. "They want to open the gates."

"If Lucifer is freed, this prophecy is the least of our problems," Isaiah says, panic rising in his tone.

I tilt my head back, closing my eyes as the possibilities of what we are up against align.

"So not only are we dealing with a world-ending prophecy involving the bloodline, falling angels, missing chunks of time, an unknown enemy hunting survivors of the fall, and hellhounds running loose in heaven, but now, someone is out there breaking the seals that separate our world from hell. Best-worst case, they plan to open the gates. Worst-worst case, they intend to free Lucifer from his cage."

"When you say it like that," Isaiah drawls, "fleeing to Mexico doesn't sound so bad."

I nod in agreement, imagining dying with a bottle of tequila, surrounded by beautiful men and women on the beach. No, that doesn't seem so bad at all. I give myself a moment of selfishness as I consider the possibility.

"So, my lord, which disaster would you like to tackle first?" Sahari asks, amusement in her tone. "Keeping in mind our numbers are few, and fewer still if you take out those who are unreliable or refuse to follow."

"I think it's time we stop giving them a choice," I tell Sahari, then address Isaiah and Ava. "Finding Michael should be a priority for your trackers."

"You assume Michael will share your priorities?" Isaiah questions.

"Michael is loyal to our father. The angels fear him, and if Lucifer is freed from his cage, we're going to need all the help we can get."

Sahari nods solemnly. "I'm glad you're here, Raziel."

"Thanks for letting me use your shower," I say, exiting the bathroom in a cloud of steam. I've got a towel around my waist and am using a smaller one to dry my hair. Sahari looks up from her position at her desk, her eyes roaming along my bare torso.

"You're most welcome," she purrs, tilting her head as she sets her book down on the table. "Your vessel is quite beautiful."

"As is yours," I say, meeting her gaze. "It's been a long time."

When Sahari smiles, it's a coy, seductive grin. "Where are your clothes?"

"In my room." I look to the door behind her and my room beyond. "Has Isaiah returned from his errands?"

"I haven't seen him." Shrugging lazily, Sahari pushes off the desk and approaches me. I still beneath her touch as her fingers brush along the back of my hand and travel up, her body closing the distance between us, as she leans to me and breathes in the scent of her soap.

"Sahari," I say, my voice shaky at the close proximity of her mouth on my flesh. "I'm not sure we have time for this."

"There is always time for this," Sahari croons, looking up through her black lashes. "You taught me that." My body reacts as her hands glide along my rib cage and across the abs of my stomach before pulling on the towel wrapped around my waist. "Impressive."

I hiss through my teeth and grab hold of her arms, backing her toward the desk. My lips part to allow her access as our hands roam hungrily over each other.

Any self-control I possess goes out the window as she moves with a swiftness I hadn't expected, pushing me back against the desk, her eyes darkening. Her blonde hair frames her body like a second pair of wings. The energy emitting from her lights a fire within, and I rise to meet her challenge for dominance.

Her nails drag along the flesh of my stomach, leaving angry red marks, while her hot breath tickles and her tongue peeks out to taste the water droplets still clinging to my skin. I reach for her, but her eyes snap to mine and her hands knock away my advances.

"Keep them on the desk," she orders.

"It's going to be like that, huh." I grit my teeth as her mouth continues its assault. "Sahari."

Before either of us can take it further, the doors to the bedroom are thrown open. Trinity, covered in blood, yells from the doorway, "We're under attack."

Screams from below filter through the open doors. Sahari moves before Trinity can finish.

"Ester is dead."

I stare at the trembling angel as a silk garment is thrown at my face. "Put it on," Sahari orders, before throwing a sword to the quivering angel. "Prepare for battle."

Trinity yells in panic. "We're not warriors, Sahari! We don't know how to fight! We'll die."

"Today, you are warriors," I tell her as I close the distance between us. "And you'll die faster if you cower in the corner," I warn, squeezing her shoulder reassuringly. "Fight or die. It's that simple."

Sahari tosses a long sword through the air. I catch it and swing it in an arc, testing its weight and balance. It'll do.

"Are you ready?" she asks.

I look at her and nod. "After you."

Sahari pauses in the doorway and looks back with a grin. "If we survive this, I want my robe back."

I raise my hand to her cheek, caressing her exposed throat, and wrap my fingers around it, dragging her closer to me as I brush my lips against hers in a promise for more. "If we survive, Sahari, you're welcome to help me take it off."

Sahari's smile widens as she twists away from the blade at her throat. Twin blades appear in her hands as a different kind of lust fills her blue eyes.

As I enter the foyer, I watch as Sahari gives orders and the remaining angels and witches hand out weapons.

Standing off to the side is a small child . . . It takes a moment for me to recall Uriel's vessel. Even in this form, he stands stoic, ready to fight alongside his brothers and sisters.

"You should be in the tombs," I say.

"Nice robe." Uriel's tone is flat. "It really shows off your calves."

"Thanks. I like the freedom of it." I match his tone as I kneel beside him, my sword resting between my legs. "You shouldn't be up here, Uriel."

Uriel's blue eyes flash to mine with a rage that only an archangel can possess. "I may be trapped in the body of a child, but I'm not vulnerable! I'm one of the most powerful archangels you have here. I'll fight with my brothers and sisters."

"I apologize, Uriel," I say, taking a dagger from a passing angel and handing it to him. "Take this and play to your vessel's innocence. When the rogues attack, they may hesitate to attack a child. Do not let them see who you are until it's too late." I squeeze his small shoulders. "Do not underestimate how valuable you are to your people."

Uriel's eyes soften, and he touches my shoulder. "Our people."

I bow my head and stand. "I'll find you after the battle, brother."

"Good luck," Uriel says, before turning and disappearing down another hall.

Sahari finishes giving out orders, and when the foyer empties and it's just the two of us, she turns to me.

I smile and stand by her side. "Where do you want me?"

I can hear the rogues surrounding the house, ascending the steps to the front and back doors. The patio windows are boarded up, but I can already hear the panels being removed.

"You're here with me," Sahari says, turning to the door in front of us. "This is the largest entrance into the house. The front door is covered by Ava and the others."

Neither of us are strangers to casualties, but this battle will leave a bitter taste in Sahari's mouth. It's one thing to send trained soldiers into battle, another to send civilians. I doubt the witches are prepared for a fight of this magnitude.

The door is kicked open, and rogue angels rush in.

I hesitate, only for a moment, as an angel's sword swings by my head. I come up swinging and slice the angel from stomach to throat. Sinking into the bloodlust, we fight through them in waves, Sahari slicing through angels alongside me like the legendary warrior from the stories.

"Raziel," Sahari yells. "Behind you!"

I spin with my sword and behead a rogue, dodging the fists of another. A sword in close quarters is only so useful. I drop my blade and fight hand-to-hand with the angel before me, trying to make sense of the vile spewing from his lips.

A blade cuts across my back, and I scream, the pain stealing my focus for a second too long, giving the angel in front of me the advantage. Throwing caution to the wind, I wrap my hands around the angel's neck, pulling him closer as I snap his spine.

I watch his body fall to the floor and move onto the next. "You owe me a robe," Sahari says in passing, as she disposes of another rogue.

I roll my eyes. "Let's save this discussion for later, sweetheart."

"Call me sweetheart again and I'll cut your heart out."

Sahari ducks, then rolls across the floor and cuts down the next rogue at his knees.

Isaiah appears, carrying a bag of groceries and clothes in one hand and a sword in the other. Blood splatter covers his face.

"Where have you been?" I growl at him.

"I went shopping!" Isaiah looks around the foyer, wide-eyed. "What did I miss?"

"Down!" I yell, picking up a dead rogue's sword and throwing it at the attacker behind him. It hits the rogue between the eyes and splits his skull.

Tossing the bags by the door, Isaiah picks up one of the rogue angel's blades. "Let's take out the trash."

CHAPTER

TWELVE

RAZIEL

Sahari caresses her blade like a lover as she circles the rogue hostage hanging from the basement ceiling. "I must have left my manners upstairs when I fell. I don't believe I caught your name?"

The rogue spits at her feet, blood dribbling from his chin as he looks at her through his one remaining eye. "Go to hell, bitch."

"I've been there." Sahari leans into him, and the tip of her blade slides across his stomach, leaving a wound six inches long. "Perhaps I'll take you with me next time. It's been a few millennia since we've had flesh to play with."

"You sick bitch—ARGHHH!" His screams echo throughout the basement as Sahari's nails dig into the wound.

"Shhhhh," she purrs, pressing bloody fingers to his lips. "You don't want to wake the neighbors. Now, I was telling you about Lucifer. You know, he once told me a trick for skinning humans. I always wanted to try it, but I was never allowed to play with the mortals. What do you think, should I give it a go?"

"Is she serious?" Isaiah whispers.

"They were very close before his fall," I tell him with a grin.

"How close?"

My smirk grows, but I don't respond.

"Were they lovers?" Isaiah asks.

"It was more than that," I admit, thinking back to a particularly pleasant time. "The bond those two shared was kindred. They shared many lovers in their time."

"Did you . . ." Isaiah trails off, sensing the answer. "Wow, really? You and Lucifer?"

"You haven't lived until you've sinned with the devil." I lean against the brick wall and smile, catching the look that crosses Isaiah's face. "It was a brief affair."

Sahari clears her throat, bringing our attention back to her. She's kneeling in front of the hostage, her blade clutched in her hand and blood smearing the side of her face. "Are you two done gossiping? I'm trying to concentrate."

"I'm done." Isaiah raises his hands and backs away. "You two have fun torturing our kin."

I should feel guilty, but I feel nothing for the rogue in front of me. I open my mouth to assure Isaiah we'll make it quick, but he's gone. Sahari nods at me and tilts her head toward our hostage. "Wanna play?"

Smiling, I push off the wall and join her in front of the rogue. She's still kneeling, and I run a hand through her hair as I let my gaze roam over her handiwork. "Beautifully done, sweetheart. You know, I was the one who taught Lucifer how to skin the humans."

Sahari tilts her head to look up at me. "Really?"

"Mm-hmm." I offer her my hand, and she stands slowly, one bloody hand in mine and her blade in the other. "Would you like me to teach you?"

"Yes," she says, her voice breathy.

I pull the dagger from my belt and look at the rogue. "This will hurt."

~

I don't know how much time passes in the basement, but by the time I finish, my nails are stained red from the rogue's blood.

I watch the naked angel rock back and forth, his knees limp beneath him and his head hanging forward. Sahari's done quite a number on him. I was slightly concerned we'd pushed it too far, but he's yet to break, despite our best efforts.

"We're short on time, brother. If you aren't going to cough up the good stuff, I'll have to unleash Sahari's full arsenal on you. Even then, it'll just be for fun."

"Oh, please keep that pretty mouth shut," Sahari taunts, kneeling in a puddle of blood as she lets the tip of her dagger draw circles in the clotting fluids. "I never get to play."

I grin and kneel beside her as the angel lifts his head to stare at us. "Tell us what we need to know, and I swear to you I'll make your death quick."

"Or you'll die slowly," Sahari purrs, leaning into me, "and in a way your limited little mind won't be able to comprehend, even as it's happening to you. And I'll enjoy every sensual second of the experience."

A throaty laugh escapes me as I lean in and nip at her ear. "So, which will it be?"

"We were sent to retrieve you," the angel confesses, lifting his one remaining bloodshot eye to mine. "Our master believes you've seen the missing prophecy."

I straighten and close the distance between the angel and me. "What prophecy?"

"The one from the journal." The angel flinches as I move closer. "Please, no more."

"Who is your master?"

"If he finds out—"

Grabbing the angel by the throat, I lift him up off the ground and let him hang. "I can guarantee you, I'm a lot scarier than whoever you serve. I'll give you to the count of three before I start peeling the flesh from your—"

"Raphael!" he screams. "It's the archangel Raphael!"

"Raphael is not behind this," Sahari says with a smirk as she stands. "Think about it, Raziel. He's not powerful enough to cast anyone out of heaven, let alone you or me."

I want to agree, but there's a nagging sensation in the back of mind. It's as if I'm seeing a memory but can't recall the details. My gut tells me the angel is telling the truth, but I'm not seeing the whole picture.

"He couldn't do it alone," I say, focusing on the angel turning an unhealthy shade of purple. I release my grip and let him fall. "How did he do it?"

The angel gasps for breath, and I watch him splutter. "He enlisted the help of a witch. Her bloodline makes her powerful."

"Let me guess," Sahari says through gritted teeth. "She's from the McCoy line."

"Yes, ma'am." His voice is hoarse, barely a whisper. The angel stares at me. "You don't remember any of this, do you?"

"No."

The rogue shakes his head. "Raphael's witch cast a spell on those thrown through the veil so that they don't remember the rogues or Raphael."

Sahari moves in. "He's lying."

"I wish I were," the rogue mutters. "Those that question him end up dead, fed to his hellhounds, get thrown through the veil to die, or lose their free will and return to camp as zombies. I was there when you went through the veil, my lord. You weren't supposed to get away, but after Nina was killed, you went into a blind rage and tore through soldiers and hellhounds. I've never seen anything like it."

"Nina," Sahari whispers. "You were there?"

I open my mouth but close it again, trying to remember. "I remember being with her." I frown as I try to clear my mind. "Nina and Reign came for me in Purgatory to find you." I lift my gaze to hers. "You were investigating missing angels."

Sahari's eyes fill with tears. "I don't remember."

Keeping my expression blank, I turn back to the rogue. "Where is Reign and the rest of the Iron Sisters?"

"They fled with those who refused to follow Raphael." A sickening smile lit up his face. "Those that weren't slaughtered made it through an unmarked veil. If they aren't dead, they will be soon."

"You son of a bitch!" Sahari throws herself at the rogue, but I catch her before she makes contact. "Let go!"

"It's time to go, Sahari." I tighten my hold and pull her back to me.

"What about him?" she spits, seething. "He can't be allowed to live."

"Kill him," I whisper in her ear. "Then meet me upstairs."

Ignoring the angel's pleas, I leave the basement, relishing in the sound of his screams as they fill the hall. I trudge upstairs to Sahari's room, strip down to nothing, and climb into the shower. The water is hot, and the room smells of the soap I used earlier. I reach for the bar and scrub away the blood staining my skin.

The shower door opens, and Sahari steps inside with tears staining her blood-splattered cheeks. No words are needed to tell me it's done.

Reaching for her hand, I pull her close and kiss away her tears. The hot water hits my back, and I lift her into my arms. Her legs wrap around my waist as I pin her to the tiles. We need this.

Our kisses start out slow, building in urgency as our hands roam, her nails leaving red marks across my back and shoulders.

After the water runs cold, I leave Sahari to collect herself as I exit the shower. Steam pours out of the room behind me as I enter the bedroom and find Isaiah sitting on the edge of the bed, a bloodied dagger in his hand. He tosses it at my feet and lifts his gaze to me.

"Don't look at me like that, Isaiah. It needed to be done." I step over the dagger on the floor and pull clothes from the bag by the bed. "Raphael has taken heaven. He's killing anyone who refuses to kneel. The rogues were sent to retrieve or kill me."

Isaiah stands and paces, his eyes wide and alert. "Why?"

"After my hearing, a journal went missing. I had my suspicions but never followed it up. Before the fall, I must have found it, or it was returned, but inside was a prophecy that must be important enough to kill for, because that's what the rogues were after."

"But you don't remember?"

Sighing, I zip my jeans and take a seat on the edge of the bed. "The memories are vague, like pieces of a puzzle I can't quite put together until something clicks. They're there, but I can't reach them."

Isaiah sits beside me, his brows drawn together. "Why is nothing ever simple with you?"

Smiling, I turn my head to look at Isaiah. "You're one to talk."

Rolling his eyes, he leans back on the bed. "The fallen speak of their memories as if they're just gone, but it sounds as if yours are locked away. It might be the product of two spells counteracting each other. I might run the theory by Uriel and the witches."

"You do that." I grab a shirt from the floor and stand. "One thing's for sure, I need to find that journal."

"Assuming it was in your possession when you fell, it wouldn't have made it through," Isaiah points out, watching me dress.

I tuck in my shirt and grab the belt from the bag. "I have a feeling it did. I need time to find it. In the meantime, you and Sahari keep the angels moving. Find the fallen, locate Michael. Set up a base for when the storm comes."

"One of us should go with you," Isaiah challenges. "If these rogues are after you, you'll need someone to watch your back."

"I'm better off alone." I turn to face him. "The fallen need your guidance. This isn't my first trip to earth. I know my way around, and if all else fails, my vessel's knowledge will help keep me out of trouble."

"And what about me?" Sahari challenges, coming out of the shower wearing only a towel. Her hands are on her hips, and she's ready for a fight.

"You're the most fearless warrior I've ever known." I don't go to her, knowing she'd likely make use of the blade at her feet. "Isaiah and the fallen need you because you'll do what needs to be done. You're a leader, Sahari. Michael is a strong ally, and I know you'll work together to guide our people home."

"If you're going after Raphael—"

"I'm not," I promise. "And even if I was, would you really leave the fate of our kind in Isaiah's hands?"

Sahari smirks, and Isaiah throws a pillow at my head as he says, "Fuck you."

I suppress a grin and keep my gaze on Sahari. "I'll do whatever it takes to get back."

"I know you will." She sweeps past me. "I'm going to go pack."

I wait until Sahari leaves before turning back to Isaiah. "Look after her."

"Of course," Isaiah says, glaring at me. "I still think this is stupid."

"You think everything I do is stupid," I remind him as I zip up the backpack. "I'd be worried if you thought it was a good idea."

"If things get worse and the prophecy comes to pass, we'll lose communications." Isaiah holds out a silver phone with a touch screen. "I've turned on the tracking app, but I'll check in every day with an update on where we're headed and vice versa. If at any point we lose communication for longer than a week, we meet up at the last check-in point. Deal?"

"Deal." I pocket the phone and gesture to the door. "Do you want to walk me out?"

"There's a taxi waiting." Isaiah stands in front of me, awkwardly shuffling back. "Be safe."

I drop the backpack on the bed and close the distance between us. Isaiah stiffens as he watches me, his gaze expressionless as I cup the side of his face, his beard tickling my palm as my thumb traces his bottom lip. I smile at the sensation and meet his gaze. "Thank you for everything."

I close the distance between our mouths and kiss him goodbye. I only intend for it to be brief, but his hands grip the sides of my shirt and hold me against him. Not since Gwen was alive have we shared a kiss, shared anything.

Reluctantly, I pull back, and he releases me. While his eyes are still closed, I pick up my bag and walk out the door.

Uriel greets me by the front door, the blade I gave him earlier in his hand as he twists and spins it between his tiny fingers. A smile tugs at the boy's lips as he lifts his blue eyes to mine. "What? No kiss for me?"

I chuckle, running a hand through my still damp hair. "I'm glad to see you survived."

"Ah, yes. I was touched that you rushed to check on my well-being." He winked, mischief in his eyes. "It seems you're leaving us."

I spot the taxi waiting in the driveway. "The rogues were looking for me. They believe I have the missing journal."

"You did," Uriel says.

I stare at my brother, raising an eyebrow. "What do you know about it?"

"I know it was stolen." He smiles, pushing off the wall. "And I know who stole it. I know it was returned to you shortly before you fell."

I stiffen, watching the cunning little bastard.

A giggle slips from between his lips. It's a frightening sound when you know the soul within.

"It was Claire McCoy. But you know this, just as you knew then. Your love for the witch made you blind. You looked the other way in order to keep her, and she led you down a path of destruction," Uriel taunts.

"She was never mine to keep." The truth of that doesn't sting as much as it once did. "Since you already know so much, do you know where the journal is now?"

"Maybe." Uriel's head shakes from side to side.

"We don't have time for games, Uriel." I grit my teeth and kneel before the child. "Where is it?"

Uriel grins coyly. "I believe it was passed onto a priest. You might find answers here." He reaches into the pocket of his pants and hands me a map. "I circled it."

As I take the map, I chuckle, seeing the perfect circle drawn in crayon. I pat his shoulder. "Thank you, brother."

Uriel speaks quietly. "I want to go home, Raziel. We don't belong here."

"No, we don't. Isaiah has a theory about our memories. He thinks it may be a product of two spells counteracting each other, which is why my memories aren't like yours or the others."

Uriel rolls his eyes. "You're one of the most powerful archangels in history, and the Keeper of Secrets. If it was that easy to crack open your skull, I'd have done it a millennium ago. Though it's possible you could recover your memories if you pulled the right thread."

I chew my lip. "Interesting."

He bows his head and leaves me as he wanders back into the house. I pick up my backpack and head out to the taxi, glancing back to the second-floor window, where Isaiah stands, watching me leave.

'Til next time.

THIRTEEN

MIA

By the time I arrive at Abigail's apartment building, half the day's gone. I ditched the bicycle after arriving in the city and kept getting detoured by those infected by the storm. I ended up taking the scenic route through some of the city's worst neighborhoods, dodging other survivors as I made my way to Abi's apartment building.

The single time I hesitated was when I came across an elderly man cowering inside an industrial garbage bin. He was tall with dark skin and haunted brown eyes, his hair gray and curly beneath his old, faded Mack-truck hat.

"It's okay, mate," I tell him, returning my gun to my holster and raising my hands up in front of me. "You look like you need some help?"

He stares at me for a long time, fear in his eyes. "You aren't one of them?"

"No, sir." I point to my eyes. "See, my eyes aren't black. I won't hurt you." I offer him my hand. "You can't stay in there forever."

After helping the old man out of the bin, I unzip my bag and hand him a bottle of water. I take out a second bottle and place it near his worn grocery bag. *"The storm last night tainted the water. Whatever you do, only drink bottled water unless you can make sure it's pure."*

He drank greedily. "I'm Keith," he says, his voice croaky.

"Nice to meet you, Keith," I say, as I return my pack to my back. "Do you have family around here?"

He nods. "My daughter, and the dog. I need to get to her. She hates storms."

"Your daughter?"

"No, the dog. I hope she's okay."

Ordinarily, I'd have a chuckle at the man's concern for his dog, but after the morning I've had, I can't bring myself to find any amusement in the situation.

"Do you have a weapon you can use to protect yourself?" I ask.

At the mention of a weapon, he reaches back into the garbage bin and pulls out a long red stick with a sharpened end.

"That's a very pointy stick, Keith."

He smiles a broad smile as he holds it up in front of him. "It keeps those damn kids from littering in my front yard."

I can't help but laugh at his serious expression. "How far away does your daughter live?"

"A few streets over," he says, nodding in the opposite direction. "Are you looking for someone?"

"My sister." I nod in the direction opposite. "Be safe, Keith."

I'm halfway down the alley when he calls out to me. "Hey, darl . . . what's your name?"

I look over my shoulder at the old man. "Mia McCoy."

He smiles, raising his fingers in a wave. "I hope you find your sister, Mia."

The door to Abi's apartment building is ajar, and I ease my way up the front steps, listening for any movement inside. The floor is littered with junk, though that isn't out of the ordinary.

When Abi first moved in, she refused to let me inside. I assumed it was because she didn't want her neighbors knowing her big sister was a cop. Well, that and she didn't want to hear another lecture about her choice in apartments.

The number of arguments we had about the building was ridiculous. But it was affordable, the apartments themselves weren't that bad, and everything was split down the middle with her roommate. That didn't stop me from worrying about the dealers and prostitutes in the other apartments, nor did it stop me from asking my buddies on patrol to do random drive-bys in exchange for morning coffees and donuts. It was a small price to pay for peace of mind.

Picking my way through the trash, I head up the staircase to the second floor, my anxiety rising with every step, and say a little prayer to whatever God exists that my sister is safe.

The door to Abigail's apartment is open, and I pause at the top of the stairs as panic unlike anything I've felt in a long time lodges heavy on my chest. I move across the hall and toward the open door, mentally preparing myself for whatever lies beyond.

I nudge open the door with my boot, my firearm raised but pointed at the floor as I scan the room, step inside, and close the door behind me. On instinct, I lock the door and latch the chain. Whatever additional senses I have tell me the apartment is empty of life.

The apartment is quiet. Eerily quiet. As I inch closer to the kitchen, the scent of death reaches me. *Please don't let it be her.* There, on the floor, a carving knife buried through her eye, is Abigail's roommate.

Relief at the sight of Samantha's body has me reeling toward the kitchen sink. It wasn't Abigail. Thank God. I throw up in the sink, then turn on the tap and cup my hands beneath the running water. I freeze as that thrum of *otherness* reaches out to me.

Throwing myself back from the water, I rub my hands on my thighs to dry them. It doesn't matter, though, as the ringing in my ears grows louder.

Feathers, still alight with the holy flame, fall upon parted lips. As the prophet's tears salt the earth, he gives his life for hope.

Collapsing to my knees, I gasp for air, sobbing and scrubbing my hands dry. When I'm finished, I'm unable to stop them from trembling.

I want all of this to be a dream. I want to wake up, to be at home in my bed. I want to go downstairs and have a cup of coffee while I call Abi. I want to go to work and argue with Garry from IT.

I want my sister to be okay.

Just like that, my moment of self-pity ends. I'm not in this alone. Abigail is still out there, and while she may not have been cursed with these damned gifts, she's still capable of looking after herself. She'd have figured out what was happening, and she'd know I'd come for her.

My gaze wanders over to Sam, and I know without a doubt that my sister made it out of here alive.

She'd have known it wasn't safe here and would have known this would be the first place I come looking.

"First rule of the apocalypse—find survivors and make them indebted to you. Become invaluable to their survival, and after that, do whatever it takes to get weapons, food, medical supplies. When the end of the world comes, people tend to look for Jesus. If you're ever separated during the storm, remember that."

It was as if Jonah was there with me in the kitchen, giving his lecture. I struggle to my feet, ignoring the dizziness, and my stomach growls, reminding me I haven't eaten since lunch yesterday. I walk to the fridge and find it empty except for yogurt.

A big tub, and still in date. I grab a spoon and eat it as I walk through the apartment. Abi's room is a mess, but that's nothing unusual. If she packed a bag, I can't tell.

I set the tub aside and kneel next to the bed to look for the backpack that holds her emergency supplies. You can take the girl out of the cult, but you can't take the cult out of the girl. The backpack is missing.

That's a good sign.

I search her bottom drawers and pull out her clothes. Her favorite pocketknife is missing, another positive. I look on top of the wardrobe—nothing except a little baggie of weed with two rolled joints.

Chuckling, I pocket the stash as I hear a commotion outside. Abi's window is open, and I press myself to the wall beside it to peer around the edge of the curtain. There's a group of men loitering as they talk about how they tracked a girl to this very building.

Great. As if the world ending isn't bad enough.

I push away from the window and head back to the kitchen. There's a fire escape that leads to the roof, and the neighboring buildings are close enough I could leap across. It's not that big of a leap between the buildings. At least, that's what I tell myself. I open the window to the fire escape and catch sight of the bright pink Post-it stuck to the salt and pepper shakers.

Mia,

Gone to find Jesus.

Abi.

I chuckle as I pick up the Post-it and stuff it into my pocket. then open the window and slip outside, heading to the roof. The gap between buildings is a little farther than I anticipated, but not impossible.

"This is such a bad idea," I mutter as I line up the jump and try to channel my inner Lara Croft.

What's the worst that could happen?

I fall to my death?

Hearing movements on the fire escape, I realize it's now or never. I take off running and leap, then land on the other side with a tuck-and-roll, just like I'd been trained to.

I get to my feet and grin at my accomplishment. What a rush! I make it across to the next apartment building and climb down the fire escape, then jump the fence into the alley. I keep myself out of sight as I run from the apartment, being careful not to take the obvious routes while still heading toward the nearest church.

The top of the church comes into view, and I could almost weep. It's still a few blocks away, but finally visible. I'm so distracted I don't see the young man moving toward me until he's screaming in my face, his hands wrapping around my throat.

"Kill me!" he snarls, his voice filled with rage and fear, his eyes black. "Please, it's going to kill you! I can't stop it!"

I pry his fingers from my throat and bring my knee up to hit him in the gut. The man barely reacts, but his grip loosens. I grab the knife from my belt and slice open his arm, and he lets go of me.

After putting distance between us, I feel the corruption within him. "How are you able to talk?"

"I don't know!" he screams, lunging for me. "You have to kill me! Please!"

"You have to fight it," I snap, holding my knife in front of me. "You can do it."

"Don't you think I've tried?" The fear in his voice brings tears to my eyes. "I don't want to hurt anybody else. You have to do it. I can't stop! DO IT!" he screams, rushing toward me and throwing a right hook at my head. I dodge and swing my leg out to knock him off his feet.

I don't want to kill him. I wouldn't hesitate if he was like Thomas or his father, but he isn't. This boy is conscious, trapped inside his own body.

The realization hits at the same time as he tackles me into a puddle of water. I scream, though the sound is muffled as he attempts to drown me in the puddle. The sound of drums filter through the fear and panic, but I fight it off as I use the boy's weight to flip us, then hold his head in the puddle, ignoring his hands clawing at my body, forcing him down until his body goes slack.

I fall back and scramble away as I stare at the corpse. His dreads float on the surface of the shallow puddle.

I throw up in the alley. Stumbling to my feet, I run as fast as I can, ignoring that voice in the back of my head. I don't look back at the man I just drowned with my bare hands.

I run from the alley, from the boy, from the memories of Thomas and his father. I run from the person capable of killing another human being and from the knowledge that the infected are conscious, trapped inside their own bodies as they watch themselves tear other people apart.

The iron fencing is well over six feet tall, with sharpened spears adoring the top. The gates leading to the front doors are chained closed and would need bolt cutters to get through.

Vaguely familiar with its exterior layout, having passed this church whenever I visited Abi's building, I circle the fence. The property is surrounded on three sides by six-foot iron fencing, but at the back of the property, it has a six-foot brick fence overgrown with bougainvillea.

While the flowers themselves are a vibrant pink and quite beautiful to behold, the thorns hidden beneath would no doubt leave me shredded and regretful. But if my sister is inside, nothing will stop me from getting to her.

Dropping my bag, I shrug out of my jacket, throw it over the wall, then toss my bag over. I pull myself up and straddle the wall, praying I'm not about to get a new piercing.

A voice calls out from the stairs behind me. "You could have rang the doorbell."

My hand immediately reaches for my gun, but I hesitate as I find a priest on the steps of the church. He's handsome, with gray eyes, dark skin, and gang tattoos peeking from beneath his white collar.

The man might be holy, but I have no doubt he's capable of all sorts of sin.

"Mia McCoy, correct? Your sister said you'd come." His hands rest effortlessly on his hips as he watches me with curiosity.

"Where is she?" I ask, pushing off the wall and landing inside the church grounds with a thud. I rise, dusting the dirt from my knees as I meet the priest's shocked gaze. "What is it, padre?"

He whispers something, but it's too quiet for me to catch. If I didn't know better, I'd have sworn there was recognition in his eyes. "You look just like her."

"Like Abi?" I chuckle, half-confused, as I look to the church behind him. "Can't say I've heard that before."

The priest blinks, shaking his head as his laughter trails off. "No, of course not. I'm sorry. Forgive me. What was your question?"

Had I asked a question? "Where is my sister?"

"On a run for medical supplies." He gestures to the church, inviting me in.

I hesitate, weighing the dangers of going inside. Do I trust the priest? He could be lying. Fear of the unknown freezes me.

"There's a radio inside, if you'd like to contact her. There are only innocents here: women, children, the sick, and the elderly. There's a few men left to defend against those infected. You have my word." He watches me closely, his gaze flickering to my hand where it rests on the gun at my side. "There's no need for violence inside these walls."

"I better not regret this, padre."

"You can call me Raziel." The priest smiles as if I amuse him. "You're not what I pictured either."

"What exactly did you picture?"

The priest takes in my stature from head to toe, and finally, he smirks. "I thought you'd be taller."

I roll my eyes. "Heard that before," I mutter.

"Let's go inside and talk." His lips tug up into a mischievous grin as he walks alongside me and opens the door to the church. "Luke, the guy in the maroon jersey, is in charge until Abigail returns with the others. He's got the radio."

I pause, taking in the church and its survivors as something Raziel said clicks. I turn to him, unable to suppress my grin. The idea of her bossing around men like Luke and Raziel amuses me. "Abigail is your leader?"

"She was the only one who knew what to do, so she took over." He shrugs and looks down at me pointedly. "She'd never have pointed a gun at me."

"Then that was her first mistake," I tell him, unable to help myself as I take in the sinful priest. "Raziel, right? Like the archangel, the lord of secrets?"

"Master of Secrets," Raziel corrects. "The full title is—"

"Lord Keeper, *Master* of Secrets, Prophet, Keeper of the Word, and the Bringer of Hope," I recall from my teachings. "I'm familiar."

He seems shocked. "Not many are *that* familiar."

I shrug nonchalantly. "Our father was a bit of a religious nut. I always favored the archangels, particularly your namesake."

"Why?"

I feel my face flush at my confession. "Secrets are a burden, big or small. I always felt sorry for Raziel and the secrets he was expected to keep. I suspect it's a lonely existence."

The priest is quiet for a long time before he nods. "Indeed."

As we move farther into the church, I spot a man in a maroon jersey—Luke. He turns and I can see him assessing me for a threat.

"Luke, it seems Abigail was right. Her sister made her way here." Raziel gestures to me. "Mia, Luke; Luke, Mia."

"Sorry to meet you under these circumstances," I say, offering Luke my hand.

His large hand engulfs mine, and he nods. "Welcome. Abigail said you're a police officer . . . do you have any idea what's happening?"

"Somewhat." I shrug. "Do you have a radio to contact my sister?"

He nods and holds it out to me. "The group is on their way back."

The words are barely out of his mouth when the radio crackles to life and Abigail's voice filters through. With a sigh of relief, I press the button. "You have no idea how good it is to hear your voice, Abigail."

"Mia! You found Jesus!"

I laugh and sink into the nearest seat as tears fill my eyes. "Yeah, I did." I pause as the knowledge of what that means sinks in. "I'm sorry about Sam."

"Me too." Her voice cracks over the radio. "Are you okay? This is it, isn't it? Like in your dreams?"

It doesn't matter who knows now. Raziel and Luke listen intently. "Looks like it." I take a breath. "The house is gone, Abs. The storm came through in the middle of the night and destroyed it."

"Are you okay?"

"I'm alive." For now, that's enough. "Where are you?"

"We're stuck on Omar. Do you think you could bring a few people out and help move some cars?"

It was a fifteen-, maybe twenty-minute walk from the church to the top of Omar street. It'd be quicker to drive, but I doubted we'd get lucky enough to find wheels. I'd have to ask Abigail how she found trucks that still work.

"I'll be there in twenty," I say, looking at Luke. "Can you spare anybody?"

"I'll go," Raziel offers, earning a wary look from both of us. If he noticed, he ignored it.

"Neil," Luke calls to a man in the back of the church. The gentleman stands and makes his way through the rows of chairs. "This is Mia, Abigail's sister. She's a cop. Abigail and the others are stuck on Omar and need help to get back."

"I'll go," he says, looking at me. "When?"

"Now."

"I'll meet you outside in five." He glances over his shoulder. "I just need to speak to Trina."

"Take your time." I turn my attention to Luke as I unclasp my camping pack and set it on the pew beside us. "Lock the doors behind us. If we're not here by dark, we'll find shelter in town. I'll do my best to bring them back."

"What's in the bag?"

"My supplies." I give him a pointed look. "If anything goes missing, I'll know."

He smirks but nods. "It'll remain there 'til you return."

Without a word, I remove my second-layer jacket and allow them to see the arsenal I carry as I adjust the rifle across my body. It's a twenty-minute trek across town, and the streets could be steep. I look at Raziel and notice him staring at me in wide-eyed surprise. "What?"

"How many guns do you have?"

"A few." It's a nonanswer, and I wasn't counting the ones in my bag. "How many do you have on you?"

"None." He pulls a dagger from somewhere inside his sleeve. "I prefer knives."

"What kind of priest are you?" Luke asks, clearly surprised.

A smile tugs on the corners of his lips. "The bad kind."

"I respect that." I wink and take a step back as I toss my jacket onto my bag. "Let's go."

As we leave the church, Raziel says, "So, you're a cop?"

"Correct."

"What did you do before, Neil?"

"I served in Iraq. What about you, Priest? Based on the ink covering your body, I'm guessing you weren't always so devout?"

"I was a soldier once," he answers, and the haunted look that all of us carry reflects in those strange eyes. "In a lot of ways, I still am. It's just a different uniform."

"Amen to that," Neil says.

"I joined the army when I was eighteen," I explain. "It was the first thing I did. Served for eight years and worked my way through the ranks until I transitioned out and took the police exam."

"How old are you?" Raziel asks quietly.

"Twenty-nine. You?"

"Older." He snorts. "Thirty-two . . . or so."

Before I can question what's so funny, we reach the top of town. It's abandoned. No sign of any cars on the street, and all the shops and cafés are closed. There's not a soul in sight. "I've never seen it so quiet."

"Then you've never wandered out of a bar at 3 a.m.," Neil muses. He steps into the middle of the street, looking down toward the train station. "Where is everyone?"

"People are still coming to terms with what's happening," I say. "The loitering and chaos aren't in full swing yet."

"If they're smart, they'll wait a few days until the threat of the storm passes." Raziel nods to the east, then looks back over his shoulder. "There's more storms brewing."

"That makes no sense," I say, thinking back over my dreams. "It should be over."

Neil looks down at me. "What makes you think that?"

I hesitate but decide to answer truthfully. "Because that's how I dreamed it." I look east at the brewing storm.

"These storms aren't of this world," Raziel explains, before I go on to explain the prophecy—the words I've heard in my dreams so many times.

"*Two hearts bend and feathers turn to ash. The blackest of hearts, the beasts take hold to overcome the soul. Death conquers 'til immortality reigns. Shadows rise, waters fall, time shifts until the waters rise again. As it began, so must it end.*"

"Nah." Neil laughs, shaking his head in disbelief. "Y'all are pulling my leg."

Frowning, Raziel stares at the man's leg. "She is not."

"He doesn't mean literally, padre." I chuckle, unable to help myself, and turn to the priest. "He doesn't believe us."

"Everything that's happened in the last twenty-four hours isn't enough proof?" Raziel says to Neil with a serious expression. "This particular prophecy was born from a curse placed long ago."

"You know about the bloodlines?" I ask him suspiciously.

"Prophecies are my specialty," he answers. "I was sent here to try to prevent it."

"How's that working out for you?" Neil laughs and shakes his head. "This is insane."

"You don't need to believe us," I say, gesturing around to the abandoned streets. "Just open your eyes and look around."

The McDonalds sign glows up ahead, and we make our way up the steep driveway. The restaurant and parking lot are abandoned.

"Question," Neil asks, "why is this storm so different?"

"Because it is not of this world," Raziel answers. "Nor is the bloodline from whence it came."

"There they are." In the distance, I can see a small moving truck, an ambulance, and Abigail. She's standing next to the truck, smiling as she talks to someone, a bottle of water in her hands.

"Mia, wait!" Raziel shouts.

It's too late. I'm halfway down the street before that ability to sense the corruption flickers and my eyes zero in on the water. Everything slows as she raises it to her lips.

"No!" I scream, the sound tearing at my throat and bringing her attention to me. It all happens so fast. One minute, she looks surprised, then happy, relieved, and finally confused as I'm running toward her. "Don't drink the water!"

The water bottle slips from her grasp, and her face slackens as she stumbles away from the truck. Those around her scatter, screaming and panicking as they pull out their weapons.

"Abigail!"

She lifts her eyes to mine, and they are as black as the abyss. A cruel, sinister smile spreads across her face. I try to run to her, to help her, but I can't move. Strong arms drag me farther away from my sister.

"No! Let me go! I can help her! I have to—"

"It's too late, Mia," Raziel whispers in my ear, his hold unrelenting. "She's gone."

Abigail makes her way toward us with a look of pure hatred swimming within her onyx eyes. She wants me dead, and I'd let her kill me.

"I'll take care of Abigail," Neil orders, stepping between us. "Get Mia and the others out of here. She doesn't need to see this."

He aims the gun at Abi's head but never gets to pull the trigger. I'm forced to watch in horror as my sister takes the gun from his hand and brings it down on his skull with a loud *whack*. Horror fills me as she—it—stands over his lifeless, bleeding body.

I watch as she grins down at Neil's unconscious form, the gun pointing at his head as she pulls the trigger. "Night night, my sweet."

"I didn't think they could talk," Raziel whispers, quiet terror in his voice as his grip loosens.

"Get the others and leave," I order, bringing her attention to me.

"What are you going to do?" Raziel asks.

"Go!" I yell, never taking my eyes off my sister. "I know you're in there, Abs. I need you to fight."

"You were always his favorite," it sneers back at me before lunging.

I sidestep and circle her, placing myself between the trucks and my sister. I hear Raziel shouting orders and the sound of an engine starting as they rush to get away.

"You have to fight it, Abi! I need you to fight it. I can't do this without you."

I see the flicker of emotion, like a ripple on a still pond, but as quick as it was there, it's gone again. The corruption within her screams, lashing out at me as its nails dig into the flesh of my arm. Its grasp is brutal, unrelenting, inhuman. It uses its grip on me to throw me across the street, my back slamming against a car windshield.

I scream as I roll off the hood and onto the gravel road. My head throbs and my body protests, but I ignore the ringing in my ears as I force myself to stand. My left ankle rolls, and I almost collapse, my vision blurring from the tears.

"You ruined my life! I hate you!" It speaks with my sister's voice. On instinct, I react, grabbing her wrist midair and twisting until I hear the sickening pop of dislocation. I use the car behind me to support my weight as I kick her in the stomach, pushing her away.

"Please, stop!" I plead, tears rolling down my cheeks as she charges at me again. Her wrist is limp and her blade heavy in my palm. I let her tackle me and I wrap my arm around her neck, holding her as I take the knife and thrust it between her ribs, straight into her heart.

I hold her as she stills and the blackness fades from her eyes.

"Mia?"

"I'm here," I whisper, pressing my forehead to hers. "I'm right here."

"I'm sorry," she wheezes through her last breath.

"I know." I sob, clutching her as her body goes limp.

"Mia." Raziel kneels beside us. "Sweetheart, we have to go."

I sob as I look up at him. "I killed my sister."

"You didn't have any other choice," Raziel whispers, placing a hand on my shoulder. "Please, let us help you. Let me help you."

"I can't do this without her."

"I will not leave you here to die."

"GO!" I scream at him as he pulls me to my feet. "I'M NOT LEAVING HER!"

"She's gone, Mia! You don't get to give up. I won't allow it."

Overwhelmed with rage, I lash out. I kick, scream, punch, and slap him so hard his head rolls back, but he never once loosens his grip on me. I scream at him, beating his chest, cursing his God and calling him every vile word I can think of, and still, he doesn't react. Raziel wraps his arms around me until I cry and shake in his arms. "I've got you."

"I was supposed to protect her."

"You did," he whispers, stroking my back. "The darkness can't hurt her anymore."

I bury my face in his chest and cry as he carries me away from the scene. I don't ask questions, I don't look up, and when he carries me back through the doors of the church, I don't fight him.

FOURTEEN

MIA

When I wake, it seems the priest hasn't moved from his place by the bed. I told him to leave, yet he remained. At first, I thought he'd try to force me to talk about what happened with Abigail, but he just sat in his chair with his research papers and worn journal, leaving only once to retrieve a glass of water, which remains untouched beside the bed.

Raziel sits hunched over the papers on his lap, his brows pinched together in concentration and his reading glasses halfway down his nose. The sleeves of his shirt are rolled up, revealing the ink of his past—beautiful, intricate designs, colorful and dark, heavily shaded in some parts to cover old gang affiliations. I recognized them from my time working organized crime.

Layers upon layers of ink and scars, but beneath all of that is writing in a language I'm not familiar with. It seemed to shimmer like scars in certain light. My fingers ached to trace the words, as if by doing so they'd reveal their meaning.

"You're the strangest priest I've ever met," I say cringing at the ache in my throat as I sit up and reach for the water.

Raziel lifts his eyes to mine and smiles. "You've met many priests, then?"

"In another life, I was the daughter of a pastor," I say, sitting against pillows that smell of him. "My parents were missionaries."

"What happened to them?"

"They died," I admit, and a bitter laugh escapes me. "I was eight. I lived on the streets for a few weeks, then found myself in foster care. Bounced around for a while, then Abigail's father found me."

"Is he still . . ."

"Alive?" I shrug. "Unfortunately. He's like a cockroach. Not even the apocalypse could kill him."

"I take it you two aren't on good terms?"

"Jonah Redwood is a con artist and a predator. He manipulates grown adults and steals their children, brainwashing young and old alike into believing he's their savior."

Someone knocks on the door, and I call for them to come in. A nun enters, bowing her head.

"My apologies," she says, looking at the priest. "Sister Joselyn requires your presence downstairs. It's urgent."

"Go. I'll be fine." I shoo him away.

Raziel walks to the bed, places a hand on my shoulder, and stares into my eyes as though searching for the lie. Satisfied by whatever he finds, he leans down and kisses my forehead. It's a sweet gesture. "Sister Marie will stay with you while I'm gone."

I roll my eyes but don't argue as I catch sight of the blood on my hands and beneath my nails. Raziel leaves the room, and Sister Marie takes his place by the bed with a bible in hand, murmuring prayers by candlelight. She is a sweet lady, but far too soft for this new world we find ourselves in.

How long will it be before the darkness claims her? Or before she ends up dead, like everybody else?

Maybe it'll be her blood on my hands next.

I squeeze my eyes closed, kick off the blanket, and sit on the edge of the bed. Bile rises in the back of my throat, and the acidic taste of vomit sits on my tongue as the knowledge of whose blood still coats my skin threatens to undo me.

"I saw a water tank out back. Looks like it was covered before the storm, as it's untainted. I'd like to shower."

Sister Marie lifts her gaze from the bible, wide-eyed. "Now?"

"Yes," I say, and stand from the bed, ignoring the weakness in my knees. "I need to wash away her blood. *Please.*"

Sister Marie looks at my hands and the state of my clothes, and her eyes fill with sympathy. "Let's get you cleaned up."

I grab a change of clothes from my pack and follow the sister into the corridor and down the hall to the nuns' sleeping quarters. She lights a single candle and sits it by the bathtub before turning on the water and retrieving a towel from the basket of fresh linens. When Raziel put me to bed earlier, he removed all my weapons, but I still have my belt and thigh holster.

I try to unbuckle the holsters, but my hands won't stop shaking, and my fingers fumble with the latches. Sister Marie kneels in front of me, gently swatting away my hands, and undoes the straps that secure everything in place.

"I'm sorry," I whisper.

She ignores me and starts humming a familiar tune. She stands once she's finished with the straps and helps me undress.

"Thank you, Sister."

"You're most welcome," she murmurs, offering her hand to help me lower into the tub. "Is there anything I can get you, Mia?"

"No, thank you. This will do," I say, hissing as I sink into the steaming water.

Sister Marie leaves but soon returns with a washcloth and kneels by the tub to wash the blood and dirt from my back. We don't speak, and she continues to hum her song. It brings tears to my eyes. "My dad used to sing that song to us when I was a girl," I say.

"It was Father Aiden's favorite song," Marie tells me, her voice soft and quiet. "I miss him."

"How did he die?" I ask quietly, the moment oddly intimate.

"It was a robbery. At least, that's what the police say."

"Did they ever catch those responsible?"

Sister Marie shakes her head, squeezing the water from the cloth over my shoulder.

"I am sorry for your loss."

"As am I," she says. She places a hand on my shoulder and holds my gaze. There's an understanding between us—grief, guilt, and pity within her kind gray eyes. "Your sister was a lovely girl, and kind, even in the face of chaos. She spoke of you with love and respect, even before the storm."

I pause, looking up at the woman. "What do you mean 'before?' "

"Abigail attended church every Sunday," she says, and I can't keep the surprise off my face. "She was my friend, and she was close to Father Aiden as well."

"I didn't know that," I admit, taking the cloth from her hand. "Would you mind giving me a few moments alone, please?"

"Of course." Sister Marie stands, wipes her hands on a hand towel, and exits the bathroom.

I sit in the water, staring at the steam rising from the tub, but I can only feel cold. Closing my eyes against the tears threatening to fall, I swallow back the scream threatening to rip from my throat.

These feelings are too much to contain. I bring my knees to my chest and wrap my arms around myself as my body begins to tremble. I reach for the cloth floating in the water and bring it to my mouth in an attempt to smother my cries so nobody passing hears me.

I want to scream until I can't anymore, to claw at the darkness until I hold its heart in my hands and crush it between my fingers. I'm so tired of losing people, so tired of fighting for a world that seems so determined to destroy itself.

How do I do this without her?

How do I survive this new world and not become the very thing I hate?

I don't have the answer.

Unsure of anything, I pull the plug and watch as the bloodied, dirty water runs down the drain. I turn on the shower and wash away the last traces of blood and dirt before climbing out of the tub. Ignoring the aches and pains, I wrap myself in a towel and set about drying my hair, then dress and set about cleaning the leather of my holster and belt in the sink before strapping myself back into them.

Opening the door, I almost trip over Raziel, who is sitting on the floor outside, reading the same old journal. "What are you doing?" I ask.

"Waiting for you." Raziel smiles and stands from the floor. "You look better."

Unsure how to respond, I gesture to the journal. "Couldn't find anything interesting to read in the church library, Padre?"

With a chuckle, Raziel lifts the journal and tucks it under his arm. "It belonged to the late priest of this parish—a descendant from the bloodline. I was hoping to find answers between the pages."

"Was the priest a descendant of McCoy?" I ask, trying to link all I'd learned today. It couldn't be a coincidence, could it? Did Abigail know? Why didn't she tell me? "The sister said Abigail knew him."

"They were friends," he admits, looking at me. "What's wrong?"

"Everything." I gesture to the book. "Did you find anything useful?"

"Only more questions, unfortunately." He pulls a flask from his pocket and unscrews the lid, pausing as he catches sight of my expression. "Would you like a drink? It's whiskey."

"You're the worst priest I've ever met," I tell him, taking the flask and tipping my head back. The liquor burns all the way down, but the aftertaste is pleasant, surprisingly smooth. It leaves a feeling of warmth in the pit of my stomach. "Did you brew that yourself?"

"Very funny, McCoy. We should talk," Raziel says, taking the flask and gesturing to the stairwell. "It leads upstairs to the bell tower. It's private."

"That kind of discussion, huh?" I fall into step beside him. "You have a devious plan to get me tipsy so you can take advantage?"

"How tempting . . ." He flashes a grin. "Though I don't think I need to lower your inhibitions to seduce you, sweetheart. I think you like me."

I can't help but laugh as I follow him up the stairs. "You think highly of yourself."

"I do." He looks back and winks. "Don't enjoy the view too much."

I roll my eyes and follow him up the narrow stairwell. I have to admit, the view is pleasing.

Raziel pulls out a key and opens the door to the bell tower, then steps aside for me to walk through first. It's a large, circular room with a bell hanging above our heads. The windows have bars on them, but it's otherwise open, revealing the city below and the storm above.

"Wow." I step up to the window. "It's almost beautiful from up here."

Raziel and I linger in silence by the window, watching the lightning as the sky changes color from green and blue back to darkness again. There isn't a star in sight, as if the storm had consumed their light too.

"You can feel it, can't you?" Raziel asks, his focus on my face. "The Darken inside the storm."

Turning my back to the city, I answer. "Ever since I opened my eyes this morning."

I flinch when I feel it feed on another soul, the sinister entity laughing as it gorged on its victim's humanity. What had Raziel called it? The Darken?

"Does it call to you?" Raziel asks, handing me the flask.

I turn the flask in my hands, the clasp biting against my fingers as I nod. "Yeah, it does."

"It calls to me too," he says, his eyes already on mine when I look up. "I suspected you felt them when we first met, but it wasn't until we found Abigail and the others that I knew for sure."

"You aren't one of the descendants." A statement of fact, not a question.

"How can you tell?"

"There's a pull between us." I take another swig from the flask. "A calling, almost. A familial bond. You don't have that."

"I'm not one of you," he admits.

"What do you know about all this?" I ask, gesturing to the city below and the otherworldly storm.

"I know it's the by-product of a curse." Raziel lifts himself onto the window, his back to the storm. "I also know the origins of where it began and the ancestors involved, and that you are a direct descendant of Claire McCoy."

"How do you know all that?" Eerily accurate, his information isn't incorrect.

Raziel leans closer, voice low as he speaks. "I have a personal stake in your bloodline. The Darken will roam, feeding on the humanity of every living being, gorging on the worst of us, the rage, despair, until nothing remains. It will last for seven days. Those that survive will greet a new world built from the ashes of those who weren't so lucky."

"How delightful," I murmur. "I always told myself they were just dreams, but deep down, I knew it was coming. I saw the meteor shower, I knew it was a sign. I knew the prophecy was closing in, but I ignored it. I ran from them. I should've been prepared. I should've been there when it hit."

I lift myself onto the window beside Raziel. I can't bring myself to look at the storm, a mocking reminder of everything I've spent my life running from.

"The blame does not fall on you, Mia. The prophecy was written long before your time. Everything that has happened since the storm was predestined. Your sister's death was a tragedy, but in no way was it your fault."

"Was it my sister's destiny to die at my hands?" I ask, my hands shaking with frustration. "Fuck destiny, and fuck Claire McCoy for cursing our family. How many lives need to be claimed before it's enough?"

A bitter laugh escapes my chest as I lift my eyes to the ceiling. Raziel's hand covers my knee, and he squeezes. I wipe away a stray tear and look down at the tattooed hand covering my knee.

"I can't remember how many broken bones or lashes I received as a child in the name of fucking destiny," I continue. "What's the point of fighting if it's my destiny to watch everyone I love die?"

"What if there was a way to stop it?" Raziel's voice is low. "The virus and the apocalypse."

I look at him, ready to retort, but it's the hope in his gray eyes that makes me pause. "I wish that there were, I really do, but I've seen how this storm ends. I've seen the red sky, the fields littered with death. I have walked through dry oceans covered with the bones of creatures we've never seen before and watched as the earth beneath my feet split and broke away. I have seen, and lived, a thousand endings like this one. If you're right, Padre, it is destined to end."

"Fuck destiny." He repeats my earlier words with venom. "I, too, have seen that red sky, walked among and alongside death. I have seen more, done more, and I have witnessed true miracles in my life. You, Mia McCoy, are a miracle. I think, with your help, we could change how this story ends."

"I don't understand."

Raziel slips off the windowsill with a sigh and comes to stand in front of me. He's so tall that I have to tilt my head back to look at him as he takes hold of both my hands.

"I came here looking for answers only to find more questions, but the moment I saw you climbing over that wall, I felt it for the first time in a long time."

I roll my eyes and give him a flirty smile. "The undeniable urge to rip off each other's clothes?"

"Hope," he corrects, though his smile widens, and his eyes drop to my mouth for the briefest moment. "I think that I was meant to find you, Mia. I think, together, you and I can undo all of this."

"How do you propose we do that?" I ask, not feeling as hopeful as he'd like me to be.

Releasing my hands, he grabs the journal from the floor beneath the window and holds it up. I raise a brow and reach for the flask to take a swing.

"I think Father Aiden held the key to a cure, but toward the end, he became secretive and paranoid."

"Aiden was the priest here, right? He was killed in a robbery?" I ask, as he flicks through the pages of the journal. "You think he was killed for this cure?"

"I think so, yes."

"Okay, devil's advocate," I say, holding up my hand. "Apologies for the analogy, but let's say you're right and this priest had a magic cure. Who would he have trusted with this information?"

"It's a short list," Raziel admits. "In the last entries, he mentioned the whitecoats." I stiffen at the reference, and Raziel pauses, meeting my gaze. "Are you familiar with the term?"

"Show me," I say, unable to keep my hands from shaking.

The whitecoats were a myth to most McCoy children, a nightmare to others who'd encountered them. A story parents at the compound told their children to make them behave. *If you don't finish your chores, the whitecoats will come while you sleep.* As teenagers, we'd sneak out and sit by the fire, sharing stories of the day the whitecoats would come.

Raziel hands me the journal, and I stare at a madman's writings. I swallow the lump in my throat—the sob, the terror—as the final words on the page sink in.

For two nights now, the whitecoats have stood across the street, whistling the melody of death. I am not afraid to die. I knew they'd find me again. The prophecy will be upon us soon. The bloodline will not end with me. My only regret is that I cannot say goodbye to my girls, but I leave them with hope.

"The melody of death," I whisper, recalling the chilling tune. "Oh my God."

"I don't understand?" Raziel reaches out to touch me, and I flinch. "You're shaking like a leaf."

I slide off the windowsill, hand him the journal, and pace. "Every culture has a bogeyman. For us, the descendants of the McCoy bloodline, it's the whitecoats, also known as the cleaners. Their only mission in life is to purify the bloodline. They don't want to stop the new world, Raziel. They want to repopulate it with their own kind. They kill most of us on sight."

"Most of you?"

"They take the children," I admit, my voice cracking. "Those young enough not to be a challenge."

"How do you know so much?"

I lift my gaze to his, tears filling my eyes. "When I was a little girl, before Jonah found me, I had a family. A mum, a dad, a big brother and sister. One night, the whitecoats came, and they surrounded the house. They killed my mum and brother first, and dragged my sister and I from the house, and that's when my sister started to fight back. She was able to get free, and I told her to run, but she wouldn't leave me. She saved me, and we ran, and I didn't stop running until I was sure we were safe. When I looked back, she wasn't there. That was the last night I saw my biological family."

Releasing a heavy sigh, I wrap my arms around myself as memories of the past flood back. The sound of my parents pleading, my brother's sobs, my sister's hand in mine. The sound of the gunshot, the thud of my mother's body hitting the floor, followed by my brother's. The warmth of their blood as it soaked the carpet beneath my knees, soaking the bottom of my nightie.

"I don't know what to say."

"The whitecoats are monsters," I tell him, clenching and unclenching my fists.

"Enough talking for tonight. You need sleep, Mia."

I choke on a laugh as I lift my eyes to meet his. "Believe me, Raziel, sleep is the last thing I'm about to do." I take the flask. "Do you think the cleaners got what they wanted from the priest?"

"I don't believe they did," he says, rocking back on his heels as he stares out at the sky in thought. "They would have tortured him for information. It was a clean kill. I'm sorry."

"Don't apologize to me." I shrug, take a deep breath, then shake my head. "You really think we can save the world, Padre? The odds are not in our favor. We're talking about facing a literal apocalypse, the Darken, religious nuts that have made a sport of killing my people, and God only knows what else."

"Don't forget trying to find the secret location of a cure that was known only by a paranoid madman?"

"Of course! How could I forget that." I smirk. "Who knew the end of the world would involve a treasure hunt?"

"That's what I like about you, Mia. You always find the silver lining." Raziel chuckles and brushes a strand of hair from my face. "We're going to make it. I promise."

"You shouldn't make promises when you can't assure the outcome." My eyes close against the warmth of his palm.

I feel him move closer, his breath on my cheek and his palm traveling to cup the back of my neck. I open my eyes and meet his gaze. He's so close. My eyes shift to his lips, and I reach up, grabbing a fistful of his shirt as I lean in and kiss him.

I hear the thud of the journal as it hits the floor, right as his hand cups the back of my thigh and lifts me into his arms. He pins me to the wall with his body, a very impressive mass grinding against me.

I tighten my grip on his shoulders as I match his rhythm and cry out as heat begins to build between my legs.

"Father Raziel!" Sister Joselyn enters the tower, her face flushed from the walk up the stairs—or our scandalous position—and her eyes wide with shock. Raziel and I pull away from each other. "I . . . Oh, gosh. Um . . . I need to speak to you in private, Father."

"Of course," Raziel says, a shit-eating grin on his face, with not an ounce of shame, as he shoots me a wink in front of the nun. "I'll find you later, sweetheart."

"You'd better," I mutter, avoiding the old nun's gaze. I'm not even halfway down the staircase when I hear her lecturing him on etiquette and sins of the body. I chuckle and shake my head as I make my way back to the bedroom.

I stand beneath a red sky. The air is thick with smoke as fires blaze across the battlefield. A wolf howls in the distance, and warriors, angels, humans, and beings clearly not of this world, run toward the horizon. Numbering in the hundreds, winged men and women dressed in obsidian armor fly onto the battlefield. Men, women, and children shift into wolves, bears, tigers, mountain lions, and rhinos. On the backs of the rhinos ride warriors with long spears that pluck the winged beings from the sky, sending them spiraling to the earth below. Explosions of dirt rise as bodies hit the ground.

This is war.

Holding the front line is a woman with black wings that shimmer blue when the light reflects off them. Her braided blonde hair and pale skin show blood splatter as her piercing blue eyes meet mine, a tilt of her head in silent acknowledgment.

The mages come next, stepping into line with me, and one by one, the elements are summoned. Earth. Water. Fire. Air. Witches gather at our backs, offering whatever protection they can summon.

I look to the mage to my right, a mirror of myself. His eyes are a dark gray, the color of a storm, his attention on the battle ahead. He holds a ball of fire in one hand as a sand tornado twists in the other.

His head snaps in my direction. Our eyes lock, and he stiffens as if he's seeing me for the first time. "Who are you?"

I look to my left to see who he's speaking to, but all the witches are staring directly at me. "You can see me?"

"Yes," he says as he reaches for me, but I pull away. "Who are you?" he repeats as I return to consciousness.

Sitting upright, I clutch my head. The room spins, and the ringing in my ears grows louder. I lean back on the pillows, my eyes still closed, as I process what just happened.

They saw me. Not just that mage, but all of them. It can't be a coincidence. I move to the edge of the bed and force myself to get dressed, thinking over the events of yesterday.

The house is gone, my sister is dead, and the whitecoats are still actively killing my people. They killed the priest of the parish and will likely be back sooner or later. A part of me wanted to be here when they came, but logic told me it was best to keep moving.

I grab my hip holster from the back of the chair and loop the belt through the hoops of my jeans, then attach my thigh holsters. My guns and knives are laid out on top of the desk, and I check the safety and rounds before strapping each one into place.

I reach for my dagger where it sits on the bedside table but hesitate as I catch sight of Abi's dagger, nearly identical to my own.

I killed my sister yesterday . . .

Pushing those thoughts to the back of my mind, I grab the daggers and slide mine back into its case on my belt, then slide Abi's into the slit inside my boot before turning and pulling on my leather jacket. I pack the rest of the weapons away and slide the duffel beneath the bed.

Before I decide on my next move, I need to speak to Raziel. And, more than that, I need coffee. Walking into the kitchen, the last thing I expect to find is Sister Joselyn breaking up a fight between Raziel, Luke, and one of Luke's men.

I pull Joselyn out of the way before she's crushed between the three men.

"What's going on?" I ask.

"Luke has taken leadership of the group," Joselyn explains, "and he's planning to leave today."

Laid out on the dining table is a map of the city, parts of it marked in red.

"Listen, I don't have the time to argue with you. These are the facts—we're low on supplies, our ammo is dwindling, and we're in the middle of a hot zone. My men are tired; we've been up all night protecting this place while you and Red suck faces in the tower. We lost half our people yesterday, and we're going to lose more if we don't leave today," Luke says.

"We're leaving with or without you," the boy at Luke's side adds.

"I don't want to leave," Sister Marie says, moving forward and looking at each man before settling her gaze on me. "This is my home."

My heart breaks for the woman, and I reach out to comfort her, but before I can, the kid talks again.

"No offense, Sister, but it's only a matter of time before this church is taken and you end up dead, or one of them."

It would have been kinder to slap her.

"What is wrong with you?" Raziel places himself in front of Marie and faces the boy. "You don't talk to her like that."

The boy smirks and steps closer to Raziel. "What are you going to do about it?"

"That's enough." I glare at the kid. "I suggest you step back before I stick my foot up your ass." I turn my glare on Luke. "You want to be in charge? Control your people, and teach this one some manners while you're at it."

"You're right," Luke says, having the decency to look ashamed. "Apologize to Sister Marie."

"What?"

"The world might've gone to shit, Ben, but that ain't how your mama raised you. Be a man and apologize."

Ben and Luke stare at each other for a moment, then Ben curses under his breath, crosses his arms over his chest, and straightens as he looks from Raziel to Sister Marie and me. "I'm sorry."

"Apology accepted," I say. "As tactless as Ben here is"—I look to those standing with Raziel and the sisters. It's clear these people aren't ready to leave—"he isn't wrong, and neither is Luke. You've been lucky to survive here as long as you have, but it's only a matter of time before we're overrun."

Sister Marie looks scared as she meets my gaze. "What chance do we have out there? People like you will survive, but people like us"—she gestures to the other sisters and seniors—"we're safe here."

"But for how long?" I ask gently. "Right now, the church is protected by these men, but without them, you're vulnerable. You might not make it out there, but out there, you have a chance. People need people to survive. If we can find somewhere to set up camp, maybe we can wait this out, but we're going to need people like you to help do that."

Raziel looks at Luke. "I'm not arguing with your reasons. I need more time."

"Time isn't something we have, Raziel." I offer a sympathetic smile. "I know what it is you seek, but if it were here, you'd have found it already. You asked for my help last night to protect these people. If they'll allow it, then that's what I'm going to do."

"Give me the day," Raziel says, looking between me and Luke. "If I can't find it, we'll leave first thing tomorrow."

"I'm sorry," Luke says, stepping up to my side. "I'm not risking my family, or these people, on something that may or may not exist." Luke turns to look at me and gestures to the map. "How did you get into the city?"

"I rode in on a bicycle." I stuff my hands into the pockets of my jeans. "I abandoned it at the edge of the city and kept to the backstreets. Saw a few strays, rats—not all of them were Darken. I dodged a few homeless people who weren't so lucky."

"What are the chances we can use that route to get out of the city?"

Staring at the map, I trace my movements backward using Abi's apartment building as the starting point. "It's possible, though moving a crowd this big through those alleys is a risk. I was on my own before. I hid behind dumpsters and garbage bags. We can't do that with a group this size."

"I didn't ask if it'd be easy; I asked if it could be done," Luke says, his tone irritated.

Resisting the urge to roll my eyes, I nod. "Yes. But if it's alright with you, I'd like to scout the route first. I can clear a path, find an alternative if required, and shelter in place if that storm comes back through."

"I don't like this," Raziel murmurs, standing by my side and glaring at Luke and me.

Luke's wife, Trina, steps forward, cradling their baby. "We're leaving on foot?" she asks quietly.

One of the men behind her shakes his head and steps forward. "That's crazy! Why would we do that when we have a bus parked outside?"

"If it's as bad as you say it is out there," Trina continues, "people will get left behind and picked off. What about our children?"

Luke's expression softens as he reaches for his wife's hand. "The streets are unpredictable, love. We lost good men and women yesterday because they couldn't get their trucks through. I won't let anything happen to our children; I swear."

"And what about the rest of us?" one of the nuns asks. "Your wife is right. We'll either fall behind or be picked off by the infected."

I turn to Luke, but neither of us can offer comfort for their concerns. The simple truth of the matter is they aren't wrong. Their deaths would likely buy us time to escape.

I hated the thought as soon as I had it.

With a sigh, Luke straightens and addresses the room. "I don't know what will happen out there, but I do know that I'll do whatever it takes to keep us alive. We will find someplace safe."

"What's safe these days?" Raziel asks, as I pick up the red Sharpie and map out a route. "You aren't going out there alone, Mia. You're too valuable."

I smile at the priest. "Your concern is touching, and unwarranted. This isn't my first time going into hostile territory, Padre. I'm the best person to do recon."

"I don't like the idea either," Luke admits, "but it's the only option available to us. I hope you understand that I can't risk sending anyone else out. If you get stuck out there, you're on your own."

"I know." I gesture to the map in front of me. "If I don't make it back, get to this building. My sister's apartment is secure and has access to the roof. You can make it across to the other apartments if needed to look for supplies."

A few minutes later, I'm standing at the kitchen bench, preparing my coffee. The water is lukewarm, but I don't have time to reboil it. I'm about to take my first sip of coffee in two days when Raziel storms up to me. "Do you have some death wish I need to be aware of?"

With a sigh, I lower my cup and lift a questioning brow. "Do you?"

He stares at me with annoyance. "Excuse me?"

"You're interrupting the first cup of coffee I've had in two days. I'm not a nice person in general, but most would agree I'm a lot nicer once caffeinated. So, Padre, I suggest you back the fuck up and take a moment to consider how you want to die, because I will end you if you interrupt this moment between me and my coffee."

A smile lights up his features as he stares at me. "You'd really kill me over a cup of coffee?"

"I'd do a lot of things to you over coffee." After taking my first sip, I smile. "You're dressed differently today."

"It's my day off," he says, taking a cup from the shelf and pouring himself a cup of coffee. "Jeans and hoodies are more my style anyway."

I lean against the bench beside him, and we drink our coffee in silence.

"Listen, about last night—"

"The kiss?" he interrupts.

My face heats, and I take a drink. "It was a mistake."

"A mistake I hope to repeat soon," he says casually, his eyes scanning the kitchen. "Listen, I'd love nothing more than to talk about that kiss. Please, believe that. It'll forever live rent-free inside my head."

"But?"

"I need your help to get more time."

"What exactly is it you're looking for?"

"The priest kept a journal that was passed down through his family."

"Isn't that what you've been reading?"

"No, that is his personal journal," Raziel answers, turning to me. "The journal I'm looking for is extremely old and valuable; it originally belonged to Silas McCoy. It potentially holds the answers to many prophecies involving your bloodline, including loopholes to prevent or change the outcomes. I suspect Aiden also hid the location of the cure within it."

"I don't know, Raziel." I'm unsure what to say. "Are you willing to risk all these people's lives on a hunch?"

"Are you willing to risk the lives of billions?" he asks, holding my gaze. "If we leave and the whitecoats find that journal, things will be a lot worse."

"You said they didn't know."

"They might not have known Aiden had it," he corrects, "but I have no doubt they know of its existence. Silas McCoy's journal isn't widely known. I've been searching for it since I arrived. I know the journal is here. It has to be."

"Have you spoken to Sister Joselyn?"

"I don't think she trusts me," Raziel admits. "I suspect she knows what I'm looking for."

"How can you be sure?"

"Aiden and Joselyn were close. He speaks of her a lot in his journal, and even mentions trusting her with the truth."

I sit my cup on the bench and take a deep breath. "Do you really believe this journal contains the key to undoing all this?"

"I believe it contains answers," Raziel admits, leaning into me. "Are you okay?"

"I've been thinking about the prophecy."

Raziel nods slowly, his fingers brushing against my own just as Sister Joselyn walks up to us, her eyes glancing down to our just-touching hands before darting back up to our faces. "Sorry to interrupt, again."

Raziel pulls his hand away and straightens as he smiles at the woman. "How are you feeling, Sister?"

"I'm okay, Father, but I couldn't help but overhear that you're looking for something that belonged to Father Aiden."

She reaches into her habit and pulls out a brown leather journal with the initials A. M. on the front.

"It doesn't make much sense—the ramblings of a madman. I almost burned it to protect the father's reputation, but it was the letter that stopped me. It was addressed to his daughter." Sister Joselyn holds out both the journal and a heavy leather antique book. "It was the only sane thing he wrote."

"I don't understand," I whisper, staring at the sister.

"Father Aiden McCoy was your biological father, Mia. Shortly before his death, he wrote you this letter. It's inside his bible."

My father?

"My father died when I was a child," I say, even as I flip open the bible, and sure enough, there's an open envelope with *Mia McCoy* written in a messy scrawl across the front, along with an old family photograph. I swallow the lump in my throat as I trace the faces of my parents.

"Your father was a good man," Sister Joselyn says, with tears in her eyes. "He was very proud of you, Mia."

What the actual fuck?

"My parents died when I was eight," I repeat, though more to myself. "I don't understand."

Raziel places a hand on my arm and turns to Sister Joselyn. "Thank you for giving us these, Sister. You have no idea how it will help. Could you give us a moment, please?"

"Of course. I am truly sorry for your loss," Sister Joselyn says, before making her exit.

I can't bring myself to open the letter, so I fold it and slide it into my pocket. I hand Raziel the bible and open to the first page of the journal.

Property of Aiden McCoy.

I flick through the first pages and feel my stomach churn. If I'd eaten this morning, it would have made a reappearance. Sister Joselyn was right. These are the words of a madman, and the more I read, the worse it gets. Only, it's not all mad. Because I understand every word.

What does that say about me?

"Mia?" Raziel whispers, staring at the open pages of the bible. "You're not going to believe this—"

"We're under attack!" Trina screams, right as a bullet shatters the window where she's standing. As the glass explodes, Trina's head shoots forward at the impact of the bullet entering the back of her skull. Sister Marie leaps over and catches hold of the baby as its mother collapses.

Screams fill the kitchen as panic erupts.

Luke runs for his children, his gaze lingering on his wife's body as he starts barking orders for his men. I turn to Raziel and hand him the journal. "You need to get them out of here."

"Where are you going?" he yells, grabbing my hand. "Mia?"

I turn to him and pull my hand from his grip. "We won't survive out there without weapons!" I hand him my gun. "Do you know how to use this?"

"Yes." He takes the gun but doesn't seem sure. "I'll wait for you."

"No! Get them out of here! I'll find you," I yell at him, but I'm already running for the stairs.

I throw open my bedroom door as gunshots sound from outside and downstairs. People scream as they flee for their lives. I kneel beside my bed and pull out the duffel and backpack.

Pressing my back to the wall, I listen to the footsteps climbing the stairs. Three people, at least. A scratching on the wall makes the hairs on the back of my neck rise, and then I hear it. The whistling tune of death's melody.

The whitecoats.

"No!" Sister Joselyn screams from the hall. "Please God—"

I step into the hallway and shoot the first attacker. He falls back down the stairs, but it's the sight of watching a man withdraw a sword from Sister Joselyn's belly that makes me hesitate. Blood pours from her mouth, and her eyes go wide as she stares at her killer.

The other smiles as he approaches, his hand raised, trailing a dagger along the wall. It leaves a mark the entire way up the staircase. The sadist's smile grows as he moves toward me. I rush back into the room and slam the door closed.

Fuck!

I search for a lock, but there is none.

I close my eyes and try to calm my racing mind, even as the whitecoats bang on the bedroom door. I have two options—let them in and fight, or . . .

Jump out the window.

The window that opens out onto a tiny ledge. It's close enough I can run and climb out onto the roof. I can make it. I unsheathe my dagger and cut the duffle bag loose, letting it fall to the floor. The extra weight will slow me down too much. I'll have to make a supply stop on the way out of the city.

I bolt across the room and push open the window, and I'm barely out when one of them grabs hold of my hand. I roll onto my back, swinging my leg out and hitting the attacker upside the head, then use the momentum to fling myself off the roof. I catch the gutter with the tips of my fingers but can feel myself slipping . . . This is a third-story fall. If it doesn't kill me, there's no way I get out of this without breaking something.

"Mia! Let go!" Raziel shouts from below. "I'm here!"

Screaming, I let go of the ledge and pray to God he'll catch me. Colliding with Raziel knocks the wind out of me, but he holds me as I fling my arms around his neck and hold on for dear life.

"I've got you," he says.

I lift my head and stare at him in disbelief. "They killed Joselyn. I tried—"

"It's okay," he says, lowering my feet to the ground. "Can you walk?"

I nod and catch sight of his bloodied shirt. "Are you hurt?"

"It's not my blood," he says, taking my hand. "Come on."

We're halfway down the block when Raziel pulls me into an alley. "As if dealing with Darken isn't bad enough. Can you believe we've also got humans trying to kill us?"

"You didn't notice, did you?" I ask, scanning our surroundings for danger. "They wore all white, Raziel. They're whitecoats."

"Mia—"

As if I summoned them, five whitecoats step into the alley ahead, weapons drawn as they approach. Raziel moves ahead, and it's only now I see the sword strapped across his back.

"What's with the sword?" I ask, stepping next to him. "What kind of priest are you?"

"The old kind." Raziel gestures to the five men in front of us. "Think you can handle the two on the right?"

"Oh, sure. Let me just pull a sword out of my ass." I can shoot them, but there's only so many bullets and gunshots would bring the infected down upon us.

"That's where you keep it? No wonder you're so moody."

CHAPTER

SIXTEEN

MIA

I was eight years old when the whitecoats came. I remember the break-in, the screams, my parents arguing, and my father telling my mother to take us and go.

I remember the warmth of their blood beneath my feet.

I remember the sight of my father begging on his hands and knees.

The cursed ones. A scourge on the Earth.

That's what they called us.

The Unclean.

Rage consumes me as the last surviving whitecoat groans in agony at my feet. I don't know how it happened. One minute, I was standing over him, and the next, my fists were pounding into his shattered skull.

Raziel wraps his arm around my waist and lifts me off the corpse. "Mia, stop. He's dead." I kick and scratch to get away, but Raziel's grip remains tight around me. "Breathe, sweetheart."

I try to hold it in, to smother the flames, but the rage and fear only fuel the fire as it erupts from within me. I scream, and for the first time in years, blue flames consume the air around us and scorch the alley, turning everything to ash. Everything except Raziel.

With my back pressed against a tree, I sit in the dirt as the remaining survivors huddle around the firepit. Luke and his two eldest children—Damien and Eliza. Wayne and his husband Eric. Ben, Sister Marie, Betty, Bridget.

We lost seven people in the attack with the cleaners.

Seven innocent people.

Wives. Mothers. Fathers. A baby.

Innocents.

"You should eat, Mia," Raziel says, bringing me out of my thoughts. He's kneeling in front of me, holding out a small tin of baked beans. "I couldn't find a spoon."

"I'm not hungry." The lie is contradicted by the sound of my stomach growling.

Raziel takes a seat beside me, his back pressed against the tree and his forearm against mine. Goosebumps rise along my arm, and I resist the urge to lean into him. "You need to eat, sweetheart. You exerted a lot of raw energy this afternoon. You need to replenish your strength."

"It'll take a lot more than beans," I snap. "Sorry, I'm still . . ." I take a deep breath and swallow down the words I can't say. "I'm sorry."

"I understand." His hand reaches out, and he squeezes my knee. "Was that your first time?"

"What?" I ask, unable to help a laugh as I turn to look at him. "You mean the flames, right?"

With an ambiguous look, Raziel raises a brow. "What else would I mean?"

I roll my eyes, though I know my cheeks have flushed. "It's not the first time something like that has happened," I reluctantly admit. "Though it's never happened on that scale before."

"What do you mean?"

I check to make sure nobody is watching, then turn into the tree, lowering my hand so it can't be seen from the fire. I take a deep breath in, unclench my fist, and watch as the sparks of lightning dance with the blue flames in the center of my palm.

It's been so long since I let myself use any of my gifts. The last time I used them was the night Abi and I escaped the compound. I'd been too afraid to try in case someone caught me, or Jonah found a way to track me through them, or the whitecoats found us.

"I lost control in the alley," I admit, staring at the sparks as I raise my other hand and watch them move through my fingertips, bright and alive. Free at last. "I forgot how beautiful it was." I lift my gaze to find Raziel staring at me. "Does this scare you?"

"I'm not afraid of you," Raziel says, and he settles next to me against the tree.

"A normal person would be freaking out." I search his eyes for an explanation. "Why aren't you?"

"You aren't the first person I've met with elemental abilities."

I lean away from him and pick up the tin of beans. "What's your story, Padre? I know there's more to it than you've shared."

"There's always more to the story, Mia." He grins. "That bible Joselyn gave you wasn't an ordinary bible. It also belonged to Silas McCoy. Written in the old fae language, and among it were coordinates left by your father."

"Coordinates to where?"

"I haven't figured that out yet, but I have a good feeling." He grins widely, before turning serious. "So, Father Adrian is actually your father."

I hand him the beans. "I thought my father died when I was eight years old."

"He didn't."

"Obviously," I snap, my palms heating. "He was alive this whole time. Living in the same damn city, right down the street from Abigail. My sister knew who he was, and still, she kept it from me. I drove past that church every time I visited her. He's been right there this whole time, and the kicker is that he knew I was alive.

"He knew I was here, he knew I'd get that letter, and instead of reaching out to say 'Hi, Mia, remember me? I'm your dad,' he waited until he was dead so he didn't have to face the consequences of his actions or answer the question of why he didn't come for me."

"I can't imagine what you must be feeling," Raziel whispers. "For what it's worth, I think he did it to protect you." He reaches for my hand when I start to get up. "Your family was killed because of the bloodline, because of *his* bloodline. He didn't change his name, Mia. You could've found him. He didn't hide from you."

"I thought he was dead."

"I understand that." He squeezes my hand. "I also understand needing to protect those you love most, and I know he loved you."

"I have so many questions, Raziel."

"I know."

"I had a dream last night," I whisper, needing to change the topic. "I was standing on a battlefield. The sky was red, and there were winged warriors and shifters. There was a woman, a warrior, with blue-black wings. She looked right at me as if she could see me."

"Mia."

"There were witches and mages who saw me."

"What do you mean they saw you?"

"A guy looked right at me and asked who I was. I thought he might've been talking to someone else, but when I looked back, there was no one else. They all stood there, staring at me." I close my eyes as the first tears fall. "It scared me."

He kisses the top of my head and wraps his arms around my shoulder. "It'll be okay."

"You keep saying that, but do you actually believe it?"

I feel his smile on my forehead as he whispers, "I have hope."

I roll my eyes. "Seriously?"

Raziel squeezes my shoulders, pulling me closer before whispering, "Close your eyes and sleep." He leans in and brushes his lips against mine, and I lean up into the kiss, but before it can deepen, he pulls back and brushes his thumb across my bottom lip.

The look in his eyes stirs something within me, and I reach for him. Our lips meet in a frenzied kiss. He stiffens against the tree, his hand tightening on my hip as his breathing grows heavier. "Follow me into the woods and show me just how bossy you can be," I say.

"When I take you, Mia, it won't be a quickie against a tree. Go to sleep."

"Fine," I hiss, jerking back from him. "Goodnight, Padre."

"Goodnight, sweetheart."

I turn my back on him and lie down on the ground. Still pissed about having to leave my supply bag behind, I contemplate going back before dawn to find it. The whitecoats likely took whatever was left behind, and they'd no doubt be out for blood for their fallen zealots.

It's safer to stay with the group.

Eventually, I drift off to sleep and dream of ash falling from a red sky and angels riding on giant beasts with wings. Warriors with swords and spears ride the lightning down to the blood-soaked battle-field. The rivers that ran dry now flow with the blood of the fallen.

I awake before dawn and find myself pressed against the sleeping priest. His hoodie is draped around me, and his arms circle my waist, holding me close. I let myself relax against him as the sun begins to rise.

"Morning," Raziel grumbles as he stretches. "How did you sleep?"

"It's not the worst I've had," I admit, holding out his hoodie. "Thank you for this."

"You looked cold." He stands. "Thanks for sharing your pillow."

I stand and shake out my jacket before pulling it back on. "I'm going to borrow Ben's crossbow. I'll come find you later."

"You know how to hunt?"

I smirk as I look back at him. "Don't sound so surprised."

He raises his hands in defeat, but his smile widens. "Guess I'll wait here and look pretty."

Later that afternoon, our group of survivors walks down the main street. Raziel and I lead the others through town, searching shops and restaurants for any food to get us through the coming days.

We meet up at the top of town and continue toward the train station.

"What is that?" Ben asks, as ear-piercing screeches echo in the trees. He raises his gun, aiming at the rustling leaves.

Raziel's hand shoots out, gesturing for him to lower his weapon. "Nobody move."

"Are those lorikeets?" someone asks from behind us as the swarm of birds turn their attention to our group. I take a step back, almost bumping into Raziel as the Darken reaches out for us from within the lorikeets. I can taste the rot on my tongue as the corrupted birds turn their focus on our group.

"Run!" Raziel orders.

The birds swoop, razor-sharp claws catching hoods and hair as we flee.

Damien trips in front of me, and we both fall to the ground. The birds swarm us before we can get to our feet. I try to cover the boy's face, but the birds are so small it's hard to do anything. I can hear Raziel barking orders not to shoot right as gunshots fill the air, but the screech of the birds continues.

"Mia?" I lift my head at Raziel's voice as he runs to me, his arms up to protect his head. He drops beside me, his eyes searching mine. I force myself to stand, pulling Damien along with me. "We need to run!"

Two people lie dead among the chaos, and others scream as the birds rip and claw at their upper bodies.

That's when I feel the power surge within me. It's different to the alley—like everything slows and I watch from outside myself. My eyes focus on a single bird, and it stills, turning to me with its lifeless eyes, but I see something there, within the abyss.

A spark of consciousness.

The heart inside its chest hammers away like a machine gun, and as my magic searches out the others, they all turn and hang in the air, the only movement coming from their wings keeping them airborne. My body aches, but my mind is sharp. I don't waver as I seek that spark within the birds. I can feel their hearts in the palm of my hand. The darkness is a thick layer of despair, wrapping itself around the muscle like a second skin. My fingers tighten around their hearts, and it fights back. They swarm me, but Raziel's arms wrap around me as disheveled wings unfurl from his back, taking the brunt of their attack.

My head spins, and I hold on to Raziel's shirt. The taste of iron assaults my senses, and blood trickles from my nose. I should stop. But I can't. I squeeze my eyes closed and focus on the heartbeats of the lorikeets, I crush them in my palm, suffocating the Darken. Their lifeless bodies plummet from the sky and hit the pavement with a thud.

A weight lifts as darkness releases its hold. Once I'm sure it's gone, I release the grip, and with each breath I take, I give back to them, encouraging their hearts to beat, watching in awe as the lorikeets come to life free of the darken.

There's a moment of silence before the screaming starts. With deafening screeches, the lorikeets take flight and flee.

I'm so in awe at the scene that I don't realize when Raziel lets go of me, moving to stand between me and a shotgun.

It's only the sight of the broken and bloody wings protruding from his back that pulls me back into myself. Raziel's hoodie is shredded, revealing every inch of his exposed flesh soaked with blood from his wings.

I stare at the wings in disbelief, unable to process the sight in front of me. Raziel is trying to speak to Luke and the survivors, who continue to scream and stare at us like we're the monsters.

Maybe we are.

The ringing intensifies, and without Raziel's support, I sway and stumble forward, bumping into Raziel's broken wing. He stumbles but turns to catch me as I fall. "Mia?"

I open my mouth to speak but can't.

"Is she okay?"

"She needs rest," Raziel tells them, lifting me into his arms.

"What are you?" Luke asks. He nods to his son. "Damien, come here. Now."

"Raziel," I choke out, and his arms tighten protectively around me. "What's happening?"

"I've got you. Don't fight it. Let your body rest." His lips brush against my forehead. "She needs to lay down, Luke. Let's get to safety first, then I'll explain."

That's the last thing I remember before I succumb to the darkness.

"Raziel?" I groan as I lift my head from the pillow and press my palm to my forehead. I can't open my eyes, but I can sense him close by. The surface dips beside me, and he's easing me back onto what feels like an uncomfortable couch. "Where are we?"

"A room above some bar." His voice is quiet, barely above a whisper.

"Where are the others?"

"Gone."

I stiffen and force my eyes open. It's night. I blink a few times, and after a moment, my vision adjusts to see a guilty-looking Raziel. "I tried to stop them, but they were afraid of me. Of us."

"That's ridiculous," I mutter, pulling myself up to sit. Raziel moves to sit beside me, his hand on my lower back as he rubs comforting circles. I close my eyes and lean into him as he relaxes back against the lounge.

"It is," Raziel whispers quietly. "We're safe for now, but we'll need to leave at first light."

"The coordinates." I lift my head to look at him. "Did you figure out where they led?"

"It's to a shipping yard." he whispers, brushing hair from my face. "How did you do it?"

"Do what?"

"I watched you," he says, his voice filled with awe. "I felt it. You stopped their hearts until the Darken released its hold. If that wasn't enough of a miracle, then you bringing the birds back to life definitely was. Do you have any idea what that means?"

"No, but I'm sure you're about to tell me," I say, leaning back against the couch and cradling my head as the throbbing intensifies.

"You cured those lorikeets."

"I don't know how I did that," I admit, staring out at the night sky. Raziel stands, takes my hand, and pulls me over to the window. Hundreds of Darken wander aimlessly through the streets. "What does this mean?"

"It means they can be saved," Raziel whispers, his hand on my lower back as he stares out at the Darken. "You found its weakness, and that gives our people a chance to survive."

"Our people?" I look around the empty room. "Our people left us, Raziel."

"They weren't our people," he says. "There is so much you don't yet know."

"So, tell me." I walk back to the couch and collapse down onto it, preparing for a long conversation. "Tell me everything, starting with what you are."

SEVENTEEN

I'm not sure what I expected when I revealed what I was, or the existence of others in this world. How does a human process that? Though, did Mia really qualify as human herself?

"Mia," I press hesitantly. "Please don't be afraid."

She scoffs and lifts her head from her hands to look at me. "I'm not afraid, Raziel. I'm just shocked." She looks thoughtful for a moment, then continues. "Your friends—Sahari and Isaiah—they've been gathering survivors and making alliances with the other leaders. Shifters, wolves, witches, mages. Those like me?"

"Yes."

"That's who was in the dream," she whispers almost to herself, as she sits up, straightens her spine, and gives a single nod. "Okay."

"Okay?"

She pushes the jacket off her lap and stands. "The place you're supposed to meet Sahari and Isaiah is a few hours' drive, at best. We're going to need supplies and wheels if we're to survive the trip."

"We'll make do with what we have."

"And what the heck do we have, Raziel?" She turns on me, waving to her near-empty bag in the corner. "You let Luke and the others take most of our supplies. We've got a few bottles of water, some knives, my old rifle, and a handgun with half a dozen rounds each. Oh, and your sword. How can we forget your sword!?"

"I can protect you—"

"No, you can't." Her eyes blaze with fire as she stalks toward me. "This is what I do, Raziel. This is what I'm trained for, and what I've been preparing for my entire life. I'm not some fragile damsel that needs your protection."

I stand from the couch. "This isn't a game, sweetheart. It's war."

"I'm glad we're finally on the same page." She raises her chin and glares at me. "I've got a stash in the city. We'll make a detour and restock. If it's safe, we'll stay the night and plan our route. There's a car in the garage that should still work."

She's got supplies hidden in the city?

"You're prepared for anything, aren't you?"

"Almost," she whispers, lifting her eyes to mine. "If you're waiting for me to break, I won't. This isn't as big of a shock as you might think. If you knew where I grew up—where I came from—you'd understand."

"Is it so wrong that I care for you?" I ask, closing the space between us. It was easier than I expected to admit how I feel. "I don't know what I'd do if anything happened to you, Mia. It doesn't make sense, but nothing about this makes sense. All I know is that you're important."

She pulls back, her expression guarded. "To your mission, or to you?"

I take her hand and place it over the human heart in my chest. "To me."

Mia closes the distance, her arms sliding around my neck and her face inching closer to mine. Everything else fades as her lips find mine. I pull her close and lead her back to the lounge, smiling as she tugs at my hair and bites my bottom lip.

Glass shattering downstairs breaks us apart, then footsteps thump on the stairs outside the room. Mia pushes away from me and rushes to her gun. Bullets fly through the closed door, and I grab the lounge, pushing it up against it. It won't hold for long, but it'll give us time to escape.

I run back to the barred window and rip off the iron bars. "Mia! Come on!"

"The supplies—"

"Fuck the supplies," I yell at her, grabbing her arm.

"We won't survive without weapons!" she hisses, pulling her arm from mine.

Fuck. I curse and send a quick prayer to God, then to Mia, say, "I'll distract them, you run for the guns, and we'll escape out the window." Her eyes bulge out of her head as she looks to the window, then back at me. "It won't kill you. Wait for my signal."

Two whitecoats push their way into the room and level their guns at me. My smile widens as I lift my gaze back to theirs. "Are guns really necessary in this situation?"

"Kneel, scum."

I deliberately move away from the couch, drawing their aim away from Mia. "I don't want to hurt you both, but I will."

"You will die."

"Someday, I'm sure." Feeling behind me, I grip the back of a chair. "But it won't be today, or by your hand."

Before they can react, I fling the chair in their direction, then close the distance, taking the knife from my belt and slicing their throats open.

Mia moved at the same time, grabbing the backpack with our supplies and her rifle. Gunshots echo and plaster explodes when the wall behind her is hit. I hold out my hand, and she takes it.

"Whatever you do," I whisper against her ear as I wrap my arm around her, pulling her close, "don't let go."

EIGHTEEN

MIA

Raziel wraps his arms around me, his lips at my ear as he whispers, "Whatever you do, don't let go."

Before I can question it, his hold tightens, and his broken wings spring from his back. My heart rises to my throat and my stomach churns as he throws us out the window. For a moment, we're just falling, but then I hear a snap and Raziel's groan as his wings expand and carry us over the buildings.

I tighten my hold on Raziel as I take in the city in complete darkness, except for the occasional fire, but it's the view of the night sky that takes my breath away.

"Mia." I hear the strain in his voice. "I need to land."

"Are you shot?" I ask him, leaning back to look, but his grip holds me still. "Raziel?"

Tears slid down his cheek, and for the first time, I see true agony in his eyes. "It's my wings."

I search the ground below and spot an empty lot. "There."

The landing is rough. On impact, Raziel's hold loosens, and I'm thrown across gravel. I groan, rolling onto my back, and hiss at the stinging where the gravel has cut my palms and lower back. Stunned, I lie there for a moment before pushing myself into a sitting position.

The area is empty except for a few cars and a large industrial bin behind a restaurant. Raziel lies face down on the gravel in front of that bin, his wings limp and trembling above him. I rush to get up, scraping my hands and knees as I trip and fall.

"Raziel?" I cry, kneeling beside him, as I take in the extent of the damage done to his wing. He flinches beneath my touch, unconscious but alive, and I lean in, pressing our foreheads together as we take a moment to catch our breaths.

As I look around the parking lot, my gaze wanders back to the bin. We need to get out of sight, but I can't carry a badly injured six-foot angel across the city. I stand up, ignoring the pain. Pushing back the lid of the bin, I almost gag. The smell alone would deter anybody from looking inside.

I kneel beside Raziel and am relieved to see his eyes open. "Are you able to stand?"

"Yeah." He slowly pushes himself up, kneeling first, his hands shaking as he straightens his spine. His wings aren't just broken—they are so badly damaged the feathers turn to ash as they fall to the gravel beneath him. "I just need a moment."

"I'm surprised we made it this far," I admit, looking up at the sky.

"As am I. For a minute, I wasn't sure we'd make it out the window."

I raise a brow as I stare at him. "Why wouldn't we have?"

"My wings are turning to ash before our eyes. Someday, there won't be anything left." He keeps his eyes on mine. "You could say I took a leap of faith." I want to yell at him, scream, and throw a rock at his stupid face, but the sound of whistling halts my movements. "You should go."

"What?" I whisper angrily at him. "Are you mad?"

"I'll slow you down." A defeated smile tugs at his lips, and he raises his hand to my face. "You said it yourself: you don't need my help, Mia. You've been preparing for this war your entire life. I couldn't see that before, couldn't see past my own fear and need to protect you, but I see it now."

"You're insane!" I whisper, grabbing his arm. "Get in the bin."

He groans in pain and looks at the bin. "I won't fit."

"Bet that's the first time you've said that to a girl." I can't help smirking as I turn to him, but there's no amusement on his face. "Our options are limited, Raziel. Put away your wings and get in the damn bin before I throw you in."

The wings fold in on themselves, crooked and trembling as embers and ashes continue to fall to the gravel at his feet, then they're gone from sight. I help him into the bin, ignoring his complaints as he falls in, gagging. "Dear God, what is that smell? Actually, Lord, I'd rather not know."

"Shut up," I order, eyeing the parking lot for my rifle and bag. I can't see it. *Fuck.* Time is running out; the whistling is getting closer. I climb into the bin, close the lid, and settle in the corner, my back pressed against Raziel's chest.

"This is not how I thought the night would end," Raziel whispers, burying his face in my hair. "Your safe house better have running water."

"There isn't enough water in the world." I wrinkle my nose, trying not to breathe it in. "Sleep. I'll keep watch."

The whole time Raziel and I were inside that bin, I was terrified. I hated not seeing what was coming. I'd hear movements outside— thump, crunch, clack, whap—and hold my breath as I waited for bullets to rain down on us.

But nothing happened, and when soft light began peeking through the crack where lid met bin, I knew we'd made it through the night. "Do you think it's clear?" I whisper.

Raziel listens and nods. "You don't sense anything out there?"

Nothing. I shake my head, and he nods before we climb to the top of the rubbish and push open the lid.

I climb out first and watch in amusement as Raziel struggles to climb over the lip, then I bite back a grin and shake my head. "There's my badass archangel warrior."

He glares, straightening his shirt. "Don't start with me, Red."

I smile and turn to the parking lot. "Let's take five to search the area for the bag. If it's not here, we'll need to be extra vigilant."

"How far is the apartment?" Raziel asks, his eyes scanning the parking lot.

To be entirely honest, I'm not sure. I tried to place our location during the night, but it was difficult with no landmarks lit up.

The only good thing to come out of Raziel's gamble last night was that he'd taken us farther into the city and not out of it.

"We're a few blocks away, I think." I turn and kick the gravel beneath my boot. "Goddamn it!"

"Mia," Raziel says, trying to be reassuring, I'm sure, but it only pisses me off more.

"Don't 'Mia' me in that tone, Raziel," I snap, raising my hands to run through my hair and cringing at the smell clinging to it. "The bag is gone."

"It is," he agrees, taking a tentative step toward me, "but it'll be okay."

"You don't know that."

"No, I don't. But I have faith." His smile widens as I roll my eyes, and he takes my hand, intertwining our fingers. "We should go before someone shows up."

I nod and hand him Abi's blade from my boot. "We need to conserve ammo."

Raziel's giant hand wraps around the hilt of the blade, and amusement fills his eyes. "I've used toothpicks bigger than this."

"Don't try cleaning your teeth with that," I warn, tugging him toward the exit. "It might look small, but it's sharp enough to cut through bone with the flick of a wrist."

~

"Let me do that." Raziel kneels beside me, taking the lockpick out of my hands. "You keep watch."

The journey to the apartment was relatively quiet, and we managed to remain hidden from any of the lurking Darken wandering the streets. No sign of the whitecoats, but that doesn't mean they weren't close by, waiting for an opportunity to attack.

I stand and watch the stairwell, listening, letting my senses expand beyond myself to search out anybody still in the area. "Where did you learn that?" I ask Raziel.

"I don't know," he admits, focusing on the lock. "I just know how."

I recall parts of our conversation earlier. "You retained your vessel's memories."

"Some of them. I guess if you do something enough times, it becomes second nature."

There's a click, and he turns the handle and pushes the door open. The curtains are drawn and the furniture covered. "What do you use this place for?"

"Protection," I tell him, flicking the light switch, and I grin as the lights turn on. "The building has its own generator, so when the power went out, it automatically switched over."

"Is the water affected?"

"Why don't you go check?" I smile at him from over my shoulder and bolt the door. "The bathroom is at the end of the hall. I'll join you shortly."

I listen for the shower to turn on before I walk to the security system. *Secure.* The entire apartment is fitted with bulletproof glass, and the blinds are on a manual setting, only able to be opened with a mobile device connected to the system.

I switch to the camera footage of the garage and smile at the sight of the familiar Volvo. I'd bought the sedan from an army buddy after our first tour, and I taught Abi to drive in that car. The garage doors would need to be opened manually from inside, but the area looked secure. I'll check it once I've gotten some sleep.

I shrug out of my jacket and head to the bathroom, pausing at the sight of Raziel standing beneath the showerhead, hot water steaming the glass and obscuring the sight of the male inside. Kicking off my boots, I unbuckle my belt and strip before opening the door and stepping in to join him.

He stills beneath the water, soap in his hand, and turns his head to see me. I'm nervous as his eyes roam along the length of my naked body. "Hi."

"Hi." I grin, closing the distance between us. "Can I give you a hand? With your back."

Raziel hands me the soap and turns his back to me. He drops his head forward, and the water cascades down his back and over his shoulders. Gang tattoos cover most of his skin—wings, prayer hands, a few areas that have been blackened out. Words written in runes, and song lyrics from the nineties.

I soap up my hands and run them across his skin, my thumbs digging slightly into the muscles. He braces himself on the tiles, his head hanging down as the water washes the suds away. My eyes are glued to his skin, watching as the water travels down his back, over the curve of his ass, and down his thighs.

Closing the distance, I press my body against his back and kiss his spine.

"You're far too pretty, Raziel," I say teasingly, my fingers tracing the ink covering his flesh. Tiny electric shocks rush through my fingertips and into my hand. I stare at the spot on his ribcage as a rune begins to form in my head, but before I can think too hard, I'm pressed against the tiles and his mouth is on mine.

The bar of soap falls from my hands, and I cling to his shoulders as he lifts me, wrapping my legs around his waist as he claims my mouth. I bury my hand in his hair and pull, breaking the kiss to trail kisses along his jaw and down his throat, his hands running along every wet inch of my body.

"This is a bad idea," Raziel whispers into my skin as his hand travels down between my thighs. My eyes close, and I arch against the tiles as his fingers slide along the spot where I want him the most. "You should stop me."

"Why on earth would I do that?" I ask, my breaths shaky, my nails digging into the flesh of his shoulders, drawing him closer.

His lips brush against my mouth as his strange gray eyes bore into mine. "Where is the nearest bed?"

I'm still giggling when his hand smacks my ass, causing me to yelp. "First door on the right. We couldn't have done this in the shower?"

"The first time I have you will be in a bed," Raziel declares, then he pushes open the bathroom door and walks us through the apartment, dripping wet.

"You have no idea what you're in for, do you?" he growls as he drops me atop the king-sized bed. The sound of his voice sends goosebumps over my skin.

No, but I can't wait to find out.

The next morning, I sip my coffee as I assess the weapons spread out on the guest bed. I pick up the handgun, weighing it in my hand as I look down the barrel and point it at the window overlooking the city below. I take another sip of my coffee, then set it on the bedside table. As I pick up the rifle, I sense Raziel enter behind me.

"Take a picture; it'll last longer," I murmur, looking through the scope. "It's quiet down there."

Raziel presses his chest to my back, his hands on my hips as he kisses the spot below my ear. "We should probably go soon."

"You'll need a change of clothes," I tell him, fighting back a grin. "You might get cold out there in just a towel."

"I don't suppose you've got a stash of male clothing in the back of that closet?"

"Well, no," I tell him, turning in his embrace as I run my hands across his chest. "But the guy across the hall was about your size. Help yourself."

"Do you have a key?" he asks, and I hold up the lockpick. Raziel grins as he leans in for a kiss and takes the pick. "You scare me sometimes, you know that?"

I raise a brow. "Just sometimes?"

"From the moment we met." He kisses me a final time, then steps back. "Have fun with your guns."

"Have fun finding your way out of Dion's closet." I suppress a laugh as I watch him leave.

An hour passes, and I've finished packing a second duffel when I hear the front door open.

The hairs on the back of my neck stand up, and I grab the gun from my belt and press my back to the wall. I can sense more than one presence in the apartment, but they aren't Darken or Raziel.

I make sure there's a round in the chamber and wait for the intruder to get closer. The fact they aren't Darken should make me feel better, but it doesn't. Nor does the fact they aren't whitecoats.

The shadow of a man appears in the doorway. He kicks the door open with his foot and peers inside, and his eyes widen as they zero in on the bags. I kick the gun out of his hands and use the butt of my gun to knock him out.

"Well, that was easier than expected," I mutter, staring at the unconscious boy as I nudge him with my foot. Famous last words. A fist comes flying out of my blind spot, and I move at the last second, but it still makes an impact with my cheek. "Fuck!"

Vision blurring, I hit the ground and see a figure coming toward me. I aim, shoot, and miss as the gun is kicked from my hand. The scumbag stands over me, unbuckling his belt.

"Well, well, well. What do we have here?" He undoes his fly as he steps toward me.

I wait for him to come closer, then push myself up, spin, and kick his legs out from beneath him. I grab the dagger from my belt and hold it to his throat as a third person enters the room.

"Mia, stop!" I freeze and lift my gaze to the old man in the doorway. I knew that voice was familiar.

"Dennis," I say through gritted teeth as I glare at my former partner.

"Get this bitch off me, man!" The man beneath me groans. "You're dead, whore!"

I press the dagger into his skin, cutting off his insults, while my eyes remain on the man in the doorway, his gun pointed at my forehead. "Make a move and I'll slit his throat," I say.

"You aren't a killer," Dennis tries to reason. "He's just a kid."

"He didn't look much like a kid standing over me with his dick out," I snap through clenched teeth as Raziel came up behind him, placing a kitchen knife to Dennis's throat.

"Drop the gun, asshole," Raziel demands. "You know this guy?"

"His name's Dennis," I say, rolling the kid onto his chest and grabbing my cuffs from the bed. "He's a dirty cop. Set me up to take the fall for his fuckup." I move in front of Dennis. "Let's talk, D."

Raziel lowers the knife from his throat and pulls him from the room. I grab hold of Dennis's arm and gesture back to the two boys. "Tie up the other one and finish packing," I tell Raziel, then I direct Dennis back to the living room and gesture to the wall.

"You gonna frisk me, baby?" Dennis asks.

"Palms up, legs apart."

Laughing, Dennis places his hands on the wall as he spreads his legs. "Are you still bitter about Dakota?"

"It's a new world, D. I don't have the luxury of petty grudges." I pat down his sides, finding an old switchblade and lighter. "You want to tell me how you knew about my safe house?"

"I read it somewhere," he lies, turning his head so his gaze meets mine. "You fucking that thug?"

"That's none of your business." I kick his legs apart. "Wider."

"I like it when you get rough, baby."

Resisting the urge to hit him, I finish my search and place the weapons on the counter, never taking my eyes off him. "Sit."

"Yes, ma'am." He grins and drops casually onto the lounge. "How's a nice girl like you afford a crib like this?"

"Let's cut the bullshit, Dennis."

"Oh, come on, baby, play with me." Dennis smiles and licks his lips as his eyes roam the length of my body. I want to shoot him, the urge growing every time he opens his mouth to speak. "Haven't you missed me even a little?"

I take a moment to study the man in front of me. I know what he wants, and I know if I play into his games, I'll get the truth out of him. I slip into a familiar role and give him a seductive smile as I approach him with a sway to my hips.

"There's my girl."

I stand between his legs, reaching for the gun at my back, and lean in as if I'm about to kiss him. "Is that what you want, Dennis? You want me to play your bad girl—"

"Mia." There's a warning in Raziel's voice. I hadn't heard him come back. I resist the urge to roll my eyes at the possessiveness in his tone. "We don't have time to play games."

Dennis's eyes light up with mischief. "Your new dog lacks imagination."

"Ignore him, baby. It's just you and me," I say, my thumb tracing the corner of his mouth. "How did you find out about my place?"

"I told you—"

I press the gun to his skull, still smiling as I tsk at the lie.

"The next few minutes will determine whether you live or die, Dennis, so listen carefully. I'm going to ask you three questions. If you answer them truthfully, I'll let you live. Don't, and I'll kill you and your boys like the dogs you are."

The feel of the metal against his skull must've cleared up any remaining lust. "What happened to you, Mia?"

Ignoring the question, I let him see the truth of my words

reflecting in my eyes. "Question one: how do you know about this place?"

"Let's be rational—"

"I will kill you, Dennis. I've already asked twice. It's best not to waste your words. It'd be a shame to ruin the curtains."

"Perez! He mentioned the general location in his report from your last case together. He spilled the address and the condo after a few drinks over poker. Mentioned you have emergency supplies. I figured the boys and I could crash for a few days."

"Good boy, Dennis. Next question. How long have you been watching me? Don't pretend you don't know what I'm talking about. I'm not as stupid as you think."

"If you know, why the fuck are you asking?"

I shrug lazily, dropping the gun from his forehead and taking a seat on the coffee table in front of him. "I'm curious how many safe houses you've ransacked. This isn't your first stop, so tell me, how many?"

"I don't know what you're talking about," Dennis lies, sitting forward. "I don't remember you being so paranoid, Mia."

I pick up the familiar switchblade and open it. "One of your boys was carrying an old favorite of mine—a gift from an army buddy. So, I'm assuming you've made at least one other stop before coming here."

"I don't know what you're talking—ARGHHH!" I stare at Dennis's face as he screams, his hands covering mine around the switchblade now buried in his knee. "You crazy fucking bitch!"

I twist the blade, unfazed. "I want an answer, Dennis."

"This was our third stop," he spits between his teeth. "I took the lighter from the other house. I'm bleeding, Mia. I need medical attention."

"You should call an ambulance." I smirk, unable to hide my amusement as I let go of the blade, leaving it in his knee. "How many others know about my safe houses?"

"Just me!"

Raziel speaks from behind me. "He's telling the truth."

"Dennis doesn't share information unless it gives him an advantage over others." I stand from the table, my eyes still on Dennis. "Thank you for being honest with me."

"I need medical—" I raise the gun and pull the trigger, his body jolting on the couch as three bullets enter his chest. One wasn't enough. His blue eyes go wide with shock, and blood spills from the corner of his lips as he stares at me. I close the distance between us and lean in close as I pull the blade from his knee. "That was for Dakota."

Straightening, I turn from the lifeless body and come face-to-face with Raziel. "Is the car packed?"

He blinks and shifts his focus to me. "You just killed a man."

"I killed a murderer and thief," I correct, pausing beside Raziel. I raise my hand to his arm, but he flinches away from my touch. "Trust me, Raziel, the world is better off without him in it."

"What about those boys?" The accusation in his eyes hurts. "Do you plan to kill them too? Or will you show mercy?"

"Mercy?" I chuckle, unable to hide my disbelief. "If you hadn't shown up, they'd have killed me *after* they'd raped me. Don't stand there and pretend otherwise. It's a new world, but not all the monsters were created by the curse."

"I can't let you kill them." He stands between me and the hallway. "The boys will wake in a few hours and go their own way. Let's not be here when they wake up."

I stare him, unable to believe his words. "Are you truly that naive?"

His eyes harden as he straightens his spine, towering over me. "I believe in second chances, Mia. If you kill them, what makes you any better?"

I half expect to feel enraged, but I can only feel pity for him. "I'm sorry, Raziel."

"For what?"

"For the blood that'll be on your hands," I say. "I understand your gesture, misguided as it is, but those boys cannot be saved."

"Anybody can be saved if they seek redemption," Raziel argues. "You can't know what will become of them."

"No, I can't, but I can see that you will come to regret not killing them," I say, while taking one last look down the hall. "We should go before they wake."

Unable to sleep, I sit in the front seat of the sedan and look to the night sky. Being just past midnight, it's the perfect level of dark to see the full moon surrounded by hundreds of stars. My eyes wander over to the restless angel attempting to sleep.

This world is so much bigger than I ever imagined.

I wonder if Jonah knew of the existence of other supernaturals. I doubt it. There's no way he'd have left that out of our teachings, nor would he have passed up an opportunity to "collect" the orphaned children of those he'd slain.

The thought triggers memories better left buried, but I've never been one to leave things alone. A little voice tells me to wait, to leave it until I've slept, but if I carry the letter unopened, there will be no sleep. I pull out the envelope and trace the name written on the front.

Mia McCoy.

Most of Jonah's children are descendants of the McCoy bloodline, but there are only a few of us who still bear the name. Jonah calls us his special ones. Abi used to call us his human trophies. He would disappear for months on end and return with a new "special addition" to the family.

Only those with "real gifts" or a direct familial link to the cursed lines were afforded rooms in the main house—to be under Jonah's watch—while others were placed with families living within the compound.

The unluckiest would be given a swag and directed to an empty spot in a warehouse, where they would need to earn their place by working or studying to contribute.

DEAR MIA,

AS I SIT DOWN TO WRITE THIS LETTER, I AM OVER-WHELMED WITH EMOTIONS—AND WITH VISIONS OF WHAT MIGHT HAVE BEEN. THERE IS SO MUCH YOU DO NOT KNOW, SO MUCH THAT HAS BEEN KEPT FROM US.

THE MASSACRE THAT BEFELL OUR HOME THAT NIGHT CHANGED ALL OUR LIVES. I WAS LEFT FOR DEAD, LYING IN THE POOL OF MY WIFE AND SON'S BLOOD. MY LAST COHERENT MEMORY: THE SOUND OF YOUR AND EMILIA'S SCREAMS. IN THAT MOMENT, I PRAYED TO GOD TO TAKE ME TOO, FOR TO LIVE IN A WORLD WITHOUT MY WIFE, MY BEST FRIEND, AND MY CHILDREN WAS NO LIFE I WISHED TO ENDURE.

THE HORRORS OF THAT NIGHT ARE FOREVER ETCHED INTO MY SOUL.

IN THE AFTERMATH, I SOUGHT REFUGE WITH A FRIEND, A PRIEST WITHIN THE CHURCH. HE HID ME FROM THE ORGANI-ZATION THAT FUNDED THE WHITECOATS AND OPENED MY EYES TO THE TRUTH OF OUR HERITAGE, AND OF WHAT WAS STILL TO COME.

TO BE TRUTHFUL, I AM NOT SURE WHICH WAS WORSE: THE YEARS I BELIEVED YOU WERE BOTH DEAD, OR THE TRUTH OF WHAT BECAME OF YOU. IT WAS NOT UNTIL A DECADE LATER THAT I LEARNED YOU HAD SURVIVED. EMILIA, RAISED

BY THE ORGANIZATION, TRAINED TO BE AN ASSASSIN, MARRIED INTO A WEALTHY FAMILY TIED TO THEIR CAUSE, AND BECAME A MOTHER.

I HAVE SEEN ONLY ONE PHOTOGRAPH OF HER WITH A BOY, THOUGH MY SOURCES WHISPER THAT SHE ALSO HAS TWO DAUGHTERS. I DON'T KNOW THEIR NAMES.

IT TOOK A LONG TIME TO FIND YOU. FOR YEARS YOUR WHEREABOUTS WERE UNKNOWN TO ME, UNTIL FATE FINALLY INTERVENED. BY THEN YOU WERE GROWN—A RESPECTED FIGURE, A DECORATED OFFICER, A WOMAN FORGED BY TRIALS I COULD SCARCELY IMAGINE.

IT WAS ONLY WHEN I MET ABIGAIL REDWOOD THAT I LEARNED THE TRUTH OF WHAT YOU ENDURED, AND THE SACRIFICES YOU MADE TO FREE HER FROM HER FATHER. I CROSSED PATHS WITH JONAH ONCE, MANY YEARS AGO. IT MUST HAVE BEEN AFTER YOUR ESCAPE. I SAW THE COMPOUND HE PREACHED FROM AND THE TWISTED FUTURE HE INTENDED TO BUILD. I TRIED TO INTERVENE, TO HELP THOSE WILLING TO LEAVE, BUT MY HANDS WERE TIED. I COULD NOT RISK EXPOSING MYSELF—OR THOSE RELYING ON ME. I THINK OFTEN OF THE PEOPLE I LEFT BEHIND.

NOW, AS THE PROPHECY'S FULFILLMENT DRAWS CLOSER, MY VISIONS SPIRAL BEYOND MY CONTROL, PULLING ME TOWARD MADNESS. OTHERS I HAVE SPOKEN WITH SAY THEIR GIFTS ARE CHANGING AS WELL. SOME GROW STRONGER AND STEADIER, WHILE OTHERS, LIKE ME, SLIP FURTHER FROM REALITY WITH EACH PASSING NIGHT.

AND SO, I MUST ENTRUST YOU WITH THE TRUTH. THERE IS A SHIPPING CONTAINER AT THE COORDINATES WRITTEN ON THE BACK OF THIS LETTER. INSIDE YOU WILL FIND A REPOSITORY OF ARTIFACTS THAT HOLD THE KEY TO OUR FAMILY'S PAST, AND PERHAPS TO OUR FUTURE. FOR TWO DECADES I HAVE NOT ONLY HIDDEN FROM OUR ENEMIES, BUT HUNTED FOR WHAT WAS LOST. I HAVE FOUND ANGELIC JOURNALS,

FAMILY HEIRLOOMS, AND SECRETS OF ROYALTY AND BETRAYAL
REACHING BACK TO OUR ANCESTRAL HOME.

AMONG THESE IS AN AMULET ONCE BELONGING TO A
COMPANION OF OUR FOREBEAR. IT'S SAID TO HOLD THE
POWER TO TRAVERSE TIME.

MY DARLING DAUGHTER, I CANNOT EASE THE PAIN OF
OUR PAST, NOR SHIELD YOU FROM THE DANGERS AHEAD. BUT
IN SHARING THIS, I PRAY I MAY GIVE YOU A BETTER UNDER-
STANDING AND PERHAPS A MEASURE OF GUIDANCE, AS YOU
WALK THE PERILOUS ROAD BEFORE YOU.

WITH ALL MY LOVE,
YOUR FATHER,
AIDEN MCCOY

Even after I read my father's letter, sleep continues to elude me. I wait until dawn before I pull onto the road. By the time Raziel wakes, stretching and yawning in the front seat, it's almost midday. He rubs his eyes and looks out at the passing scenery. "Morning," I say.

"Morning." He blinks and turns his head to look at me. "Where are we?"

"Middle of nowhere." I smile as I hand him the map. "We should reach your friends within the hour."

He's quiet as he looks the map over. "Did you get any sleep?"

"Not really." I ignore his pity-filled eyes. "I'll sleep once we're there."

"Should we talk about what happened?"

It hasn't been easy to look at him since the incident back at the apartment. Every time it looked like we'd discuss it, I could see the way he looked at me and flinched beneath my touch. I wasn't usually one to dwell, but the moment kept playing on a loop.

"You made a choice, Raziel," I say to keep the peace.

"You'd have killed those boys." It's a statement, not a question.

"This life is about survival now. Dennis knew that. It was either him or me. I don't regret my decision."

"I don't accept that. You cannot be that heartless."

Heartless! My knuckles tighten around the steering wheel, and I keep my gaze on the road. "Why does it bother you so much? I've seen you kill people."

"That's different." He turns in his seat to face me. "I have never executed a single soul that wasn't trying to kill me at the time. If peace can be reached, I will always favor the side that spares lives."

"Even if it results in more loss of life—innocent lives?" I catch the smallest of flinches from him. I'm too angry to process what it means. "After all this time, you still don't get it."

"Get what?" he asks, defeated.

"It doesn't matter what we do, Raziel. Peace is no longer an option. The weak will die, and the strong will live. I've seen how this story ends, and—spoiler alert—it's not a happy ending."

"I don't believe that, and neither do you. You wouldn't be here if you did. You're a warrior, Mia, and what is a warrior without something to fight for?"

A survivor.

Before I can respond, the car jerks and swerves off road, spinning, the world coming in and out of darkness before a massive impact rattles my bones. I come to with Raziel's hand on my face, brushing my hair away. "Mia? They ran us off the road. Mia."

"I'm good," I say groggily, taking my hand off the wheel as I push myself up and rest my head back against the headrest. "Go."

He leans across the seat and grabs his sword from the back. I catch his arm and hand him my gun. "Gun versus sword? Gun always wins."

He rolls his eyes and pushes his door, but it's stuck. Shuffling down in his seat, he brings both knees to his chest and kicks with all his strength, ripping the door off its hinges and sending it flying across the road. My head is still spinning, but I can hear voices coming from the road as someone says, "No survivors."

Rage settles in my stomach, and I unbuckle my belt, ignoring the pain ripping through my ribcage and back. My head still spins. Orange flames flicker in the distance, and the smell of smoke reaches me. The car is on fire.

I lift myself over the console, biting back my scream as I use my arms to push myself up. I fall into the passenger seat and hear gunshots ringing out through the bush. Raziel is behind a tree, his sword across his back and my gun in his hand. He turns his head and meets my gaze.

I grab the gun hidden beneath the seat and peer out, spotting the car. Three whitecoats creep around it, one of them making their way toward me. I take aim and shoot, but the shot misses, and the ringing in my ears intensifies.

I swallow the pain and take aim again, this time trying to get the whitecoat to take cover. The ringing is so loud now I can barely focus, but I push myself up and out of the car. I duck behind a tree as gunshots whirl past my head.

Bringing the gun to my chest, I close my eyes and push the nausea and pain to the back of my mind until I am empty of thought and feeling. I seek out the power within, find the flames, and draw it close, wrapping it around myself until my blood runs hot.

Stepping out from behind the tree, I come face-to-face with a female whitecoat. Her eyes go wide at the sight of me. She raises her gun, finger on the trigger.

I shoot and hit the whitecoat behind her as her bullet whirls past my head. Before she can pull the trigger again, I close the distance and kick the gun from her hand, then pull my fist back and slam it into her nose. She grunts and stumbles back before rushing toward me.

Our bodies collide, and all the oxygen leaves my lungs as we hit the ground and her hands wrap around my throat. Rapid gunfire fills the air, and we freeze, registering the new threat. Using the distraction, I use the whitecoat's weight to roll us over until I'm above her and bury my elbow into her ribs. Her grip loosens, and I lose sight of her hands as a knife gets buried hilt-deep in my thigh and ripped out again.

I scream and throw myself back as she crawls away from me, wiping blood from her lip and holding the dagger out in front of her face.

I half expect the ringing to return, for the world to go black, but as soon as the pain appears, it disappears again, replaced by pure rage. I reach for the woman's ankle and drag her back to me, ignoring her attempts to kick me in the face. Since it's so close anyway, I tighten my grip on her ankle and snap it at the joint, taking a sick pleasure as her screams echo through the clearing.

I stand and spin to face a new threat, only to find a muscular figure dressed in leather armor, with hair that fades to orange flames just above the shoulders. Amber eyes framed by thick black lashes look curiously at me, and they take in the scene with a sinister grin.

Breathing heavily, I back up a step, fighting the urge to flee. I don't know who they are, but there's no denying the lethal beauty.

"Settle, kitten. We're on your side." The creature circles me like a predator would its prey. Their voices send chills down my spine. *Voices.* One body, and yet sometimes, it's as if the words are spoken by more than one.

"We?" I ask, only now taking in the wolves and warriors in the clearing. They stand ready for battle, waiting on a command— looking to the creature circling me a little too closely. My eyes linger on a man shadowed by a gray wolf, and a sense of familiarity passes between us.

"Get away from her," Raziel orders, stumbling into the circle. The warriors make their way around the clearing I found myself centered in. "Mia, come here."

The creature with two voices speaks, ignoring him. "I like this one, Storyteller."

"She's mine, Nyari." Raziel inches closer but maintains a respectful distance from the strange creature. "Mia." He gestures again for me to join him.

"Is this true?" Nyari asks, tilting their head to the side. I can't stop staring at their eyes, the masculine yet feminine features.

"No," I say, snapping myself out of the trance I'd fallen into. I take a step away from the creature but don't move toward Raziel. "What are you?"

"My name is Nyari," they answer, raising a hand in offering. "Such a feisty little kitten."

"I prefer Mia." I place my hand in theirs, and they bring my bloodied knuckles to their lips. The moment is interrupted by the whitecoat on the ground behind us, who screams, rises to her feet, and launches at me with a dagger.

Nyari slides their arm around my waist, shielding my body with their own as they pull a sword from thin air and behead the whitecoat at my feet.

"What the hell?"

"What the hell indeed." Turning to see who spoke, I watch as a silver-haired gentleman with tattooed arms enters the clearing, wearing blue jeans and a white T-shirt. He looks as if he just stepped off the set of a GQ photoshoot. "Hello, Claire."

Claire? Was he talking to me?

"Isaiah," Raziel greets, placing himself in front of the gray-haired man. "Let me explain, please. It's not as it looks."

"Explain? I should thank you." He grins, though there is a crazed look in his eyes. "I have waited a long time for this."

"She's a descendant of the bloodline," Raziel urges. "Her name is Mia. Not Claire. Mia McCoy."

Isaiah sidesteps Raziel, and his eyes roam every inch of my body, a look of disgust on his face. He approaches me, ignoring Raziel's warning. "She looks *just* like her."

Nyari's chest is pressed to my back and their arm tightens around my waist. It doesn't feel like a threat, more like an instruction to remain still.

The gesture does not go unnoticed by either Raziel or Isaiah. "Sahari is waiting, Isaiah," Nyari says. "Take the storyteller to her.

Elijah and I will tend to Mia's wounds while the pack scouts the area for threats."

"I'm not leaving her." Raziel reaches for my arm, but I pull it out of his reach. "Mia—"

"I'm fine, Raziel. You should go." Even as I say it, I can feel myself growing tired and weak from the adrenaline wearing off. The pain starts to trickle in as if I summoned it by thought.

The arm circling my waist takes my weight, and a warm cheek brushes against my own as they pull me back into their chest, holding me up. "She needs to rest."

"She needs to stay with me," Raziel insists, but before I can argue, Isaiah shoves him in the opposite direction. "Don't push me, Isaiah."

"Oh, brother. Perhaps it is you who should not push me. Perhaps in your sick obsession with redheads you've forgotten what it is we're trying to accomplish."

"What's he talking about?" I ask, feeling nauseous.

"Stop it, Isaiah," Raziel snaps, looking at me. "He doesn't know what he's talking about."

Isaiah laughs, a bitter and cruel sound as he looks at me with disgust. Hate drips from his every word like venom. "You poor thing. You fell for his pretty human package, didn't you? You aren't special, love. My brother has a fatal attraction for your kind."

"Enough," Raziel snaps. "I'm going to go with Isaiah to meet Sahari. Please be careful." He reaches for me, but I pull away. "Mia, I'll explain everything, I swear."

"Come now, Raziel, it's not that long of a story. Take your time. Explain to your new human lover how you betrayed your own people to plant your seed between the thighs of her ancestor, the one who cursed us all?"

"What?"

"Isaiah." Nyari's tone was quiet but firm. "This is not the time. The girl is hurt and bleeding. Your gripe is with Raziel, not her."

Moving to stand on my own, I look to Isaiah, then Raziel. Nyari's hand presses to my back, and a white kind of heat emanates from their palm. It travels up my spine and pumps through my bloodstream. I feel stronger already.

"I don't need you to protect me," I say firmly, hating the look in his eyes—as if I'm weak. Vulnerable. "Go. I will be fine with Nyari."

"You cannot trust that fae."

"You speak as if I can trust you," I say flatly, "and yet you have proven more than once that is not the case. Go."

"Perhaps you aren't as foolish as I thought," Isaiah comments, though his glare doesn't soften. In fact, he seems to take satisfaction at the look of hurt in Raziel's gaze. "Do what you need to do and then bring her back to meet Sahari."

"Of course." Nyari gives a small nod. "Safe travels."

After Isaiah and Raziel leave, Nyari guides me to a rock and calls for a healer. "This is Elijah McCoy."

Nyari kneels beside me, holding my hand, thumbs circling my wrist as they stare into my eyes. It's oddly intimate, as if they're peering into my soul, searching for something.

"Where did you learn to fight like that, kitten?" Nyari asks, tracing a faded scar with the tips of their fingers. "You fight like a trained warrior."

"I've been trained in combat since I was a child." I watch as their fingers graze my skin. "After I finished my homeschooling, I joined the army, then the police force."

"Is this normal for humans?"

What an odd question. "Not typically, no. But for the special children of Jonah, it was deemed necessary for survival. He believed the end of the world was nigh, and he wanted us to be ready for it when it arrived."

"That was smart of him," Nyari muses quietly. "The children back home also start training at a young age, but I imagine our training is quite different to yours."

"Possibly." I'm unsure of what else to say. I refuse to think of the broken bones, the tears, the torture, and the consequences if we failed to please him. "I'm feeling better now."

"You heal quickly," Elijah comments, reminding me of his presence and that of his grey wolf. "It's quite impressive considering the extent of your injuries, even for a McCoy. How are you feeling?"

"Hungry," I admit, and my stomach grumbles louldy. "But otherwise okay."

Chuckling, Elijah reaches into his pocket and pulls out a granola bar. "This should tide you over until we reach the house."

"Thank you, Elijah."

"The 'special' children?" Elijah asks. "I assume they're like us? Descendants of the McCoy bloodline?"

"Yes. Direct descendants, or those who display powers."

"Are there a lot of you back home?"

"Last time I was there, there were. My sister and I ran away before my sixteenth birthday."

"Why?"

"For reasons severe enough to run away." I stand and brush the dirt from my ass. "I'm sure we'll have an opportunity to swap war stories." I hope he takes the hint to leave it be for now. "Thanks for the granola bar."

I take a few steps, pausing to look back at Elijah, and am hit by a wave of déjà vu. He's the mage from my dream. "I know you."

Elijah rises to his feet slowly, bows his head, and a cocky grin appears on his face. "It's nice to finally meet you in person."

I sit on the blanket by the stream and peel the skin from my apple. It's been a long night, and the day isn't shaping up to be any easier. My gaze wanders around the camp. Spotting my fae warrior in his beast form sleeping high in a tree, the giant black panther's whiskers twitching in the breeze, I smirk and resist the urge to throw a rock at the dumb cat.

He opens his eyes as if sensing my thoughts, and the tiniest growl of challenge escapes from between his teeth. I smile sweetly and pop a sliver of apple into my mouth.

After the witches came looking for their lost sister, we made an alliance that opened the doors for similar arrangements between other supernaturals, for information and protection. When my powers grew too strong and unpredictable, the witches decided I needed a familiar—a conduit to help channel my power and maintain control. The vessel I inherited came with its own power, and the combination with my gifts can make things . . . explosive.

The witches selected three alpha wolves willing to bind themselves to me, but unbeknownst to anyone, when I fell from grace, Jeremiah sensed my power and followed it from the Fae world. The witches called it fate. Two halves of a soul. It sounds rather romantic to hear them tell it, but I found myself bound to a resentful, grumpy, eight-hundred-year-old and two-hundred-pound jungle cat, prone to shedding and scratching the furniture if left unattended.

In his fae form, though, Prince Jeremiah was glorious, and just as lethal on two legs as he was on four.

After the ceremony was complete, Jeremiah returned home, to the Fae realm and his people. He needed to tie up loose ends and make arrangements for his children. When he returned, he wasn't alone.

He'd brought four of his siblings. Three strong fae warriors—Fallon, Artemis, and Malik—and Nyari, a legendary fae-mage hybrid with hair that danced with flames. A former spy for the late heir of an ancient fire bloodline.

I had heard stories of the warrior spy, even from heaven, but nothing compared to meeting them in the flesh. It was rumored that the Fae had once been friends with Claire and Silas, and that the late heir was in fact Claire's lover and the sire of her children.

Nyari speaks with an ancient lilt that is neither alive nor dead, neither male nor female, neither singular nor plural. The gift that makes Nyari such a skilled spy is their ability to move through the veil—the space between life and death, time and space.

If I sound like a fangirl, it's because I am. There was a time when my sisters and I spent many nights around a campfire sharing stories of the fae.

Raziel, Isaiah, and Gwen were the only ones given permission to leave the sanctuary of heaven, and when they returned home after a mission, they'd regale us with stories they'd heard in taverns.

Then the Great Fae War changed everything.

It was selfish, but I admit that I had never considered how much the Fae had lost during the war. Hadn't even cared until I found myself bound to the warrior prince and his people.

Sometimes I catch Jeremiah staring off into the distance and feel his longing to return home. I understand the feeling well, yet it only seems to fuel his resentment further. And so I meet every glare and cold shoulder with one of my own.

The whimper of a werewolf in the distance brings my attention to the mage kneeling by the contaminated river. I sit up a little straighter and watch as Elijah McCoy, a direct descendant from the cursed bloodline, lowers the bucket into the water.

His wolf creeps closer to the edge, sniffs at the water, and pins her ears back as she growls. I suppress a smile as Elijah shoots a charming grin at her over his shoulder as if to say "Don't worry, love. I've got this." He reaches out to ruffle the fur on her head.

After the last storm, we learned that even our kind were just as vulnerable to the Darken as the humans. We lost many. The only ones who showed partial resistance were those who descended from the McCoy bloodline. Even though they aren't fully immune, just... slower to succumb, if they did at all.

According to the scientists back at the camp, the Darken isn't just a virus, it's a mutagen. It rewrites your DNA. That's why elemental users like Elijah were assigned to collect samples. Their unique bond with the elements seems to delay the mutation, allowing them to withstand the virus longer without succumbing.

Across the field, angels work alongside shifters to disassemble the tents, while the wolves maintain the perimeter, keeping watch for any signs of the Darken.

Isaiah left at first light with a band of warriors to scout the road for today's journey.

The cracked surface of the ruby scratches my palm, and I look down at the dagger in my hand. One of the first things I did after the alliance with the witches was to seek Nina's final resting place, and in the rubble that remained, I found her short sword broken in two.

I tried to rejoin the halves back together, but every attempt failed, until I turned the sword into a dagger. The handle was small enough, but the bulkiness of it meant I kept it in my travel bag, so now it only comes out for rituals and when I'm peeling fruit. I smile, thinking of what Nina would say if she were here.

"Admiring your handiwork, Sahari?" Ava—the high priestess's great-great-granddaughter and my tutor in all things witchy—towers above me. Apparently, my vessel's original host was a little more than a hobbyist, holding great power that the coven desperately wanted to keep in the circle.

"Good morning, Ava." I sit up a little straighter. "What is it?"

The witch takes a seat in front of me. "Are you ready?"

"For what, exactly?"

Ava smiles, unzipping her jacket as she reaches inside her breast pocket and retrieves a long white feather. Not just any feather, but that of an angel. "Where did you get that?"

"Uriel gifted it to me." She smiles, stroking the near-perfect feather. "It's beautiful."

My fingers twitch to feel the soft velvet beneath my fingertips, but even as my hand rises from my lap, the ache in my heart deepens, and pain trickles through every nerve of my wings.

"Have you been taking your potions?" she asks.

A part of our deal with the witches was they help treat our injured, which means helping to heal our wings. It's a brutal process that leaves a few of us comatose for days at a time, but once the initial shock and pain wears off, some of us notice a change.

"Every morning," I tell her, lifting my gaze from the feather. "What's the lesson today, kiddo?"

Her gaze hardens at the nickname, and she places the feather in front of me. "It's simple," she says, with a sadistic grin. "I want you to make it float."

Bitch. "How does this help?"

She crosses her legs and straightens her back as she raises a challenging brow. "It's an endurance test, Sahari. The coven needs to see you're maintaining control over your powers."

Jeremiah's voice filters through my mind. *Stop being stubborn. You throw heavier things at me in your sleep.*

What makes you think I'm asleep? I counter. I suppress a smile but straighten my spine as I focus my attention solely on the feather.

Jeremiah's right. I'm stubborn because Ava annoys me, but also because I'm sick of playing games with her. I have better things to do with my time.

"Very good," Ava whispers as the feather hovers in front of us. "You've been practicing."

"Turns out Jeremiah is good for something," I remark. "I'm ready."

"I disagree," Ava argues. "You're powerful, Sahari—no one is arguing that—but you're still adjusting to life on earth. It's only been six months since your fall. Your wings are healing, but you can't fly yet, and you might never be able to fly again. I'm sorry, I know that hurts, but I'm not here to coddle you or protect your feelings. I'm here to make sure you're in control of the other half inside of you."

"I'm in control."

Ava's gaze moves to the feather spinning in the air erratically. "Maya was a young, powerful, naive, and arrogant witch. She could have been a priestess someday, but she sacrificed her future, our coven's future, for you—"

"She didn't do it for me. She did it for the survival of your coven."

Ava blinks, staring at me in disbelief. "What?"

"She knew what was coming." I stab the dagger into the ground as the feather floats down beside it. "She sacrificed herself so the coven would survive the storm, and you did. Your grandmother didn't tell you that?"

"No," she whispers. "She did not."

"She was young and naive," I agree, reaching for her hand and holding it until she lifts her gaze to mine. "But every day I am on this earth, I'm mindful of her sacrifice, and all that I do is so it wasn't in vain. I can only hope that if the time ever comes, I can be half as brave as she was."

"Thank you, Sahari." Ava's hand covers mine and squeezes, her gaze soft. "But I stand by what I said. You're not yet ready to walk through the shadow world. I understand your need to find your missing sisters, but if you go in now, you'll never return."

We arrive at the safe house a day late, but there's no sign of Raziel. If he beat us here and left, the shifters would have caught his scent on the way into town.

The safe house is an abandoned bed-and-breakfast. We passed it on our way through before the storm hit and marked it as a meeting ground. It also serves as a safe place to rest when our people are out searching for survivors.

I leave Isaiah to sort out patrols and head for the stairs, having spotted the water tank attached to the house. As I run it, I'm grateful to find the water supply is pure. I find one of the master bedrooms with a private suite and strip down to nothing as I walk into the bathroom and turn on the water.

It's been days since I last bathed. I test the temperature and almost dance for joy when the sting of the hot water hits my fingers. I step up into the shower and tilt my head back beneath the spray.

It won't be long now.

Do they suspect anything?

Not a clue.

Soon.

Soon.

The shower curtain pulls back to reveal Seth, my favorite among the alphas. He's naked before me, every muscle rippled from his arms to his abs and legs, the scars from his past visible but only adding to the beautiful package that makes him so unique.

"May I join you, Sahari?"

I smile and turn my back to him, making room in the small shower. I lean into his touch as his hand trails across the curve of my hip and along the length of my thigh as he presses himself against my ass.

He gathers my hair in his hand, baring my neck to him as he kisses and nips at the flesh, nuzzling my ear.

"Seth." I moan, arching into his embrace as he slides a finger between my lips, circling my clit. His touch is soft and teasing. It's not enough, and he knows it. His fingers retreat and flatten against my stomach, traveling higher and higher until he's cupping my breast, his thumb and forefinger pinching at the nipple until I'm standing on my tiptoes, crying out from the pleasure and pain.

"He told me to make you beg," Seth whispers, his nose still tracing the shell of my ear. "Will you beg for me, Sahari?"

"No." I grit my teeth and force my eyes open. My vision blurs as his grip tightens in my hair and he pulls my head back, his cock sliding back and forth between my legs. Dammit. "Seth!"

"Mm-hmm," he growls, parting my legs. "Just like that." The head of his cock slides between my folds and rubs against my clit as his fingers dig into my hip.

"Holy—"

"Beg," the bastard wolf challenges. "Beg and I'll give you what you want before I take you to him."

"Where is he?" I ask, my body trembling, as he sinks the tip of his cock inside. I brace myself against the tiles and push down on his length. He doesn't fight me, but he doesn't rush to pull out either. I want to cry out and scream my frustration. "*Please!*"

A dark chuckle escapes him as he pulls almost all the way out before thrusting his hips forward again. My body launches forward, and I cry out as he pounds his cock in and out, his balls slapping against my clit.

"Yes!" I scream, reaching back for him. "Please, please let go."

"You're mine," Seth snarls in my ear as his cock fills me. He pulls me away from the tiles and forces me to the ground. His hand in my hair forces my head to the floor, his entire body exerting his control over mine.

"I'm yours!" My orgasm tears its way through me as his teeth sink into my shoulder, his thrusts coming short and quick as he fills me. Closing my eyes, I let the warmth of him sink into me. The shower runs cold, but it doesn't bother me now.

Seth lifts himself up and falls back against the tiles, a satisfied grin plastered across his face. I smile, take his hand, and lean back into his chest as he lowers his lips to mine.

"I am yours," I whisper softly against his lips, his eyes opening to reveal his wolf, "but don't ever forget that you're mine."

His smile softens and he leans down and kisses me. "I love you too, Sahari."

I stroke his cheek and smile up at the sweet, broken man whose heart captured my own. He lifts me into his arms, and I wrap myself around him, my lips finding their way to his as he carries me into the bedroom.

Seth lowers me onto the bed, his weight pinning me down for the briefest moment. He breaks the kiss and looks at me beneath him. "I'd love to stay and watch, but Isaiah needs me downstairs."

With a sigh, I reluctantly let him go, but not before I take in the sight of his fine ass once more. "Be safe."

"Always." His smile widens as he steps back. "She's all yours, gentlemen."

Gentlemen? My eyes widen as I recall his warning in the shower. I sit up and look toward the window, where Kody sits wearing only denim jeans, his eyes glued to my breasts. His husband, Jensen, sits on the other side of the bed, his arm bent behind his head and a wide grin on his face.

My God, they're beautiful. But it's Jeremiah who steals my attention. He stands by the door completely naked, staring at me with a mixture of lust and hate. Most days, I'm not sure if he wants to fuck me or kill me. Seth closes the door behind him, and I'm left alone with two alpha wolves and a fae prince.

Jeremiah closes the distance between us, and I crawl across the bed, away from him. My back hits Jensen's chest, and he chuckles as Jeremiah crawls onto the bed, stalking my every move. The smile on his face is almost feral. "You've got nowhere to run."

Something about the fae triggers my fight-or-flight response. Fighting with him is intoxicating—it's almost as good as foreplay— but the chase is also appealing. His large hand wraps around my calf, and he squeezes as he leans down and kisses my stomach, his green eyes never leaving mine as Jensen nuzzles my throat. "Three on one isn't exactly fair," I complain.

"I'm just here to watch," Kody pipes in from the window. "I'll help with the cleanup."

I glare at the wolf, but it's short-lived as Jeremiah's fingers find their way between my legs. My eyes flutter closed, and I lean into Jensen's body, giving into the pleasure. "I want to hear you beg again."

Squeezing my eyes closed, I dig my nails into Jensen's arm as Jeremiah's tongue lazily circles my clit, his fingers curling and increasing their movements. It's not fast enough. I buck my hips and bite my lip, swallowing the whimper, but I cave. "Please, Jere."

I sit on the edge of the bed lacing my shoes while Kody lounges by the window, strumming the strings of an acoustic guitar he found downstairs. The melody fills the room, drowning out the chaos of the world outside. I stand from the bed and pause as I take in the sight of my lovers in varying degrees of undress.

Jeremiah lays on the pillows and watches the wolf, a crease in his brow as his fingers drum a pattern on the abs of his stomach. Jensen slides to the end of the bed with the sheet wrapped around his waist and leans in to kiss my bare stomach.

"Are you sure I can't convince you to come back to bed?" Jensen asks with an adorable pout.

Smiling, I tilt his head back as I lean down and kiss him, moaning as his teeth graze my bottom lip and his nails dig into the backs of my thighs. I sigh, arching into his touch, giving him better access, but the moment is ruined when the bedroom door opens and Isaiah appears in the doorway.

"What is it now?" I ask, trying to keep the irritation from my voice. Jensen's lips distract me as his arm slides around my waist and travels lower.

Isaiah's eyes follow Jensen's hand, and he smirks as he meets my gaze. "Your presence is required downstairs."

"Can't it wait?" Jensen asks.

"It's Raziel." At the mention of the truth-keeper, I grab hold of Jensen's hand and give Isaiah my full attention. "He and a companion were ambushed on the road to the safe house. His wounds are being tended to by Seth, and his companion is being escorted by Nyari and Eli."

"What happened?"

"The same thing that always happens when Raziel finds himself involved with a redhead."

Sighing, I reluctantly step out of Jensen's reach, then grab a discarded shirt from the floor and pull it on. By the size and smell, it's Jeremiah's, and immediately, a sense of calmness settles over me.

I follow Isaiah out of the room. I can feel the men behind me but don't look back as Isaiah walks alongside me. "What has he done this time?"

"He's managed to *befriend* a McCoy descendant," Isaiah says through gritted teeth, "who happens to look *exactly* like the witch herself."

TWENTY-ONE

NYARI | THEY/SHE

My thumb circles the smooth surface of the rock, the energy causing a slight electricity to run through my hand. I can't seem to forget the feeling of the way Mia's skin felt beneath my palm.

Not looking forward to the reaction of those back at the safe house, I look ahead to where the fiery redhead strides alongside the large gray wolf. Mia is beautiful, there's no denying it, but her resemblance to Claire McCoy leaves me feeling uneasy.

It feels wrong, as if I'm betraying my friend, and yet the pull I feel toward Mia is inescapable. Her spirit calls to my own in a language lost to our kind for thousands of years. Even the magic within the last heir had not felt this powerful.

She reminds me of home, so it irks me to no end that the archangel seems to think she's his. The scent of him lingers on her, causing ugly emotions to stir within me. I do not hate the storyteller, but I don't particularly like him, either.

"What do you think?" Elijah asks. "She's powerful."

"Sahari will not react well upon seeing her."

"Because she looks like Claire?"

I nod, and he lowers his voice so that only I would hear his next words.

"Do you think she's in danger?"

The thought troubles me. An inner voice laughs at the foolishness and reminds me of the battle in the clearing. I wonder if the others saw it. She was pure fire, lethal and beautiful—just as my friend, the last heir had been.

I have no doubt that had she been born in the homeland, she'd have been chosen to rule as the next heir. I could feel it, and I wanted to protect it. She would have been a symbol of hope. And after the war, that wasn't something we had a lot of back home.

"She can take care of herself," I say, unable to resist the urge to look her way. She's standing on the other side of the creek with Elijah's wife, Mack, now in her human form. Mia looks back at me, and our eyes lock. I feel myself held captive. I wonder if she feels it— the call of the ancient familial fire that runs through our veins.

She smiles, and my heart skips a beat. I pull within myself and step through the veil, closing the distance as I wrap myself around the air surrounding her body, breathing in her very scent. I reappear beside her, and she jumps, her face flushed, as she smiles at me with shock and wonder.

"How did you do that?"

"Stick with me, kitten, and I'll show you things you only ever dreamed of."

She chuckles, rolling her eyes, but falls into step beside me. Mack falls back to talk to Elijah. "Are you flirting with me?"

Smiling, I keep my eyes ahead. "Would it upset you if I was?"

"I'd be disappointed if you weren't," she murmurs quietly, and I know I wasn't supposed to hear it.

"Do you not belong to the storyteller?" I ask her.

"Excuse me?"

"He seems to believe he has a claim to you. And you smell of him."

"I . . . what?"

She pauses, her face flushing in embarrassment or anger, I'm not sure. Human emotions are complex.

"Not that it's anyone's business, but yes, we had sex a few days ago, but I do not belong to him, or anyone. I'm my own woman."

"I did not mean to offend you."

"I'm not offended," she corrects, turning her head to meet my gaze. "A little mortified."

"Don't be." I smirk. "Raziel is rather attractive, if your type is tall, dark, and damaged. I meant no judgment, kitten. I simply wanted to know if you were spoken for."

Her green eyes brighten curiously, as she returns my smile. "Why do you call me Kitten?"

"It's that look in your eyes," I admit, the words slipping free before I can stop myself. "When you look at me like that, well—it's hard not to take notice. It's even harder to believe anything as beautiful as you could be entirely human."

Her mouth curves into a smirk, though her eyes remain serious. "That's one hell of a line, Nyari. You always talk like that, or am I just special?"

My gaze drags over Mia's form, unhurried, and unapologetically lingering, as the air between us thickens. Desire stirs low in my belly, and when my eyes meet hers again, there's no mistaking the effect I have on her. "I think you already know the answer, Kitten."

Mia curses under breath, the sharp edge of the word lost to the thunder in my own ears. Her steps falter, and she glances my way. I'm unable to hide my amusement as I watch her physically trying to restrain herself from acting on her natural instincts. Her lips part, then close, then open again as if to speak. When she finally does, I'm almost disappointed that it's to talk about the storyteller.

"Raziel is looking for a cure, a way to prevent the Darken from destroying everything, but he also mentioned Sahari is gathering survivors—the fallen—and making alliances with other communities of supernatural beings. I'm still wrapping my head around all this. Do you think there is a cure?"

"I can't speak for Raziel's intentions, but my sisters and I followed our brother Jeremiah over after he completed the bond with Sahari during a ritual involving an alliance with the pack. Since the fall, Sahari has allied herself to the covens, the packs, the Fae, the mages, and those of the McCoy bloodline."

"Sounds like she's building an army."

"She is. The Darken are a temporary threat, but there are those who seek to capitalize on the aftermath. There are rogues hunting the fallen and anyone who aids with them. Then you have the hypocrisy of the cleaners, whose only goal is to cleanse the world of those they deem unclean."

"The whitecoats—*cleaners*—I'm familiar with," she admits cautiously. "But the rogues?"

"Rogue angels sent from heaven to kill survivors of the fall."

"Why would God send angels to kill other angels?"

"He wouldn't," Elijah says, appearing alongside us. "Talk among the angels is that the archangel Raphael has usurped the throne, bewitched the angels with the help of a McCoy witch, and turned them to his side. They seek a missing journal."

"According to Isaiah, this particular journal contains the prophecies related to the McCoy bloodlines"

"Why would Raphael want that?"

Elijah shrugs. "Perhaps he's looking for the same thing Raziel is. A cure."

"Isn't that a good thing?"

"Depends on how he intends to use it."

"Do you think there is such a thing?" Mia asks, looking between Elijah and me. "A way to undo all of this mess?"

"No," Elijah admits. "But I do believe we can come back from this."

"The only way forward is through," I say, looking at Mia. "What do you believe, Mia?"

"In all honesty, I don't believe in magic cures. I think all we can do is make the best of a bad situation, and hopefully leave the world livable for those that come after us."

"Raziel does not share those same beliefs?"

"Raziel is a complicated character," Mia muses, looking up at the safe house. It's nothing special—a simple old two-story cottage surrounded by trees just off from the main road.

"It's seen better days," I agree, hesitating when we get closer to the house. I can feel Sahari's irritation and power even from outside, mixed with annoyance and anger from both Raziel and Isaiah. "A word of advice, kitten," I say, gesturing to the cottage before us. "Don't get on Sahari's bad side. If she decides you're a threat, especially during times of war, she won't hesitate to kill you."

TWENTY-TWO

Raziel stands as I enter the study with Jeremiah and Isaiah. The last six months have not been kind to the archangel in front of me. Raziel bows his head in respect, and the corners of his mouth rise into that familiar arrogant smile. "It would seem you've been busy, Sahari."

"After our last meeting, I made alliances to further our cause." I gesture for Raziel to sit at the table. "Your vessel has seen better days."

"It has not been an easy journey since the storms began," Raziel says, lowering himself into his seat. "I did not see many of our brothers and sisters on my way in. I can only assume they have not fared well either."

"We've lost many to rogue attacks." Ignoring the hollow ache in my chest, I move to sit across from him. "More still to the storms that carried the curse."

"I'm saddened to hear that," Raziel says, meeting my gaze. "I'm sure you did everything you could to protect them."

"And yet it wasn't enough." I rein in my irritation and anger as I hold his gaze. It's hard not to blame the male sitting across from me. "What news do you have? Did you find anything in your travels?"

"I did." He grins. "I just need a little more time."

"Time is not a luxury we have to offer you," Jeremiah says, speaking my thoughts aloud.

"I don't recall asking for your input," Raziel snaps. "You shouldn't even be here."

"If it weren't for you, none of us would be here," Jeremiah reminds him. "Perhaps you should have more respect for those who helped clean up your last mess, or have you forgotten the part you played in the war?"

"Enough." I raise a hand, silencing Raziel before he can say anything stupid. "The past cannot be undone. If you don't have the journals or the cure, what information do you have for me?"

"I know the location of the priest's storage container," Raziel says, smiling as he reaches into a backpack that is laid on the table. "I also have in my possession Silas McCoy's journal, along with Aiden McCoy's personal journal."

"Who is this Aiden McCoy?" I ask, watching Jeremiah reach for the old leather-bound book. His fingers hover above the ancient tome. I know it's the genuine artifact by the pained expression on my lover's face.

"Father Aiden collected artifacts relating to the McCoy bloodlines. I believe we'll find what we're looking for there. It's only a two days' drive. Mia and I will go—"

"Ah, yes. I had heard you were traveling with a new plaything," I say, mockingly. "What is your fascination with redheads?"

"Well, you know what they say—blonds have more fun but reds give better head." An eerily familiar voice come from behind me, I turn my head to find Claire McCoy's doppelgänger standing in the doorway.

The girl is short, with an oval-shaped face, a dimple in her chin, and curves hidden beneath her leather jacket, though it is her eyes that unsettle me—strikingly green, like those of a prowling cat. Her skin is darker, as if she has spent a lot of time in the sun, but her hair is the color of copper, with natural highlights when the light hits it. She is beautiful, strikingly so, just as her ancestor had been all those years ago.

Raziel rises from his seat, ready to intervene, but the girl stops him with only a gesture, her challenging gaze focused solely on me.

"My name is Mia McCoy. You must be Sahari." The human steps forward and extends her hand to me.

Jeremiah and Nyari move in sync, and I can't help but notice the way Nyari places herself in a protective stance, slightly to Mia's right. Jeremiah's expression hardens as he observes his sibling.

I stare at the redheaded human, a smile tugging at the corners of my mouth as I appraise her. "I was told you'd been injured, but you seem fine to me."

Sensing I'm not about to take her hand, she lets it drop and perches herself on the corner of the dining table. She seems to do her own assessment of the room, quickly taking in Jeremiah, Isaiah, myself, and the exits, where Elijah and Nyari remain.

"Nyari and Elijah took good care of me," Mia says. "Elijah tells me you're preparing for war? That you've been making alliances to fight alongside the other communities?"

"Does he now?" I say, looking at the mage standing against the wall. He straightens and meets my gaze with a submissive bow of his head. "What else does our Elijah tell you?"

"He tells me I can trust you," Mia says, holding my gaze in a challenge when I return it to her. "Is he wrong?"

"The question, Mia McCoy, isn't if you can trust me." I rise from my seat and approach the legendary fae warrior while holding Mia's gaze. "It's if I can trust you. Nyari seems fond of you, but if I've learned anything, it's that even the strongest minds can be easily manipulated by a pretty mouth." I brush my thumb over Nyari's bottom lip.

Nyari jerks back from my touch, their amber eyes lit with that ancient flame as they expose their fangs. "I'm no one's puppet, Sahari."

"Of course not, my little firebug," I murmur, unable to keep the patronizing tone from my voice. "However, I'm sure you cannot blame me for being cautious about the company we keep. After all, who knows better than you, Nyari, of what the McCoy are capable of in times of war."

"They are not the same, Sahari." Nyari looks at the human, affection and wonder in their eyes. "Look at her. Don't you see it."

"See what?" Jeremiah asks, his tone bored.

"Everything." Nyari's tone is full of curiosity and wonder.

"Leave them alone," Mia snaps, rising off the table. "I'm not my ancestor. I kept my word and got Raziel this far. As far as I'm concerned, I've paid my debt. So trust me, or don't. I won't lose sleep over it."

The room goes silent as Mia wraps up her pretty speech, while I suppress a grin, sensing the others' weariness as they await my reaction.

"Is that right—"

"I wasn't finished," Mia interrupts, now standing directly in front of me, placing herself conveniently in front of Nyari. How sweet. "I'm a soldier, Sahari, and I'm willing to help if you'll have me, but I will not beg to belong where I'm not wanted."

"I trust her," Raziel says. "And she's a good fighter."

Looking to Raziel, I'm unable to keep the cynicism from my voice. "Once, your word would have been enough."

Isaiah rises from the table, looking between Mia and Nyari. "If Nyari vouches for Mia, I will not object of her staying in camp."

Nyari straightens, holding Isaiah's gaze with respect and trust for their friend. Nyari looks at Mia, and a small smile tugs at their lips. Mia returns their smile as if they'd just exchanged words.

Jeremiah speaks in their native tongue. "*Think carefully, Nya. She will be your responsibility.*"

"I know," Nyari says, looking from their brother to me as she moves to stand next to Mia, their arms brushing together. "I vouch for Mia McCoy."

"Thank you," Mia whispers, her words only meant for the fae at her side. "I'm not quite sure of the significance, but it feels important."

Jeremiah glares at the human. "If your intentions are not pure and you seek to betray us, your punishment will not solely be yours to bear."

"What do you mean?" Mia asks.

Without looking at Mia, Nyari speaks in a calm and emotionless tone. "Your crimes are now mine, kitten. If you seek to betray Sahari or the course we fight against, they'll kill us both."

"That's barbaric," Mia mutters, then shakes her head. "I don't have a death wish or ulterior motives."

Ignoring the human, Isaiah gestures to the journals on the table. "Now that the unpleasantries are out of the way, can you tell us more about these?"

"The journal was last in the possession of a priest named Aiden McCoy," Raziel explains, "Mia's biological father. I posed as a priest for the parish for months, gaining the trust of the sisters closest to him, and was able to piece together information regarding the journal. Its exact location wasn't clear to me until after the storm."

"That's an awfully big coincidence, Raziel," Isaiah says, taking a seat on the edge of the table and looking down on the exhausted archangel. "You just happened to stumble upon *this* McCoy descendant?"

The two males stare each other down, but I grow tired of the cat and mouse games. "What am I missing?"

"This journal belonged to Silas McCoy. It was handed down through the generations and was eventually in the possession of Aiden. He hid it before the whitecoats killed him."

At the mention of the whitecoats, Mia pales. If her history with the zealots was anything like that of the covens, I'm sure it wasn't a happy story.

Keep an eye on that girl.

I keep my features neutral at the intrusion, refocusing my attention on the conversation.

"Inside are coordinates to a shipping yard about two days' drive from here."

Seemingly deep in thought, Mia traces the side of her father's bible. "What about the cure for the Darken?"

"While I do believe we'll find more answers amongst your father's research, we have an alternative option for a cure from the virus."

This news has all our attention. "What is it?" Elijah asks.

"It's her." Raziel nods to Mia, ignoring the irritation appearing on Mia's features as Raziel continues to talk. "We were attacked by a swarm of birds, and Mia was able to stop their hearts. The moment the hearts stopped beating, the Darken released its hold."

"Killing the infected isn't a cure," I tell him. "Believe me, we've killed plenty."

"Did you ever bring them back?" Raziel asks, his tone full of confidence as he holds my gaze. "Because Mia did, and the birds flew away unharmed."

Elijah looks at Mia. "Is this true?"

Mia nods. "It is."

"How did you do it?" he asks excitedly. "This could change everything."

"I don't know exactly. I was scared, angry, and desperate. It was like I became separated from myself and stepped through the darkness, until there was only me and the Darken. I was able to visualize the bird's heart and the darkness coating it. I squeezed until the heart stopped beating, and it fell from the air."

"Did the bird come alive on its own?" Jeremiah asks.

"No. When I stopped the heart, I took a life. In order to bring it back, I had to offer up a sliver of my own." Mia seems unsure of how to explain it. "I'm rusty when it comes to using my powers. I didn't even know I could do it."

"It's okay," Nyari assures softly. "I'll teach you."

Isaiah opens the bible and waves at the pages. "What is this language?"

Nyari pulls their gaze from Mia and zeros in on the text. "Curious."

"Do you know it?" I ask, staring at the unfamiliar script.

Nyari reaches for the bible, turning its pages. "Parts are scripture, but the scribbles are notable events in your family's lineage. Information, locations, spells, warnings, prophecies, and recordings of new life."

"What is that?" Mia asks, pointing at a symbol.

"That is an angelic rune." I look to Raziel for answers. "What does it say?"

Raziel squints, looking concerned as he lifts his eyes to mine. "I don't know."

"You don't know?" Isaiah questions. "Is that not one of yours?"

"It is."

"I've seen it before," Mia says, peering down at the paper. "The other night in the shower, when I touched you, that rune appeared in flames. Before I could think too much about it . . . well, you know what happened next."

"That I'll never forget." Raziel winks at her before looking back to the rune. "It's definitely mine, but I've never seen that rune before."

Isaiah and I share a look of concern, and I nod for him to take the lead. "I think someone has tampered with your memories," he says.

"That's your rune," I say, gently. "You said it yourself."

There seems to be a war waging inside of Raziel as he takes in all the information. "Where is Uriel?"

"He's back at the main camp. I'll send for him."

Raziel nods and sinks back into the dining chair.

"We're here for a few days before we return home," Isaiah says. "Uriel will want to examine your vessel, but I suspect you'll need to upgrade sooner rather than later."

"I'm not returning to base without making a stop at the shipping yard," Raziel insists, meeting Isaiah's hardened glare. "We have a location, Isaiah. It's our best hope to end this chaos."

Before Isaiah can argue, Mia pulls a map from her back pocket. "The shipping yard isn't that far. A day or two."

"And on foot?" Elijah moves to examine the map.

"Worst case, a week, but I can get us there," Mia says to the group. "I have a safe house stocked with supplies and weapons in that area."

"I'm not risking my people—" Isaiah starts, but I wave a hand and cut him off. "Sahari?"

"I haven't agreed to anything, but I'm willing to hear what she has to say."

"I'll run into town, find a car and a few supplies for the road. We're here"—Mia points to the map—"and the shipping yard is here. The safe house is not too far from the yard. We'll rest, restock our supplies, and travel on foot. In and out, grab whatever we can, then circle back to the safe house. We'll rest for the night and be back on the road by dawn."

"Assuming you don't run into any trouble," Jeremiah says, shaking his head as he looks at the map. "It seems too easy. Both the safe house and shipping yard are central to a major city—those places are swarming with Darken. There's no way you get in and out unnoticed."

"I can," Mia says confidently, though as she looks at Raziel, I can tell she's worried. "Are you sure you're up for the mission?" she asks him. "I can go alone."

"Give me a few nights to sleep and I'll be ready."

"I don't like this," Isaiah snaps. "You can barely stand."

"I'll be fine, Isaiah," Raziel insists. "Keep this up and I'll start to think you actually care."

A howl silences the arguing, and the room falls quiet right before chaos sets in. Gunshots, windows shattering, someone screams. A battle breaks out in the front yard.

"We're under attack! The cleaners have surrounded the property," Kody tells me, his eyes shifting to reveal his beast. "My brothers are out there."

"Stick to the plan, wolf," Isaiah snarls at the man. "We've trained for this."

Jeremiah hands me my sword and dagger, grabs the back of my head, kisses my forehead, then leaves with Kody and Jensen. Nyari hesitates, looks back at Mia, nods, then follows their brother.

Mia turns to Raziel and places her hand on his shoulder. "You need to sit, Raziel. You don't need to fight this battle."

"Mia," I say. She turns to face me. "You're with me."

"No," Raziel argues, but his will is weak. "She stays with me."

Mia's head snaps in Raziel's direction, the irritation visible on her face. "I'm not a dog, Raziel. I don't sit when you command it."

Smirking, I look at Elijah. "You and Isaiah stay with Raziel. Do what you can for his injuries." I pause at the door and look back at Isaiah. "Break his legs if he tries to leave."

Mia turns to me with a familiar spark in her eyes—the adrenaline and lust of battle. "Let's do this," she says.

She isn't at all what I expected.

TWENTY-THREE

"You fought bravely today, kitten."

The sound of their voices sends chills through my spine. The pain in my body and head fades with every brush of their fingertips. Nyari is a healer of some kind, but I also feel a pull toward them. I can't stop staring at their eyes, the sharpness of their cheeks, and the unnatural point of their ears. They're beautiful.

Nyari stands between my knees while I sit on the step. They assess the cut on my brow and wipe it with alcohol. It seems like a waste to me, but when I point it out, they only roll their eyes and smile as they hold out the vodka. I take a swig of the clear liquid before pouring a little onto the blade of my dagger. I clean the steel and wipe it on my jeans, trying to focus on anything but their close proximity.

God. They even smell good, like the bush after rain, with an undercurrent of sweetness.

Sahari is speaking with Elijah about Raziel's injuries, and Isaiah is in the living room getting reports from the wolves. A few surviving whitecoats have been taken down into the basement for questioning.

My eyes close as Nyari's fingers brush my temple. Electricity rushes through my body and settles in my stomach. I open my eyes and find myself staring at their lips, the urge to reach out and taste them almost overwhelming. Nyari's finger tilts my chin, and I meet their gaze. "What is it you're thinking, kitten?"

Warmth floods my cheeks, and I can't stop myself from saying, "I'm thinking I'd like to see if your lips taste as sweet as they look."

A smile lights up their face, and they kneel on the steps between my feet. I raise my hand and see that it's still covered in the white-coats blood. I hesitate, but Nyari grasps my hand, holding my gaze as they bring my hand to their lips.

My thumb traces the outline of their mouth, and their eyes close as I lean in to press a kiss to their lips. It's chaste to start, but quickly unravels as my free hand grasps hold of the back of their neck, pulling them closer, our lips growing hungrier with every passing second.

Nyari climbs into my lap, their hands in my hair as the kiss deepens. In this moment, breathing no longer seems important, even as my lungs burn from the lack of oxygen. The kiss doesn't slow as my hands slide beneath their leathers, or as theirs slip beneath my shirt. Their nails claw at my skin, causing my back to arch as a moan escapes my throat.

Nyari's growl sends goosebumps along my entire body. I hold them close as their mouth trails along my jaw and nuzzles my neck. I don't care where we are or who sees; all that matters is Nyari's touch.

Biting back a whimper, I tilt my head to grant them better access to my throat.

Nyari shivers against me, their lips still at my neck. Neither of us try to move, our hands continuing to explore.

With a reluctant sigh, Nyari withdraws and stands. I look up at them, grab the blade and the bottle of vodka from the steps, stand, and offer my free hand to Nyari.

Nyari takes my hand but hesitates at the door. "What about the storyteller? I know you aren't his, but he cares for you."

Curiously and hesitantly, I ask, "Would you like him to join us?"

Their eyes widen. "No! I certainly would not like that."

Chuckling, I lean in and kiss the strange fae. "Raziel is a *friend*, that's all."

"A friend whom you've shared your body with? He believes you're his."

"Nobody owns me, Nyari." I tilt their chin and force them to look at me. "He does not understand me."

"You think I understand you?"

I trace their cheek and brush a lock of hair behind their ear. "You see the world as I do." I drop my hand and step back. "I'm going to go find a shower and crawl into bed. I hope you'll join me, but it's your choice." I press one last kiss against the side of their mouth, then walk away.

The next morning, I sit on the steps with a cup of coffee and watch the others train. The attack last night was the first taste of battle for a lot of them. It was thanks to the warriors Jeremiah, Nyari, and the sisters Harlow and Artemis, that our loss wasn't greater.

The few mages among the group were skilled in their elements but lacked the knowledge of how to use it defensively. I couldn't fault them. As a child, I'd been trained to wield the elements, but decades of suppressing them had rendered my own abilities unreliable. My outburst in the alley was the first time I'd expelled fire in years. I could barely summon a spark otherwise.

Nyari stood in the center of those gathered in the yard, giving instructions, correcting postures, and offering words of encouragement. Occasionally, one of the younger wolves would get too arrogant, and they'd promptly find themselves being made an example of.

Elijah stood off to the side with a few mages, watching the lesson closely. His wife, Mackenzie, is in the ring with Nyari. Earlier, Elijah and I went for a run along the perimeter, and I learned before the storm, he'd been a firefighter, and his wife a paramedic. They'd known each other before the storm and had been together for seven years. Mackenzie has two children from a previous relationship. The kids are with her pack and their father, back at the camp. I like Elijah and Mack. Aside from Nyari and Raziel, they are the only two who don't curse or spit on the ground when I walk past.

My attention returns to the fighting ring, and I can't help but smile as I watch Nyari make quick work of two shifters at once. The fae taunts the shifters, arms open wide, giving them a free shot. I set aside my coffee mug and shrug out of my jacket.

It isn't that the shifters aren't as fast or strong—it simply comes down to experience. Nyari is a trained warrior who has honed their craft. Light on their feet, every strike and foot placement planned— they themselves *are* the weapon.

The shifters lack the experience and the patience, but in time, with the right leaders, they could become a formidable force.

Nyari straightens from their position, and their eyes lock with mine. We haven't spoken since I left them on the stairs last night. I waited for them to join me, but they never came.

The battle last night was brutal. I'd fought back-to-back with Sahari and then Nyari. There were a lot of swords flying around. I preferred hand-to-hand, or my gun, but with so many people in close proximity, it wasn't a safe option.

The shifters separated, allowing me into the makeshift ring. Murmurs run through the onlookers as they watch Nyari and I size each other up. I hold Nyari's gaze as the wolves on the ground roll out of the way. We circle each other, taking each other's measure. The air thickens, and flames dance in Nyari's eyes moments before they attack.

It feels more like a dance than fighting. Every attack is met with a counterattack, even as our breathing grows louder and sweat beads on our foreheads. Occasionally, one of us lands a blow. I forget about those around us and become all too aware of Nyari—of their hands, their breathing, of the knife at my throat moments before I swivel and pin them to the ground, straddling their waist, my own blade against their neck.

I feel the trickle of blood as it slides down my throat. The scent of iron is unmistakable. Nyari reacts beneath me, their eyes zeroing in on the blood.

"You win," Nyari murmurs, and the knife at my throat disappears. The moment is broken, and those around us erupt into shouts and hollers. Neither of us miss the shouts of "get a room" and "fuck already." I feel my face heat as I stand and put space between us, my entire body burning as if it's been engulfed with flames.

"Where did you learn to fight like that?" Mack asks, her voice full of awe and disbelief. "I've never seen anything like it."

"Neither have I," Jeremiah says, watching me curiously. "You surprised me today, Mia McCoy."

"Thank you." I bow my head in respect. As I lift my head, my eyes shift to Nyari's retreating form before they disappear into thin air, leaving only embers behind. I excuse myself to the house, grabbing my jacket and my now-cold coffee from the steps on the way.

Entering the kitchen, I toss my jacket onto the back of a chair and put my cup in the sink, then turn on the water and splash my face. My entire body feels as though it's on fire. I can still feel their hands on my body, their lips on my throat. I touch the cut on my neck, and my fingers come away bloody.

Grabbing a napkin from the bench, I clean away the blood, willing my body to calm down, but there's no use. Cursing, I toss the napkin into the trash and go upstairs for a shower. I ignore the sneers from Isaiah, and Raziel's worried glances.

After an hour in the shower with the water scalding hot and leaving my skin deliciously pink, I finally give up. I soaped and sudded every inch of my body. My hands soothed every ache as I imagined they belonged to someone else. Even as my back arched off the tiles and pleasure found me, I was still left aching and frustrated.

I wrap the towel around my chest, open the bathroom door, and step out into the hallway. My face heats at the thought that anyone could have heard me. I'm in a house full of supernaturals; there's no way nobody knew what I was doing.

I open my bedroom door and step inside, my free hand running through my damp curls. I halt at the sight of Nyari sitting on the edge of my bed in only a shirt that stops midthigh, revealing a large tribal tattoo.

Neither of us speak as I close the door behind me and press my back against it. My heart races, and I wonder if they can hear it.

Slowly, Nyari stands from the bed and closes the distance between us. My hand twists in the fabric of their shirt as my breathing quickens.

"Will you still have me?" Nyari whispers, their lips brushing against my jaw and their nose grazing my skin as their arms circle me.

I turn my head and capture their lips in a kiss, then slide my arms around their neck, dropping the towel. Their hands grab the back of my thighs and lift me, pinning me to the door.

"You are precious," they whisper. "From the moment we met, I felt it."

My heart races with every word. "I feel it too."

"I cannot fall for you, kitten." The thought seems to pain them, even as they squeeze me tighter to them. "Yet I fear that it is too late . . . I don't think I could bear to lose you."

I grasp hold of their face between my palms and kiss their lips, cheeks, eyelids, nudging their nose with my own until they open their eyes to look at me. "Let's enjoy tonight. We'll worry about the future tomorrow."

"Tonight." They seem to almost purr at the reminder, their hands caressing my cheeks before lowering my feet to the ground. "Get on the bed, kitten," Nyari orders, a smile tugging on their lips to reveal sharp canines.

Reluctantly, I let go of them and walk to the bed, pull back the covers, and crawl beneath the sheets.

Nyari climbs into bed and straddles my lap before lifting the T-shirt above their head. My hands settle on their hips, the pad of my thumbs tracing the twining scars before traveling higher over their abs. I kiss every available inch of their flesh within reach.

It's unlike anything I've ever felt before. Their skin isn't like mine. Every inch of them is hard, filled out with muscle like a swimmer or runner, and yet it feels softer. I can't stop touching, exploring. My lips refuse to leave their skin, even as they grab a fistful of my hair and tug, exposing my throat, and their teeth sink into the flesh where their knife had sliced the skin earlier. I cry out in pleasure as I *finally* get exactly what I need.

The sun shines through the blinds on the window, and the bed shifts behind me as the scent of coffee fills the room. I twist, half rolling onto my back as I look at the beautiful fae dressed only in a pair of shorts. "Good morning."

Nyari grins as they lean down and press a kiss to my lips. "I made you coffee."

I shuffle up the bed and lean against the pillows, unable to keep the sleepy grin from my face as I reach for the mug and take a sip. "I love coffee."

"I know." They slide down on the bed and prop their head up on their hand as their other hand trails up and down my thigh. "You kept talking about it in your sleep."

I cringe. "I talked in my sleep?"

"Mm-hmm." Nyari leans over and kisses the bare skin of my thigh. "It was very cute."

I roll my eyes and take a drink of the bitter black liquid. "Cute, huh?"

"Yes, kitten. Cute." They grin, looking up at me through their lashes. "Sahari has postponed your travel plans. Uriel is expected to arrive in two days' time, so we'll remain here at least until then."

"Is it safe to wait?"

Nyari shrugs. "Here's as safe a place as any." They lift themselves off the mattress and take the coffee, placing it on the bedside table as they straddle my lap. "And it means I get to keep you for a little longer."

I slip my hand through their hair and pull their lips down to mine, flipping Nyari onto their back as I hover above them. "You said two days, right?"

"Mm-hmm." Nyari moans as I trail kisses down their chest, my tongue circling their nipples before I close my teeth around the tip and bite. Their back arches off the bed, and their cries fill the room as I slide a hand down between their thighs. "Kitten—"

A knock sounds on the bedroom door, and I pause, cursing. "What is it?"

"Nyari's presence is required downstairs."

"Fuck," Nyari curses, before sitting up and pressing their forehead to mine. "Rain check."

I collapse back on the bed and smile as Nyari kisses their way up my naked body until their lips meet mine. "Drink your coffee."

"Yes, boss." I smile, watching as Nyari disappears into tiny embers. "I'm never going to get used to that."

TWENTY-FOUR

MIA

The house is quiet as I step over the sleeping fae in the hall. I grab the nearby throw blanket and drape it across the warrior's lap, smiling as she stirs slightly and clutches the blanket to her chest.

I head to the study and pause in the doorway as I find an unfamiliar man sitting cross-legged in the office chair, the early morning sun shining through the window and reflecting off his mousy brown hair. He's overdue for a haircut.

The man is clearly tall and shouldn't be comfortable in that position, and yet he looks entirely at peace as he flicks through the pages of the book in his lap.

"Do you intend to stand there gawking all day?" he asks. His accent has a slight twang, like a southerner.

"I haven't seen you around here before. I'm Mia."

The man lifts his gaze from the book, and his smile widens. "So you're the doppelgänger I've heard so much about. I'm Uriel."

I take a seat on the sofa. "We weren't expecting you until tomorrow."

"It's not wise to keep the fearless leader waiting," Uriel jokes, closing the book and resting his elbows on his knees. "The resemblance is remarkable."

"So I keep hearing." I cringe inwardly but keep a smile on my face.

"I'm sorry. Does the comparison make you uncomfortable?"

I shrug and sink back onto the sofa. "I've been compared to Claire since I was ten. You're the first person I've met since the storm that hasn't made the comparison with disgust or mistrust, or tried to kill me."

"Folks aren't too fond of your ancestors."

"For good reason, it seems." I pull my legs up under me.

"What happened to you when you were ten?"

"I was adopted by Jonah Redwood; a collector of the McCoy bloodline."

"What happened to your family?"

"Up until recently, I believed they'd been murdered by the whitecoats." I frown as I look at the angel. "I don't make a habit of telling people this."

"Perhaps you like me."

I roll my eyes and smirk. "You're cute, but not that cute."

Uriel laughs and shakes his head before meeting my eyes. "I like you too, Mia."

"Settle down, Uriel, we've only just met." I enjoy the sound of the man's laughter. "It must be something to do with the archangels."

"What do you mean?"

"You're only the third archangel I've met, but there's this aura surrounding your kind. It draws people in and makes them want to serve, I guess?"

"I wouldn't quite say it like that, but it's certainly a quirk among us. Take Sahari, for example. She is the original Avenging Angel, the Goddess of Death, and the Commander of War. A natural leader, as I'm sure you've witnessed."

"I have. It makes sense then that Raziel is the Lord Keeper of

Secrets, Prophet, Protector of the Word, and the Bringer of Hope. So what does that make you?"

"My title isn't nearly as fancy as those belonging to my brother and sister."

"Humor me."

"My official titles are the Guardian of the North and the Bringer of Flame. Really, I'm just a glorified librarian and unpaid therapist."

"That sounds pretty fancy to me, Uriel."

The archangel shifts uncomfortably in his seat and opens his mouth to speak as Sahari, Jeremiah, Raziel, and Isaiah enter the study.

Sahari is wearing a nightgown, and Jeremiah is in only jeans, leaving his chest bare and tribal tattoos and markings on display. Isaiah and Raziel are both dressed in sweatpants, having just gotten back from their morning run.

"It's nice to see you, brother," Uriel says, looking at Raziel.

"Uriel," Raziel greets with a curt nod. "Thank you for coming."

"I see you've met the witch's—"

Uriel cuts Isaiah off. "We're acquainted. Mia is a breath of fresh air."

"Thank you, Uriel. You're too kind." I smile and stand with him.

"You can stay, Mia," Sahari says as I make to leave. "You're the only one who has seen the rune." She gestures to the table with the journal and bible sitting on top. "Let's begin."

Uriel walks to the table, sets his book down, and flips through the pages. His fingers trace the runes as he murmurs in a foreign language. Occasionally, he'll make a sound, or his brows will rise in thought.

"And you are sure this is the rune you saw?" Uriel asks, holding the sketch I'd drawn and placed on the page with the one in the bible.

"Yes. When I touched it, I could see it inside my mind, engulfed in flames."

"Interesting," Uriel murmurs. "I want to see what happens when Mia touches it."

"Nothing happens," Raziel protests.

"That you know of," Sahari counters. "Do as he says."

I approach the half-naked archangel and try to ignore the racing of my heart. I haven't been this close to him since we arrived, and I can feel the heat between my palm and his skin. The fire engulfing the rune calls to me, pulling me closer, as my fingers caress the smooth skin.

"You see it?" Uriel asks, moving closer. His hand slides over mine. "Open your mind, Mia. Let me see."

"I don't understand what you're asking."

"We can't see what you see," Uriel explains, his voice patient and gentle. "Focus on the rune and listen to the sound of my voice." Sighing, I do as he asks. I feel the moment he's inside my head, just on the outskirts. *Let me in, Mia. It's okay. You're safe.*

"The rune is definitely one of yours," Uriel says, his voice sounding far away. "It's a rune of memories, tweaked for protection against mind control."

"Mind control?" Sahari asks. "Are you sure?"

"Yes," Uriel says. "It won't be easy to access, but I can unpick the spell. I just need time."

"We don't have time." Jeremiah repeats his words from our first meeting.

"There is always time," Uriel counters. "You have no memory of marking your flesh with the rune?"

"It's like I'm in a room full of smoke," Raziel says. "I can barely make out shapes or see the hand in front of my face. How long do you think it'll take for you to remove it?"

"I need to gather supplies and speak to the witches. It'll take me a week to get everything ready. After that, it's hard to tell."

"Thank you, brother," Raziel says, then turns to me. "Our mission hasn't changed."

"The shipping yard?" I ask, and he nods. "I'm with you."

Isaiah speaks from his position on the couch. "I don't think that's a good idea. I don't think it's worth risking your lives for, not before we find out what that rune is protecting."

"The cure—" Raziel pushes, but Jeremiah cuts him off.

"There is no cure, Raziel. We cannot undo what's been done. The most we can hope for is to get Mia back to the base and have her show us how she cured the birds. All you'll find at the shipping yard is empty promises, false hope, and more Darken."

"You don't know that," I counter, turning to Sahari. "My father died protecting the location of that container. I'm not saying we'll find a cure to fix all this—I don't entirely believe it exists—but I do believe we will find answers that could help us navigate the new world you're trying to save."

"You'd risk your life on a hunch?"

"I've risked my life for less." It's the truth, but I also need to know what was more important to my father than having a relationship with me. I need to know what got him killed. "I trust Raziel."

A bitter laugh escapes Isaiah as he looks at me. "Then you're a bigger fool than I originally thought."

"I won't risk my people for a suicide mission," Jeremiah says, before leaving the study. Isaiah stands from the lounge and follows.

"Give us the room," Sahari says to Uriel and me.

Once we're out of the room, I dejectedly take a seat on the steps. "They don't trust me, do they?"

Uriel shakes his head and leans against the wall. "It's not you, Mia. My brother has a history of making poor decisions that result in catastrophic consequences. Consequences that cost lives and have left Jeremiah's people in mourning for hundreds of years. There are parts of the Fae realm that I doubt have recovered, even now. This storm—the Darken—is a consequence of Raziel's blind devotion to your ancestor."

"Raziel was in love with Claire McCoy?"

"Irrevocably," Uriel confirms. "It's dangerous when our kind falls for a human, but when the archangel is as powerful and old as Raziel and the human is a black-magic-using vengeful witch, it's always going to end in chaos and flames."

I fall silent as I take in the information. I look toward the study and try to listen, catching fragments of the conversation.

"You can hide it from the others, but you cannot hide it from me. You are of no use to us dead, nor will I jeopardize my people for the sake of your pride."

"None of your people are coming with us."

"Elijah has requested to accompany you, and I've chosen Seth to keep lines of communication open as well as serve as extra protection. Elijah is one of our strongest mages, and Mia has proven to be quite the asset for our cause. You can leave two days from now."

"I do not take my orders from you, Sahari." Raziel's voice rises in anger. "Or have you forgotten that?"

"Perhaps, brother, if you took orders, we wouldn't be in this situation."

Even from the stairwell, I can feel the power boiling with quiet rage beneath her calm demeanor.

"Need I remind you, *My Lord Keeper*, that you once walked away and hid from your duties in Purgatory while I cleaned up your mess? We are not in heaven. This is a new world, and you can either obey my orders, or you can find yourself a new Purgatory to hide in while the rest of us continue to clean up yet another one of your mistakes."

"This isn't my fault!"

"I wonder where I've heard that before. I'm done speaking to you, Raziel. You have your orders."

My head snaps up as Raziel passes through the living room. I jump from the stairs and run after him into the foyer. "Can we talk?"

"Now's not a good time, Mia." Raziel pushes past me toward the front door.

"You were in love with Claire? Is that why you were so interested in me?"

A bitter, angry laugh escapes him as he turns to look at me. He's guarded, hurt, and lashing out. "Is your fae mutt not doing it for you?

Because I'm not really in the mood to fuck—" His words are cut off by my slap across his face.

"You don't talk to me that way," I seethe, my vision red and my entire body boiling with rage.

Raziel turns to look at me, his cheek red and his teeth clenched as he wraps his hand around my throat. He pins me to the wall, his white eyes darkening to a stormy blue.

I don't cower from Raziel's rage. I let his rage fuel my fire. My hand wraps around his wrists. Blue flames engulf his flesh, then I use his hold to bring my knees up and kick him in the stomach. He's still healing from his injuries, but he gives as good as he receives, grabbing my leg and throwing me across the room. I crash through a table.

"Mia!" Nyari pushes through the gathering crowd to get to me, but Jeremiah pulls them back from the fight. I summon the air from Raziel's lungs and choke the life from him as I stand amongst the broken table. A supernatural wind rips through the room, shattering the windows. Blood drips from my nose, and Raziel falls to his knees, gasping for breath.

Nyari breaks free of Jeremiah's grasp and inches closer. "Kitten, you're killing him." They ignore the wind and the glass flying around the room, cutting their arms and face, but just as my own cuts heal, so do Nyari's. "You wield the power. It does not wield you. Focus on me, kitten. On my voice. Let go. I'll catch you."

I hear them. Nyari's words register in my raging mind, but I can't let go. The first tears spill down my cheeks as I admit through gritted teeth, "I don't know how."

Nyari reaches out their hand, offering me an escape. "Trust me," they say.

The moment our fingers touch, Nyari pulls me into their arms. One minute, we're standing among the rubble of what used to be the living room, and the next, we're flying through the abyss between worlds.

TWENTY-FIVE

MIA

Blue flames spark at my fingertips and spread past my wrist, tiny sparks of lightning crackling at the tips. Storm clouds gather above, but the thought of going back inside that house makes my skin crawl. I walk until I reach the edge of the border surrounding the property.

I stop, staring at the invisible wall, and feel the flames grow hotter. "Control it," I scoff.

Nyari's voice floats on the wind, surrounding me with the warmth of their embrace. "Control is all well and good, kitten, but knowing when to let go is also necessary to one's sanity." I close my eyes and turn to the bush, half expecting to find them standing nearby, but find only empty air. "Come find me, kitten. I'm lonely here all by myself."

"I'm not in the mood for your games, Nyari," I call, and yet I follow the pull of their voices.

A chuckle caresses my ear, and I shiver, spinning in place. "You rather liked our games last night."

Memories of the night before filter through my mind, and I smile as the ache between my thighs returns. "That was a little different, Nyari."

"Perhaps it was." This time, their voice is too close, and I turn to find them leaning against a tree, still dressed in their warrior leathers but with twin swords at their back. "We can't stay out here for long, kitten. There's a storm coming."

"I can't go back inside like this," I say, raising my hands, which still burn with blue flames.

Nyari stares at my hands and unfolds their arms from across their chest, then closes the distance between us. A flick of their wrist, and flames appear like a second skin. The embers of their eyes brighten and dance as they reach for my hand and intertwine our fingers until the red and blue fire become a single flame.

"How did you do that?" I ask, my voice barely a whisper.

"Like calls to like." They raise our hands to their lips. "Feel better?"

I nod, staring at their mouth as I begin to relax. "Thank you for getting me out of there," I say. "I'm sorry I lost control."

Nyari leans in and kisses the tears from my cheeks. "You needn't be sorry, kitten. He does not understand you, and it frightens him."

"Does it frighten you?"

"It does not." They tilt my chin back, searching my eyes. "But I can sense that it frightens you." I jump at the sound of lightning hitting the earth nearby and the boom that follows. "I know of a spot where we can wait out the storm."

Before I can ask, the world tilts, and the bush surrounding us shifts and changes into a cave lit only by a tiny pit. There is a blanket spread out on the floor a few feet away, and the storm rages outside, but it's barely audible from inside the cave.

"Are you okay?" Nyari asks, their hands traveling the length of my arms and stroking my cheek. "There was not enough time to properly prepare you for jumping."

I look at the cave. "Where are we?"

"We're in a cave not far from the house." Nyari takes my hand

and leads me to the fire. "Patrols use the cave between shift changes." I sink onto the blankets as Nyari removes their armor and sets it aside. "What is it that frightens you, Mia?"

"I haven't stopped running since I was eight years old," I say, as they sink onto the blanket in front of me and take my hands in theirs. "For the last twenty years of my life, I have been running from who I am. What I am."

Nyari raises their hand to my face and brushes the hair from my cheek. They kneel in front of me. "You still don't understand, do you?" Nyari whispers. They lean in and kiss me, tangling their fingers in my hair before pulling back to stare into my eyes.

"Understand what?" I reach for them, bringing them into my lap. The sensation of their claws upon my skin makes my back arch and shiver in delight. "Tell me, oh wise one."

A chuckle escapes them as they straddle my lap, their hands retreating from my hair and resting atop my shoulders. "You will never be able to outrun the storm, kitten, because you *are* the storm. I can feel it inside you, and those with the gift of true sight can see it too. If one dared to listen, they would hear the sound of fire crackling with every beat of your heart. The whistle of the wind is upon your lips, and the taste of rain lingers on your flesh. You are no more a part of this world than I am."

"If that is true, where do I belong?" I ask, searching the embers of their gaze.

"Silly girl," Nyari whispers, cradling my face between their hands as they lean in. "You belong right here, kitten. With us."

While time passes outside, it seems to stand still for us inside this cave. I lie on my stomach and stare at the flames as Nyari runs their fingers up and down my back. Their fangs nip the skin on the back of my shoulder, and I shiver. I smile as I feel their lips turn up in satisfaction.

"I love how responsive you are, kitten." Their voice is quiet in the cave, and their breath tickles as they move lower down my back, kissing and nipping as their claws trail behind the kisses. "Your human flesh is so soft, fragile, but beneath it, your muscles are taut and lean. You have the body of a warrior, but the curves of a woman."

"Thank you?" I smile, lifting myself up onto my elbows to look over my shoulder at the disheveled fae. Their hair is wild from where my fingers ran through it. "What are the women like where you are from?"

Smiling, their eyes glint with mischief. "Sizing up the competition, kitten?"

I roll my eyes and reach for their arm, bringing them to me. I cup the back of their neck and kiss them, deepening the kiss, before I bite their lip hard, earning a growl of pleasure as their arm snakes around my waist and brings our naked bodies flush.

"You were saying . . ." I nip softly at their swollen bottom lip, looking up at them through my lashes. ". . . something about competition?"

"There isn't a single creature in existence that could compete with you," they whisper, their lips trailing along my jaw. "Someday, when this war is over and it's safe to return, I'll show you our home."

I lean into their touch, my fingers threading through their soft curls. "Tell me what it's like."

Nyari pulls back, their hand rising to my cheek. A smile tugs on their lips, and there's a faraway look in their ember-flecked eyes. "It's not all that different from this world, only there is no electricity like there is here."

"What do you do without power?" I ask, my eyes widening at the thought.

Amused, Nyari shakes their head and pulls me close as they lie back on the rug. One arm rests behind their head, and the other curls around my butt, tracing symbols on my hip. "You have much to learn, kitten. Our power comes from the sun, the earth, the water and air."

"The elements?"

"That's right." Lips press to my forehead, and I close my eyes, laying my head on their chest. "Jeremiah would say that it comes from our people, that our lives give life to the realm. After the Great Fae War, our land was desecrated, villages destroyed, crops burned and entire bloodlines wiped out, but as our people recovered, so did our lands, and in time, our power."

"Did you fight in the Fae war?" I ask quietly, not wanting to bring it up but curious. Their fingers hesitate on my hip, but after a beat, continue tracing their path.

"I was still a youngling when it started. Once I came of age, I was sent to serve my mother's people. I'm considered a bastard, but I'm the bastard of a king. Prince Rey, last heir of the fire fae and my friend, was Claire's lover. I was his spy and his squire, but after his death at the hands of Lord McCoy—Claire and Silas's father—I was sent to serve on the frontlines as a spy within the enemy's camp."

"Did you know Silas?" I ask.

"He was a friend and a brave soldier." I glance up at them, taking in the faraway look in their gaze. "You're curious about her," Nyari says.

I grew up surrounded by those who adored her, and who looked upon me with awe simply because I resembled an ancestor like her. And now? Now, I'm amongst the survivors of the Fae war, victims of her manipulation and torture. They stare at me with disgust. "I am."

Nyari lifts my hand to their lips and squeezes my waist. "I knew Claire when she was just a girl. The first time I met the twins they hadn't hit puberty, but she was kind, shy. Even as a child she was powerful. Lord McCoy knew this, and he resented her for it, was jealous that a girl could inherit such power. He was a hateful, cruel man, and he treated his children and wife as such.

"The moment Rey and Claire met, I knew it wouldn't end well. I warned Rey to stay away from her, but he was in love. I suspected they were mates, but the bond hadn't been completed at the time of his death."

"Lord McCoy killed Rey because he was in love with his daughter?"

"If only it were that simple, kitten. The royal houses were discussing terms of peace. Lord McCoy killed Rey because he wanted a war but couldn't justify the murder without getting himself into trouble. Rey and Claire went to him, unguarded. They told him she was pregnant and asked for permission to marry. The bastard killed Rey, in front of Claire, Silas, and their mother, and then threatened to kill Claire if she did not tell the king and the Fae that she was raped."

"That bastard."

"Indeed." Nyari is quiet, their breathing steady. "It all happened quickly after that."

"Do you know what happened to Claire afterward?"

"Not entirely," they admit. "She was sent away to give birth. Silas was shipped off to serve Jeremiah, and I was on the front lines. Many years later, I was passing through a village that had been destroyed by an army. Hundreds lay dead, dying, or broken in the mud. She was guarding her med-witches while they tried to help."

"That doesn't sound very evil."

"It doesn't, does it." Nyari's gaze flickers down to my own, their fingers grazing my arm. "I often find myself wondering if the villain she's portrayed to be is a disguise."

"Would it make it easier if it was?" I question, sensing the conflict within them. "She was your friend, Nyari. You cared for her."

"It's more than that." Sitting up, Nyari pulled the blankets across their lap. "She was carrying twins, Mia. A future heir to our people. I don't know what happened to those babies. Obviously one of them survived or you wouldn't be here. Regardless of her reasons, her actions in that war decimated our kind. Hundreds of thousands lost their lives that day."

"What was Raziel's role in that?"

"She wasn't meant to be there," Nyari tells me. "None of them should've been. Isaiah and his wife, Gwyneth. Raziel is the reason she died, the reason they all died. Five thousand warriors walked onto that battlefield, and only a quarter of them made it out.

Hundreds of thousands were lost in the decades following Rey's death."

Silence falls in the cave, and I think about Raziel. "I don't understand."

"Understand what, kitten?"

"How she did it," I admit, lifting myself off the blankets. "Raziel is good, isn't he?"

"Humans have this warped sense of right and wrong, black and white, but life is so much more complex. I do not believe Raziel is entirely good, nor is he entirely bad."

"He was there when I killed my sister, and he refused to let me die with her. Even back at the church, he never strayed too far, and after the attack, he came back for me. I fought at his side, and I found comfort with him after."

"Mia—" Nyari slides their arms around me and pulls me into their lap, their lips pressing to my temple as they murmur, nuzzling my cheek. "You care for him."

I roll my eyes and lean into their embrace. "It's not like that, Nyari."

"You had sex with him."

I glance back to the naked fae, my defenses rising, but stop when I see the glint in their eyes.

"Sex is just sex, kitten, but it is more if you care for him. Why did you invite me to your bed after the whitecoats attacked? Why have you not returned to him?"

My cheeks heat under their penetrating gaze. "The sex was good, Nyari—it really was—and maybe it could've been more, but there was a moment when Raziel saw who I was and flinched. That is all I see when I look at him now."

"He still cares for you," Nyari says, releasing their hold as I turn in their lap. "I don't think that has anything to do with Claire. I think that has everything to do with you."

I push Nyari back onto the blankets as I lean over them, my thighs straddling their lap. "He loves her, Nyari. I knew it when I saw the look in his eyes, the guilt. I am not her, nor will I ever be, but I don't think the version of her in his head is real either."

Their hands run up my thighs and settle on my hips, their gaze roaming my body. "I find that I do not want to speak of the archangel any longer."

"Good." I grin, flipping my hair back over my shoulder as I lean down and kiss them. Nyari smiles against my lips as their arm wraps around my back, pinning me above them, our chests pressed together as our kisses deepen.

Nyari purrs, arching as I grab a fistful of their hair and pull them into a sitting position. I kiss along their jaw, nipping at their earlobe. "If you continue to bite me, kitten, I will not be held responsible for my actions."

I chuckle and feel the shiver that runs through their body as their hold tightens. "From the moment I saw you, I wanted you, Nyari."

"Did I not scare you?"

"You did. Still do," I admit, kissing the shell of their ear. "The thought of losing you scares me. The thought of never holding you, kissing you, riding you—that frightens me." My eyes close as they fill me, the heat of their body pressed against mine as our bodies move, seeking pleasure. "You're who I want. Just you, just this."

The next morning, we split off into three groups. Raziel, Seth, Elijah, and I will take a car back into the city to locate the shipping container. We'll pick up supplies from my safe house nearby and use the spot to rest for a night before continuing on.

Everyone else is doing a supply run in the opposite direction. The plan is to meet up with them in seven days before returning to base, where the rest of the survivors gathered.

Nyari tosses my duffle into the boot of the car, and even with their back to me, I know they struggle to maintain control. I suspect it's not easy for them to show emotion in front of others, but at this moment, I don't care. I walk up behind them, slipping my arms around their waist, and bury my face in their back, breathing in the scent of their leathers.

Nyari's hands cover mine and bring them to their lips. "Seven days."

I loosen my hold and allow their body to turn in my arms. I slide my arms around their neck and press my lips to theirs, and their arms circle my waist and lift me. Their hands grasp my ass as my thighs wrap around them, holding me off the ground.

"Be careful," I quietly plead, knowing the others will hear regardless. I fight back tears as their lips kiss the pulse on my neck.

No words are needed as we stand there among our people.

"It's time to go, Nyari," Jeremiah says from behind us.

I unwrap my legs from around their waist and slide back to the ground, looking into Nyari's ember-flecked eyes. "I'll see you soon."

Nyari presses our foreheads together, intertwining our fingers. "Remember what I told you, Mia." I nod and press my lips to theirs. "Be careful."

Seth calls from the front of the car. "Don't worry, Nyari, I'll bring her back in one piece."

"I'll see you soon," I whisper.

"Yes, you will." Nyari smiles, though it doesn't quite meet their eyes as they walk me to the passenger door, leans down, and kisses my cheek once more, then looks to Seth. "Be careful with this one, Mia. Road trips make him gassy."

"Fuck you, Nyari." Seth flips them the bird, and Elijah and Raziel wind down the windows in the back. "Fuck you both!"

Nyari drops a kiss to my forehead, and their hand cups the back of my neck. Then they pull away, nodding as they shut the passenger door. Seth starts the car, and as he drives, I feel Nyari reach out and say the words, "I love you, kitten."

I can't be sure I heard correctly, but before I can look back and ask, Seth hits the gas, and we're driving away.

I wonder if I'll ever get the chance to say it back.

TWENTY-SIX

MIA

Sitting by the campfire, I watch the flames writhe and crackle as I recall my night in the cave with Nyari. Embers dance as they are swept up in the wind, carrying them off into the night before they fade into the abyss.

"You should eat," Elijah says, handing me a can of beans. "Tomorrow will be a long day. Get this into you."

Reluctantly, I take the offered beans. "Thanks."

I must look miserable, because as Elijah sets up his swag beside mine, he says, "Don't worry, Mia. You'll be back with your fae in no time. They'll be okay."

"I'm not worried," I lie, pulling the blanket over my shoulders and taking a mouthful of the offending beans. "Where are you from, Elijah?"

"I grew up in Ipswich. My father was first generation, and after my parents' deaths, I was raised by my Irish grandfather, Arthur McCoy. He was a weather mage like me and you. Taught me how to control it. When I was a bit older, we discovered my abilities for healing. I believe that comes from Claire. My cousins never showed any traits from the bloodline. What about you; what's your story?"

"After the storm, I went into the city to find my sister—"

"I know this part of the story."

"Then why ask?" I tease, knowing it's only fair. Elijah opened up about his life. I owe him answers. "What would you like to know?"

"How old were you when your powers developed?"

"I'm not actually sure," I admit. "I've dreamt of storms for as long as I can remember, but the other powers didn't start to develop until Jonah found me."

"Jonah? Your father?"

"After the whitecoats killed my family, I was on the streets for a while until I landed in the foster system. That's where Jonah found me. After that, my life consisted of journaling, training, and learning the histories of our bloodline."

"What was that like?"

"It was a prison camp. It barely beat living on the street. In some ways, it was worse. We had a warm bed, full bellies, and a roof over our heads, but every day we had to earn it. We weren't people to him —we were weapons, soldiers to be used for mass destruction."

"Do you think he achieved that before the storm?"

"I have no doubt he did," I admit.

"Why—or rather, how—did you escape?"

I thought about not answering, knowing Elijah wasn't the type to push. But, if not now, when?

"Jonah has been purchasing the land and housing surrounding the compound's property for years. It's essentially a small town now —population of two thousand or so. He has housing developments, farms, a doctor's surgery, and even a small hospital. There was this one man who refused to sell. After he died, the property was left to his son, who met with Jonah the day of the funeral.

"Jonah called me and Abigail into the visitor's room, and he introduced us to the man and told him he could have his choice of his 'daughters.' The man circled us like prey, stopped, stroked Abi's cheek, and said, 'I'll have this one,' as if he was simply picking out a new bitch for breeding."

"How old was your sister?"

"Twelve." I could feel myself slipping into the past. "Papers were signed, and they were to be married. It took me a year to come up with a plan to help her escape, but she wouldn't leave without me.

"My social worker visited a few weeks after that, and I told her everything. She left me her phone and went for help. When nobody believed her, she called, and we came up with a plan to escape. She put Abigail and I on a bus heading out of state and sent us to live with relatives of hers. She died a few weeks later.

"Abi and I were shuffled around for a few years until I joined the army when I was eighteen. I made contacts in the service, and they helped me get custody of Abigail and put her through school. We'd been homeschooled at the compound, and she was smart. She graduated early and lived on the base with me. It was the first place we ever felt safe."

"He sold your sister for land?" Elijah asks, shock clear in his voice.

"She wasn't the first, nor would she have been the last. I tried to have them shut down, but there wasn't enough evidence."

"Have you seen him since you escaped?"

"Once. A few years ago. I don't think I'd ever seen him so angry. The hate in his eyes as we stood facing each other, with a street between us. He doesn't have an ounce of McCoy blood, but if he could've killed me with his mind, he would have."

"Did you ever tell Abi?"

"She was at university and had even started dating. I wasn't going to allow him to ruin her life."

"So, what did you do?"

I couldn't help a smile as I recalled the night I confronted him in his hotel room. "I waited until nightfall, went to his hotel, and talked to him."

"You talked to him?"

"Yes." I smirk, meeting Elijah's questioning gaze. "I used persuasion and reason to make him leave town, and in return, I wouldn't interfere with his plans."

"Plans?"

"Jonah intends to rebuild humanity in his image, using our bloodline to repopulate a stronger race."

Elijah looks horrified as he searches my expression for any sign of a lie. "He plans to breed our kin?"

"He's been doing it for years, Elijah." I suppress my own guilt for bargaining my freedom against the suffering of my friends, my family.

The sound of a stick breaking in the darkness pulls my attention to the trees. My hand wraps around my blade as I move to defend myself. Amber eyes are the first thing to appear from the darkness, and my heart quickens as I resist the urge to call their name.

"Seth." Elijah releases a sigh of relief as he lowers his gun. "You scared the hell outta me."

The large black wolf emerges from the trees and approaches my swag. I swear there's a spark of mirth in his wolf's eyes as he plops himself down beside the fire. Sighing, I lie back and stare up at the stars.

"We have to stop him, Mia." Elijah's voice is quiet in the darkness. I think of the compound. "They're our people."

"One problem at a time, Eli. For now, they're safer where they are."

"Why are you so scared of Jonah?"

"If you knew him, you'd be scared too."

"He's only human."

He says it as if we aren't, and maybe he's right. "Most monsters are." Exhausted, I sigh and let the darkness of my thoughts take me.

I've faced suicide bombers, conducted interviews with serial killers, and hunted down the lowest of the low—scum who torture and rape for pleasure. I've even been tortured a time or two behind enemy lines, and yet no monster ever compared to Jonah Redwood, or the place I once called home.

Jonah was entirely human, not an ounce of McCoy blood, but he wields power through those loyal to him. Elijah underestimates his influence, but he doesn't know Jonah. He hasn't seen the plans, hasn't witnessed the cruelty and devotion of his followers.

"Mia—"

"Go to sleep, Elijah. Tomorrow is another day."

The next morning, I'm woken by the sound of birds fluttering in the trees above. Smiling, I watch them fly back and forth between the trees, singing. Reaching out with the invisible force within me, I feel no corruption within them.

I sit up, stretch, and look around the camp, or what's left of it. The guys have already packed their swags and loaded up the car while I was sleeping. Raziel and Seth stand in front of the car, hunched over a map.

"Good morning." Elijah smiles and holds up his canteen. "Thirsty?"

I nod and take the offered water. "You should've woken me."

"You didn't get much sleep," Elijah says, kneeling in front of me. "Raziel insisted we let you rest. He said you'd need your energy in case we ran into trouble."

"I appreciate that," I say through a yawn. I pour water into the palm of my hand and rub it over my face, then lift the canteen and pour some in my mouth. "The dreams are getting a bit rough."

"Do you remember anything?"

"It's the same old storm, just different," I admit, handing him back the water. "It's always mostly the same. You don't dream, do you?"

"Of the storm, no." He pauses, his face etched in contemplation. "Sometimes I get glimpses of things before they happen, but it's not always accurate. The general feel is the same. Funnily enough, it's usually most accurate before a storm. The atmospheric pressure shift triggers it, I suspect."

"Must be nice," I say, unable to keep the envy from my voice.

"Every time I close my eyes, I'm swept up in a storm dream. Every storm is different, but the little girl is always there."

"Little girl?" Elijah asks, his eyes shooting to mine. "What little girl?"

"I don't know her name, and she doesn't talk, but she's always there." I watch his reaction curiously. "What is it?"

"This girl, what does she look like?"

"She's thin, pale, has catlike green eyes and long—"

"White hair. I see her too."

"Really?"

"She appears to all of us at some point. Especially those like you, who dream of the storms. The witches call her a guardian. There's a legend that she was the daughter of Claire and Silas McCoy, and that Claire sacrificed the child to bring Silas back from the other side."

Seth whistles from across the camp and waves a hand for us to pack up and get on the road.

Six hours later, Raziel pulls the car onto the side of the road. We're on the outskirts of the city, and from the higher ground, we have a good vantage point.

The Darken calls to us like sirens in the ocean.

"Do you feel them?" Elijah asks, as I strap my weapons into place. "Are you sure this is a good idea? There's got to be hundreds of them down there."

"It's a terrible idea." Seth shifts into his wolf form and paces back and forth, his eyes focused on the city below.

"Aiden McCoy sacrificed everything to protect the location of this container. I need to know what was worth that. Stay close," I say. "And don't be a hero. We'll mark our way in, and hopefully come back out the same way. If we get separated, we meet back at the last checkpoint. Understood?"

I pat the wolf's head and force a smile as I look into his amber eyes.

"I know you've got your orders, Seth, but this is my mission. If I give you an order, you will follow it. Understood?" The wolf bows his head, but I can see the defiance in his eyes. These were my people now. Their lives are my responsibility. "Let's get this done and get you boys home."

Raziel falls into step beside me, his sword strapped across his back. "I owe you an apology."

"It's water under the bridge, Padre. We're good," I say. "I forgive you."

"Do you? I was an ass."

Screaming pierces the eerie silence around us, and I throw my arm out to stop him from going farther. Raziel pulls his sword as a woman comes around the corner, dragging her child behind her.

The woman sees us and her steps falter, but she's close enough for me to grab her arm and swing her into the alley behind us. "Run!"

Seth takes the lead back down the alley. I can feel the Darken closing in on us.

"Mia!" Elijah shouts. A Darken jumps from the roof and lands on top of me, throwing me to the ground. "Get up!" Elijah yells as a wave of darkness attacks, but he can't get to me. None of them can. I can hear myself screaming, feel the heat of their breath on my neck and their suffocating stench as it fouls the air.

Sinking into myself, I slow my breathing and reach into the darkness, seeking out the decayed heart of the Darken. There was nothing left. Just death. Every happy emotion, thought, and memory had been stripped away.

There was no saving these people. No way back from the brink. The kindest mercy would be to snuff out the darkness and let their bodies succumb to their injuries, hoping they have a quick and painless death.

The Darken on top of me falls away screaming, and I slowly come to my knees, unseeing, only visualizing the Darken surrounding me. I hold them in my palm and squeeze until their hearts cease beating.

The Darken fall to their knees, their features twisted in pained and silent screams as the darkness disappears from their irises. The attacker closest to me was the first to fall, and a single tear slid down her cheek. I hope that means she found peace.

Elijah rushes to my side, taking my hands in his and tilting my head up to look at him. His green eyes, identical to my own, fill with fear, wonder, and hope. "Are you—"

"We need to go," Raziel orders, wiping the blood from his sword. "Mia?"

"I'm here." I force myself to stand as I look to the cowering woman against the wall, cradling her traumatized son. "If you want to survive, you'll come with us."

"Do you have somewhere safe?"

"We do," Elijah answers, stepping to her side. "We're on a supply run, but after that, we're meeting up with friends and heading home."

"Mama," the little boy whimpers with a trembling bottom lip, looking at the wolf. Her arm tightens around the boy as she takes in Seth and the rest of us. "What is that?"

The wolf inches forward and takes a seat by my side. I place a hand on his head and scratch behind his ear. "This is Seth, our friend. He won't hurt you." As if in response, the wolf lets out a low whine and lies on the ground. "But if it makes you feel better, we can send him away."

"Is he a good boy?" the child asks, his eyes never straying from Seth.

"Define good." Elijah chuckles, earning a wicked side-eye from the wolf. "He's on our side, kid. I like to think we're good guys."

"We need to hurry," Raziel insists. "More are coming."

The woman looks to her little boy, back to the three of us, and to the wolf now standing beside me.

"We need to go now." I kneel by the boy and place my hand on his shoulder. "Stay with your mom, okay?"

Raziel leads us out of the alley and into an empty street, scanning the map for street names.

"We're not far away now," I assure him. "Stay close to the kid."

"Stop," the woman urges in a panicked whisper. "The city is overrun with those things."

Seth lets out a huff, and I can see the suggestion in his amber eyes. It was dangerous enough when it was just the four of us. Now we've got two civilians to worry about.

"Turning back isn't an option." Raziel echoes my thoughts. "We stick to the plan, Seth."

"It's not safe," the woman pleads.

"You are free to go your own way," I tell her, keeping my voice calm as I turn to meet her gaze. "You might make it out of the city."

"We're not leaving them," Elijah hisses. "She's got a child, Mia."

"We're not turning back, Elijah. We came into the city for a reason."

"The safe house is two blocks away," Raziel interjects. "We can make it."

Elijah reassures the woman and promises to keep her son safe, and we're able to continue toward the safe house. You can't access the building from the outside without a key, and luckily, I kept a spare master key hidden in a loose brick. I kneel by the door and jiggle the brick out of its hole.

As I retrieve the key, Elijah says, "I'm in this with you, but how do we know it's any safer inside than it is outside?"

Seth shifts back to human form. "Don't worry, Eli. I'll protect you. We've got this."

"Take a knee in the laundry while we sweep the building," I instruct Elijah and Raziel. "If things go bad, be ready to leave."

Locking the door behind us, I take a moment to drink from my water as Elijah tends to the woman's and child's injuries.

Raziel approaches and leans against the wall beside me. "You good?"

"Never better," I mutter sarcastically. "You?"

"They complicate things." Raziel nods to the boy and his mum. "A part of me wants to get them out of the city, but I know we've only got one shot at this."

"Everything is going to be okay." I reassure him by patting his shoulder. "I made you a promise we'd find the shipping yard, and I meant it. If it's safe, we'll rest here tonight and continue tomorrow at first light."

"The first floor is clear," Seth says, coming back into the laundry. "Ready to go up?"

Elijah hands me a walkie-talkie set to a station. "Shout if you need help or if we need to be ready to flee."

I pocket the walkie and pat his shoulder as I pass. Lowering my voice so that only he and Raziel can hear, I say, "If she panics and wants to leave, don't try to stop them. This won't take long."

Elijah nods stiffly while Raziel holds my gaze. "Be safe," Raziel says. I nod, then exit the room.

TWENTY-SEVEN

MIA

S eth and I take the staircase, clearing each level as we make our way toward the top. It only takes half an hour to clear the building, and then we've reached my floor.

My apartment is one of two on this level, with access to the roof and fire escape if we need to make a quick exit.

Seth pulls the walkie from his belt and radios down to Elijah. "Building's clear. Come on up. We'll leave the fire escape door open."

I punch in the keycode to my apartment and push the door open. It's been a while since I was last here, but I paid a neighbor to come in once a month to wipe down the dust and update the software.

I look to the door across from mine and pause, wondering what I'd find.

"I wouldn't." Seth raises his hand, stopping me as I unconsciously step in that direction.

I turn my head to him as his nose crinkles. "She's dead?"

"If that smell is her, then yes."

"I don't smell anything."

"You wouldn't. Not yet."

I pull away from him. "Get the others—"

"I would feel better if we stayed together."

"I can take care of myself,"

"Of that I have no doubt."

Ignoring him, I turn back to my apartment and walk inside to where my security screen is set up. I take the tablet from the wall and check through the live security cameras. They're motion sensitive and record whenever movement is detected in the building. I check the basement and log into the generator's data. All three backup tanks are full, and the one in use is at seventy percent.

When the others walk in, I'm sitting at the dining table. "Make yourselves at home. There's food in the pantry; take what you need."

Elijah sits at the table and releases a sigh. "That was exciting."

"Can't wait to see what tomorrow brings." Seth sinks into the seat beside Eli, his voice low as he echoes Raziel's earlier statement. "Those two complicate the mission."

Raziel stands beside me. "They can't come with us to the shipping yard."

"Splitting up is a bad idea," Seth protests.

"It might be the only option," Elijah throws in. "Mia?"

"Let's take a moment to breathe," I suggest, rising from my seat. "I need a shower, a change of clothes, and food in my belly. There's a secondary bathroom down the hall, along with two bedrooms. The building is secure—there's no way in or out without tripping off the sensors."

An hour later, I emerge from the shower wearing leggings and a worn army shirt that hangs off my shoulder. I pause at the sight of Raziel sitting on the edge of my bed with a cup of steaming coffee.

Raziel lifts his eyes to mine, and to his credit, masks his own emotions.

"Is that for me, or . . . ?"

"It's for you," he says, holding out the mug as he stands to his full height. I can't deny that he's beautiful—tall, muscular, and covered in ink. "Can we talk?"

Blinking, I shake myself out of my daze and take the coffee as I sit on the bed. "Sure."

"Seth is doing another sweep of the building, and Elijah is taking stock of the pantry. I don't think he's seen that much food in a while."

"We'll take what we can with us tomorrow." I sip the coffee. "Are you nervous?"

"I'm terrified," he admits. He sits beside me with his elbows on his knees, hands clasped. "If anything happens to you—"

"Don't think like that."

Raziel turns his head to meet my gaze. "How's that working for you?" I roll my eyes, unable to help but smile. "You're a leader, Mia. You know how this goes. Those men might only be here to protect you, but this is my mission."

"It's our mission," I correct, reaching out to touch his arm. "I need to find that container just as much as you do. And once we do, we'll get what we came for and head home. Wherever that is."

Turning his hand, Raziel intertwines our fingers. "I'm sorry, Mia."

"So am I." I search his eyes and squeeze his hand reassuringly, seeing only sincerity. "I forgive you."

Raziel's smile is sad as he holds my gaze. "You aren't her, Mia. I should have told you about her—about our history—but I was scared you wouldn't understand. If I'm honest, I don't entirely understand either, but I swear my feelings for you are real."

"Raziel." His name is like a plea, even to my own ears. "This is weird for me. I understand you need this, and I'm on your side, *always*, but if you're looking for more than an ally or a friend, I can't be that for you."

"Because of the fae?" he asks, his tone harsh. He shakes his head and releases my hand. "You can't trust their kind, Mia."

"The same could be said for yours, Raziel." As I wait for his response, daring him to argue, I stand from the bed and set my mug on the bedside table. "I'm really tired."

"Understood." Raziel rises from the bed. "Get some sleep."

"Thanks."

I turn my back to the door and sink onto the mattress.

I close my eyes and think about the cave—the warmth of Nyari's body pressing against my back, and their breath at my neck as their fingers traced my stomach. My heart breaks as I hear Nyari's voice in my head, saying, *"I love you."*

"I miss you," I whisper into the cave.

"We'll be together again soon, kitten."

The next morning, I wake to the view of the sunrise through the window. It must be about 5:30 a.m. I sit on the edge of the bed and rub at my itchy eyes as I watch the sun.

I'm starving, and my mouth is dry. I shower, change, and head into the kitchen, where I find Elijah preparing eggs, bacon, and pancakes on the stove.

"Good morning," Elijah greets. "I thought you might be hungry. You missed dinner. Seth ate your leftovers."

I smile and empty last night's coffee down the sink. "How did you sleep?"

"Good." He shrugs. "I miss the family, but Seth checked in last night before bed. They're safe." A weight lifts from my shoulders at that news.

"Raziel was in a good mood last night," Elijah comments, his tone heavy with sarcasm. "Did you two get into it?"

I lean against the bench.

"Do you want to talk about it?" Elijah leans against the bench beside me, our arms touching, and lets the silence sit for a moment between us. Eventually, he asks, "Do you love him?"

"It's been two weeks," I say.

"And in that time, you've fought side by side, faced death together, and almost killed each other. It's my experience, Mia, that when it comes to love, there is no time limit. I fell in love with Mack the moment she walked through the door at the fire station. She was married at that time, separated, and a single mother with two wild kids. It didn't matter to me."

"I think the circumstances are a bit different."

"Very different back then. The world wasn't ending—I was able to take my time. That's not a luxury people have these days. Now, if you find the one, you tell them and deal with the consequences later, because in a few hours you might be dead."

"I don't love him," I whisper. "I could have, if things were different, but I do care for him."

"Do you love Nyari?" he asks, his tone equally quiet.

Sighing, I think about the fae whose fire and soul calls my own. The way their skin feels beneath my fingers, the brush of their lips against mine, and the way their lips turn up into a crooked smile, showing their fangs. "It's certainly something else," I say.

Elijah brushes my arm with his. "The look in your eye says it all, darlin', and that's okay. If Nyari didn't scare the fuck out of me, I might fall in love with them too."

"Thanks, Eli."

"For what?"

"For listening to me. And for caring."

"Anytime," he teases. "I'll always have your back."

I reach into my pocket and pull out a little black booklet. "Here," I say.

"What is it?"

"It's a list of all my safe houses in the country." I watch as he opens it. "I've written them in coordinates. The ones with red dots have possibly been blown. My ex-partner found the location for my last safe house. I don't think he shared what he knew, but just in case, be cautious."

"What happened to him?"

"I killed him." I met his gaze. "Not all these locations are as nice as this one, but they'll have supplies and ammo, if you're desperate. The ones marked with a T will have wheels."

"There's got to be at least thirty houses in this?"

"Forty-two," I correct with a smile.

"How does a federal agent afford all that?" Seth asks, coming into the kitchen and obviously having overheard our conversation.

"I was good at my job."

"I bet you were," he says, a knowing glint in his eyes.

Truth is, I wasn't always a police officer. I spent most of my career as part of a special task force that handled high-risk missions. There was even a time I acted as a mercenary for anyone who paid enough.

"What's the plan for today?" Elijah asks, placing two plates of pancakes, bacon, and eggs at the dining table. "What are we going to do about our guests, Tori and Jan?"

Seth and I take a seat at the table as Raziel walks into the kitchen. "Good morning," Raziel says.

"Morning. This looks amazing, Elijah."

"Dig in." Elijah grins as he takes a seat at the head of the table.

"Tori and the kid won't make it to the shipping yard," Seth states, shoveling eggs into his mouth. "As long as they remain in the apartment, they'll be safe."

I nod in agreement. "What happens if we don't make it back or can't come back the same way? We can't leave them here alone."

Seth pauses his eating. "You want to split us up?"

"No, I don't, but I don't see any other choice." I meet his gaze. "I'd like you to stay with them, Seth. If you would. The mother clings to anyone with authority, and the boy has taken a liking to you. You'll keep him calm."

"She's a bit skittish," Elijah comments. "You'll have to remain in this form to maintain control of her. Otherwise, she'll flee soon as you run into trouble."

"I agree," Raziel says with a nod. "If she were to run, you'd have to make the decision to save her, the boy, or yourself."

"Excellent," Seth grunts, reaching for the coffee pot. "So while you three go on the suicide mission, I'm stuck babysitting the humans. Pretty sure this is not what Sahari had in mind when she assigned me this post."

"I'm sure it's not," I agree. "Will you do it anyway?"

Seth meets my gaze. "If this is what you believe is best, then yes, I will."

"Thank you." I release a sigh. "The shipping yard is an hour's walk from here. It's five thirty now. We take with us only what we can carry. If we're not back by midday, head back to the car without us and wait for as long as you can."

"You want me to leave without you?"

"We might not be able to make it back to the building. If we have to bunk down for the night, we'll get back on the road at daylight. If we don't make it, leave."

"I—"

"If it comes to that," Elijah presses, "go."

"What do I tell my sister?" Seth asks.

"You tell my wife that I love her," Elijah says, holding the man's gaze. "She knows the risks, Seth."

"It's not going to come to that," I say, looking around the table at each of them. "Every one of us has a job to do."

Seth and Elijah nod, and Raziel meets my gaze. "We're all going home after this."

"Yes, we are," I say, giving Raziel a smile. "Together."

TWENTY-EIGHT

MIA

Elijah and I hold the fencing apart as Raziel carefully maneuvers his way through the opening. I reach down, grab hold of his bag with my free hand, and pass it through the fence.

"Ouch!" I snatch my arm back, tearing the flesh as the fencing wire cuts through my palm.

"Are you okay?" Raziel asks, jumping to his feet and peering down with concern from the other side of the fence. "Mia?"

"Let me see." Elijah lets go of the fence and takes my wrist. I cringe, pulling my hand from my chest as blood soaks through my white shirt. Elijah curses, pulls a hanky out from his pocket, and presses it into my palm before kneeling by his backpack.

"We don't have time for you to play doctor," I tell him through clenched teeth, even as blood quickly soaks the hanky and trails down my arm. "Fuck."

Raziel starts back through the opening, but Elijah stops him. "It'll take me five minutes to clean and wrap the wound. I'll take care of Mia. You go scout the path ahead."

"Mia?" Raziel says, genuine concern in his gray-white eyes.

"I'll be fine," I promise, nodding toward the shipping yard. "Go. We'll be right behind you."

Reluctantly, Raziel picks up his bag and moves between the containers. I kneel by the fence, using my uninjured hand to steady myself as Elijah makes quick work of cleaning the wound and wrapping it tight with a bandage.

We stiffen at the same time as the familiar pull of the Darken alerts us to someone approaching. With a finger to his lips, Elijah gets up and moves to the fence, widening the opening. I slip through and take the bags from Elijah, then attempt to help him through.

"Are you okay?" I whisper as he lets out a hiss.

"I caught myself on the fence," he whispers, looking at his jacket. "I liked this jacket."

I roll my eyes and hold up my bloody palm. "Poor you."

"Touché." He chuckles as he grabs our bags from the gravel. "Let's go."

"Do you feel that?" I ask, grabbing hold of Elijah's arm. It's a slight tugging in the pit of my stomach—a pull toward something, telling my body to go, go now.

"Mia? What are you doing?"

I take off running toward the shipping yard, Elijah close behind. I don't know how to explain it, but within minutes, I find myself standing in front of a shipping container, Raziel standing next to me.

The unsettled feeling eases as I look up at the container. "This is it."

"I'm convinced," Elijah says, huffing as he comes to stand on the other side of me. He looks up at the container. "I thought it'd be bigger."

"It doesn't exactly scream 'lost treasures of a cursed bloodline,' does it?" Raziel muses, raising his hand to touch it.

Elijah makes a sound of agreement, then looks at the lock. "I don't suppose either of you have a key?"

"I do." I pull the envelope from my back pocket and retrieve the key. I step up to the lock, but I can't get a grip on it with my hand in a bandage. I hand the key to Elijah. "Do the honors?"

"You ripped your hand open on purpose, didn't you? If I get blown up opening this damn container—" He continues to grumble as he turns the key. "So far so good."

"Are you done being dramatic?" I ask, as he drops the lock opening the doors to the shipping container.

"For now." He peers at the contents within. "*Wow.*"

Every inch of the container's interior is covered in symbols. "What are these?"

"Runes for protection," Raziel answers, his fingers tracing one on the door. "Runes of invisibility. You should photograph these for Uriel."

Elijah retrieves his camera to take photos. Inside the container are rows upon rows of bookshelves, each one overflowing with books, journals, and boxes. My fingers brush along the spines and over the top of a small wooden box. My palm heats from the contact. *Odd.*

I move toward the back of the shipping container, passing Raziel as he rifles through books. I find a box in the corner with writing on top.

To my daughters, Emilia & Mia McCoy.
May you find your way.

With shaking hands, I kneel by the box and tear it open. This must be it—the book Aiden wrote about in the letter. I open my bag and shove the contents of the box inside, but at the very bottom is a yellow envelope with my father's name scrawled across the front. Inside the envelope are photos of me. Walking to the gym, grabbing coffee with Abi, leaving work. The other photos are of Emilia holding the hands of two young boys on their way to school. *My sister . . .*

I look over my shoulder to speak to Raziel and find him pocketing a golden chain and amulet. "Raziel—"

"Honey, I'm home . . ."

Freezing at the feminine voice, I watch as the color drains from

Raziel's features. I place the photos into my bag but miss one, so I fold the photo and pocket it. Left in the bottom of the box is a golden chain with a blue stone accompanying a tiny golden sparrow.

I subtly pocket the necklace and stand. Raziel is already moving toward the exit—toward Claire McCoy and her twin brother, Silas.

I watch in horror as Raziel falls to one knee and bows his head. A sickening, satisfied smile covers her face as she looks from Raziel to me. "He's always looked better on his knees, don't you think?"

"What did you do to him?" Elijah asks, voice shaking.

Claire steps forward and reaches for Raziel's head. Faster than should've been possible, I reach for my gun and aim it at her. Thunder rumbles in the sky above as Silas reacts, blue lightning at his fingertips.

"Don't touch him." I sneer at the powerful witch before me, her green eyes identical to my own but lit with pure amusement as she stares at my gun.

"Really? A gun?"

"You think this is a game, Claire? I won't hesitate to put a bullet between your pretty green eyes."

"Mia," Elijah warns.

Silas takes a step forward, but Claire halts his movements with a raise of her hand. "I must admit, Mia, you're every bit as beautiful as they say," she taunts, tilting her head. "It's a shame, though."

"Step away from him," I warn her, inching closer. "I won't tell you again."

Smiling, Claire raises her hands and steps back, eyeing me. "Mm-hmm. I see."

"You don't see shit, bitch," I spit from beside Raziel. "You're a monster."

"I am whatever I have to be." She shrugs lazily as she stares at her brother. "Isn't that right, brother?"

A look passes between the twins before Silas bows his head. "Of course, sister."

I place a hand on Raziel's shoulder and feel the control Claire has over him. *Raziel.* Slowly but surely, he lifts his head. His gaze is still cloudy, but there's a consciousness to him now. *Come back.*

I feel Claire's eyes on me, feel her power testing my defenses. The pressure on my skull causes me to lose my balance. I meet her gaze and feel my own power roar to life. The bandage on my arm burns up beneath the flames and falls to my feet.

"Is that all you've got?" I ask.

"That was but a taste." Claire smiles arrogantly as Elijah falls to his knees, screaming and clutching his head. I rush to his side, cover his hands with my own, and press our foreheads together, lulling him back into himself.

Elijah collapses in my arms, his breathing ragged. I lift my gaze to the twins, still staring at us with curiosity. Claire is powerful, but it's more than that. She's testing me, and for whatever reason, she doesn't seem to like what she found.

The sound of whistling is like a bucket of ice-cold water. Elijah stiffens in my lap and struggles to lift himself as the whitecoats surround the area. Regaining his bearings, Raziel moves to Elijah's other side and helps him stand, a trickle of blood slipping from Raziel's ear.

"I'm fine," Raziel says, trying to assure me.

Not having any other choice but to believe him, I focus on the bigger threat. Claire and Silas McCoy are backed into a corner with us. All in white, the whitecoats surround us, swords and chains in hand and whistling that God-awful tune of death.

Burn it. A voice that isn't mine echoes inside my head. I look at Raziel and Elijah, but neither of them seem fazed. *The container. Burn it down. I'll buy you as much time as I can. We cannot let the whitecoats have what's inside. We're not the enemy; they are.*

I withdraw into myself and pull from that bottomless pit of fire magic, conjuring every ounce of fury and flame that I've suppressed my entire life. It's been there this whole time, waiting. I shrug out of my backpack and turn to Elijah.

"What are you doing?" Raziel asks, his voice full of panic.

"What needs to be done," I tell him, forcing Elijah to look at me. "When I tell you to run—"

"I can't go back without you," Elijah says.

"Listen to me, Elijah. You have a family that needs you. Sahari needs you." I lower my voice to a whisper and tug on the straps of my bag for emphasis. "Make sure she gets what's inside. Protect the contents of this bag with your life. Do you understand?"

"What do I tell Nyari?"

For a moment, the entire world seems to slow. My flames falter, and I forget where I am. Holding back tears, I lift my eyes to meet Elijah's gaze and manage a small smile. "Tell Nyari I'm sorry."

I turn my back on Elijah as the first cleaner lunges forward, then stops. He's held midair by invisible talons. His screams pierce the air, and blood gurgles from his mouth. Chaos erupts as the rest of the cleaners attack all at once. Raziel draws his sword and meets a handful of them with his blade.

I throw myself into the fray of cleaners, fighting them off hand-to-hand. Silas defends my back as a cleaner springs into the air with his sword. The air gets ripped from his lungs as Silas clenches his fist, and a wave of cleaners drop like flies.

I pull the dagger from my thigh and slit the throat of the white-coat gasping at my feet. Silas and I make an opening for Elijah. It's now or never. I turn to Elijah.

"Run!"

He hesitates, and it almost costs him his life.

"Go!" I scream, as blue flames that don't burn engulf his body. "Go!"

Without looking back, Elijah takes off. Claire is distracted by Elijah's escape and doesn't see the cleaner come up behind her. It drops to the ground at Claire's feet, a bullet hole in the side of his head. Claire's green eyes meet mine as she looks up, her face covered in blood.

"You're welcome," I say, lowering my gun.

A snarl escapes from between Claire's teeth as she takes a step toward the container.

I release my power from Elijah and direct it all toward the shipping container. Where the blue flame didn't burn Elijah, it now engulfs the contents of the container, sending it up in flames. Silas appears by Claire's side, taking her arm. "It's time to go."

"Not until I have the amulet—" Before she can finish, they vanish, leaving Raziel and I alone with the remaining cleaners. Raziel backs up beside me, his face covered in blood, his clothes torn and bloody.

"Any ideas on how we get out of this one?" he asks, his chest heaving from the battle.

"Now seems like a good time to run?" I say halfheartedly, as the cleaners creep toward us. I summon fire from the container and direct it in their direction as a wave of Darken comes up behind them.

TWENTY-NINE

The battlefield is muddy with blood from the fallen. I stand on top of the hill, fighting side-by-side with Gwyneth, my dearest friend and lover. Even now, she's beautiful, covered in sweat, dirt, and the blood of Fae.

She shouldn't be here. None of us should be. But I'd gone to them, fallen to my knees, and they'd come back for me. I did it all to save her. As the last warrior falls, I hear her voice inside my head.

Kill her and bring me the amulet.

I sweep forward, my sword raised for a killing blow, but even caught off guard, Gwen catches it with her sword. Hands shaking, her expression shocked, eyes wide with betrayal.

"Raziel—"

"Forgive me," I plead, tears trailing down my cheeks. I disarm her, grab the back of her neck, and run my sword through her heart. I lower my friend, my lover, to the ground and kneel by her body as the realization of what I've done sinks in. "I'm sorry."

The amulet.

Trying to shake her voice from my head, I focus on the golden chain that hangs from Gwen's bloody neck. I blink back tears, and when I open my eyes, the amulet shimmers and disappears as Gwen's soul leaves her body.

The memories shift, and I'm standing in the garden, a page of my missing journal in my hand. I retrieve the dagger from my belt and cut open my palm, using it as ink as I draw a rune onto my ribcage.

Gritting my teeth as the rune etches itself into my flesh, I press the page to my ribcage and embrace the pain as the page and the truths written upon it are absorbed into my body.

"We're closed," Cherry calls from behind the bar. She pauses, hands on her hips as she takes in my appearance. "You look like shit, Raziel."

"I need a favor."

"Purgatory doesn't involve itself in the matters of heaven." Cherry picks up a bottle of scotch from the top shelf. "A drink for the road?"

"I'll pass." I smile, pulling a letter from my pocket. "Things are about to get bad, Cherry. The lives of my brothers and sisters depend on you getting this to Reign or Michael. I've made arrangements for sanctuary over the border. It's a one-way trip."

"The Guardians agreed to this?" Cherry asks, taking the letter and slipping it into her pocket.

"They did. And there's one more thing." I slide my journal across the bar. "I need you to deliver this to the priest. He'll know what to do."

"Is this what I think it is?"

"Yes." I rap my knuckles on the bar, smiling to myself at the old habit. "Take care of yourself, Cherry. It's been fun."

Cherry takes the journal off the bar and looks up at me. "Goodbye, my lord."

I lean against the wall beside the cracked window and breathe in the fresh air. A few Darken and wandering strays amble around, but it's otherwise quiet. Mia is curled up in the corner, asleep. I hope Elijah made it back to the apartment before dark. If they follow orders, they'll be on the road already.

Reaching into my pocket, I pull out the amulet. Claire has been trying to get her hands on this for five hundred years. I slip it around my neck and tuck it inside my shirt.

"I saw you take that from the shipping container," Mia says, sitting up in the corner. She rubs the sleep from her eyes with her good hand. "I'm assuming that the amulet is the same one Claire was searching for?"

"It belonged to my friend," I tell her, guilt weighing heavy on my chest. "I killed her for it."

"Why?" When I don't answer, Mia stands from her spot and walks over to me. "Back at the shipping yard, when you heard her voice . . . you changed. She calls you and you go."

"I don't know why—"

"She's got a spell on you."

"She did," I admit, and I lift my shirt to reveal the rune. "While I was still in heaven, I realized what she'd done to me. That she'd manipulated my memories. I drew this rune on my ribcage to protect myself, but I tweaked the spell so that if she ever tried to enter my mind again, it'd only give her access to information I wanted her to have, and it'd return the memories she'd taken from me while also giving me access to her."

"Did it work?"

"It did," I admit, fighting back tears. "I remember everything." Mia's arms wrap around me, and I realize my body is shaking. I wrap my arms around her slender body and draw her closer as I breathe in her scent. "I'm so sorry, Mia."

"For what?"

"For everything," I whisper. "You deserve all the happiness this new world has to offer you."

Mia pulls back, tears in her eyes as she stares up at me. "So do you, Raziel. It's not too late."

"I hope not." We remain quiet for a few moments longer. "We should get moving."

Mia nods and takes a step back, wiping her cheeks. "Elijah and Seth would've left by now."

"If we don't run into trouble, we might make it back to the car before they leave."

"It's better to take our time," Mia says, picking up my backpack. "I don't want to rush it and alert the Darken or whitecoats to our location. It's a miracle they didn't find us last night."

"I'm sorry."

"Stop apologizing," Mia says, handing me a bottle of water from the bag. "Neither of us were in any condition to run."

It was the truth, but I still felt guilty that I hadn't been able to protect her.

After Mia finds a granola bar in the bottom of the bag, we split it and hit the road. We stick to the back streets and are lucky enough to have a clear run all the way through.

"Are you sure this is where we left the car?"

"I'm sure," she answers, kneeling in the gravel by the fresh tire tracks. With a sigh, Mia looks up at me, squinting against the sun. "We must have just missed them."

"Perhaps we should go back into the city for a car."

Taking a moment to weigh up our options, Mia pulls out a map from the side pocket of my backpack. "On the way into the city, we passed through a small town. There was a supermarket there with a few cars in the parking lot. If we're lucky, we might be able to get one working."

"It'll give us a chance to restock supplies and maybe rest for the night," I add, taking the map she offers. "You're really good at this."

"Survival 101." She smiles, though it doesn't quite reach her eyes. Mia gestures to the bush around us. "Let's stay off the road. I don't want to risk running into whitecoats or any unfriendly types." Mia picks the path ahead as we enter the thick bush. She looks back at me and gestures to the ground. "Make sure to watch your step. You don't want to step on a snake or anything deadly."

I nod, following her to keep an eye open for any stray movements. Soon, we fall into a quiet silence, with only the sound of the trees rustling and the birds singing. If I wasn't worried about tripping over a brown snake, I might have enjoyed the walk.

"You grew up around here, didn't you?"

"Unfortunately," she admits, a haunted look in her eyes. "We're a little closer to Redwood than I'd like. How does it feel to have your memories back?"

"In some ways, it's a relief to remember. It also feels like I've had my heart cut out with a blunt knife."

Mia is quiet for a moment before she says, "My sister is alive."

"What—"

"My biological sister," she clarifies. "Emilia. Aidan mentions it in the letter. There was also a box addressed to Emilia and Mia McCoy. Inside were photos of us. Surveillance photos. She's a mum living in Brisbane, assuming she's survived the storm."

"I don't know what to say," I admit, watching her sift through her emotions at rapid speed. "How are you feeling about it?"

"Angry," she says, after a few minutes of walking in silence. "Sad. Mostly, I'm pissed off. My father has been here this entire time, Raziel, within a thirty-minute freaking drive! I drove past that damned church every time I went to see Abigail. I'm mad that Abi knew who he was and kept it from me. I don't understand why."

"He was trying—"

"Stop!" she pleads, turning to me with tears in her eyes. "I don't want to hear that."

"Okay."

"He's been here this entire time, just lurking," she whispers, shaking her head as she wipes the tears from her cheeks. "And yes, I know why, but he could have found a way. He could have tried harder, Raziel."

"Maybe he did," I whisper, reaching for her hand. "Abigail knew who he was, Mia. She knew, and she was his friend. Maybe that was as close to you as he could get without putting either of you in danger."

Shrugging, Mia looks up to the sky, her brow furrowed. "Do you hear that?"

Thunder. "Where's it coming from?"

Panic creeps in as I look around for shelter and find none. Mia starts toward the thunder, and I curse as I run to catch up, dodging fallen branches and ant nests.

This woman will be the death of me.

After twenty minutes of running at full speed, Mia slows to jog as a pawnshop appears through the trees. I come up behind her, both of us breathing heavy, and take in the fifty or so Darken gathering in the parking lot. Storm clouds hover above, and from this distance, I can see three people in the store.

"It's the boy," Mia whispers, her eyes darting from the store to the Darken. "He's summoning the storm."

"How can you tell?" I ask curiously.

"There's something in our blood that allows us to recognize each other. I can feel it. It's him. He's afraid, Raziel."

I tug on her arm, and we make our way around the parking lot, keeping deep enough to remain hidden from the Darken. I spot the back entry to the store—the path is clear. "If we can get to that door, we'll make it inside."

"And then what?" Mia asks, gesturing to the parking lot. "We're trapped inside with them? The Darken will eventually get in too."

"Do you want to help the boy or not?"

"I'd prefer it if we had a plan."

"This is the plan," I argue with a smile. "We get inside, we make friendly chitchat, and we get the hell out of there."

"And what about the storm?"

"We'll figure that part out once we're inside."

"This is stupid—Raziel! Are you nuts?"

"Shhh," I hiss, exiting the tree line and reaching back for her hand. "Hurry up before they see us."

We've made it halfway across the rear parking lot when gunshots echo from inside. Mia lets go of my hand, and we run for the back entry. It's locked. "You've got to be kidding me—"

Mia steps back from the door and scans the building. "The fire escape!"

I give Mia a leg-up, and she climbs the ladder. I take a run and jump, my hands wrapping around the bottom bar, then pull myself up, ignoring the pain shooting down my back.

Once we're on the roof, there's a door to the stairwell into the building. With her gun already drawn, Mia pulls open the door, waiting for me to come in behind her. The stairwell is dark, but my vision adjusts quickly as we descend. I reach for the next handle and push it open. Another gunshot rings out through the space, and I grab Mia, pulling her back behind me.

"Who's there?" a man shouts. "I'll fucking kill you! I swear!"

"We're friendly!" Mia calls back, pushing me off her. "My name is Mia, and I'm with my friend Raziel. We saw you guys in the window and thought we could help."

There is the sound of a woman praying, and of a boy crying for his mum. We need to get this situation under control.

"We're going to come out," I call. "Don't shoot, or I swear, as God is my witness, I'll leave you here for the Darken."

I look at Mia, gesturing for her to stay put. Reluctantly, she nods, and I exit the stairwell. I raise my hands and step into the chaos that was the pawnshop.

The Darken have already gotten through the outer layer of security. It won't take them long to get past the bars and into the store.

The man with the gun is older and pot-bellied with a gray goatee, wearing a sun-faded blue singlet, footy shorts, and the unmistakable smell of beer. "What's your name, sir?"

"Richard, but my friends call me Dick."

Makes sense. "Well, Dick, it seems you have a bit of a problem."

"I ain't have no problem 'til this kid showed up." He stands taller, waving his gun at the cowering child. An older woman is in the corner, half-dressed and with a busted lip. "Now I got those lurkers banging down my doors."

"I'd trade you, but I never much liked kids," I say, trying to put the man at ease and bring his attention back to me. "I was just trying to get back into town, find a car, and get on the road, but this broad saw your kid from the window, and before I knew it—"

"Women." The man spits on the ground. "Too soft."

I hear Mia snort in the stairwell and resist a smile. "Listen, Dick, it seems like we've both been dealt a shitty hand with travel partners, but what do you say we get out of here?"

Mia slips out of the stairwell, and Dick refocuses on her. Mia's gun is already aimed at his head, and I sigh. "Relax, sweetheart. I've got this."

The window behind Dick cracks as a brick comes flying from the herd. The boy screams, lightning flaring at his fingertips. Dick's eyes widen in fear, and his hand shakes as he aims his gun at the kid. Before Dick has a chance to pull the trigger, a bullet enters his skull, and Dick's brain splatters the window behind him. The roar of the Darken grows as the smell of blood sends them into a frenzy.

The woman screams and cries, her eyes wide, tears staining her cheeks. "RICHARD!"

Ignoring the fresh body on the floor, Mia holsters the gun and approaches the boy. She kneels a few feet away from him and whispers, "It's okay, bud. You don't need to be afraid anymore. I won't let anyone hurt you."

The boy lifts his head to Mia, then looks out at the sea of Darken.

I was so focused on Mia and the boy that I didn't see the gun 'til it was too late. The boy screams. Mia spins around, her eyes wide and mouth open. The woman, beaten bloody and only half-dressed, aims a gun at Mia.

There's only time to react. It's not even a thought, it simply is. One second, I'm across the other side of the room, and the next, I'm throwing myself in front of a bullet. Mia's screams are the only thing I hear as my body hits the ground. The pain—a white, searing pain that radiates from my chest—is secondary. I lie on my back and stare at the ceiling. I can hear Mia's voice, far away until her face appears over mine.

"Raziel? Can you hear me?!"

The wound is bad. There's a lot of blood. It's as if I'm outside of myself, watching as Mia's hands try to stop the bleeding. The irony isn't lost on me that I'm dying in the same way my vessel's original host had.

I'm running out of time.

"Help me—"

"I'm trying!" Mia sobs, her hands warm against my cold chest.

No, beautiful girl, don't cry. "No, Mia." I summon all the strength I have and grab hold of her hand. "I need to get to the roof." Another window shatters behind us, and I see the panic in her eyes. "It's okay, Mia. It's going to be okay."

I use the bench to pull myself up and pause at the sight of the woman's sightless eyes, blood still seeping from the bullet wound between them. "Remind me not to piss you off," I say.

"Too late." Mia chokes on a sob. "Raziel—"

"The roof," I tell her, struggling to move one foot in front of the other. Mia supports my weight as we stumble toward the stairwell. I pause at the entry and look back to the window. "Stay with the boy."

"Raziel—"

"Mia," I whisper, stroking the side of her cheek. My thumb leaves a bloody smear on her sun-kissed skin. I smile and press my forehead to hers. "I love you, Mia McCoy. It's time to let me go."

"I can't do this without you."

"Yes, you can," I whisper, forcing her to look at me. "You will survive this world, Mia. I believe that you will build a better world, for Hope."

"I don't understand," Mia cries, reaching for my hand as I pull away. "What does that mean?"

"You will soon." I press one final kiss to her cheek before stepping back. "Once the path is clear, take the boy and run."

Climbing to the roof is painful. My joints feel like sandpaper. The cool wind hitting my face is a welcome relief. There isn't a drop of rain, only wind and thunder. I make my way to the edge of the pawnshop that overlooks the parking lot now filled with Darken.

Summoning all my strength and power, I unfurl my wings and leap into the air. I aim for a spot far enough away that the blast won't hurt those inside the pawnshop, while still close enough to lure those Darken at the windows away.

I make sure my landing attracts the Darkens' attention. They turn as one, their eyes vacant of emotion, even as their lips peel back to reveal bloody and rotting teeth. I look beyond the sea of Darken and find Mia standing in the window, screaming as her fists bang against the metal security bars.

For Hope. I do this for Hope.

In these final moments, I summon the holy flame, letting it uncoil within. The Darken ascend upon me, their claws, teeth, and fingers sinking into my flesh, tearing me apart, but I feel nothing.

I think of my friends—of Sahari, Isaiah, Reign, Nina, and Gwen. Tears spill down my cheeks, and I smile as I open my arms and heart.

Through this holy anointing, may the Lord in his love and mercy help you with the grace of the Holy Spirit. May the Lord who frees you from sin save you and raise you up.

My last thought before unleashing the holy flame in all its glory is, *for Hope.*

THIRTY

MIA

"Wake up!" a small, broken voice pleads. Tiny hands shake my shoulders, and sobs rack his body as he kneels over me, tears spilling down his cheeks. "Please wake up! The monsters are coming."

Cringing, I roll onto my side and push myself up onto my elbows. The windows of the pawnshop exploded inwards, showering us in shards of glass. The parking lot is an empty crater where Raziel sacrificed himself, and only Darken outside the explosion radius made it out.

I had thrown myself over the boy as blinding white light erupted from within Raziel, completely vaporizing the Darken mauling his body and smoldering wings.

Time to go.

Rifling through Raziel's bag, I grab our supplies.

"They're coming!" the boy screams, pointing to the Darken stumbling toward the open windows. Ignoring the lost souls, I kneel in front of the boy and take his hand in mine.

"What's your name?"

"Tobias."

"I'm Mia," I say to him, pausing as I spot a folded piece of paper on the floor with a familiar font. I unfold the map, and my blood runs cold as the words *Redwood Crystal Creek* appear in bold red lettering across the top. We'd come closer than I thought.

"What is it?" the boy asks.

"We need to get out of here, now." I head to the window and jump out, then turn back to help Tobias climb over the broken glass. "We have to run, Tobias. Can you do that?"

"Yes, ma'am. I'm a really good runner."

"I bet you are," I say, pulling my gun from my belt as I make my way to the side of the store. "We need to get as far from here as—"

Movement in the sky catches my attention, and I get to my feet as I see bright red flares shooting into the now blue sky.

"Look!" Tobias points to the sky as three more flares appear. I curse as I take Tobias's hand, shouting for him to run with me. Together, we leap over fallen logs and dodge between branches. Tobias trips and falls face-first into the dirt.

I kneel beside him, catching my breath as I pull my backpack around to retrieve a bottle of water. "It's okay, it's just a scrape. Have a drink, then we'll have to run a little farther."

"Why are we running from the flares?" he asks, gasping for air between gulps of water. "Shouldn't we find whoever shot them?"

"No," I tell him, sitting back on my knees and trying not to be impatient. I take in the wheezing boy's appearance and can't help but feel that same familial tug that I'd felt when around Elijah and other descendants. "Can you feel the Darken, Tobias?"

"I'm not supposed to talk about it." He shifts uncomfortably, fidgeting with the bottle cap.

"It's okay." I pat his back, lowering my head to catch his gaze. "You can talk about it with me. I can feel when they are close too."

His eyes widen with surprise and a little fear. "Really?"

"Really."

"Can you summon the rain?"

"Sometimes," I admit, taking in our surroundings and expanding my powers to feel for Darken and the others in the bushland around us. "I can control fire too."

"Wow," Tobias says in awe. "Do you think we're superheroes?"

"Wouldn't that be cool?" I ask, unable to hide my smile at the innocence of his question. "Have you ever heard of a man named Jonah Redwood?"

He seems genuinely confused. "No, ma'am."

"How did you end up in that shop back there?"

"Pam said she knew a man with a farm who'd help us. I got scared, and a storm was coming. We hid in the store, and that's where that bad man found us. He killed Pam and then you and your friend came."

"Where are your parents?"

"Gone, I think." Tears fill his eyes. "My mama got sick after the storm, and I haven't seen my dad in a long while."

"Do you know his name?"

"Noah McCoy."

"So you're a McCoy too, huh? I guess that makes us family." I smile and reach out to pat the kid's knee. "Which means we've got to stick together."

His smile was small, but it was there. "Yeah, it does."

I stand up and offer him my hand. "Do you think you can run a little farther?"

"I can try." Tobias takes my hand and lets me pull him to his feet.

A few hours later, it's starting to get cold as the sun goes down. "How much farther do you think you can go?"

"I'm pretty tired," Tobias says, and rubs his stomach. "And hungry. Do you have anything to eat?"

I unzip the backpack, pull out a granola bar, and hand it to him.

To his credit, Tobias doesn't once complain as he munches on the bland bar. I ruffle his hair and keep him close as we make our way along the creek until I spot a small cave opening hidden from sight. I search the ground for any tracks or animal droppings.

"Can you be my lookout?" I ask. "I need to check if the cave is safe, and then we'll set up camp and get you something decent to eat, okay?"

"What if the monsters come?"

"Sit behind the bush," I say, pointing at a bush by the cave and setting my backpack down beside him. "If you stay low and quiet, nobody will be able to see you. I'll be right inside. If anything pops up, whistle."

"I don't know how to whistle."

I manage a smile and kneel in front of him, looking into his eyes. "I'll teach you. It's gonna be okay, Tobias. I promise—"

"Don't promise things you can't see through," he says, cutting me off with a hard look.

I nod and stand up. "Don't move. I'll be right back."

"Okay," he says, dragging my backpack to his lap, "but hurry."

I withdraw my gun and torch from my belt and enter the cave. The tunnel into the cave is narrow, the only way in crawling on your belly through the space. It opens into an alcove large enough to kneel upright, but it's still a tight fit, and the only exit is the way I came in.

I return to Tobias, then send him through the tunnel ahead of me, taking a few minutes to gather supplies and set up a trap for anyone who wandered too close before following.

I enter the cave and crawl through to find Tobias looking around in awe. "This is so cool."

I kneel in the center of the cave and begin making a firepit, digging out the ground with a sharp rock and arranging the twigs. "Do you want to see something else cool?"

"Yeah." Tobias kneels beside me, eager to watch. I hold out my hand and summon the flame. Small blue embers appear in my palm. I lower the blue flame into the firepit and watch as it ignites the twigs and shifts from blue to orange. "How did you do that?"

I lean back on the ground next to Tobias. "The same way you summon storms, but using a different element."

"Can I do that with fire?"

"I don't know, maybe." I unpack my backpack, pulling out a

sleeping bag and food supplies. "Let's make dinner and we can practice."

Tobias helps me cook the dehydrated soup and then we practice summoning fire. When the embers ignite in his palms, he gets so excited. "Did you see that, Mia? I did it!"

"You did." I chuckle and high-five him. "Good job."

Beaming widely, he collapses on the sleeping bag. "Are there other people like us?"

"Yes." I lie beside him and stare at the roof of the cave. "My friend and I got separated from our group, but we'll find them."

"It's lucky you found me," he says, yawning as he rolls onto his side.

"It is." I think about the odds of finding another McCoy on the road, miles from the Redwood compound, where my adoptive father gathered our kind. "Get some sleep, Tobias. We've got a long day ahead of us."

I let myself drift off and relive Raziel's final moments until the early hours of the morning.

When I wake up, Tobias is still asleep, curled into a ball with his fists tucked up under his chin. He's so small and innocent. The worry of what today will bring weighs heavily on my shoulders.

I know how close we are to the compound. Flares had been going off all night to keep the Darken from gathering. There's no way his men aren't searching the surrounding bush with orders to bring back any survivors. The chances of us getting away from the area unseen are slim.

A cold chill runs along my spine. It's cold inside the cave. I sit up and stare at the dwindling flames, willing them to brighten as sparks kindle and the tiny fire fills the cave with warmth.

I think back to the parking lot—the look in Raziel's eyes as he lifted his face to the sky and spread his broken wings, alight with fire. I run a hand over my face and stretch, contemplating the meaning of Raziel's final words.

You will survive this world, Mia. I believe that you will build a better world, for hope.

Hope? Hope for what? A future? A cure?

Looking at the sleeping child beside me, I know he was right about one thing.

"It's going to be okay, Tobias," I promise, brushing the hair from his forehead. "I'm going to make it okay."

I grab my jacket that I used as a pillow, pull on my boots, and crawl through the tunnel.

The morning fog is just beginning to lift as I exit the cave. I let my mind wander, searching for Darken, and find only a slight tug in the distance.

Kneeling by the creek, I raise my hand above the running water. The supply is tainted, and the Darken reaches out from within, trying to grab hold. A twig breaks behind me, and I freeze, rolling to the right as a large male throws himself at me and barely avoids falling into the creek himself.

Dodging his attacks, I get to my feet, coming face-to-face with one of my father's men: Joshua.

"You don't have to do this," I tell him, raising my palms. "I don't want to hurt you."

A cruel smile tugs on his lips, and I can see a retort forming, though it falls as he catches sight of my face. "Mia?"

"You can let us go," I continue, even knowing it's pointless.

"Your father will reward my—"

I pull my fist back and hit him square in the nose. "I warned you," I say, as he screams and stumbles back. He rushes toward me, tackling me into the hard earth. I flip us over and go for the blade at my thigh, bringing it to his throat, when a weak cry shatters all hope.

"Mia!" Tobias screams as he's dragged from the cave.

Staring down at Joshua, I hold his gaze. Even with my dagger at his throat, the man smiles up at me, blood coating his crooked yellow teeth. If it wasn't for the boy, I'd have gladly slit his throat and let the men kill me. At least this death would be quick, which is more than what awaits me back at the compound.

"Let him go, Mia," another familiar voice says, as a gun is pressed to my forehead. "I don't want to kill you."

With a sigh, I toss the blade into the dirt but catch Joshua's fist as he aims for my face. I snap his wrist and bury the palm of my hand into his nose. Blood gushes over his mouth as I'm pulled off him by my hair and thrown into the dirt right before I get a boot to the ribs.

I scream as I roll into the kick, keeping my body loose as a second person joins in on the attack. I can hear Tobias screaming for them to stop, but it's not until the man in charge gives the order that the beating finally ceases.

"Get her up."

I'm forced to my knees with a hand in my hair as a man approaches, dragging Tobias. I don't recognize him, but I know the type. "What's your name, girl?"

I spit blood at his feet, then smile as I answer. "Mia."

Recognition flashes in his eyes as he looks to Kevin for confirmation. "The doppelgänger?"

"Yes, sir."

Of all the things they could have called me. "If it's all the same, fellas, I prefer Mia."

"Get the iron," he orders, ignoring me as he puts the gun to Tobias's temple. He looks at me then and smiles. "If you resist, I will put a bullet in your son's head."

My son. I mean, the familial similarities are uncanny, but I can't have them believing he's mine. "He's not mine, asshole, but he is a child of McCoy blood. You kill him without Jonah's blessing and it's an automatic bullet with your name on it. Unless the rules have changed since I left?"

"Get the bitch in the truck," he orders, as my wrists are wrapped in iron shackles and my eyes blindfolded. Ignoring the pain, I let them drag me to my feet and push me toward the truck.

Desperate, I reach out to Tobias using the methods Uriel had taught me and whisper his name.

Tobias?

Mia?

I need you to listen carefully, okay?

Okay.

Don't fight them, Tobias. I know where they're taking us. You'll be safe there.

I don't like them.

I know, but they won't hurt you, unless you try to run.

They hurt you.

You don't need to worry about me, Tobias.

Yes, ma'am.

The drive lasts forty-five minutes. I know the moment we pass through the gates of the compound. I hear bells as it closes behind us, and by the time the truck comes to a standstill, voices begin to filter through.

The iron shackles around my wrists are tugged as rough hands pull me from the truck. I bite back my pain as I land on the gravel, the sharp edges of the rocks cutting into my exposed flesh.

"The blindfold was a bit redundant, don't you think?" I ask as it's removed. The morning sun leaves me blinded and trying to adjust to the sight before me. My shock upon seeing my home can't be hidden. The houses, buildings, and people gather to see who the guards brought back.

They whisper in shock and awe. "The savior has returned."

"Claire McCoy."

"That's not Claire."

"It's Mia—"

"Mia McCoy."

"Mia Redwood."

"The doppelgänger."

"The traitor."

"Where's her sister?"

"Who's the boy?"

I search the crowd for a familiar face and smile to myself. As I spot the older woman with graying hair and green eyes, I find myself fighting back tears. Her wrinkled hands cover her mouth, and there's dread in her gaze.

Auntie Grace?

Her eyes widened at my intrusion.

My sweet girl, what trouble did you find this time?

I've missed you too. The boy, his name is Tobias. I found him on the road. Watch over him.

Jonah has become cruel. He'll want your blood.

He's always been cruel, I think to myself as I cut the connection and hold my head high as I'm escorted through the streets. If Jonah wants to make a spectacle of my return, I'll let him. but I will not give him the satisfaction of hearing me beg for my life.

As we approach the center of the compound, Jonah's house comes into view. Memories come rushing back as if no time has passed at all. I half expect Abi to run around the corner.

Jonah Redwood stands on the top step of his home, watching the spectacle with a mask of boredom. Everything has a purpose. He could've chosen to avoid the walk of shame, but he brings me through the center of town in front of everybody, and with a single raise of his hand, the streets fall silent.

"Welcome home, daughter."

"Jonah. I'd give you a hug, but . . ." I meet his gaze as I raise my hands, still bound by the iron shackles.

"A necessary precaution," he says, his eyes hard. "After last time, it's best to be safe."

"Of course. I understand," I say mockingly, then gesture to the buildings. "I like what you've done with the place."

"You could've been part of it had you stayed." He makes a show of looking around me as if in search of someone. "Where is Abigail?"

"I killed her," I admit, and a ripple of whispers runs through the crowd. "She became infected."

"You had no choice," he said flatly. "A small mercy, I suppose, though perhaps she'd still be alive had you not taken her."

"At what cost?" I spit, unable to keep my temper in check. "You sold her like a prized pup—a child bride. I saved her from you and from that sadist pig and gave her a life outside this prison."

"A life cut short too soon," he snarls, real emotion flaring in his gaze. "It's clear you haven't changed your ways. Take her to the doctor."

Since I'd last been here, the compound has expanded to include a small medical center at the edge of town. There, I am forced into a shower and made to change into a hospital gown.

The doctor performs her tests, taking my sugar levels, blood pressure, and a vial of blood, along with a urine sample. She's quiet, head down, scribbling in her notebook.

"What's the point of all this?" I ask the doctor when the silence becomes too much. "You and I both know he's going to kill me."

The woman lifts her face and meets my gaze. "You don't recognize me, do you?"

"No."

She nods slowly, unsurprised. "My father was killed for helping you and your sister escape that night. He was the senior officer in charge of security."

"Paul Dawson?" I ask, thinking back to that time. "Paul was Jonah's best friend. He—"

"It didn't matter." The doctor, Hannah, opens the top drawer of her desk. "And those he didn't kill wished they had been."

"I'm sorry," I whisper, meeting her blue eyes. "I didn't know."

"You were just trying to save your sister," Hannah says, turning my hand over and placing a bottle of pills in my palm. "The guards will come for you shortly. Whatever he has planned, you won't feel it."

Opening my palm, I stare at the bottle of oxy and feel my throat tighten. "How often does he do this?"

"You'll be the first since the storm," she admits. "At the end of each month, he chooses one of us to pay for the sins of our brothers and sisters."

A knock sounds on the door, and I lift my head to see a young guard step into the room. His eyes are kind, concerned, and grief-stricken. "I'm sorry, Mia. It's time to go. If you're going to take those, I suggest you do it now."

Placing the pills on the desk, I stand. "I won't give him the satisfaction." I reach for my clothes, but the guard shakes his head.

"You won't be needing those," he says, almost regretfully. "You're to be taken to the post."

The doctor covers her mouth, her eyes wide. Memories filter back into my mind, and I remember it all.

"He intends to use the iron whip," the guard says.

I swallow the lump in my throat, remaining silent in case my voice betrays me. The door opens, and Auntie Grace McCoy—stands there with sorrow on her frail face. "You shouldn't be in here," the guard says to her, panic in his voice.

"It's okay, Locklyn." The old woman dismisses him and steps into the room. I straighten as she approaches, shaking her head. "I'm sorry, sweet girl."

I bow my head in respect, fighting back the tears as she lifts my chin and embraces me. It's my undoing. I wrap my arms around her slender body. "I tried to keep her safe, Auntie. I tried," I whisper, barely containing the sobs. "The Darken—"

"It doesn't matter now." Auntie pulls away and brushes aside my tears. "I wish there was something I could do."

"It's okay," I lie, forcing a smile as I take her hands in mine. "I always knew I'd die here." She opens her mouth to argue, but I cut her off. "I don't want you out there when he does it."

"Mia—"

Ignoring her, I turn to Hannah. "Keep her here, Hannah. Drug her if you must." I step back from the old woman currently cursing at me. "I won't have your death on my conscience, Auntie Grace."

Hannah catches the woman's arm, earning a death glare. "It's better for you not to see this," Hannah says to her.

I look at Locklyn and nod my readiness. "She doesn't leave this room until it's over."

"Elliot will remain at the door," Locklyn says, as the man behind him nods his agreement. "You won't run?"

"I'm tired of running." I say, stepping up to walk alongside him.

The walk through the compound is quiet. It seems like everybody is already assembled at the post.

After a few moments of silence, Locklyn says, "I was just a boy when you ran away. I didn't understand back then, but I want you to know I do now."

The crowd comes into view. "You aren't like the others, Locklyn. You still have your humanity. You know this is wrong. I don't expect you to save me, but there will be a day when you'll have to fight. Jonah is a cancer that needs to be cut out, and only then will this place thrive."

"Are you suggesting I kill your father?"

"I'm not suggesting anything," I tell him. "I'm simply stating the truth of what will come."

Jonah stands on the dais in blue jeans and a white T-shirt, his hands grasping the worn iron whip as he speaks to a member of his council. Memories of the last time I felt its sting leave me in a cold sweat. I regret not taking those pills.

"This is your last chance," Locklyn whispers. "You could take those pills and slip into darkness before the worst of it."

"I can do this."

"You have nothing to prove."

"Not to you," I agree.

My father stands tall, menacing, his legs parted and his arms crossed. At his side hangs the iron-tipped whip of nightmares. I've seen and felt the effect of its lashes and watched with my own two eyes as it split the skin and spilled the blood of McCoy.

Our bloodline didn't originate in this world, and as a result, certain elements react like acid to our skin. The iron shackles have already left my wrists blistered and would no doubt scar; fortunately, that isn't something I'll need to worry about after today.

I hold my head high and feel myself dissociate as Locklyn raises my shackles to the hook on the post. He grabs the leather bit and eases it to my mouth but stops when Jonah speaks. "Does the traitor have any last words?"

I meet his gaze and let a smile creep across my face. "I should've killed you that night."

His gaze burned as it shifted to Locklyn. "Don't gag her. I want to hear every scream."

I close my eyes as Jonah circles behind me. I hear his knife being unsheathed from his belt, then feel as he cuts the ties of my hospital gown, leaving my backside exposed to the gathering crowd.

I suppress a shudder as I feel his thumb trace the scars on my back and hear the beginning of thunder echoing in the sky above. He leans in close, his hot breath on my ear. "I'd say this is going to hurt me more than it hurts you . . . but I'd be lying."

I slip inside of myself and enter a cave far away from this place. Nyari is there, naked and sitting among the blankets. Flames dance at their fingertips as their ember-flecked eyes roam my body. "You're wearing too many clothes, kitten."

My body jolts with the first strike of the whip, and my mind screams out in agony as rage and anger tear through my consciousness. The thunder grows louder, and I could swear the ground shakes, though that could just be my knees as I struggle to remain standing.

Nyari stands in front of me, ember-flecked eyes searching mine, hands cradling my face. "Mia."

I feel myself breaking with every crack of the whip, every white-hot lash across my back, then one of the iron-tipped lashes grazes my cheeks.

"Stop!" I vaguely hear a voice call from within the crowd, but I'm so far gone. My body trembles, my knees have long since given up the fight, and I dangle from my wrists as blood and sweat run down my body and piss runs down my thighs. I beg for it to end, though the words never leave my lips.

"Mia." Nyari's voice pulls me into myself, and I stare into their eyes. "Please don't leave me, kitten. I just found you."

Our foreheads press together, and our lips meet in a final farewell. "I'm sorry we didn't have more time," I whisper.

Pain pulls me from the illusion, and I feel a scream rip its way from my throat as I'm lifted off the ground and into a strong pair of arms. "Take her to the infirmary," I hear my father seethe from somewhere in the darkness. "Keep her alive but do not heal her wounds."

"Yes, sir."

My head falls back onto Locklyn's shoulder. "What's happening?"

The man looks down at me with tears in his eyes. "You're pregnant, Mia."

"I can't—" I whisper, and from a great distance, I can hear someone shouting my name.

THIRTY-ONE

After five hundred years, sleep isn't as necessary as it once was. I can go days, weeks, even months without more than a few hours. Since my siblings and I arrived in this world, a lot has changed—more than any of us could have predicted—but this new need for sleep was a surprising side effect. An hour every other day had once been enough, but the toll was becoming harder to ignore as exhaustion grew heavier, slow and relentless, with each new day.

I couldn't explain what it was about Mia McCoy. Human, yet undeniable other. From the moment we met, my world tilted off it's axis, and everything that once made sense unraveled in her absence.

There was a word for it in the old language. There were many translations for it, but the phrase used by our people today was "soul bonded." Two hearts becoming one . . . It's how I know Mia is still out there somewhere—because from that first meeting, our lives became bound to each other.

Please, God, give her back to me. I'll do anything, I'll give anything. My life, my sword. All that I am . . . I give myself to you. "Bring her back to me."

Footsteps approach, and I steel myself for the confrontation. My grip tightens around the cold metal of the railing, and flames begin to creep down the flesh of my arms. Footsteps falter, as he takes a steading breath.

"Nyari," Elijah says, sounding as exhausted as I feel. I consider him my friend, a brother. He's a good person, a powerful mage, and a respected leader amongst the mages who traveled with us. Loved by his wife and stepchildren.

I remind myself of these things as he continues to approach. Mia cared for him. They'd become close in a short time, like brother and sister. Both leaders, they complimented each other's strengths and weaknesses, able to predict each other's movements and decisions as they made them.

And yet, when she'd needed him, he'd run away to save himself. I'm sure there was more to it, but I didn't care to hear it, not when he was here and she wasn't. If it weren't for all the reasons I listed, I might have killed him when he'd returned without her.

I almost did. It had taken Jeremiah and three of my siblings to keep me from him. Even now, my fists tighten around the cold metal bar of the railing, the metal turning black against the flames engulfing my hands.

"Go away," I growl. It was a testament to my own self-control that I hadn't murdered him already. "I'm not in the space to hear your excuses, Elijah . For your own safety, run away. It's what you're good at."

"That's not fair, Nyari, and you know it," Elijah objects, though he comes no closer. "We're stronger together, Nyari. I miss my friend. I miss you."

Despite his words and the truth behind them, I can't move past the betrayal. I imagine what it would be like to rip out his throat with my fangs, and the thought alone makes my mouth water. My stomach churns, but not in horror. No, in hunger.

When was the last time I fed? I couldn't remember at first, until a memory hit so hard it stole the very air from my lungs.

The warmth of the fire by the makeshift bed, blankets and furs spread out as my lover lay naked atop them. Her sun-kissed skin glows with the ether of her Fae heritage, the light of the fire making her appear almost divine. Not even the scars could take away from the beauty. They were healed, and most had faded to the human eye, but I could see every tiny sliver where iron had sliced through her flesh. The ones on her back were the worst.

"What are you thinking, Nya?" she asks, her eyelids heavy with sleep and exhaustion. She expelled a lot of power during her fight with the archangel, and during the last few hours of love making.

I sat back against the furs, simply observing the sated creature. "I'm thinking you're the most beautiful female I've ever seen, and that I am the luckiest bastard-born Fae to have been chosen to share your bed."

Even half-asleep, she rolls her eyes and smiles lazily at me. "Aren't you tired?"

"I've never felt more rested." I stretch my foot to trace the curve of her thigh with my toe. I want her again. My appetite knows no end. But it's not what she needs. "Go to sleep, kitten. I will watch over you."

I turn my focus to the flames and use my own to dim the brightness until it's just a soft glow and the crackling of the firewood. Looking to Mia, I find her watching me, an unsettled expression on her beautiful face.

"What wrong, kitten?" I ask, reaching out to run my fingers across her flesh in comfort. "Tell me what's bothering you."

"It's stupid." She looks down at her hand fidgeting with the fabric before looking back up at me from beneath her thick lashes. Her face flushes when I raise a questioning brow, not letting the question go until she tells me what she needs. "Why are you so impossible?"

"Tsk tsk, kitten." My fingers curl around her ankle, and I squeeze, holding eye contact as my thumb traces circles on the soft flesh. Sensing her need to be vulnerable and the walls slowly erecting themselves between us, my mind reaches for her, and I caress the inside of her mind. Her eyes close at the contact, and goosebumps rise along her flesh.

Tell me what it is you need, I demand softly.

"It's silly," Mia protests quietly. "You don't have to—"

"Mia McCoy." At the use of her full name, her eyes snap open, and she looks at me. I resist the urge to smile at the smallest sign of irritation. My girl does not like when I use her full name. It's cute.

"Will you hold me while I sleep?"

I rise from the blankets, letting the sheet I'd used to cover myself fall to the ground. Her eyes brighten, and her face flushes a deeper shade of red as she watches me with lust in her beautiful green eyes.

"Enough of that, kitten. You need your rest," I purr, teasingly as I kneel behind her, adjusting the blankets and pillows around me before lying down. I can't help but chuckle at her sigh of frustration as she takes my left arm and places it across her pillow before snuggling back against me, intertwining our fingers then brushing her lips across my knuckles. Such a tender gesture.

I kiss her ear, and she arches her neck for me, exposing her slender throat where I'd fed from her earlier this evening. *Mine.*

I close my eyes, content to hold my woman. My free hand rests on the curve of her hip as she fidgets with my fingers, soft kisses fluttering across the scars that cover my knuckles. There's a tenderness I've never experienced with other lovers I've taken to bed. There has been many, sure, but none of them brought me . . . peace?

"Thank you," Mia says, so quietly I almost miss it. I open my eyes and watch our hands as our fingers move together in a dance, our fingers interlocking until our palms touch. She giggles as I hold her hand captive. "Nya."

"What are you thanking me for?" I ask, genuinely curious, before nipping at the sensitive spot behind her ear, causing her to giggle again.

"This." Her voice is quiet, vulnerable. "I can't remember the last time I felt . . . safe."

"Kitten." I say, lifting myself up on my elbow, the change in position causes her to roll onto her back.

Sighing, she avoids meeting my eyes, holding back unshed tears. I lean over her until our gazes are level, cup the side of her face, and pepper her face with kisses as her body trembles.

"Listen to my words, kitten, and know them to be true." I kiss the corner of her mouth, nipping at her bottom lip as I wrap my hands around her wrists, pinning them above her head with one hand. "From the very first moment in the clearing, to the kiss on the stoop, the training session in the yard, our first night together, every moment between then and now and until my last breath, I am yours, and you're mine."

"Nyari—" She gasps as I nip at the flesh of her breast. I know what she needs from me, even if it isn't what she wants at the moment. "Stop fucking teasing!" She cries out as I slap her trembling thigh. "Argghh!"

"We're having a conversation, kitten." I growl against her flesh, barely restraining the hunger clawing inside me. "If you need me to hold you so you can sleep, my arms are yours. I'll kiss away every tear, every ache, every bruise."

I smile as I settle my weight over her, the hard length of me pressing against her entrance, hot and insistent. I allow myself a moment to take in the beautiful woman beneath me. Wild, willing, and trembling. Perfection.

"I will get on my knees every night, for you and only you." My tongue flicks over the wound at her throat, still raw and tender. "And because you've been such a good girl, I'll allow you to thank me for what comes next."

"Bastard." Mia gasps, bucking like a wild beast, pleading for her release. My grip on her wrists doesn't waiver, and neither does the rhythm I set. Slow, deep, and teasing . . . I know what my girl likes.

"Manners, kitten." I growl, gripping her jaw with my free hand as

I kiss her roughly, claiming her mouth as I claim her body. She is mine. She bites down on my bottom lip until the taste of iron fills my mouth, and I growl, wrapping my hand around her slender throat. She lets out a throaty moan. Bad girl.

"Bite me," she begs, ever the defiant little spitfire. Taking in the smeared blood on her mouth, I chuckle and release her hands from above her head, then grab a fistful of her hair, angling her throat as I sink my teeth into the healing wound and drink deep. It's only a moment before her orgasm shatters whatever remains of my self-control.

Mine.

~

"Nyari!" Elijah shouts, grabbing hold of my arm, fear in his voice. "Stop it! You're hurting yourself. Stop!"

I jolt back into myself and stumble away from the railing, taking in the blistering, bloody flesh of my hands. *What is happening to me?* Elijah takes my hands by the wrist and holds them up to look at the damage.

"What the hell was that?" Jeremiah's voice is raised in concern as he rushes to my side, his eyes still wild from the sudden shift. He must have been close by. "Fire has never burned you, Nyari."

It's one thing to feel your lover's bond begin to fade, and your own life along with it, but losing control of your own abilities in this manner is something else. "Is this the fade?"

"Nyari," Jeremiah growls, grabbing hold of my face in both his hands. My face feels cold against the warmth of his palms. His words are as frantic as his emotions. "I know you care for the girl, but she's just a human. You cannot do this; you cannot leave me. I forbid it, as your prince and as your brother."

I take a step back, letting Jeremiah's hands drop from my face as I stare up at him. Jeremiah is my favorite sibling, despite our differences, and I have always respected and heeded his advice, but in this case, he's wrong about so many things.

"Her name is Mia McCoy," I tell him, pride in my voice. "She's not just another human, Jeremiah. Do you not see it, or are you so blinded by your own lust for Sahari that you have forgotten the one thing our people need most?"

"You want to talk to me about being blinded by lust?" Jeremiah sneers, disgust evident in his tone. "You follow that witch's spawn like a lost puppy."

Elijah tries to interject. "Let's not say something we'll later regret—"

"Lost puppy?" I seethe, biting back a laugh. "That's rich. I'm not the one sharing my female with a pack of overgrown lapdogs. Tell me, brother, how do you enjoy sloppy seconds, or is it thirds by the time she gets to you?"

I barely step out of the way of the fist that's thrown in my direction. I step through the veil and reappear behind him. "What's wrong, brother? Did I hit a nerve?"

Jeremiah's face turns red with fury as his beast's eyes glow green. "Cheating, Nyari. I never took you for a coward. Then again, I didn't think you'd be foolish enough to let the little witch bitch get under your skin either."

"Don't talk about her like that," I spit back, and hit him square in the jaw. He stumbles back a few steps before he pounces, our teeth bared as our fists connect, my own blood filling my mouth as his hand wraps around my throat.

"ENOUGH," Jeremiah screams in my face. "I do not wish to hurt you."

I barely recognize myself as he forces me to see through his eyes. My eyes are lifeless, the circles under them black as the night sky. "Kill me," I plead, unable to keep my chest from cracking open. "I'm tired, Jere. I can't do this without her. I won't. I'm not like you—I'm not strong enough to survive. Kill me!"

Jeremiah pushes himself away, landing on his butt. He stares at me in horror as realization of what's truly happening hits him. "You poor bastard," he says, shaking his head and running a hand over his face. "Of all the humans you had to go and fall for . . ."

Slowly, I sit up, mirroring his position in the dirt with my elbows on my knees. My chest feels as though it's about to cave in, and I choke back tears. "It wasn't exactly a choice, brother. She is mine, and I am hers."

Those words are the final nail in the coffin. "Wherever Mia is, she's dying," Jeremiah says quietly, looking at me. "Because of the bond, she's draining your ether and causing you to fade along with her."

I hadn't thought of it like that. "As long as I live, she lives."

"What the heck is going on here?" Artemis asks, coming into the clearing with Elijah hot on her heels. Elijah must have run off for help rather than getting between us. I guess his survival instincts are still intact. "Eli said you two were trying to kill each other?"

Jeremiah sighs, looking to our sister as he rises from the ground. "We sorted it out."

"With your fists?" Artemis glares, taking a step toward me to inspect the injuries. "Almost two thousand years between you and you still haven't learned to use your words?"

I swat away her fingers from my jaw. "I'm fine, Art."

"That's a bit of a stretch," Jeremiah says. Artemis turns to him and arches a brow for him to elaborate. "Nyari has bonded with Mia, and wherever the mage is, she's dying. Her body is drawing on the bond to stay alive. They're fading."

"How is that possible?" Artemis asks, looking between us. "Mia McCoy is just a descendant . . . with powerful mage abilities, but for all intents and purposes, utterly human. Humans cannot bond with Fae."

"She's not human," Jeremiah and I say in sync.

"At least, not entirely." Jeremiah looks to me. "Do you have any theories?"

"She's not human, not in the same sense that Elijah or Sahari's vessel is," I explain cautiously, looking between my siblings and noting the fear in their eyes. They loved me, that was their only crime. "She's able to control the elements like other mages in the bloodline, but the fire that burns within her is old Fae."

"Let's assume that's true," Artemis states, processing the information. "It would explain the bond, and her ability to draw from it to remain alive. You're both powerful. It's safe to assume your bond would be as well. Wherever and whatever is happening to Mia is bad enough that she's now fading, and you along with her."

"I guess it's a good thing we know where your girl is," Fallon says, coming down the path alongside Malik. Another sibling who had recently returned from an assignment tracking the fallen angels. Walking between them is a third unknown man, dressed entirely in black. The unmistakable red hair of the McCoy Bloodline peeks from beneath his hat, and an empty gun holster hangs at his hip. "Meet our new best friend, Locklyn McCoy. Head of Security for Jonah Redwood."

Malik threw an arm around Locklyn's shoulders and grinned at the four of us. The male didn't look entirely comfortable but couldn't get away if he tried. "Just so we're clear, this was all my idea," Malik adds.

"I mean, technically, I found you—" Locklyn falls silent but shrugs at the glare Malik and Fallon send his way, as if to say *sorry not sorry*. "And I was sent by Mia, so technically it was all her idea— WOAH!" The male shouts as I appear out of thin air before him, my hand around his throat. "Fuck!"

"Where is she?" I ask, ignoring Fallon's hand on my arm. "Where is she?!"

"She's at the compound." Locklyn gasps as I release him. "Jonah's men brought her in almost six weeks ago."

"Where?" I seethe, barely registering Jeremiah's hand on my shoulder. "Take me to her."

"It's not that easy—" Locklyn stumbles back when I reach for him. "I have a letter for you, from Mia. S-she wanted me to give it to you."

I snatch the letter from his hand, rip open the seal, and walk away, leaving Jeremiah and Artemis to interrogate the male.

I need you to know that I love you.

I'm pregnant . . . at least for a few more days.

Raziel is the father. I'm sorry. I won't survive this pregnancy, but I will not leave my baby to be raised by Jonah Redwood. If I don't make it, promise me that you'll take Hope and return to your world. Show her everything that we talked about. I know it's selfish of me to ask, but I never claimed to be selfless.

I love you, Nyari. I would have enjoyed forever with you.

Yours always. Xx.

"How can you trust that letter was written by Mia?" Artemis challenges, though when I turn back to face my siblings, any doubt they have disappears. "What is it, Nyari?"

"She's pregnant with the archangel's baby," I tell them, barely recognizing the sound of my own voice. "That's why she's fading. The pregnancy is killing her."

"A Nephilim," Jeremiah says, approaching me cautiously. "We need to take this to Sahari and Isaiah. They'll know more about her condition than us."

"Wait," Elijah says, looking directly at Locklyn as he says his next words. "Mia warned me about Jonah Redwood—the compound, the mission, child soldiers . . . She wouldn't talk much about her experience, but I know she went through hell in that place. Aside from this pregnancy, what else is being done to her?"

"I've only had access to her during visits with the doctors," Locklyn admits, shifting uncomfortably as he takes the hat from his head and runs a hand through it. "She refuses to talk to me, or let me help her. She insists that it'll draw Jonah's attention. The last time I saw her was when she wrote that letter, five days ago."

"Will you show me?" I ask before I can second-guess myself. Locklyn's eyes snap to mine, confused. "If you open your mind and think about the last time you saw her, I will be able to 'view' it like a memory."

"Mia said you could do that," Locklyn admits. "Said that I might be required to let Sahari or Uriel inside my head to confirm my story." He hesitates, seeming conflicted. "She wouldn't want your last memory of her to be in that place. I will share it with your leader, and whoever else, but I ask that you don't make me share that with you."

"I ask your permission only out of respect," I say, taking a step toward him, though I'm cut off when Jeremiah grabs hold of my arm and pulls me to a stop. "Jeremiah."

"We're wasting time," Jeremiah says, nodding for the others to begin moving. "Malik, Fallon, return to camp with our guest. Find and update Sahari and Isaiah." Malik and Fallon each place a hand on Locklyn's shoulder, and the three of them fade from sight. "You can hate me, Nyari, but until there is no hope left, your last memories of her should be your own."

· CHAPTER

THIRTY-TWO

SAHARI

S taring at the mage seated at the other end of the table, I replay the redheaded man's memory over and over in my head, sharing it with Isaiah, my wolves, and Jeremiah as I do.

Jeremiah's hand tightens on my knee as he sits beside me, the only sign of emotion he'll allow. The alpha wolves behind me remain quiet, unmoving, taking everything in.

"I underestimated the girl," Isaiah says, looking toward the male being guarded by Malik and Fallon. "Do you know what she is?"

"She's a McCoy descendant," Locklyn says, looking around the room. "Like most of us."

"She's different." Nyari's knuckles turn white as they grip the back of the dining chair. "The magic, the ether, that runs through her veins is old Fae—like our ancestors. *Pure.*"

"You aren't suggesting she's—"

Malik cuts Art off excitedly. "Are you saying she's the heir of our people?"

"She could be," Nyari admits. "Had she been born in our world, she'd have at least been considered."

"What of the princeling?" Fallon asks, looking between her siblings. "The male heir of Prince Rey? Zephyr."

Isaiah leans forward in his seat. "Who is Zephyr?"

"Prince Zephyr is the true heir of the Fae," Jeremiah says. "Also known as the lost heir. His father was my cousin, Prince Rey."

"Zephyr and his twin-sister, Valyria—the current ruler of our people—are the children of Prince Rey and Claire McCoy," Nyari says, allowing an appropriate amount of time for the news to sink in for those Fae in the room. "Only a handful of Fae know the truth. I served Prince Rey during the war, and I witnessed them fall in love. I tried to stop it, but I suspect they were bonded. When Prince Rey was killed for false crimes, Claire was sent to a nunnery to give birth. The details of what happened next aren't clear, but five summers after the birth of the twins, Claire brought the princess before the king and he claimed her as his kin, but only if Claire swore to return the rightful heir to the Fae realm."

"Why am I only hearing about this now?" Jeremiah asks, rising from his seat. "We could have helped find the heir."

"It was the king's decision," was all Nyari said. "Claire made a vow that day. I believe everything that has happened since has been to find her son and deliver on her promise to return the heir to our people."

"Do we know where this lost heir is?" I ask, looking around the room at the bewildered expressions. "Are we assuming he's here . . . on Earth?"

"There are rumors he's in a hell dimension," Nyari says cautiously. "According to the whispers beyond the veil."

"Does Claire know this?" Jeremiah asks.

"It's a safe assumption that she does."

I rise from my seat, contemplating everything I knew about the witch, and our history; the timing of events, and the seals being broken. There must be some truth to the matter. How else could her bloodline have passed through so many worlds and generations and remained so powerful?

Did Raziel know the truth? Could that be why he helped her? I wasn't sure if that made his betrayal better or worse.

"How many children does this princess have?" Mack asks.

"Fae don't track heirs like humans, but from my knowledge, there could be more than fifty by now. She's five hundred years old," Jeremiah answers. "If what Nyari is saying is true, every McCoy descendant could be traced back to Princess Valyria. It would explain why some descendants are so powerful."

"What are you thinking, Sahari?" Isaiah asks.

I look at my brother, friend, right hand and trusted adviser. From the moment I arrived on his footstep, broken, and disorientated, he'd taken me in, sheltered me, and helped forge the alliances that remained today.

How was I meant to tell him that I was considering a new alliance with his worst enemy, the woman that not only killed his wife and destroyed his life, but who was also responsible for all this mess?

We need her.

Despite the voice in my head, I find myself replaying the worst moment of Isaiah's life, and the grief he still carried—not only for his lost wife, but also the pain from Raziel's betrayal. I allow myself to recall my own grief, the loss of my friends, and the most painful betrayal of all.

Raziel had chosen her. Not just over his people, but over me.

From the beginning of my creation, he had stood at my side—my friend, my ally, my protector and my lover. We'd fought many times, almost killing one another in the process, but when the opportunity for a final blow presented itself, neither of us could take the shot.

I loved him. Not in the same way I loved Jeremiah, Jensen, Kody, or Seth. Raziel used to say that our father created us to challenge each other so that we'd never grow complacent in our duty to serve and protect his creation.

Yet he'd betrayed everything we stood for . . . for her. Now, five hundred years later, I stand amongst the descendants of her line and the Fae who had stood in the bloody fields and fought in a war that she started.

I force myself to meet the eyes of my friend, my brother, and the only other being that felt as I did when it came to Claire McCoy.

Isaiah hated Claire more than any of us, and if she stood before him, I had no doubt he'd kill her or die trying. If it weren't for the new information laid out in front of me, I might have helped him.

Raziel betrayed our people for her. Everything that had happened was because of her—wasn't it? The deaths, the fall, the storm?

"No," Isaiah says, his eyes wild with rage as he stares at me. He seemed to know where my mind was going without me even saying a word. "Sahari."

"I'm sorry, Isaiah." I shift my gaze to Nyari. "Do you think you could get a message to Claire McCoy? Set up a meeting?"

"I haven't had contact with Claire since the war," Nyari says, deep in thought. "I could try putting out a call through the veil, but that would take time—time Mia doesn't have."

"I might be able to set up a meet," Elijah says. Several shades paler than usual, he rises from his seat and looks at me. "Since the shipping yard, she's been visiting me, trying to recruit me into joining her course."

Mack glares at him accusingly. "You never told me that."

"I wasn't interested," Elijah says, looking at his wife with guilt. "I would never leave you, or the kids. I'm loyal to our people, Mack. It never crossed my mind to take her up on it."

"You still should have told us," I tell the mage, only slightly annoyed.

"I didn't want to give you reason to question my loyalty," Elijah says, looking around the table. "I've earned my place here. I have fought at your side, spilled blood, and almost died on more than one occasion. As far as I am concerned, we're family, but if I'm wrong in my assumption, tell me now and I will show myself out."

Elijah's wife stands at his side, her hand on his arm, her wolfish eyes blazing with pride. She looks to each person at the table, daring them to say something.

It's Nyari who responds first, raising their hands in submission to the angry wolf. "I never doubted your loyalty to this group, Elijah. We're family."

"Okay," I say. "Did the witch give you a way to communicate with her if you changed your mind? A location?"

"Just a spell."

THIRTY-THREE

NYARI

A full day has passed since Locklyn left. Every second feels like acid bubbling away beneath the flesh of my skin. Time is running out, and I need to be there.

Instead, I'm here, in a clearing just outside the small town of Redwood. Teams are in position, ready and awaiting orders.

Only three others stand in the clearing with me. Sahari, Jeremiah, and Elijah. If this works, our next stop will be the gates of the compound, where we'll meet Jonah Redwood.

"What are the odds this goes to plan?" Elijah asks as I complete the summoning ritual. "There is a lot of hate amongst our people. When Mia first arrived, you were concerned she'd be killed just for looking like Claire, and now we're summoning the very witch your kind wants to see dead?"

"I don't know how this will end," I admit. "The only people who can make this happen are Claire and Sahari."

"No pressure." Sahari chuckles dryly, and I straighten as a breeze passes through the clearing, ruffling her golden-blonde curls.

"She's coming."

Jeremiah's hand settles on the sword at his side. "And she's not alone."

I rise from my place by the circle and take a step back, taking in every shift and change to the surrounding environment. A cloud gathers in the sky above as raindrops begin to fall in a soft shower, dampening the dry grass beneath our feet.

As quickly as the clouds appeared, they dissolve, and in their place are Claire and Silas McCoy. Behind them, I see familiar faces. Princesses Astrid and Hyacinth—daughters of the Fae ruler Valyria. A pirate siren named Mira. And two cloaked beings I don't recognize.

Jeremiah's shock is evident as he recognizes the royals. "Princess Astrid; Princess Hyacinth."

"Prince Jeremiah," the twins echo in sync. "We've missed you, cousin," Astrid teases, their black eyes bright with mischief.

"Cousin Nya." Princess Hyacinth bows their head toward me in acknowledgment. "It is an honor to see you again."

"The honor is mine," I tell them genuinely as I bow low. I'd searched for the twins after their disappearance. Our people assumed they'd been slain, but I never found them beyond the veil.

"Talk about a family reunion," Elijah mutters under his breath, though it doesn't go unnoticed. Claire McCoy's focus zeros in on him.

"A little heads-up might have been nice," is all Claire says to the mage, as her eyes take in our small group. She zeroes in on me and takes a step toward where I stand. "It has been a long time."

I bow my head in respect. "It has."

"You do not look well." She raises a hand to touch my cheek, and I freeze beneath her touch. "What is wrong?"

"I'm dying," I admit, ignoring the shocked expressions on my cousins' faces.

"You aren't physically ill, yet you are weakening?" Claire asks.

"Mia McCoy and I have bonded," I explain, watching as recognition fills her features. "She's with child, and she's being held captive by a human called Jonah Redwood."

"I'm familiar with the name." Claire sighs. "I was not aware you were capable—"

"The child she carries isn't mine," I answer, cutting her off. "She was with Raziel prior to our meeting."

"*My* Raziel?"

I nod in response as she processes the new information.

"How interesting . . . most humans aren't capable of carrying a Child of Grace to term."

"Mia McCoy is not *most humans*."

"You want our help to save the girl . . .?"

"We don't need your help to save the girl," Sahari says flatly. "We're capable of doing that ourselves. What we're offering is an alliance."

Claire laughs at this news. "Is that right? Tell me, Sahari—*yes, I know who you are, even in that vessel*—why on earth would I want to ally myself to you and your people? I know how you feel about us, even as you wear the skin of my kin." She gestures to the four of us. "Fae, mage, witch . . . you are no different to us, and yet you call us your enemy."

"For five hundred years, you have been the enemy," Sahari says, taking a step forward. "I won't stand here and rehash the past with you. We're all painfully aware—some of us live with the reminder on a daily basis. I'm offering you an opportunity to make peace and reunite our people."

This captures Claire's attention. She holds Sahari's gaze, a silent discussion passing between the two powerful beings.

"Can you really open the gates to the demon world?" Claire asks.

"I can," Sahari states. "If we can work together, we can bring peace to the Fae realm and reunite the lost heir with his people and homeland."

Claire shifts her gaze to mine. "You once vowed to serve the heir of your people. Do you still honor that vow?"

"I do," I admit.

"Do you swear on the life of Mia McCoy that Sahari intends to honor her agreement made here today?"

"Do not ask that of them," Jeremiah snarls.

Silas speaks for the first time. "Do you not trust your lover to keep her word? Are her promises false?"

"Silas," Jeremiah warns. "My friend—"

"Answer him," Claire demands.

"I trust Sahari with my life," Jeremiah says through gritted teeth. "I trust that she will do what she thinks is best."

"That's not convincing—"

"I swear on the life of Mia McCoy. You might not always agree with Sahari's methods, but every decision is considered and calculated. She would not have agreed to this meeting if she did not intend on honoring it."

What I didn't need to say was that if Sahari betrayed my people, not even her bond with my brother would keep me from trying to kill her. It was an unspoken vow that extended beyond myself. I doubt even Jeremiah will be able to stand with her if she turns on us.

CHAPTER
THIRTY-FOUR

MIA

I've been reserving my strength—slowing down my own healing, pushing down the power and allowing it to build for this very scenario.

In my current condition, I'm not sure how much of a physical fight I can put up, which means I have to rely on my elemental defenses, which aren't all that reliable. If I can get hold of a guard and take his weapon, I'll have a better chance.

The moment I lift the barrier, power rushes to the surface, engulfing my body in blue flames. The iron cuffs around my wrists and ankles melt away into a blazing puddle on the ground. The iron collar around my neck disintegrates, melting in rivulets down my chest and between my breasts, leaving an angry trail in its wake. I wait for the pain, but it never comes.

The ringing in my ears intensifies, and I clutch at my head to drown out the sound until I realize it's the sound of an alarm, and the flashing lights are to alert the guards of my attempt to escape.

Acting quickly, I make it to the door and, unsurprisingly, find it locked from the outside. I smile to myself as I press my palm to the door, watching as the fire engulfs it. The guards are trying to put out the fire on the other side, but it's useless against the raging blue flames. It falls off its hinges out into the hallway, right at their feet as I step out and stare at the five guards with their weapons raised at me.

"That's enough," one of the guards says as I tilt my head, taking him in. "I will put you down." I can tell by the looks on the others' faces that they aren't entirely on board with that plan. If he kills me, Jonah will kill all of them. "Get on your knees."

Unfeeling and unafraid, I stare at the guard. "Make me."

"Don't—" one of the guards warns, but it's too late. Their foolish comrade reaches for me, and I unleash myself upon the five of the guards until they lie at my feet, unconscious and bleeding.

I step over the unconscious guard, kneel to pick up his weapon, and give his face a little tap until his eyes flutter open. "I could have killed you, but I didn't. Threaten me or my child again, and I will burn you and anyone with you alive. Understood?"

Unable to speak, he nods.

"Good." I reach for the security pass on his vest. "I'll be borrowing this."

I rise to my feet ignoring the spasms of pain beginning to come more frequently. I'm just about to walk away when I hear a call come in over the radio.

"Code Black! We're under attack—" I look down at the guard, his eyes wide in surprise. *"They're coming in everywhere!"*

I knock the guard unconscious and take the radio. Making my way down the hall, I stop by a supply cart with hospital linen and gowns. The gown barely covers the bump, but I feel mildly better not being completely exposed.

I make it to the room where Archangel Michael is being held. A metal slab sits in the middle, with the angel strapped down with chains, wires, and an IV going into his arm. He appears unconscious at first, until I approach his side and see his eyes are wild and surrounded by dark circles, his face drawn from starvation. I didn't know it was possible for angels to look hungry.

His gaze drops to my belly, and his expression softens. "She's coming."

"Not yet," I tell him, willing her to remain where she is for a little while longer. "We need to get out of here, Michael. Now. It's happening. Locklyn is back, and Sahari's people are infiltrating the compound."

"Sahari." He says her name with a smile. "I didn't think I'd ever see her again." He flinches as I use fire to melt away the restraints, my movements slow and shaky as another contraction threatens to bring me to my knees. "Where is Jonah?" he asks.

"I don't know." I brace my palms on the cold metal slab, breathing in through my nose. Once the pain passes, I pick up the radio and my gun. "Locklyn? Do you copy?"

"Mia?"

The smile that splits my face is genuine. "You did it."

"It's not done yet," he replies. "Where are you? I've got someone who really wants to see you."

Nyari. Tears well in my eyes at the thought of being reunited. "Where is Jonah?"

"He's surrounded," Locklyn says. "Are you okay?"

"I'm—"Another contraction hits, and this time, I can't keep myself upright. The radio falls from my hand and shatters on the floor. Michael appears at my side and allows me to lean back on him as a scream tears itself from my throat.

"I've got you," Michael promises, lifting me into his arms. My head falls back onto his shoulder, and my free hand clutches the fabric of the gown. "You did it, Mia. I'll take care of the rest."

"Nyari," I whisper against his chest. "Take me to Nyari."

Claire and I watch from beyond the veil as Sahari, Seth, Elijah, and Isaiah approach the gates of the Redwood compound. A silver wolf trails at Elijah's side, the tips of his fingers brushing the fur of her head. Mack had insisted on being here. Elijah objected, but in the end, she'd won.

Claire stiffens next to me as the spirits of the beyond sense our presence.

"He's a monster," Claire states as the memories of those spirits begin to filter through. "So much pain and destruction. For what?"

"The answer is the same as it always is," I tell her, catching her curious gaze. "Greed."

Claire releases a heavy breath. "It's the stupidest reason of all."

"Would it be better if he'd done it for love?" I question, unable to help myself. "For family?"

"Are you implying something, Nyari?"

"I'd never do such a thing." I resist the urge to smile at the irritation in her voice. "It doesn't matter if it was done for greed, love, wealth or power. Any one of them is a powerful motivator on their own, and in the wrong hands, can be wielded as a weapon for mass destruction."

Claire is quiet for the briefest moment before she speaks again. "It's a heavy burden, Nyari, to live with the things I've done. And yet —for my children, my son—I'd do it all again."

"Is there a line?"

"You tell me." Claire nods toward the iron gates. "What wouldn't you do to protect the woman you love, and your child?"

"The baby is Raziel's."

Claire nods. "Biologically. But love isn't defined by DNA, Nyari. You will love that child as if it were your own, because of the love you have for her mother. If anyone were to threaten or harm the child—"

"I'll kill them," I answer, without missing a beat. "Is that what you want to hear?"

"Yes." Claire's eyes meet mine, and for the first time, I can see the exhaustion she's been masking. "Five hundred years ago, my son was taken from my womb into a hell dimension. I've spent every day since trying to find him and return him to our world. I have become the villain in many people's story, all to get here."

"Is he waiting for us to ring the bell?" Seth complains in frustration as he shifts from foot to foot, drawing my attention back to the scene at the gate.

"Patience, love," Sahari teases, her tone patronizing. "Let the little man play his games."

"She's running out of time," a voice whispers through the veil. "The baby is coming."

Claire grabs hold of my arm, halting my movements. "Patience, Nya."

The gates open, revealing a gravel driveway with guards lined on either side, guns aimed at the ground. Each of them assessing, alert, ready for a fight.

"You can trust them," says another voice from within the veil. "They are Locklyn's men."

"Thank you," Claire says to the spirits beyond. "Do you know where he's keeping Mia McCoy?"

"She's with the archangel."

"Archangel?" I ask, looking around the veil, cloaked in shadows. "What archangel? Raziel?"

It's quiet for a moment until the spirits whisper, "She's with the one they call Michael."

This is news . . . "Where are they being kept?" I ask again, noting the middle-aged man with white hair approaching the gates.

He comes to a stop just inside the gates, his eyes taking in his visitors with a greedy assessment. His eyes linger too long on Seth before focusing solely on Sahari. "My goodness . . . Locklyn failed to mention how beautiful you are."

"Huh. I thought he'd have led with that." Sahari shakes her head in mock outrage. "What would be a befitting punishment? Ten lashes? How about fifty?"

Jonah chuckles. "Perhaps we can discuss it over tea," he suggests, gesturing to those around her. "Who are your friends?"

Sahari places a hand on Seth's forearm. "This is my wolf, Seth McCoy; my adviser, Isaiah; and Elijah McCoy and his wife, Mackenzie."

"Wife . . ." Jonah trails off as Mackenzie shifts into her human form, entirely naked, undeniably beautiful, and unmistakably inhuman. The look in Jonah's eyes is like a boy at Christmas. "My oh my."

I watch as Elijah takes a step forward, shrugs out of his coat, and holds it out for his wife to slip on. Mack never takes her eyes from Jonah's. "It's a pleasure to meet you, Mr. Redwood."

"The pleasure is mine," he promises, shifting his gaze to Elijah and then back to Seth. "You're also a wolf?"

"If you're expecting a striptease from me, you'll be disappointed," Seth replies, his disgust barely concealed. "There's no full-frontal in this scene."

"I thought your kind was a myth."

"Lucky for us," Seth retorts.

Sahari released Seth's arm and takes a step toward Jonah. "Perhaps it's time the grown-ups take this conversation somewhere more private?"

"Forgive me." Jonah offers Sahari his hand. "Will you walk with me, Sahari? I can show you the grounds before we retire for lunch."

"It would be my pleasure." Sahari bats her lashes at him. "I must admit, my companions don't quite see your vision the way I do. It's rather inspiring. You truly have a gift, Jonah. You must tell me how you did it so that I might imitate it with my own group."

Patting Sahari's hand as if she were a simple girl, Jonah makes a show of leaning down to whisper in her ear. "We're going to have such fun, you and I. I look forward to teaching you a thing or two along the way."

Isaiah exchanges a look of disgust with the others as Sahari giggles obnoxiously, playing to Jonah's ego.

Crossing the boundary into the compound sent a physical wave of goosebumps over every inch of my flesh, a thousand tiny iron needles penetrating my skin in waves from head to toe. Seth and Mack both react physically as well. Elijah's hold on his wife tightens to catch her step. He looks back at the fence line, sensing the elements. "There's an iron boundary."

"The entire property is lined with iron," one of the guards informs Elijah. "You get used to it after a while. I'll have one of my guards bring you bottled water and something to help the nausea. The sensation of cold water helps distract from the element."

"Thank you," Elijah responds respectfully, slowing his pace to walk alongside the guard. "Do you live with this feeling constantly?"

"If we're on the compound, yes," the same guard answers. "I'm Jye, by the way. Locklyn's cousin."

Seth bounds forward, and the two shake hands. "I'm Seth. This is Elijah, and his wife, Mack."

"It's a pleasure to meet you both," Jye says, shaking both their hands. "Locklyn will be joining us shortly."

"I look forward to catching up with him." Seth sounds indifferent, but there's a spark of eagerness in his expression for the fight to come.

"It's time for us to go," Claire says, bringing my attention back to the veil. "Your friends will be okay, Nya."

"I know they will be," I say, turning to her. "Let's go."

Half an hour later, all hell has broken loose. Gunshots are being fired, people are screaming, fires have been started, and an explosion rang out so strong it shook the very ground we stood on.

"Mia," I whisper, sensing the familiar power emanating from the explosion. I exit the veil, Claire following my lead as we run through the compound toward the center of the blast.

Standing in the field is a naked, bloody, brutally tortured archangel, wings of purest white dragging in the mud and the blood of those dead at his feet.

"Michael." Sahari's voice appears from nowhere. "You're alive."

Lost in his bloodlust, he tears limb from limb those attacking him, but his eyes are focused on Jonah Redwood, cowering behind guards.

"I'm going to kill you slowly, Jonah! Very, very slowly. I will make you suffer in ways your pitiful human mind cannot imagine."

Jonah pales as he takes in the pissed-off archangel. Even weakened, his wrath is mighty, but that is secondary to the sight of Mia being held up by a mage in scrubs. She wears a hospital gown, her thighs slick with blood and her belly round with a child.

Locklyn shouts his orders to stand down as his own men begin to surround the area. Seth holds Locklyn back from approaching. "He will kill you if you try to get closer."

Jonah runs behind his guards, and before any of us realizes what he's planning, he pulls a gun and points it at the doctor holding Mia upright.

"NO!" Locklyn screams, and this time, the air itself seems to burn with his powers. "It's over, Jonah. Put your weapon down."

Mia's eyes light with fire as she stares at Jonah. The gun shifts from the doctor and is pointed at Mia's belly. Any attempt Mia might have made to defend herself fades. She won't risk the baby.

Shifting through the veil, I appear behind Jonah Redwood, my swords in hand and blue flames igniting the steel as I run it through Jonah's spine. Michael's roar of rage rattles the ground, but none of that is my concern, as a moment later, Mia's body collapses in agony.

"Mia!" I jump through the void and catch her, drawing her body to mine. "I've got you."

A gurgling sound captures my attention, and I turn my head in time to watch as Michael lifts Jonah from the ground and, with one hand, rips out his heart. He shows it to him as he speaks in the old language, cursing the bastard to hell.

"Nyari." Mia's voice is weak, and I look down at her. "I love you."

"I love you," I say, pressing my lips to hers. "You have to stay with me."

"I'm so tired," Mia cries, tears spilling down her face as she stares at me. "I love you so much. I'm sorry—"

"You have nothing to be sorry for," I whisper, crying as I stroke Mia's cheek. "We're going to be okay."

She shakes her head, sobbing as she grips my shirt tighter. "It's not, Ny. I'm sorry—" Her hand goes to her stomach.

"The baby is coming," Claire says, rushing forward. "We need to get her inside."

"She's going to need blood," Mack tells Claire, before looking back at the guard named Jye. "Please tell me you have a blood bank?"

"We do," Locklyn answers, coming closer. "Follow me."

Mia's body trembles as I lift her from the ground. "It's going to be okay, Mia."

"I'm so tired of fighting," she cries, staring up at me through the tears. "I'm not afraid to die, Nyari."

Something inside of me breaks at her words.

"I can't lose you twice," I whisper, kissing her forehead as tears trek down my cheeks, my heart splitting in two as I feel the life literally draining from her being. "A world without you is not a world I wish to explore."

I rise from the ground, lifting her lifeless body, ignoring the dismembered limbs littering the garden as I follow Locklyn toward the hospital. Claire, Mack, and Elijah cover us as we move.

The moment I lay Mia down on the bed, Claire, Elijah, and Mack get to work. A hand lands on my shoulder, and I look up to find my brother surveying the scene in front of him.

"She's in good hands," Jeremiah offers, knowing that's all he can do. Claire McCoy is one of the most powerful witches and healers in her line. Elijah is a gifted healer himself, even if he is still learning.

Mack was a gifted midwife amongst her pack.

Hospital staff come in to assist as machines are hooked up and bags of blood hung. Orders from Mack fly about as she directs the staff. Claire and Elijah work alongside each other to bring Mia's body back from the brink of death.

A terrified scream fills the room as Mia's eyes shoot open and blue flames engulf the bed. Elijah was able to throw up a shield in time to protect his wife and Claire, but the flames forced them to back away from the bed.

"Get away from me!" Mia screams, tears rolling down her cheeks, the flames keeping those trying to help her at bay. "Please—I don't want to die!"

"Kitten," I whisper, approaching the bed and extending my own flames to caress her own. "You're safe. Elijah and Mack are here to help you. The baby is coming, sweetheart. You need to let them help you."

"You can't let Jonah have her," Mia cries, clutching my hand. "Promise me."

"Jonah is dead, Mia. He can't hurt you, or anyone, ever again."

THIRTY-SIX

She's the one, the voice tells me.

Humans aren't equipped to survive Nephilim births, I send back. *I don't think I can save her.*

It all happens so fast, and I find myself witnessing the birth of a Nephilim. Mia brings forth her daughter, covered in her mother's blood. As Mia's screams fade, so do her flames, and with Hope's first cry, another seal shatters.

Save her! The voice demands.

Tell me how, and I will!

I stare at the tiny bundle in Mack's arms—*a girl!*—as she's checked over and wrapped in a blanket, then handed off to a nurse, who brings her to me.

Jeremiah pulls Nyari away from the bed, and the healers continue to work. I step into the hall, staring at the crying Nephilim as Isaiah approaches, his face pale as he stares at the baby pressed to my chest.

"How's Mia?"

"She's fading," I tell him, "and Nyari with her. Brother," I greet, spotting Michael walking toward us.

"Sister." He pauses to look down at the baby in my arms. "She's finally here. Hope."

"Hope?" I ask, looking up at him.

"That's her name," he declares. "It's the prophecy, Sahari. Mia McCoy is the Bringer of Hope." With that said, Michael walks straight past us and into the room.

We watch as Michael raises his hand to Mia's chest. Holy light shines through his fingertips, and her back arches off the bed, eyes opening wide as a silent scream tears itself from her throat. Michael grabs hold of the bed, his head bowed, as Mia's body drops back down, and her once lifeless body begins to stir.

"Michael." The name is barely a whisper. Michael lifts his head and meets Mia's gaze. "Thank you."

"My debt to you is paid."

Nyari collapses to their knees before Michael as they thank him through sobs. Michael barely acknowledges the warrior at his feet as he walks from the room. Nyari rises and returns to Mia's side, pulling her into their arms as silent tears flow.

The newborn fusses in my arms, bringing the couple's attention to me. Mia reaches a hand toward us, and I approach the bed as Nyari shifts to make room.

"She's perfect," I say, placing the babe in her arms. Nyari stares in awe as Mia cradles her baby.

"She's beautiful," Mia cries, looking up at Nyari. "Don't you think?"

Nyari's thumb caresses Mia's cheek, wiping away tears. "She's perfect, kitten. You both are."

"I love you," Mia whispers.

Nyari leans in and brushes a kiss to their lover's lips. "I love you, kitten." Then they pull back, looking down at the baby between them. "Both of you."

EPILOGUE

MIA

Tied to a chair, beaten, bloody, and with a knife wound in her thigh is Emilia McCoy. She looked just as she did in the photos Aiden left for me to find.

The years have not been kind . . . not that they've been kind to any of us.

She is still beautiful, of course, but there is a hardness to her, a cruelty that can only come from years of being exposed to the worst of humanity. Her blue eyes, identical to her mother's—our mother's—have the ability to pierce straight through you and bare your deepest insecurities.

I stand before her, waiting for recognition, but it never comes.

She stares at me as if I am nothing, less than nothing, then she spits at my feet and grins. Blood has stained her teeth red. Fallon raises her hand to strike, but I halt her. "Leave us."

Fallon stares at me, eyes wide. "I don't think that's a good idea."

"If I wanted your opinion, Fallon, I'd have asked for it," I snap, my eyes darting to the warrior. "Out."

I pull up a chair in front of Emilia and let the silence linger between us. Occasionally, she'll glance around the room, test the restraints, and glare at the two-way mirror behind me.

"If your plan is to bore me to death, it's working."

A smile tugs at my lips as I stare at my sister. Even as children, she was always the first to break the silence.

"They will come for me," she says with a sneer.

"Will they?" I ask, deciding to push things along. "You're nothing to them, Emilia. You might be a soldier in their war, but you're one of us. A descendant of the McCoy. In your heart of hearts, you know it to be true."

At the mention of her name, something changes. "How do you know that name?"

"Is it not your name?"

"Who are you?" Emilia asks, suddenly all too focused on me.

"Do you not recognize your own sister?"

"My sister is dead."

"Up until recently, I thought the same."

Emilia stares at me and shakes her head. "You look like the McCoy witch," she whispers. "My sister died twenty years ago. They all died. Steven, Mum, and Dad."

Steven was our older brother. The cleaners had killed him after shooting our mother. The memory of it is vivid in my mind. The warmth of their blood soaking the carpet beneath my knees had made my stomach churn, and I wonder if Emilia is reliving that night along with me.

"Mia," Nyari says from the door behind me.

Ignoring Nyari, I push forward with Emilia. "I got away, Millie. I ran. I thought you were behind me, but when I finally stopped, you weren't there. I tried to go back for you, but I was lost."

"No." She shakes her head. "No."

"The whitecoats killed our mum and brother. I thought they'd killed Dad too," I tell her, watching her expression. Her eyes lift to mine, and I realize she'd thought they had. "You didn't know, huh?"

"Know what?"

"The whitecoats didn't finish the job that night. Our father—Aiden McCoy—escaped and found refuge in a church. They protected him, and he even became a priest, but he didn't stop gathering information about our family line. Six months before the storm hit, before the darkness came, they found him."

"The priest?" She looks almost sick. "No, he wouldn't do that—"

"Who wouldn't?"

She stops herself, squeezing her eyes closed. "None of it matters."

"What did they do to you, Millie?"

"Don't call me that," she snarls. "That is not my name."

"Mia, sweetheart, we need to go."

Millie looks at Nyari and smiles cruelly. "I'm not even surprised you're screwing the abomination. Go spread your whore legs for it. At least you won't be able to breed."

I don't let her cruel words get to me. As I stand, I pull our mother's chain from around my neck and drop it into her lap. "I'm going away for a few days, but we'll talk when I get back. You won't be harmed; I swear."

"Why are you doing this?"

"Haven't we lost enough?" I ask her. "I don't want to kill you, Millie, but I'll do it to protect my people."

"They'll come for me."

"I don't think they will."

Millie calls my name as I'm about to close the door behind me. I turn back, meeting her eyes. "I don't want to kill you either, little sister, but if I have to, I will."

T*o be continued . . .*

THANK YOU & REVIEWS

Thank you so much for reading my debut book. If you enjoyed this story, I would be very grateful if you would leave a review on your favourite reading platform as every review helps me achieve my author dream.

AUTHOR'S NOTES

A special thank you to my incredibly quacked support system! R.A. Wright Editor—I love you, and I'm sorry for all the changes made after edits. Thanks for putting up with me, and reminding me of deadlines.

My OG writers Caroline Slade, Cassandra Kelly, Tasha Broom, Sofia Aves, Joanne Creed, Monica Shultz, Neen Cohen, and Jem Gowen.

Genuinely—thank you.

Ipswich Qld Writers & Illustrators.

Romance Writers of Australia.

Shoutout to the fabulous Jacinta Peachey. Thank you for all the support, and encouragement over the years and for kicking my butt to enter competitions.

To everyone else, thank you for the support, the catchups, coffees, late night phone calls, and listening to my ideas and fictional adventures even if you didn't understand a single word.

And finally, thanks to my beautiful niece Mia for letting me borrow her name. It was an accident, but after a while, I couldn't imagine calling the MC anything else.

I love and appreciate you all.

This story began with four girlfriends, from different backgrounds, ages, and stages in their lives sitting around a table in Zarraffas. A lot has changed in this story since then, and the same can be said for those women. None of us are the same . . . and while friendships might come and go, and stories evolve into their own, there are moments in this book that wouldn't have been written without those late-night writing sessions at Zarraffas.

Thanks for being a part of my story.

Xoxo. Cinna.

ABOUT CINNA STONE

Cinna Stone writes dark fantasy romance with a wicked grin and a cup of coffee that's definitely gone cold. Fueled by ADHD hyperfocus, too many half-finished notebooks, and an unhealthy love of morally-gray characters, she creates worlds where angels misbehave, monsters brood, and survival is never guaranteed. When she's not wrangling words, she's probably wrangling cats—or plotting her next twist that will make readers yell at her in the best possible way.

You can find out more about Cinna Stone via her Instagram: Cinna Stone @cinnabunreads